GUNK BABY

ALSO BY JAMIE MARINA LAU

Pink Mountain on Locust Island

GUNK BABY

JAMIE MARINA LAU

A NOVEL

∧ ASTRA HOUSE
NEW YORK

Originally published by Hachette Australia in 2021

For information about permission to reproduce selections from this book, please contact
permissions@astrahouse.com.

This is a work of fiction. Names, characters, places, and incidents are products of the author's
imagination or are used fictitiously. Any resemblance to actual events, locales, or persons,
living or dead, is entirely coincidental.

Astra House
A Division of Astra Publishing House
astrahouse.com
Printed in the United States of America

Library of Congress Cataloging-in-Publication Data

Names: Lau, Jamie Marina, 1997– author.
Title: Gunk baby : a novel / Jamie Marina Lau.
Description: First edition. | New York : Astra House, [2022] | Summary: "Gunk Baby
    is a black comedy workplace thriller set in a sprawling indoor shopping mall about
    a cabal of low-wage workers who plot violent acts of "resistance" against their
    managers"—Provided by publisher.
Identifiers: LCCN 2022019775 (print) | LCCN 2022019776 (ebook) |
    ISBN 9781662601453 (paperback) | ISBN 9781662601460 (epub)
Subjects: LCGFT: Black humor. | Thrillers (Fiction). | Novels.
Classification: LCC PR9619.4.L378 G86 2022 (print) | LCC PR9619.4.L378 (ebook) |
    DDC 823/.92—dc23/eng/20220622
LC record available at https://lccn.loc.gov/2022019775
LC ebook record available at https://lccn.loc.gov/2022019776

First edition
10 9 8 7 6 5 4 3 2 1

Design by Richard Oriolo
The text is set in Arno Pro.
The titles are set in Champion HTF Lightweight.

Dedicated to Anna and Caroline Lee

One who knows does not speak;
one who speaks does not know.
Block the openings;
Shut the doors.
Blunt the sharpness;
Untangle the knots;
Soften the glare;
Let your wheels move only along old ruts.
This is known as mysterious sameness.

—LAO TZU, *TAO TE CHING*, BOOK TWO, LVI

CONTENTS

GUNK BABY

THE OPENING

1 **WELL, I HAD TAKEN MY** Chinese ear-cleaning service to the West, because my mother had told me that tourists to the East liked to be fondled around the eardrum.

Back in the New Territories, she had started a healing business near Lai Chi Kok. She kept a leather case of various-sized ear scoops and rods and found a space where she would perform the ritual, welcoming both traditionalists and tourists. The manner of her business relied on creating an accessible space for both.

"The marketing," she explained, "is the blueprint. The way you approach it varies according to the location, particularly in a city like Hong Kong." If the studio was in, say, Central, the aesthetic would deviate from the way she would present it if it were located in an isolated little borough in Lai Chi Kok. Often she would send me email links to playlists she's made to soundtrack the excavation of sebum from the ears of curious strangers and monthly regulars.

When I was a child, she would lay my head in the enclosure of her lap and shine a light into the hole on either side. Take me at the cheek with one hand, then take me by the ear. It was similar to a sort of tickling, only more euphoric. As if the feeling of constriction from being tickled had been replaced with a feeling of gentle, spacious inquiry. The delirium felt its way between each hair as the scoop shrank its way in. Like the curved tip of a fingernail patiently chiseling a sculpture. Like a fly soaring around inside.

At age eleven I developed a brief obsession with this feeling. I would ask my mother every night to perform the ritual, anxious about the mud that might have clotted there, in the caverns, during the day.

Addictive. What you can't see, you trust someone else to be able to somehow.

And so, I'll be owning my own healing studio in the outer suburb of Par Mars, fitted into a storefront at the Topic Heights shopping complex. In with the lime and pale rouge diamond-shaped tiles of the food court, the off-white square tiles everywhere else. In with the big arches of skylight, the second-level balconies, rusted gold banisters like those in motels, the phone-repair stall in the center of the corridors. Every corridor organized by its genre of lifestyle, encouraging you to see and consider everything you might need.

2 THE SUBURB HAS LITTLE SECTORS. The sun sets orange on the Home store, a bold stripe intruding upon its signage. The suburb sits just off a major highway, a McDonald's planted at its entrance. There are never any children in the PlayPlace there. This McDonald's establishment only seems to appeal to the morning commuters, the truck drivers. The streets behind the Home store and the McDonald's are where the residential neighborhoods begin to germinate, a healthy mixture of young families and parents with older children, an area with a fairly even ratio of recent immigrants and long-time settlers. The wealthier have migrated out here for the estates, pools of carefully thought-out architecture, often following a thematic scheme design. Surrounding the estates are leftover swaths of suburb. The only way to tell the status of a household is by the state of its garden and how awkwardly it is distinguished from the rest of the street.

If you drive down this highway at the coil before sunset, the reflection of the sunlight on the road bounces up to pierce your eyes, preventing you from seeing the cluster of traffic lights ahead.

Traffic is allowed between forty and sixty miles per hour, varying according to how many concrete warehouses are established on either side. The scatter of palm trees every so often keeps the grayness subsided, keeps the grid-like formations from looking too much like an abandoned military site.

If you have the windows down you can smell summer even if it happens to be winter.

And as you make a right turn down Brandt Boulevard, the sun peeling itself through the trees in the front yard of somebody's home.

The first house on the corner still has its Christmas lights up, you'll notice. Red ones, which match the sign reading NO PARKING AT ANY TIME. Regardless, a few feet up, someone has hoisted a Volkswagen up onto the curb the way cops do.

Gradually down Brandt Boulevard the street begins to widen and an extra lane of gravel forms. Here at the corner there is a swift turn and a group of units on the left. They are not currently inhabited, and even after three years, the local council has still not decided what to do with them. The unoccupied units have been such a regular topic of community discourse that asking about them has become a pleasantry, as mundane as asking about the weather.

One house has a purple tree in front. Next to it starts to form another industrial area: empty parking lots, wire fences; you can see folds of mountains from this parking lot. One of the Office Mart storage sites is here. A youth group I'd attended rents one of these on Friday nights.

Drive further and you will come to an intersection with a coin laundry and a liquor shop.

Past this intersection the roads open up into lakes lined with short white metal pole fencing as if to imitate white picket.

The left side is certainly prettier than the right.

We live on the left side. A flat, open lawn between two concrete houses. Steep driveways on either side that lead to four more condominiums in the back. Overgrown garden and children's toys. Three tall palm trees, some succulents, and orange roses. In the back, a pool sits in resin-bound gravel, fenced off with aluminum.

Dominique owns the second-to-last condominium in this arrangement of units. Where she lets Vic and me live too.

If you were to keep driving from our house and head east for another ten minutes or so, you'd arrive at some of the estates. These are the real treasures of Par Mars. Where the roads narrow into quaint rivers. Within these lush networks of houses, each property is larger, with more effort put into the transplantation, the foliage; imported, rare flowers. There is the Beverley Estate, where palms fan over the peculiar, box-shaped models wearing timber awnings. It takes after the organic beauty of a kind of woodland; a labyrinth highlighting the precious fabrics of a forest. A few minutes' drive over, you arrive at the most recently erected community—two hundred southwestern-style homes, appropriated from the style of Native American villages during the sixteenth century. This is another common discussion between locals: which aesthetic will be adopted for the next land package investment.

The Topic Heights shopping complex is at the heart of all these clusters, a perfect centrum, the exact summation of every need and personality of the people residing in its hem. It's where we get our clothes, where we find things to eat, where we determine what the inside of our houses will look like.

The Topic Heights shopping complex sits on the same highway as the Galleria shopping complex, ten minutes down. Only, the Galleria, with its domed white body and spiraling roundabout roads that spill into the different parking lot sections, is spectacular to look at.

Hilly roads lead off to State Route 96, directing you out to other zip codes and, if you wish, eventually to the coast.

When I get inside, Doms is sucking a splinter out of her hand.

She'd been making soaps when I left for my final shift at the public school a few hours ago. She plays the Leslie Cheung I showed her last week, lets incense run through. Doms has a habit of stopping halfway through the soap-making process to walk around our condo village. She stares at the flowers by the fencing of the pool and checks the fruit and marijuana trees she and Vic planted two summers ago.

"Vic still at work?" I ask.

"I think so." Doms blinks at me, then looks at the television, which is playing a K-drama. Her cheeks have a hot boredom about them; she tells me to come sit beside her. Our couch is situated against the window, where she is able to tan easily; often she will be there, her legs stretched out. Peeling fruit or organizing dried flowers, barely looking at what she's doing. Her white skin, drowning in evening sun.

The drama is in Korean, which she understands a little of and is learning as a way to connect to her maternal grandmother, who she otherwise knows very little about. She doesn't usually keep the English subtitles on because she is looking to improve her speaking of it as quickly as possible. She can be selfish like that, and often dreamily involved with the idea of domestic possessorship. She enjoys making the point very clear that these are *her* floorboards, *her* walls that we rotate within.

I stare outside, which is looking nice. A warm breeze blows and the palm trees gesture. A Lord Jagannath SMILE sticker is stuck on the window. It blocks the sun from piercing the side of my eyes if I'm sitting on the couch in this position, watching television at exactly this time.

"So where'd you go?" Doms stands up from the couch, pausing the television from her connected laptop.

I tell her I finished my last day at the after-school program. Doms raises her eyebrows.

It's felt like the same day repeating itself for some time now. I come home around five, Vic gets home around seven. The excitement of our workdays ending merges with Doms' restlessness, finding us in the same position by nine.

Our internal chemical environments mirror our external natural environment. Lethargy reflected in the dry leaves sitting atop my fold-out bed in the corner of the living room, the laptop still attached to the television with a taut cable, the once-novelty, boxed almond milk on the bench.

The rhythm of our schedule of emotions is dictated by the free and almost stylistic disorganization of this condo.

Our bodies may appear to be *yeet hay*, a term my mother uses to describe the disruption in one's equilibrium caused by *hotness*, the acidic boiling of blood or hot air present in the body from subtle stressors that cause subconscious anxiety. Depending on the body, these stressors can be spawned from different elements: processed sugar in sauces, the energy of excessive peanuts, the constancy of television, not the smoking of cannabis itself but perhaps the lingering of its cold resin.

This rhythm of living felt exciting and uncontrived at first, like how it feels to be *raw*. It was our attempt to draw closer to our own skin. But it's been a year now since Doms won the lottery on the cusp of finishing her degree in chemistry and we keep falling into this rhythm. We make up our days as we go, letting our habitat speak for our moods and anxieties. We suppose this must be happiness.

Sometimes Doms and I will walk around the poolside, circling a few times before jumping in. Feet are more sensitive to temperature variations because they're at the ends of us: thresholds for our bodies' heating and cooling. We let our soles start to burn, then jump in, the adrenaline bloating us, the impact collapsing us. It's exciting every time.

This evening, Doms and I are sitting in the living room watching a TV Western when we sense that Vic is back from work. Broad headlights are riding across the ceiling, then back down the wall again, scouring. A car door slams out front. The place smells like cinnamon and hemp.

"You're not eating that, are you?" Doms points to the cheesecake on a napkin.

I shake my head and she takes it.

We hear a cough, then a knock, keys jangling, then watch as Vic comes reluctantly through the door. A slight barbecue wind wisps through the air along with him. As his body becomes visible in the light from the television, we notice blood on his white pharmacy coat, dried up and molasses-like in his facial hair.

"They saw me," he says quietly. "I just was walking home and they cornered me."

"Who?" Doms stands to hold him, hanging her arms around his neck, patting his body as if to feel that it's there. She hurries to the kitchen and runs the tap.

"No, I'm fine, it's just—" Vic looks down at his combat boots, still on. Licks his bottom lip. Shakes his head and exhales.

Doms returns and wipes him.

At the dinner table, sitting a few feet from the couch. We've just finished a joint, now taking turns to rip a baguette, dipping the bits into leftover jarred chipotle mixed with Greek yogurt, conserving the flavor of the more expensive product.

Then, without considering the rhythm of the moment, Vic says, "I thought I was going to die, but everything seems ridiculous now."

After I've showered, I find it's half past two in the morning. I come out and see Vic and Doms wrapped in each other's arms, talking softly, smoking cigarettes on the couch. Doms has her arm around Vic's head, her fingers playing through his hair. His face has been cleaned up. My fold-out bed is beside the couch. Doms offers me a cigarette when she sees me in the archway. I shake my head and go stand in the kitchen.

3 I FOLLOW THE NEWS LIKE it's a series. It's the way they run network television in the suburbs, the way it plays nicely, as if *for* its citizens. As if everything was always meant to happen.

Back in the Territories, they program the television as if it's a time machine. My mother watches a kung fu period soap in a frosted-blue-glass apartment, seated at the dining table drying clear plastic cups. Laundry hanging out a small window and the city lights hovering across the harbor.

For a few days, we turn the television up while eating prepackaged dinners. In recent news, they've been trying to catch a brunette dad-looking man who is described as a local basketball team manager, a retired cop, and now a member of his local neighborhood watch council. According to the first presenter, his behavior has been *self-serving, strangely cultlike, and "religiously" driven*. The other presenter remarks, *Doesn't sound very religious to me*. They show surveillance footage of him walking around the shopping complexes, wearing a father's camping-gear fleece and New Balances. He's the antihero inside every suburban house.

Vic is sitting on the floor between Doms's legs, painting his fingernails with the white polish he took from the pharmacy.

"That was the guy," he says softly.

Doms says, "Which?"

"That was him, the guy who attacked me."

Doms stares miserably. She doesn't seem to know what to say and Vic is avoiding eye contact.

"Religious?" says Doms.

Vic flashes his eyes at me briefly, his tongue seated on the inside of his cheek, nodding from side to side. Doms is shaking her head, watching intently on the edge of the couch.

The program shows the man browsing through clothes in the Target. Once or twice I think I catch him skimming his translucent eyes over the camera's lens.

On Thursday night's program they finally decide to catch the man and wrap up the segment. Some of his close accomplices from the ex-cop club too. He and the line of police that march him out are looking straight into the pupil of the camera. There is hot rain tonight. We change to the TVB Korea Channel and arrive on a game show. Doms seems to understand a lot of it and is laughing loudly. Vic gets up to continue scrubbing at his pharmacy coat, blood still stained in the collar.

I return to the video I'd been watching earlier in the afternoon: an analysis of the first scene in *Blue Velvet* when a lovely man suffers a heart attack on the front lawn.

It seems as if the violence will be over for a little while.

4 I'M SITTING IN MY FOLD-OUT bed this morning with a very milky coffee, watching Vic put on his new pair of Adidas. He's rubbing the top of one of them with his thumb. I slide my shoes on as well and ask Vic if the Topic Heights pharmacy gets many customers early in the morning. He says, "Some." I'm driving him in this morning.

I'm going in to collect the keys for my new ear-cleaning studio. I'd been hoping, also, to spread the flyers I'd made around the complex. The visual cues of a store are very important. The decor, the number of people inside, the number of people interested. Even if I only bring in five people, it'll still create a mental snapshot for any passersby that this studio is accepted and therefore accessible for them.

I ask Vic if the center's staff community is kind and supportive.

"No," he answers, "*nobody* is friendly."

He half laughs. When he does this, there is fatigue in his eyes. He hasn't been sleeping much lately, he tells me. "Sorry, that's not the answer you wanted."

We're driving into Topic Heights. Vic has my flyers on his lap, his palms lying over the sheen of them. I've asked him to press down so they don't become creased.

The flyers read:

I'm proud of these flyers. Printed on thick, linen cardstock at the Office Mart. I promised myself that I wouldn't be passive, that I would make sure this business is seen. I promised I would not let it become one of those storefronts that appear for a few weeks before slinking away into a vacuum. A new business occupying its spot a week later, transforming the habitat of what had once been somebody else's aspiration.

This thought has been reoccurring to me as a sort of anxiety recently, materializing once again as I drive past the valet, up the ramp to the rooftop staff parking lot. Vic is saying something about the shrinkage of body size in fish as heating continues in the ocean. After three attempts to park, I unclick the belt and break my nail. "Oh well," Vic sighs, staring straight ahead. Then, "I could get used to being driven here every day." I show my nail to him and he says, "Oh shit."

We walk toward the automatic doors. I make a mental note that we're on level 3E, where staff are to park. Usually I park in 1C as a casual shopper. It allows immediate access to the supermarket on the lower level and is in close range to the phone-repair store.

Near the bins at the entrance, two pharmacy sales assistants Vic knows are kicking a hacky sack between them. They nod at Vic without saying anything, their focus intently on the sack.

As Vic approaches, the one with a beanie says, "Hey, man, how do you make that grapefruit soap your girlfriend made? It's really nice. But my girl's allergic to olive oil. She got an itch last night between her legs."

Vic says, "Animal fats, lye flakes—that's the sodium hydroxide part of it—distilled water, sugar and salt, lavender oil, synthetic colorant, the mixture of a sodium paste, and grapefruit-scented serum. No olive oil."

Vic has an impeccable memory. When he talks of substances, it's as if they are visually synthesizing before him, the logical, chronological equation for each compound he describes.

Vic unlocks the plastic screens at the pharmacy. He switches the lights on and pulls the racks of sale bins to the front. At the back, behind the pharmaceutical desk, he puts on his white coat, loops on his lanyard, which reads VICTOR and STORE MANAGER, then ties his hair back. The Vietnamese couple who own the pharmacy seem to urge only him, out of all their staff, to wear a net. Because of its texture, they had said. So he sometimes wears it and sometimes doesn't; it depends, I guess, on how he's feeling.

He goes to the back to get me nail clippers and I sit on the bench, poking my thumb with the sharp of the leftover nail, the vulnerability of it left half standing. Bending like a visor.

I go to spray a Marc Jacobs on myself and regret it because I see that there is a YSL sitting out for trialing too. It is embarrassing to want to smell of something.

Vic appears again, sniffing the air. "You're ridiculous." He passes me the clippers and wraps a hairnet over his head.

We personify the scent. A feminine or a masculine thriving on interior paradises, who decorates with house plants but not so much that it seems like they do hot yoga, because they just do the regular yoga, even so casually as to be guided by a YouTube yogi. A person who goes to a car wash and doesn't clear their belongings from the car because they've got two of everything. A person who brings a two-liter water bottle with them on a visit to the bank. A person who cooks without an apron, but with their hair up and hotel slippers on.

Vic goes to inspect each aisle. He looks carefully at the products, referring back to his notepad. I watch from the bench, flattening my hand over the flyers.

The silence before the music is turned on throughout the complex is ethereal: feels almost as if we're in a spaceship and the processing of time has shifted.

It was this strange comfort in the design of a shopping complex that prompted me to convince my father that Topic Heights was the right place for my business. In every city we had moved to for my father's work, it was the natural ecosystem, separated by climate and light, which would differ immensely. Think the difference between Malaysia and London. But in a shopping complex, the climate and light remain the same. It is the landscape of familiar logos, the behaviors of shop assistants. It is the indoor planting, the skylights, all designed to replicate what the land had once been before it was bulldozed. The climate is regulated to suit the likes of the common shopper. For someone who has come from a different one. And though I know this, I had grown up searching for a sameness, as most children do. It is a guilty pleasure to want so badly to be encased in it.

I go and look through the snacks shelved at the front desk. I take a pack of jelly beans and open it, ask Vic to come over and guess the flavor. He covers his eyes with his hand and opens his mouth a little. He guesses licorice. I tell him that was an obvious one.

He says, "You know, licorice is associated with cold and flu syrup because the plant they use for it is the exact same. Its flavor is so pungent that it masks the original medicinal taste."

He guesses orange for the next one, though it's strawberry. I tell him he's right anyway to see if he'll notice.

In a bit, the other employees arrive and report to Vic, who notes this on the timesheet. At nine, the presence of the first customer modifies the atmosphere, noticeable in the way Vic's face and the manner of his gait change. I hop off the front desk and go to sit on one of the fold-up stools in the back. My phone is in my lap, in progress of playing an analysis video about the movie adaptation of *No Country for Old Men*. I notice someone in the sectioned-off shelf area that meets the storeroom, eating out of a tin obnoxiously. Scraping the fork around inside. He works at the prescription desk too, I suppose.

He looks up at me, catches some beans back in his mouth, and says, "Hey, hey, do you even work here?"

He looks as though he's carried over the vigor of his eating into the act of intimidating me. I feel the weight of my jacket around me. Hold it into myself.

"Well?"

He looks a bit older than me and Vic, though I cannot tell for certain. He's a skinny Caucasian guy with minimal toddler hair. Wearing a short-sleeved shirt and a bland tie. Some tattoos showing, one of a beckoning cat. Chains on his teeth, I notice when he opens his mouth to speak.

"No," I say. "But I'm opening an ear-cleaning studio on the next level."

He points his fork at me, nodding. "You know, you've got to be careful in this industry. It isn't about skill or product as much as it is about socialization . . ."—he scoops more food into his mouth—"and charisma."

His teeth look as though they're squirming between his lips when he smiles. As if for attention. He chucks the bean tin into the bin beside the cabinet storing asthma inhalers. He turns back around on his heel with a swivel. I cannot really tell how old this guy is. His mannerisms don't seem to match his body. The mannerisms look as though they've occupied space longer than his body has.

The analysis video is talking about how Chigurh often checks his boots for blood.

He sees me watching my phone, continues to talk. "It's easy to move up the scale, you just gotta watch your every word. One minute you're hired. If you're sweet-talking them, complimenting their hair. The next minute you go on and imply they're gaining weight or, or you know, you've got yourself fired. Put on small-talk lists between *friends* and *colleagues*," he says theatrically. "Entertainment for the dogs."

"I run my own studio, so I don't really need to worry about that."

"I mean, your *customers*. Your customers hire you, never forget that."

The video is talking about how there is no musical score. His eyes are wide with a sort of expecting.

I pause the video.

He unfolds his arms, reaches out, shakes my hand with his bony one. He's wearing a silver Rolex, which slides a little down his wrist according to such drastic movement.

"I'm Jean Paul."

"Like Sartre?"

"You saying that right? You tryna say Sartre? You know who that is, right?"

I decide he must be at least thirty-three. There is too much practice in the way he reacts. He could be offensive but somehow is not. He could be brash, yet there is something endearingly vulnerable about him.

"I could be the manager here and I'd have every right to ban you from the store for being back here," says Jean Paul. He laughs disgustingly. Then a comfortable, silent moment. He goes to look at my flyers lying on the bench beside me, thumbing his chin. "You want me to hand these out to customers today? I could."

"Sure. Yeah, that'd be great."

He is the kind of person you cannot for the life of you tell the age or even culture of, due to the way their soul moves around in their hand gestures, the way their shoulders are held comfortably around their neutral chest. Could be twenty-six, could be forty-five. Could be from the south or could be from the north. Regardless, his body looks as though it's been in routine and is attempting to crawl out of itself.

He pulls a pharmacy coat on and I remember a time Vic complained about being brutally scolded by the owners for wearing a tie. As store manager, Vic seemingly holds a lot of the control here, in charge of everyone else's demeanor, but it is Jean Paul who is wiping his lip and tucking his tie back in between the buttons of his pharmacy coat without blinking.

5 **IT'S NIGHT AND MY TEXAN** dad stares at me across the table of a smorgasbord restaurant that opened six months ago beside the Home store. He's back visiting Par Mars, on leave from his current contract job somewhere in Japan, one of the smaller cities, Nagasaki or Nagoya.

He tells me, "I've always found oak timber walls so soothing." He knocks the wall with his knuckle. "But these are plastic."

It seems we're inside a caricature of a restaurant, but this is supposed to be the charm of it.

After a while he offers to pour me a glass of champagne.

I tell him, "But there is no champagne."

To him, this is the punch line of the joke. We laugh it off and the waiter comes to refill our glasses with water.

"How is your romantic life?" he asks.

"No one, at the moment."

"Have you tried online dating?" He fixes his cuff links. The way he says *day-ding* in his unique accent.

"I did. I tried it once," I say, eating a lamb shank.

"And why no more?"

"I'd rather not talk about it."

Between then and now, there has been the massage therapy course, my secondhand Saab 900, Doms, the lottery, the after-school program, the shopping complex.

The first time I met Doms was the last time I'd dated properly. My parents had just divorced and my father wanted to keep moving on as a contractor, would do so with less baggage. They divorced entirely in Cantonese.

He'd packed his suitcase in silence, then, as he left, he said to my mother, "What are you going to do then?"

And my mother and I remained here; for the first time we remained.

It was then I tried some online dating because my mother bought me a phone so I could catch the bus on my own. The dating app is where I met Travis. I remember leaning against his Nissan behind the local Anglican church. Ironing out my spine against the hot windows. The youth group he brought me to was run in one of those industrial-type buildings, asphalt parking lot with wire fences. We liked to smoke a cigarette, looking at the way the mountains curled, before we went in.

Travis often led the Christian-rock songs with his guitar, someone else on the tambourine. He'd talk to me about the Rapture and often, every time, he would express how much he wanted me to be baptized. He wanted for me to mention him in my testimony. He told me this girl, Dominique, had been baptized when she turned nineteen, actually. She received it for her birthday present. It was only seventy dollars to do it. You got a T-shirt, a Bible, and eternal life.

It had been summer, two whole months with Travis, and I found myself always in his Nissan, passenger seat, shotgun. We had been driving to youth group one night when his iPhone 5 rang. The name DOMS showed up on his phone, a panda beside her name. In her picture she had brunette, boy-cut fringed hair, Chloë Sevigny in the nineties. Smooth white skin, different from my own beige bumpy skin. He held on to my hand tightly. When I asked him why he was squeezing so hard, he told me he loved me very much and didn't let go until five minutes after the phone stopped vibrating, as if he'd forgotten he was squeezing, refraining.

I cut my hair that night. It seemed like the right thing to do at the time. But I see how it'd been childish, as though I were attempting to mediate myself, to shape myself into the perfect in-between of me and Doms.

He didn't seem to mind about the hair, though it didn't suit my round head the way it suited Doms's.

We had been in his bedroom, slow-dancing to the singing of his mother showering in the next room, when I asked him if he had made Doms get baptized. He said, "Well, I certainly had a core part in it."

Everything was fine until I woke in his bed naked the following day. I felt for my hair and started crying. The sky outside was a white-blue, the slight branch of a tree rattling against the window. Travis woke up, patted my head, and held me close, then I took the bus home around midday.

I messaged Doms via her social media. She messaged back immediately saying my hair would grow back and she didn't really care that Travis was seeing other people. A few weeks later he left both of us, left the country. He was going on an indefinite mission trip to a Southeast Asian country. It was important for him to do this. There were many signs that he was to do this, it was always going to be.

Doms and I hung out outside of the youth group a week after he left. We sat in the food court of Topic Heights, where she had a part-time job at the doughnut store. She'd brought me two, smiling tight-lipped as she slid them to me across the table. Then, after her shift, she invited me back to swim in her pool. Her mother was still around then; she ordered us food to eat. For a while I wasn't sure if I was in love with Doms or if there was just something so beautiful in the way she appeared not to care for anything much, still working with relentless focus on whatever she had in front of her. This was four years ago.

. . .

The next day my Texan father and I are at the grand opening of a new K.A.G. store at the Topic Heights shopping complex. He's only in Par Mars for a couple more hours and he wants to try and buy some reasonably priced undergarments in the K.A.G. welcome sale. He says these ones fit him best; something in the fabric, a kind of polyester. He knows the franchise and follows it religiously. He could spend hours in the original store, the one in Hong Kong. Singapore, New York, Shanghai, and London. He is a big fan of their company philosophy. Simple is better. "What I've said *all* along," he says.

We are watching the spectacle on the ground level of the Topic Heights, clapping as the store manager cuts the ribbon stemming from one side to the other. A sharply dressed Asian man films on his phone in close range.

The staff standing out in front are wearing plain shirts. My father tells me that with every new season comes a new color arrangement. Often still a shade, rather than an outright color, different types of off-whites, different types of gray. "It's subtle," says my father. "Very subtle, very smart." The staff looks like the cast of a modern-day television series playing at five p.m. Like they've got just *one* of every kind of ethnicity in the Par Mars range. They all wear aprons. Except the manager, who is wearing a muted red collared T-shirt.

Nine people have shown up for the opening and other shoppers have stopped to take a look while passing. A woman toward the front asks if they're doing wine or snacks. Nobody answers. The woman shrugs for herself, and her husband meanders over to the store window to take a closer look at the cargo shorts on display.

My father notices the man observing the shorts and leans across to me. "They'd be about forty-seven dollars, those ones."

When they let us in, there are hangers of T-shirts and pants that are gray, brown, beige, off-white, and black, and one other "theme" color. There are belts and bags. SIMPLE, EVERYDAY WEAR, reads a banner.

Afterward, I show my father the empty studio he's seen only in photographs. He stands in the middle of the reception area with his arms folded.

"Hmm," he says. "It doesn't look as big as in the photos."

He inspects the corners to see if there is rotting.

He'd lent me money for the deposit, and for the first two months, he'd agreed to help with the rent costs. It's not the kind of place he would've wanted for me, but what he fails to understand is that there will be more foot traffic in a shopping complex than if I were to lease a store on a sidewalk here in Par Mars. He'd only lived here for a few months before he left again, so he never knew the place the way I did, a whole ecosystem separate from any other.

He looks out the shop window. Diagonally, down the escalators, is K.A.G. "Very good location, though. Good proximity."

I'm in my fold-out bed in the corner of the living room. I have the lamp on and my feet under the covers. I'm revising the plan for my grand opening. I'll be needing more than nine people to attend. I open the document for my grand opening invitation. I type: *Snacks and wine included.*

I call a catering company that charges fifteen dollars per head with a minimum of ten guests.

I'm deciding whether or not to specify the genre of snacks and wine on the invitation, but as Robert Greene says in *The 48 Laws of Power*: *Always say less than necessary. When you are trying to impress people with words, the more you say, the more common you will appear, and the less in control.*

I realize the windows are open, a passive night breeze seeping in, shifting the dry leaves on the couch beside me. Doms and Vic went up to their loft a while ago. I pull down the window and the hiss of cicadas numb out. My laptop is right under the metal poles of my fold-out bed. It creaks as I adjust myself. There are plants climbing up our curtains, which we never use. See, being situated in the back of a block means there is no streetlight shining through. If there was, I'm sure we'd stick a sticker right in the spot where it would shine through to hit my eye.

I fall asleep excited.

6 **FACETIME WITH MY MOTHER. SHE** uses English in front of Doms. Doms is to my right on the other end of the couch, lighting up a saved roach in tweezers. She's out of frame, but the smoke dribbles in. My mother straps a headlamp to her forehead, distracted. I strap my headlamp on too. We're speaking about politics. Then Doms comes into frame.

"Hello, auntie," she says, waving tepidly.

I'd told her to say this, say *auntie,* and to this Doms had said, "But she's not."

My mother has never liked Doms much.

"Ah . . . hello," says my mother, moving her glasses down slightly.

"Yes."

Doms pulls herself closer and offers me her ear. My mother and I mimic each other with our tools, wiping them down. "Cerumen comes in many shapes and sizes," she begins. "Sometimes it's hard and sometimes it can feel like a . . . soft dough."

I listen intently.

My mother explains, "If you think too much about stabbing the eardrum, you will do it. The way you break the auditory ossicles is if you think too much about them. You have to feel through the canal, meditate through it—*not* study it. The lining of one's ear is very delicate, like you're probing a flower. Do not only use the end of your scoop, but the bamboo stick or rod that holds it."

I begin to insert the rod into Doms's ear canal.

She shivers. "Sorry, I'm ticklish."

My mother watches me, leaning in close to her phone. "That's it," she coos.

I twirl the rod.

After a moment, she says abruptly, "Change sticks."

I swap to a small feathery one.

"No, the tweezers—you don't want to push the cerumen further into the ear."

I reach over for the tweezers, wipe them down with a cotton pad, and use them to grab the little orb of paste before putting it to the edge of Doms's ear.

"No!" my mother says harshly. "Put it straight to the tray."

I pull the tray closer and dispense the sticky, almost wet sebum on it.

My mother then teaches me how to massage the canals by generating small vibrations of the stick.

Doms lets out a sigh.

She advises me to caress the outer ears and along the side of the head. The motion is like twisting a bottle cap off with one finger.

"The final stage," says my mother, "is to do a therapy clean. The healing clean with your cotton swab."

"The Ming dynasty . . ." says my mother.

I'm cleaning the tools in the sink, the phone propped up, watching her eat between chicken bones with her hands.

"The Ming dynasty is when it all started, in tea houses and social settings. You are carrying a *long tradition* in your fingers now, Leen."

She says about 80 percent of her clients are folks who come from places like the UK or Sweden, and all their friends stand around to watch and video her. Their paper cups of tea and sugarcane in one hand, phones in the other. She says there is an old woman from Guangzhou who comes just to chat about the soap opera they both happen to watch.

She barters for a cheaper price every time. She tells me that while Asian and Indigenous folks tend to have flaky, dry earwax, Caucasian and African folks have yellow, sticky wax. "Interesting," I say.

"Yes," she says. She gets up without announcing, taking her box of chicken bones with her. In a moment I hear a rubbish-tin lid snapping back, and she returns wiping her fingers with a wet wipe. She says, "Yes. Do you know, Leen, the *spirometer* has a race-corrected feature. It measures differently if you are not Caucasian?" She tells me that she found it difficult to use when practicing as a GP, because it required her to enter in a person's ethnicity prior to enabling the device and she was often unsure about her patients' details. She had found out later down the line that there was no way around this feature, as it had been built in by its manufacturer.

Without looking up, she says, "But with ear cleaning, ethnicity is told by what the earwax looks like." She laughs, sticks a note to her desk, and folds her arms. "People come to get their ears cleaned, all types of people," she continues. "People learn from the internet. They find us on the internet. Ear is a pathway to the brain. It is as though you are dusting it. Maintaining hygiene is a way of coming closer to, to be *shu-fuk*, comfortable, balance takes you closer to the Dao."

My mother is a Taoist and a believer in God. She has never expressed any emotional language toward it. My mother stares at nothing.

I detail the plans I have for my grand opening, and she tells me I'm "very business-minded," like her own father, who sold opium in the thirties. The sun is yawning in the middle of the sky.

Later, Jean Paul comes by the house with some books and pill bottles for Vic, who'd had a panic attack while waiting for the bus this morning. Vic came home and lay in bed for a few hours. He comes down from the loft to thank Jean Paul for the things and politely offers that he stay for dinner—we're having a big pasta pot.

After dinner, when Doms and Vic have gone for a bath, I drive Jean Paul to the Glenvale Estate to look at the houses. After four, the estate is only seven minutes from Doms's.

It's coming to sunset at half past eight nowadays. The appeal of these estates is the sanctitude. There is an absolute quietness you cannot achieve anywhere else unless you drive out to the forests or the mountains. Built into the marketing packages is the promise that there is marginally reduced police presence, no commercial properties, constant park maintenance, and high-quality tech surveillance. A body corp fee is paid for an honorable neighborhood watch council, security camera installation, pathways that encourage community accountability. This body corp fee is rumored to add up to about fifteen thousand a year.

We go to use the adult exercise park. I'm spinning a wheel and Jean Paul is opening and closing some handlebars. We're standing a few meters apart, but if Jean Paul were to speak I could still hear him quite clearly. These estates, they're formidably quiet past six.

What eventually triggers any sort of conversation between Jean Paul and me is a man who's walking past in jogging shorts, his head down. Between his hands is the blare of pixelated gasping, then moaning. At first he doesn't notice us, but when he registers our movements in the corner of his eye he turns the volume down on his phone without looking up. The gasping becomes quicker. He continues walking as though being unreactive toward us will make us forget about him quicker. He disappears through the swab of darkness into one of the identical-looking houses.

Jean Paul says suddenly, "Did you know that in the nineties my aunt was part of a group that maintained this conspiracy theory that heteronormativity and feminism were fabricated by a commercial government supreme in the sixties, encouraging rapidly changing genres of fashion for gender identity? They wanted to enforce power over predicted marketing demographics—the fed-up housewife, the city-slicker woman, the empowered woman, the tuxedo woman, the tomboy woman . . ."

I tell him I've never heard this theory.

We swap equipment naturally. I watch him spin the wheel with his arms ending in a twist. He untwists and twists again, as though he's never known how a car is meant to be driven.

He has a strange attractiveness about him, though I cannot tell where it comes from' perhaps it is the extreme earnestness he maintains. The shape of his nose is assertive, and there is nothing fascinating about his eyes except that they sink deeply into his head. His eyebrows come too close to his eyes. And yet when he speaks and the crease around his thin mouth forms, there is something dishy about it.

He says, "I think I've adopted the same type of thinking as her. Inherited. Like *intergenerational* . . . For example, this is me, this is my thinking: a multimillion, multistory shopping complex. The appeal is not that there are stores where you can buy things for yourself, the appeal is that the tiles are new, and the plants are green and you never see them yellowing. And it's likely that the people may not be as good or as cool as you. And the people who serve you want you. You go to see people watch you. Mmm . . . and the cleanliness."

I say, slightly defensively, "Well, ear cleaning is meant to be good for you. And casual indulgence in it is meant to balance out our equilibrium."

"Ear cleaning, or really the entire massage business, is intimate, suggestive, and voyeuristic."

"No. That may be how others have chosen to consume it, but it isn't inherently *suggestive*."

"But isn't that what happens to all businesses, my friend?" he says. "So there is nothing all that special about it. Every business and every person in charge of that business wants to tell themselves that it's important because it benefits somebody else, even though most of the time, they really just overcharge others to benefit themselves. They want to tell their customers—and not only *them* but their employees too—what their lives are to look like and what they are to feel like, and it doesn't give their customers or employees a chance to think for themselves. I mean, they're not awful people, but they're upholding a false reality on behalf of their ego, no?"

I pause. I begin to resent any of the defensiveness within me. "Well, I guess people like to *feel exotic at times.*"

He laughs. When he genuinely laughs, it seems both fantastic and psychotic. His face eases. Mine does as well, though I notice my breath is changed.

"Poor friends," he says. "People can just drink coconut water, don't they know that?"

I've started to deflate, pulling and pushing the handlebars.

He stops spinning when I stop pushing. "I'm sorry," he says. "I don't mean to be culturally insensitive. I know what you mean. Your service might be less empty than others, but the people are never less empty, Leen. And they'll approach it that way. Anyway, I'll be coming to your opening. I can invite friends too."

The pavement is slightly damp for no reason, like the air tonight, not cold but nipping softly at our knuckles. We walk back to my car, parked half up on the curb. We get in. It's dark now, and some houses have their warm, earthy lights switched on. There's a family of four sitting around a table inside the house we're parked in front of. When my headlights come on, they all turn to look out the window at us. I see the mother saying something to the father and they all continue eating. As if forgetting.

Jean Paul mutters something about the brand of my car.

"I've never had a car in my life," he says after a moment. He tells me the bus allows him time and space to write in his notebook and to read. He'd love if he could just live in a car, though. It'd save him a lot of rent. He laughs.

I tell him, "The best thing about this one is the storage in the back. I also like the steering wheel, and the top is *big* and *open* like a half moon." I grip around it.

He admires the steering wheel. I feel him staring.

"I've worn crocodile skin," says Jean Paul as we pull into the driveway of the condo.

I pull the key out. "Crocodile skin, isn't that expensive?"

"My crocodile-skin cowboy boots," sighs Jean Paul.

He leans back into the seat. "Let me estimate the cost. It was more than a grand, less than two." I make a surprised expression. "I sold them, though," says Jean Paul.

We go inside and I hear Doms and Vic in the bathroom down the hall. Doms yells gutturally, as we enter the living room, "Shut our door, Leen." I go down to shut the bathroom door. The smell of candles, the smell of rose and lavender burning. As I come back into the foyer, Jean Paul is preparing to leave again. He pulls his worn, thinly suede bomber jacket on and walks out to the street into the tangle of blackness and stark electric whiteness.

I watch a news segment from my fold-out bed. Sometimes it feels as though Doms and Vic have each other and I just have their television.

This particular segment is about a middle-aged local named Helen. The neighborhood she lives in looks strangely familiar to the one my mother and I lived in, three or four suburbs closer to the city than we are here. It was the place my mother had rented for four years before moving back to the Territories; the place we'd stayed in for the longest amount of time, the two of us.

In the segment, Helen had noticed the "new woman" next door, who she describes as a foreigner, moving things in for weeks. Once the neighbor had settled in finally, she came to Helen's door bearing fruit. She'd brought grapes, but tiny ones that squirted easily and had no desirable texture. Two days later, the neighbor brought sauces, a sweet one and a pickled one. Helen says the sauces were in unlabeled jars, as though the neighbor had made them herself. She had also started noticing how the neighbor's indoor lights and television were never turned off.

I imagine Helen, the white-haired woman on the screen, standing outside her neighbor's window and peering in, only her eyes visible from the inside.

Helen is saying that she sometimes heard yelling and would feel tempted to call the police, but she didn't because she is a woman taught to mind her own business. The final straw was when the neighbor brought her a little 100-gram bag of coffee beans. On closer inspection, Helen realized it was a small animal's shit inside a bag. Helen was now more serious about going to the authorities, hoping they would consider evaluating the woman's legitimacy in this country.

In the end, the segment is really about Helen's persistence and the friendship and cultural understanding that ensued between the two. The neighbor explains that kopi luwak originates from the Asian civet defecating coffee cherries, the process of digestion removing the acidity to result in a smoother blend. This was beneficial for Balinese and Indonesian farmers during colonization because they were not allowed to access the colony coffee bean plantations. These small civets would carry the beans over in their stomachs. The segment ends with an image of Helen and her neighbor drinking the kopi luwak together.

I stare at Helen, who is smiling gently, seeming pleased. Then I look to the ecstatic smile of her neighbor. The first presenter says, *Well, that was lovely and very touching, wasn't it?* The second says, *The luwak coffee is fantastic by the way . . . Oh is it? Quite an amusing concept . . . Well, I'll need to try it . . . We'll be right back.*

7 A FEW DAYS LATER MY mother sends me an article about Chengdu ear cleaners being put on the World Heritage List, followed by five exclamation points in a separate message. I reply saying: *Does this mean I can charge more.* She sends back: *L.O.L.*

. . .

Today I am hanging rusted gold frames with traditional floral art on the walls. There is one ultra-wide shan shui I inherited from my mother, which I decide to hang behind the reception desk. I look at it.

I'll make a habit of smoking cigarettes as soon as I become a studio manager. I like to imagine myself in the corner where the hall peels off to the studios, French inhaling, a vest on me, or some kind of wrap thing that gives off the impression that although I am stern, I am also easygoing.

There is no noise. I check the time. It's seven a.m. I find myself forgetting what ordinary behavior at a shopping complex looks like. What time do the shoppers come? The bakers came at five a.m. You can smell that.

I look at the empty wall. I am grappling with fitting a mountain into a room; more than this, making the room as prosperous as one.

I walk from one room—the main studio with the hanger for the less-wide shan shui painting—immediately back into the short, tight hallway and into the next room. It is a smaller studio, almost like a cupboard, with a sink. All throughout, the walls are slightly off-yellow, attempting to become beige in the eyes of an optimist.

I walk back into the reception area, stand in front of the desk, and look out the glass storefront. A person who looks like my cousin walks past with a backpack over their shoulder, eating an apple. They walk straight ahead without looking into the store.

People know what they want when they come into a shopping complex. They will often be here for the franchises, because these franchises are the ghosts that have been lingering around the peripheral of a civilian since birth.

A complex is unlike the city, where they are happy to stumble across something, an independent store, where they are happy to explore. They make art out of the randomness, the meandering. *Here* it is a curation. This tiny store in a larger carefully thought-out ecosystem of many choices, fit to the likes of many. It is through the decoration, the smell, what the staff look like. On top of this, the infinite maze design of a complex is what frustrates and creates the conclusiveness of a customer, so they will usually try not to stray from their immediate needs. They will walk without looking through the windows.

Robert Greene says: *Court attention at all cost. Everything is based on appearances, and appearances happen in crowds. Never let yourself get lost in the crowd.*

I hang up an LED OPEN sign. It's the final touch.

I call Doms. "You can come set up the soaps now."

Doms arrives half an hour later with a box of candles and a bag of soaps. Each candle and soap is wrapped in beautiful origami paper. I open the door for her. We set her box and bag on the reception desk.

"Hmm . . ." We look around for a moment.

"I don't know what's missing," I say, staring around the room.

"Well, it doesn't entirely look like . . . like a healing studio," says Doms.

"I'll have biology posters up in the studios too," I tell her, pointing at the rolled-up paper in the corner.

Doms shakes her head, humming. "No, no, that's not what I meant. Like, that's . . . *too* clinical."

"I also have diffusers to set up."

Doms shakes her head again. "What you need is one of those, you know, those bamboo dividers."

"To divide what?"

"You need to make it look like there is *something* going on. It needs to look like anything could be going on . . . do you get what I'm trying to say?"

"Well, nothing would be going on, except for what is said to be going on."

"I don't know, Leen, like, it just could be less clinical, right?"

I smell one of the soaps through the wrapping and place it back down again.

Doms says, "Not to sound insensitive, and don't judge me. But I think there's an element that's intriguing about places that look like brothels or something. That's what people are buying, right? The enigma of it. They want *different*. Not like in a racist . . . even sexual way . . . I think people who come specifically to Topic Heights would only come into yours because they've just discovered gua shas and jade rollers and weed, or chia seeds on the internet. But you want more depth than that. You want people to be curious, people to wander in like they would at any other shop. I think the only way to do that is through the aesthetic of it."

"Did you ever consider that someone might just have a sore back and Topic Heights just happens to have the closest massage place to them?"

Doms sits herself up on the reception desk, takes each soap from the bag, and lines them up.

She explains, "It has to be like theater. People aren't just going to try a new thing because it's there. They want to buy the whole experience, you get me? You need to make it look quite oriental. I hate saying that. But it's so people will come in and feel as though they're experiencing an alternate reality. They're having a novelty moment. It's like if you think about going to get your nails done or something. The plastic tub of lunch beside them, that shit's all part of the experience. The loud manager, the music videos on an old plasma, all that."

What Doms is saying makes sense. The novelty is half the package, the mannerisms of the furniture, the implications of the supposed randomness of the decor. I think of the massage studios I've been to, what they imply when I enter. In Kowloon, massages are much cheaper, a popular form of service, a popular way to spend time. The staff shuffle around as if they are hiding something in one of the rooms. The massage itself is effective and not tied to time, but to how the body feels. Here in Par Mars I've only ever been to one session. It had been extraordinarily clinical, as if I had something about my body I needed to be defensive about; tense the entire time. I google "established massage businesses in Par Mars." The four of them are all named with words like Silk, Lotus, Touch, Fusion, Thai, in different arrangements.

"Maybe I'll try a different name," I say to Doms.

"What's the name now?" she asks, scratching at the acne developing along her jaw.

"It's listed as Healing Studio. But I think I'm going to try Lotus Fusion Studio."

I look through the search results and observe the online presence of the other healing and massage studios. Some don't have any pictures, only their street view and reviews.

>>>*Waste of money. My "masseuse" had no knowledge of the body. Could have gotten the same massage from my husband. There was no Thai aspect to any of the massage.*

>>>*The girls is really chatty. I could tell she doesn't like her job from the beginning, it's not good value.*

>>>*All they do is talk loudly and laugh while u are trying to relax and they do not speak English.*

>>>*Not happy at all. Went in with my husband for us to have a massage, obviously. A girl came in within 10 minutes and offered him a happy ending. I'm disgusted how dare you offer my husband a sexual favor in front of me. I hope you close down, I'm reporting to the police. hope that this closes down.*

>>>*Manager is rude and does not understand a word I am saying . . . but fine massage.*

I turn to Doms. "Okay so you're only rated badly if you don't speak English, or you talk during the service or you offer them a hand job."

"A fucking hand job."

We're silent.

I say, "You don't want to come work with me sometime?"

"What would I do?"

I shrug. "You can make your soaps here and sell them.Contribute to the energy."

"Right. But then I'd have to pay rent."

We're at a standstill with this conversation, me and Doms. We always end up here lately, and from here we'll usually go for a swim or turn on the television to iron out the silence.

"I think you're asking me to offer the extra services," says Doms, blinking rapidly.

I'm still looking at the reviews. I put the phone down and start rolling out the posters of organs and muscle. "They are *big*. How do I flatten these out?"

Doms helps me hold one end. "Are you trying to get me to do the sexual favors, Leen?"

"No."

"Then what? What would I do here?"

"Well, like I said, I thought maybe you'd like the space to make the candles and soaps."

Doms is now setting up the display of candles and soaps, making tiers. I'm looking on my phone at the Target website. I'm deciding to make investments in the Fiber Weave Room Divider—Oriental Furniture edition. That or the Shoji Screen—Oriental Furniture edition.

Doms has been living on Powerball money, so she doesn't know when to start looking for work again. She has a real skill and knack for the lottery business. She draws the lucky number seven from her maternal grandmother's Korean ancestry. Draws from her maternal grandfather's

French side: the lighting of a candle before she sits down to fill out the ticket. Rituals that make her feel connected to it all. There is a meditation involved and a recording of all the numbers she witnesses in a day. *There is a mathematical algorithm*, says Doms. She is running on lottery money and her candle and soap sales at the Sunday market. Her mother had also left her some kind of inheritance.

We all stay at Doms's condo for free. The property had been paid off before her mother passed. And although Doms had wanted it to be an investment property, she never got around to beginning the process. She makes Vic pay the bills, mostly, or they'll split it and he'll buy her fresh flowers every odd week, but I've been a ghost there for a while and it hasn't been mentioned. There have been a few pieces of furniture I've bought here and there, and we get our own groceries. The second bedroom, used as an off-limits storage room, is full of old nostalgic things. It needs to be cleared, but maybe the quicker they do it, the more comfortable I might get; perhaps this is why it hasn't been done. Regardless, we have fun, and when we get into the difficult, money-related conversations, there is enough space in Par Mars to spread out, at least for a couple of hours.

"I'm just opening the offer up because I know staying at home all the time can be difficult for freelancers," I say. "I'm returning the favor. You can have the spot for free."

She considers this and shakes her head. "Oh my God, Leen."

When we get in my car, parked on 3E, I head toward the mega Target along the 96. I get an odd feeling that Jean Paul is going to steal my car one of these days. It smells like him in here. Doms makes a comment about it. On the radio, 103.8: *Just last night, Wi-Fi service outages across the country result in large data usage... Over the time of... mammals! So many of them...*

We drive past all the car showrooms and arrive at the sprawling parking lot. People with trolleys. I almost run a child over. And Doms screams, "Watch out," after it would've already been too late.

"I saw," I say.

The sun glaring in where we park. Hot air, and my breath is tangled. There's a sweetness to the slight wind as I step out of the car, and I stretch my arms out.

"Did you hear?" says Doms, slamming the door shut. She's chewing on some gum now. "Apparently, people think the outages were deliberate, done by the government. Apparently some really serious evidence of the Winstead investigation got leaked on a mass level and they needed to shut everything down."

We go inside where the air is cold and regulated and a Rihanna song is playing. I ask for the oriental furniture section and show the store assistant the specific designs on our phone. The woman points to the far end of the store. "The furniture section."

We head toward the checkout with the room divider and a lantern, when we see a Rosewood Korean Tea Table, in a box that reads *Handcrafted by Chinese artisans*, and decide to pick it up too.

Back at the studio I FaceTime my mother, who's in her dressing gown. I set my phone with her face inside it against a vase on the front desk, and we show her the furniture boxes. My mother instructs me and Doms as we lift out the first divider and position it in various sections of the reception area.

"Your clinic is already lacking flow because there are no windows to natural light." She puts her reading glasses on. "Now. When you walk in, you want to see the whole place. Don't put the thing in the way of the door. Place it so that it runs along the storefront glass, it will soften the sharp edges of the place." She adds, "And put the tea table in front of it."

"Why would a table be in the storefront like that?" I ask.

"You can use it to lean the price menu and candles or . . . vase of flowers."

Doms says, "She's right."

My mother, when she's been validated, purses her lips and raises one eyebrow.

I carry the Korean tea table to the window and Doms moves the divider back. "There."

I tell Doms and my mother that last week I bought an egg and inside there were two yolks. While I'm telling the story, Peggy, the CEO of the complex, knocks on the glass door. *Hold on*, I mime through the glass. I grab my phone from the desk and go outside to see her."It's Ling?" she says, referring to an iPad.

"Yes, Leen."

"I'm Peggy. Is that your 1994 Saab parked on level three in the permit-only disabled parking spot?"

"Yes."

"It's only for people with the permit."

"We had a lot to unload and no one's here yet. We'll move it."

I check my phone and it's nine. The stores open between nine and ten.

"Do you have a permit?"

"No."

Peggy is a muscly blonde woman wearing a pink blouse and a necklace with what looks like mothballs on it. She is taller than I am and seems to enjoy looking slightly down at me. She says, "Not off to a good start, I suppose."

She leaves me standing there.

I hear from my phone in my palm, "Leen, you shouldn't park your car just anywhere—it can be towed." My mother's public voice. "If you park where people need to park, they will not be able to access the door."

As Peggy's about to turn off right to go down the escalator, she suddenly decides to turn around again and meander back over.

Robert Greene says: *Keep others in suspended terror.*

I tell my mother I'll call her this evening and hang up.

Peggy hovers in front of me, tapping her forehead as if thinking. "Any hint of funny business and you're out. I've hosted these sorts of businesses before. I know what's up."

8 MY FATHER ONCE SAID TO me: *People are treated like resources and sometimes that makes them happier. The illusion that you're special is only something that'll hurt you when you realize you're not.*

I'm annoyed about the interaction I had with Peggy, though it seems I couldn't have done much about it. She seemed to enjoy that I had done something wrong. The faces she'd made, gravitating somewhere between smutty and complacent.

I go home and watch a film. I've always found myself to be an escapist. I advised my father once, if he ever felt alone or sad traveling around so much, not to go getting himself into any kind of trouble but to watch many films. Watch some mumblecore, I suggested.

A few months ago, I went alone to the Star Cinema and bought a ticket for a session playing a rerun of *2001: A Space Odyssey.* Someone had told me to see it, said it would help me "discover myself." And that night Doms and Vic had been fighting.

Halfway through the film, someone walked down the aisle and began dancing in front of the screen. I thought for a minute it might've been a flash mob, which was popular for a moment in time, and I'd seen many videos of it happening before. Still, this person continued just dancing alone, then started screaming; people videoed it with their phones, finding it humorous. Nobody stood up to leave or to help them, so I stayed seated too and figured it was to be expected. It confuses me, measuring the temperature of seriousness. Because sometimes something out of the ordinary does happen, and often it's okay.

The movie was paused then, and this was really the big thing above it all. I remember thinking: *I have never sat in a cinema while the screen is still.* What do you even look at? Do you still look at the screen? You feel like a maniac. But maybe this was why people continued to attend the cinema beyond the movie-watching itself—because when the process is working, there is somewhere definitive to look, even if just for a moment.

Doms is sorting financial documents and numerical notations at the dining table. She tells me to turn down *Love in the Afternoon*, which is the movie starring Zouzou. Halfway through, Doms comes and stands in the living room, staring at Zouzou's nude body. She says something in French and then moves back to the dining table. I wonder momentarily where Vic is, and then find myself scratching excessively. From the table, Doms is talking about her maternal grandfather being French and the small town he grew up in before meeting her grandmother while she was studying in Paris. After the story, Doms returns silently to the documents. She never speaks about her father. All I do know about him is that he was always from here, a settler who settled in Par Mars long ago. And that he works in real estate, sending money occasionally.

In bed that night I'm watching "Petit Garçon," a music video of Zouzou's. She's wearing an orange hat and a feather boa. Cuts of her are exchanged with unsettling stills, textiles of sketched children in overalls and bonnets.

When I wake it's dark, but my phone is lit up with the still image of the sketched children. I turn it off. The living room is cold. I switch on the panel heater and hear Vic coming through the front door. "Hey," I murmur, sitting up slightly. Speaking to someone after having woken up from a deep sleep is a lovely feeling. Your pineal gland is hovering. You are crossing conscious and unconscious thresholds. You are lonely.

I say, "You're getting home at *four*? Did something happen again? Doms was so worried, she didn't sleep for ages." Which is a lie because Doms had been, all this time, just calculating her money and placing more bets until she'd fallen asleep against the table before relocating wearily upstairs to the loft.

But I find myself performing this "upset" *at* him as if *for* her and, for a moment, I wonder if I am actually growing into serious anger. Unsure whether I feel betrayed at having missed out on something so interruptive of routine, or whether I feel apprehension, concern for his safety. Vic has never expressed any urge to remove himself from the life he and Doms have set up. He is often happy being home most of the time. A nostalgic man, making himself juice and organic food, reminiscing about his childhood often, speaking to his grandparents regularly on the phone in Yoruba, watching movies with Doms, sedated by the harvest of their garden.

"I was at a party," he mumbles. His mouth is twitching.

I ask him what had gone on at the party, if he needed water. "I'm fine. Just acid." He swallows, the hardness of his face beginning to recede. He goes upstairs. I hear him running a bath.

In the morning Doms approaches me in the kitchen while I'm drinking a sweetened coffee. Last week we'd purchased some Coffee Mate to try. As I turn the container around, I stop drinking, noticing how there are corn syrup solids involved—something my mother has always warned against.

Pouring herself some coffee from the Bodum coffee press, Doms says, "Hey, so . . . I've decided, I'll take the room." She taps some Coffee Mate in.

I pour my coffee out. "Great," I say. "You're part of the team."

She ignores this, comes closer, and quietly asks me what time Vic got home.

I shrug.

She says, "He's taking the day off work. *Weird*."

Doms reappears later in the living room, now dressed, and shows me her phone. Vic's posing in an unrecognizable interior, somebody's share house, wearing a Balmain cardigan he bought off a gym friend a few weeks before the incident.

"Where does *this* look like?"

The person who tagged him attends the same gym as Vic, we figure out.

We ignore it and go out via the back door by the kitchen, locking it behind us. Head over to the 900.

The thin trees wave kindly. The sun is nice on my skin too. I steep in it. Being in a business that promotes sun or, at least, circularity, it is important to meet the requirements of balance. Internal and external. Round and sharp. Sharp like the edges of this car. Round like the bulb of the sun swathing the curvature of exposed shoulders. I stand with the keys in my hands for a moment to enjoy it.

I ask Doms casually, "Is Vic coming later to support us?"

In the car Doms begins to sob, propping her elbow against the window, staring out along the gutters of the street. "He's just . . . he's been *so* obsessed with the gym. Have you noticed? In the last few weeks?"

She opens the window slightly to let the wind rustle through her hair.

"Tell me," I say. Doms is in a cubicle in the Topic Heights restroom. "Who are the types of people who perform well in life?"

An assistant from the department store Shiseido booth is doing her makeup in here too. It's as if observing a painter, her blending the red into yellow to imitate a sunrise, finding the equator with a softer brush.

"The type of people who are *larger than their thoughts*," I say.

The sound of Doms pissing.

Peggy walks in with her iPad under her arm. She and the make-up assistant exclaim when they recognize one another and plant a kiss on each other's cheeks. I'm hoping to gain a similar sort of relationship with Peggy—it would be good for the studio. But for some odd reason, I cannot locate this image. It is a completely intangible one. It is not so much the age difference, nor do I think it might be racial or cultural. I wonder if it must be the thought of the awkward power dynamic between us.

The two of them begin to talk about a reality program that aired for the first time the night before. Peggy talks about the lip fillers on one of the women, says, "Well, Lil, you know I've had them done a few times now, but what Veronica had was drastic work, I can tell. This was a case of not waiting the six months before getting a touch-up. This was a bit sad, it was too obvious!"

When they leave together, Doms comes out and murmurs, "Oh my God." She stands in front of the mirror, reapplying her eye makeup.

"It's okay." I smooth her shoulders out.

She flattens her lips. "I know, I guess it's just a phase he's in. I think the incident really hit him hard. I get it."

I decide to call Vic so they can talk about it, but he won't pick up. Well, it's 9:30 a.m. and Doms keeps crying and smudging her makeup.

She says, "Why wouldn't he just invite me to the party?"

By the time she stops, it's around ten to, and we take the trays of catered food from the boxes, setting them up on my small fold-out table in the main studio.

I'm glad I hung the smaller shan shui in here. There is now a multi-functional massage table, disinfecting tools, and a little stereo beside the sink. There are also the plants. Plants that clean the air: lady palms, kalanchoes—the money plant for financial fertility. My mother says round-leaved, drooping plants are yin. They are calming and should face north.

A warm Akida Lamp—Oriental Furniture edition is flicked on in the reception area, casting no shadows on important, functional areas of the room. Doms sits at the reception desk, which faces slightly opposite the door. She is rearranging the candles, putting price tags on them. If only we could bask in this moment, really enjoy it, before having the eyes of others come and *define* the layout we've so carefully set up. It would be harmonious here.

Right at 11:30 a.m, nobody comes. I gather the food in my hand and eat away at it slowly. The front door is open and wedged with a newspaper to let qi flow through. There is a sign that reads: GRAND OPENING.

Vic is the first to come at around quarter past twelve. He has his hair in twists. I ask when he got it done and he says he drove out to his auntie's right before he came here. Then Doms shouts from behind the reception desk, "Why'd you ignore my text if you were awake!"

You can only see the top of her head. She stands, approaches us with her arms crossed.

Vic explains, "My auntie Nifemi's leaving the country this afternoon and I don't know anyone else who can do my hair here. I was in a rush, I'm sorry . . . sorry." He reaches out, grabs Doms's hand.

She stares at her hand in his and exhales, discontented.

Silence.

He fills it: "No one's here."

Soon, three people come in: two from K.A.G. and one from the supermarket.

Separate, but together. When you walk into a store with barely anybody in it, there is a hidden thread among those who *do* choose to enter. The demonstration of a clump invites for more to attach to it; it happens like this.

Nobody who enters dares to mention the ear-cleaning service. One of the visitors takes a moment to smell the candles and soaps. I watch the transaction with Doms, who is looking unsure whether to provide the visitor with more information. The potential customer has a flowing ponytail of long black hair tied to the side and carries a visible air of nonchalance about her. She is one of the workers from the new K.A.G., wearing a canvas apron and a pair of Lacoste sneakers.

When she's about to leave, I tap her lightly on the shoulder. "There *is* complimentary food in the studio," I say.

"No thanks."

You can't be too prideful if you're running a business. *Do not build fortresses to protect yourself,* especially if it's to do with pride. Something Robert Greene says.

I say, "It's vegan and there's also wine."

She casually follows me into the main studio. She takes a sandwich and a glass of wine and leans against the massage table, looking at the bench with the tools. I stand in the doorway, looking out the glass storefront, people just ignoring the opening. They will not come in unless they see others. Even if they are interested in the service. It's the Asch paradigm, the hidden secret to successful shopping center businesses. I turn to look at the potential customer now. I press my lips together into a smile. She smiles back, eats her sandwich, peeling it in half before eating them separately.

She is comfortable with us staring at each other. She presses her stomach in, having drank half the portion of wine. "Bread bloats me."

"You probably shouldn't wash it down with wine."

"Oh, why?"

"It disrupts the digestion process. Because it . . . dilutes the saliva and it ends up fermenting in the stomach."

"Oh, wow. I had no idea." She sculls the last few mouthfuls of residue.

"Will your boss notice you drank?"

"My boss at K.A.G.? Well, she might. I'm so over it though. I don't really care. My boss is a drunk too."

I nod. I think about my fantasy of being the sort of shop owner who floats through the day on cigarettes and sips of vodka in a flask, dazed, unusually romantic.

"You know, she doesn't even *get* the store. You ever been to a K.A.G.?"

"I can guess the vibe . . . It's very nice in there. I've only been once."

"Yeah, so nice."

"I'll visit again."

"I mean, do whatever, *she's* just"—she holds her stomach and huffs out an exhale—"she's the worst. The company, like the K.A.G. franchise, they've hired all these ethnically and culturally diverse people. Like, the job listing literally prioritized non-English speaking backgrounds. But then to have her as the manager? It's almost—it's as if she's just used her opportunity to justify any intolerances she has."

"Maybe she's not *intolerant*, maybe she's stressed about opening a new store. It's *huge*."

She looks discernibly offended, confused. "Um, probably not. Anyway, I don't care what her intentions are. You cannot make a terrorism joke at emergency procedure meetings. It's not right. She's the worst. You'd think so too, I'm sure."

"Oh."

"Right."

"That's quite bad."

"Anyway."

I suggest she could possibly get her manager fired with that sort of behavior. She says she can't be bothered.

She pours a tinge more of the red wine. "Hope you don't mind," she mutters. She swallows it and exhales, that big stomach huff. "Anyway," she says. "What's the clinic like?"

"It's alternative healing systems," I say. "Ear cleaning is self-care."

"Oh yeah. I know. They do that all over Asia."

She points. "They do it in Malaysia!"

She appears to warm to the idea in a way that others I've told haven't seemed to. I tell her I'm passionate about relieving stress and tension in physical bodies and that we often abandon the concept that our nervous system, muscles, joints, and organs carry the weight of us around. So much of our soul lives in our eyes and our fingers. The rest of our body gets heavy from being a vehicle for it. It needs relief. We have to start from the nervous system, the mind. I tell her I'm the owner.

"That's so sick," she says. "I wonder if you need any help."

I say no immediately, though I'm in need of a receptionist. There is a bit of loaned money put aside for one, enough for a few months.

Robert Greene says: *Make other people come to you. When you force the other person to act, you are the one in control.*

"How about you give me your number before you go back to K.A.G.? And I'll call you for an interview?"

"Ugh, I fucking hate K.A.G.," she says, her body slumping again. She writes down her number and labels it: *Farah.* "They only pay fourteen-fifty an hour too. Man, I have no idea how they get away with it."

My eyes dart up. Something my mother always says is to keep people waiting and wanting. Even if you know that what they want is not particularly desirable—make it seem as though it is.

When I go out to the reception there are two people with Vic, pointing at his new hair, complimenting it. Farah exits past them with a napkin of two more vegetable-and-vegan-cheese sandwiches, looking hopeful.

Vic explains, "Animal fats, lye flakes—that's sodium hydroxide—distilled water, sugar and salt, essential oil, synthetic colorant, the mixture of a sodium paste, and grapefruit-scented serum, *just* a bit, and *CBD oil*. The benefits of the CBD are endless."

You don't realize until it's too late, plays from the main studio. *That you need all the time you . . . that's why . . .*

When the day is over, I take the leftover tray of catering down to the food court and make a show of handing out free mini sandwiches. People walk directly to me to grab a sandwich; little do they know, they must take a flyer too. Some people read the flyer and stand right in front of me, buoyantly displaying their interest in hopes of receiving another sandwich.

Peggy marching over. "Aren't you just full of ideas, Ling?" She laughs, plucking one of the flyers from me.

"I couldn't get anyone inside."

"*Yes*. It's like that," says Peggy. "But if you had referred to your handbook, you will have seen that there is to be no hawking in Topic Heights. Not here, please."

"Sorry, I misread."

Peggy scrunches her mouth up and rolls her eyes. "In other *news*"— she hands me a lanyard with a thick white pass card hanging off it—"I finally got one of these done for you. Let me know if you need others. Now that you're part of the family: no hawking and no signs out in the walkway—you have to keep it within your doorway. You can use the staffroom when you like between the hours of five a.m. and seven p.m. Microwave is a bit old so don't heat anything up for longer than three minutes. Don't store anything in the lockers you wouldn't want stolen. We aren't a freaking Pack 'n' Go, Jesus Christ."

And then she strides off slowly, all physical power reserved in the muscles along her calves, the definition of them showing through her opaque stockings.

When I'm upstairs again, the door to Doms's studio is closed and I hear her and Vic laughing. I take the newspaper out from under the front door so that it slams shut and the sound of their laughter halts. There's a huge silence.

It's already five p.m. I put the rest of Doms's items in her box and knock on the door of her studio. I leave the box there without waiting for a reply and decide to go down to K.A.G. with the candle Farah never purchased.

They're beginning to roll the plastic doors across to remind customers that their consumption time is over. To quickly purchase anything in their baskets and exit. A store assistant stands there holding the rolling door open with a rod, guarding the little gap left for any final customers. He looks at his watch as though meticulous about the time. I wait outside and our eyes meet briefly. I feel a sort of guilt. I flash a quick smile at him. He smiles back politely and looks down at his watch again. Then Farah comes through the gap with a Fila jumper pulled over her K.A.G. shirt.

I think about how many employees they must already have, how many potential employees would be on their waiting list. I reassure myself it's *okay* to bring a disgruntled worker into a job with a better cause—and likely an infinitely better employer.

"Aren't you hot?"

"Big Red Boss turns up the cooling system in K.A.G. Apparently, it's supposed to make people want to buy the warm clothes we got in stock yesterday. Also, coldness gives the impression of cleanliness and minimalism. Which is an important philosophy in the K.A.G. handbook."

I nod. I pass her the candle. "I'm feeling a good vibe from you. Congratulations, we'd love to have you as our new receptionist. I can do fifteen an hour for the first few months as we slowly start up but a cut of the commission too."

"*Thank you.*" She loops her backpack around and places the candle inside. She lowers her voice so that the store assistant at the rolling doors can't hear her. "That sounds fine, to be honest. I'll quit tomorrow."

The manager, Big Red Boss, emerges from the store wearing her muted red T-shirt. It interrupts the aesthetic of ecru and acacia and the variations of white that K.A.G. offers. She pats the store assistant on the back and he jerks up slightly. Her eyes lag on Farah and me and then she shuffles over, a limp on her left side.

She gives Farah a double whack on the shoulder. "*Okay?* See you tomorrow. And you better be early. Today you had a long lunch, remember? God knows what you were doing," she mutters, and leaves us.

Farah's jaw is clenched.

"Want to go see the staff room?" I ask.

"I've already been, but sure," says Farah, shrugging. "You can bless it."

Farah and I walk down the long passageway, make a right at the dollar store. At the end of another little passageway of immense dim light, there is a pinboard and a single door that reads: STAFF ONLY.

Inside, it's faded green carpet and a kitchenette, its benches with rounded corners and edges. The microwave has pasta sauce splattered around it. There are two couches facing toward each other in the far right corner and between them is a coffee table, magazines on top. The lockers run along the farthest wall on the left. Most of them hang open. Another fire door beside the couch setup.

There is a man on his phone sitting on one of the couches. He's bald, wearing a short-sleeved supermarket shirt and a name badge. He tries not to look up, but when he does, he does so in a way that shows he is amused by us.

"Cool," I say.

We walk over to the kitchenette and Farah opens one of the cupboards under the sink. She brings out a jar of milk biscuits and offers it to me.

I take two. She takes three. I say, "I'm so exhausted."

Farah eats one of her biscuits, looking over at the man on the couch.

"That's Freddy," she whispers. "He works at the supermarket."

Freddy doesn't flinch at his name, so we can't tell if he's heard.

He is singing softly to himself, not as if he's unaware that we're here, but as if he's unaware he's even doing it.

Farah says, a little quieter, "He's always here."

I take a third biscuit as I finish my first and lean against the counter.

Farah takes the jar from me and hugs it into her stomach. "You know I worked at BookLand? Before all of them shut down? I've been *really* lucky with my jobs, I'm not shitting you. I don't know how it happened."

I take out a flyer from my bag and go over to the coffee table. "Here," I say to Freddy.

"We're the new store upstairs. A massage and health studio."

Freddy raises his eyebrows. There is something unsightly about the intensity of his physical reaction; his nose wrinkles up and he puts his hand to his chin, crosses one leg over the other. "This flyer, will it grant me a free massage?"

"Twenty-five percent off."

Freddy starts pulling at some threads in the couch, the way an infant does when bored. He is chewing something, beginning to sing to himself again. His mouth isn't really moving. He considers. "Okay," he says, taking the flyer from me. He folds it neatly, pressing his fingers along the crease.

"If you don't mind me asking, what kind of a massage do they give there? I have a wife."

Farah rolls her eyes behind me, I can feel it.

I turn to her and see that she is taking two more milk biscuits from the jar. She breaks half of one and eats slowly at each of them.

Freddy leaves.

Farah shares with me her interest in film and literature. She tells me her favorite movie adaptation of a book is *Gone with the Wind*. She expresses a love for Clark Gable except for his infidelity. She is a true romantic, she knows she doesn't seem it. But it's the Aquarius in her and yes, Clark Gable is also an Aquarian—there is something captivating about him.

"Did you know," she says, "Oprah and Bob Marley are *also* Aquarians?"

I shake her hand and thank her for coming to the store today before going to my 900. She catches the bus—she's only ten minutes down the road.

9 **I'VE BEEN SPENDING SUNDAYS LYING** by the living room window, where the sun shoots straight through. While Doms is making her soaps, while Vic is painting on a canvas. They don't speak to each other while in a state of creation so that later they'll have a lot to talk about.

By evening, I'll be hot and I'll be comfortable with my body being nude because of the sweat lathered on my limbs. I'll undress when Doms and Vic have retired upstairs and I'll fall asleep without any clothes on and, in a sense, it'll make me feel like an artist too.

I try to watch *2001: A Space Odyssey* again. A channel on Doms's television is playing a rerun and it interests me why they want so badly for us all to have seen it. I half watch the first part, scrolling on my phone and reading various forms of reactionary texts on the movie. I assume Doms and Vic are out. They could be out, or they could be up in their loft—they don't let me know anymore.

Recently, I've felt like their baby. Not the good kind, like the eyelash baby or a sugar baby, but the kind of baby that doesn't understand how the same machine can give you feelings of goose bumps and feelings of love at different times. Babies that watch these machines play with them as though they've always existed. They let these machines make them feel without knowing it.

In the movie there's an artificial moon that belongs to both the people inside the screen and to me.

While I'm watching I begin to cry. It's been like this a lot recently. I don't have a lot to cry about, so the movies help.

At the exact same moment the movie was paused at Star Cinema, I hear a banging on the door.

"Who is it?" I call out, sniffing and wiping my eyes with my fist.

I feel paranoid, thinking about Vic's incident and the concept of surveillance which has become a popular form of reportage in the news of late. I think about the mind playing tricks on you, the eternity of all versions of time.

"Who is it?" I ask again.

After a beat, the voice calls back, "It's Jean Paul!"

Jean Paul has a duffel bag, which he drops as he enters through the door. He's been absent for the last week and a half, did not show up at the opening with friends as promised, and has not been at the pharmacy while Vic's been there. His face is haggard, he's grown a bit of hair on his chin, like underarm hair.

He hugs me briefly and says, "Sorry to *barge* my way in here. I came on a bus, and it's raining outside. I'm European." I look outside. "Oh, it *was* raining." His mouth enhances his prominent nasolabial folds. His thick brown eyebrows, heavy with sweat.

I bring him a glass of water and we sit on the couch. The television is still on. He keeps looking out the window at my pretty 900 model, parked under the garage shelter. Glancing out in quick darts. He lights a cigarette, starts to breathe a little more. I watch his teeth.

"So, I've come to ask you a favor."

Jean Paul talks in a way that makes him seem as though he's always slightly perplexed about something.

"I was just admiring your car again," he says, motioning toward the driveway. "What is it, some kind of convertible? Early nineties?"

"With the leather seats. It's secondhand, though. The leather's a bit—"

"I need to borrow your car, Leen."

"What for?"

"I'm just asking as a friend."

"Well, I mean, you can't drive it. It's too risky with the insurance and everything."

"As a *dear friend*."

"Yes, but why?"

"There are these discussion groups I've been attending. You may've noticed, I've been off work. Because I had an epiphany. I've been thinking my life purpose over."

"Hmm?"

We look into a fish eye on the television.

You don't mind talking about it ... Do you, Dave? ... Very abnormal stories floating ... Rumors about something being dug up on the moon.

"I started going with my friend, he's, um ..." He snaps his fingers on his knee. "Anyway, you'd like him. His name is Huy. You pronounce it like *hoo-wee*, *H-wee*. His parents own the pharmacy."

"Oh. He works at the pharmacy too?"

"No, no. He gets some stuff from me at the pharmacy sometimes. But I barely *know* him, no."

Jean Paul picks at the walnut-and-peanut mix left on the coffee table, which I had been unaware of up until this moment.

"He studies. I think it's science or engineering, at the community college. So they run those ... these talks there. They rent one of the little ... uh, group rooms, the tutorial rooms."

"I see."

"Yes." He crosses one leg over the other, as if in deep thought. "Yes, I'm learning a lot. They talk about many things. A lot about Heidegger—you know about Heidegger?" He swoops more walnut nodules into his palm and jostles them about.

"Maybe."

"See, Heidegger thinks about the nature of technology and its integration with human action," he says.

"Genetic engineering?"

"Not so much. I might absolutely mistranslate this but, see, to me, it's all about why technology is dangerous. Not that it's: *Technology and technology is powerful.* But because man will become competitive with it because . . . we see ourselves in it. You understand, right?"

"Sure."

"And so at these discussions, we talk about how they're trying to get those automatic cashiers at the supermarket. We talk about how . . . *managerial staff* are trained to speak to their staff as if they're digital assistants. It's all very real, it's all *real-life stuff*. It's like a community group, but there's some really brilliant people going. These ideas, I think they're important. I'm sure you'd agree, no? I'm sure you'd like it, maybe you'd even like to come along? Then you could drive me, and we could go together? It's a lot quicker to drive, it takes so much longer on the bus."

"Sure, but you know, I'm very tired, Jean Paul. I just started a business. I'm not free."

"Oh, yes! How'd that go anyway? The opening?"

"It was okay. We had a pretty good turnout."

"Wonderful."

We both rotate back around to the television. I exhale. He is still concerned with gathering the remains of the walnuts and pieces of caramelized honey left in the bowl.

"You know," he says, "it's fascinating, *it is*. I'm not going to force you to come, obviously. But I have to be honest, Leen. You just seem like the kind of person who would really care about this sort of thing."

I get up to boil the kettle and lean against the kitchen counter to face him in the living room.

"Especially because you're about to start your own business."

I wonder about my defensiveness again, why I get the feeling that Jean Paul couldn't care less about the concept of my ear-cleaning and massage business and why I can't help but feel as if he's mocking it.

"Tea?" I ask.

"Yes, please."

"What sort?"

"Surprise me."

I untangle a teabag of peppermint for him and a lemon-infused green for myself. I say through to the living room, "What's the point of going to these things if you're not able to change it? You know what I mean? I think you'd be happier if you implemented smaller changes rather than trying to preach theories to everyone. For example, my line of work is somewhere you'd never be able to *not be human*. If you care, do something that challenges it."

Jean Paul frantically spins to face me. He points earnestly, raising his eyebrows. "*Yes*. This is another thing about the community."

"What's that?"

The kettle whistles. I remove it from the flame and pour it into Jean Paul's mug first, slightly burning the skin at the tip of my finger.

"Fuck."

"You okay?"

"Yep." I suck on my finger.

"Wonderful."

I bring the tea.

He continues, "There's an entire plan of action tied to this community group, Leen. The end goal is to help these franchise managers begin to understand that the people they employ are not just their digital assistants, not just their uh . . . their automatic *vehicle* to sales."

He sips his tea. "Oh, Christ, it's hot."

"Careful."

"Thank you." He rubs his lip. "Could I get a juice? It's just a bit hot."

I go to get him a glass of Doms's cranberry juice. I pour it. Check my finger, pulsating a dark cherry red. Press it against the now-perspiring glass.

He continues from the couch, "Like a *branch* of a neighborhood watch, if you will. The end goal, Leen, *is* to make something happen."

I'm driving in my 900 with Jean Paul and his friend Huy.

Though Huy's parents are Vietnamese, he was born and raised for some of his life in Singapore, he is telling me from the backseat. He attended high school in Par Mars, then returned home to do the two years of military service, learning cybersecurity. He's back now, with a crew cut. He's skinny around the arms, heavy around the cheeks.

"I *would* study to be a pilot," says Huy, winding down the window. "I actually don't like airplanes because I get bad allergies, but I like the flying itself."

I look at him in the rearview as if to acknowledge what he's said, though I have nothing to reply with. He's staring out the window.

"I knew you two would get along," says Jean Paul. Suddenly, he adds, "Actually, can we make a stop first? We're a tad early. I bought some books from this retired philosophy professor online." He unlocks my phone. My eyes dart over. "Sorry, don't mind me. Just checking the GPS. It's nearby, just a bit farther out."

"Sure, okay."

"Wonderful. Thanks, Leen."

Continue on State Route 96 toward Lyndon . . .

"Do you have Bluetooth? Or an aux cord?" asks Huy, leaning between me and Jean Paul.

"Oh, they don't work. Just radio."

"Bummer," says Huy.

Jean Paul presses the FM button.

That one was Mozart's sonata for piano and violin in F . . . lovely bouncy one for your late-afternoon drive home . . . will clear of any rain by midday . . . when you get home . . .

I pull over in front of the house and Jean Paul gets out. We watch him ring the doorbell.

Huy asks, "Hey, do you know how old Jean Paul is?"

When we enter the meeting room, there's a plastic basket of biscuits in the center of a large community table and an electric kettle for tea in the corner.

When the meeting begins, it feels like neither a sermon, nor a classroom, nor a dinner party. The seating has been arranged so that the discussion facilitator, Aden, sits among us, welcoming everybody back and giving a warm welcome to the first-timers. He's wearing glasses and an old football fleece, and while everybody else chatters around him, he's looking at the papers on the table in front of him.

"Please," he says as the room quiets down, "feel free to take a biscuit and a cup of tea."

"Before the discussion commences, there's a few housekeeping things to note," says Aden. "But firstly, a 'grave statement' about a member of this discussion group, David, who had also been the head of the neighborhood watch at Glenvale Estate. David has been sentenced to community service and mandatory rehabilitation for two years and will not carry on within this community group.

"The problem," sighs Aden, "is that a lot of these neighborhood watch council members treat themselves like policemen. Some of us center control over communication. Unfortunately he was *a bad egg.*" Aden tilts his glasses down at someone with their hand up. He points to them and says, "Cody?"

"You know it was on TV a week ago. Did anyone else see that?"

"Yes, that's right, Cody. Very unfortunate."

Then, without any further comments about it, the discussion begins.

A man begins to raise some concerns he had about the new apartment blocks being built on top of the old storefronts. In response a woman across the room suggests to him a book by Jane Jacobs about urban planning policy in America. Jean Paul leans over to me and says, "That's Tanya, she acts so *bohemian. It kills me.*" Jean Paul then takes a turn to speak immediately after Tanya finishes. He launches into monologue:

"In Par Mars, the way we live is like a stage show for people in their houses. Someone will always notice if something is not the same as it was the night before. Everybody in Par Mars dresses the same, walks the same, walks with a dog, walks the dogs the same route so that the dog becomes the same as the next dog. So that the people in the houses—they aren't scared. It's like a courtesy. Why is it that we are courteous?"

"Mmm." People nod.

Aden writes a few notes and gives Jean Paul a promising smile.

I think about massage chairs. About online yoga. I want to say something intelligent, but I'm sure they wouldn't expect a first-timer to contribute. I think about the customer being my employer and the employer—whether a franchise manager or a small-business owner—being just another organ, holding up the wider skin, the exterior fabricated by larger corporations and ideas, all contributing to Peggy's nucleus. The pumping of her calves, the vein in her forehead. And how this contributes to the idea, the ideal.

"Would you like to say something . . . Sorry, I've forgotten your name already."

My eyes meet with Aden's. "It's Leen."

"You look like you're having a bit of a think there. Anything you'd like to add, Leen?"

Jean Paul turns to me and raises his eyebrows encouragingly.

I begin, "I think it's interesting how they put all the popular franchises in the shopping complex. They're the ones that generally survive in there. And all the family-owned stores seem to be on the street . . ."

Some people nod.

"I guess we begin to associate safety and cleanliness with franchises. Because the complex has the security to keep the shoppers satiated, there are people who walk around wiping everything down, air-conditioning. I think it's . . . I think it's strange."

"Excellent point, Leen."

"I think it's a bit cultlike. You have to buy your way up if you want security."

"Mm-hmm." There is a tone to the general hum, a kindness and empathy to the nodding.

Aden writes something down and I exhale. From the other side of the room, Tanya continues to expand on my point. We smile at each other as though I'm transferring my energy over. I sigh again and place my hand on my stomach, feeling good.

She continues, "Perhaps it was Hegel who described the unhappy consciousness in which the only space for an individual to recognize themselves as self-conscious beings is when they are recognized especially? Would this not be a fascinating way to see those franchising managerial positions?"

When the meeting concludes, everybody stands and continues to chat in separate groups, and Aden approaches me from the other end of the table. "Lovely to have you this evening, Leen, some great thoughts. Very constructive. We love to hear your perspective. Sometimes people are more concerned with things that only directly affect them. But your thoughts about the complex structures were interesting." He shakes my hand and straightens his glasses. "See you next week. Huy, Jean Paul, next week." He goes to the bench where the kettle is to grab his backpack, and slinging it over his shoulder, he exits.

It seems quicker to drive home than it had been to drive there. There is little traffic. The windows are down. We drive Huy back to his parents' just a few minutes from the community college. Then I drive Jean Paul back to his apartment, a newer building, ten minutes down the road from Doms's.

As Jean Paul gets out of the car, he says, "You liked it, no? See, I knew you would get it."

It's just after midnight when Jean Paul sends me a message: a link and a password. When I access the page, it seems to be a forum housed on an unquestionably dated create-your-own website. I'm on the couch, high after smoking Doms's ceramic bong, which she got a few months ago from the community pottery center.

I take a handful of chocolate pretzels and curl them in my palm. There is a low-frequency hum throughout the whole neighborhood tonight. I assume it's something to do with the electrical wiring.

On the forum there are expandable, threaded discussions you can click through. *Jean Paul has become an administrator* is the latest update, updated around nine p.m., a half hour after the meeting had concluded.

There are rules at the corner of the site, which say:

> **Respect others' opinions. No harmful language (sexism, homophobia, transphobia, ableism, racism, classism are not tolerated). Credit resources. Do not invite members without permission from an administrator—they will be immediately removed and you will be suspended. We value diverse members and encourage you to recruit diverse members, especially, but ask before adding them to the forum. Post videos privately and exclusively to this group. Any video posted publicly that references the group will be traced back to the member and the member will be removed.**

I scroll for a thread to open. There is one called *Thinking about the Hegelian concept of the State and enforcing a moral logic within societies... but where is logic from and why does it differ so much across the global arena . . . ,* another called *Thinking about quitting and suing my boss, how do I go about this effectively? People with law background, please?!?!,* and a thread initiated by Jean Paul, *Palpable action for palpable change.*

In Jean Paul's thread, a member has posted a video with a laughing emoji. In the video, the manager of a fast-food chain finds her employees smashing open the windows using kitchen tools late one night. The employees explain afterward that they had received a call from the local council's emergency department saying there would be a serious gas hazard leading to a leak or explosion if the windows were not busted open. Later, they realized there was no such thing as a local council emergency department where they are from.

I'm falling asleep on the couch with no intention of moving to my fold-out bed. The low-frequency hum acclimatizes, finding space in the shape of my ears.

10 I'M SCROLLING THROUGH THE FORUM constantly these last two weeks. At the studio, when I'm not talking with Farah about the future, which she seems to enjoy talking about, or answering questions for the occasional visitor before they leave without booking, I am on my phone. Reading discussions about the boom of technological AI sales assistants.

Tonight is my third time at the discussion group. I haven't been seeing Jean Paul outside of it. Vic's been complaining some nights about how exhausted he is, how he has to carry the load because Jean Paul keeps flaking. The owners refuse to hire anyone else, saying it would be too expensive.

The people in the discussion group always seem to be sitting in the same spots around the table. I take mine next to Jean Paul. During tonight's meeting, I raise a concern about my independent ear-cleaning and massage business to the group. Many people sympathize with the difficulty of my geographical positioning, which I described to be "near the new K.A.G."

One person mentions, "Oftentimes a shopper might choose to visit a store to fulfill that longing for self-care rather than commit an hour, removing their clothes and getting oily at a massage studio for sixty to a hundred bucks. Products are always more attractive, like souvenirs."

Across the table, Tanya adds, "Absolutely. The store gives them something physical as well as the browsing experience. A massage studio gives them the experience but it doesn't let them show off their identity in a meaningful way."

A man of about forty says, "Yes. The eyelash extension business is fantastic right now, I've heard."

When walking out of the meetings, I feel a sense of ease, rolling my shoulders back differently. It seems to take the load off a depressing day of chasing after curious but mostly uninterested visitors who've reluctantly left their numbers with us. To feel as though I'm not the only one experiencing the implicit misery of sustaining a business, or keeping consumers happy. The exhausting puzzle it is to "sell."

Walking out to the 900, Jean Paul tells Huy and me, "I'm thinking of doing something. I'm thinking of a way to *spook* a big franchise. The supermarket keeps buying out sections of Topic Heights for their umbrella companies. *Lord*, it's freezing . . . Anyway, I'm thinking of a harmless, silly way to *spook 'em*."

When I arrive at the studio the next day, Farah is cleaning the top of the reception desk.

"Morning," I say.

"Hello!" Farah helps me by taking the white pharmaceutical coat slipping out from under my arm. Vic had generously given me one of his.

One that couldn't fit his arms anymore, given how much muscle he's built going to the gym every evening after work.

I put my bags down in the studio and come out to swap my jacket. I begin cleaning utensils, playing the Tibetan bowl playlist through the stereo system and wiping each silver and wooden tool with a long stroke.

Farah appears in the doorway.

"How're you feeling after these last two weeks?" she asks, arms crossed over her chest. Slightly nervous to ask the question.

"It'll be better this week. I think people need time to get used to a new store. They need to familiarize themselves and feel comfortable coming in. It just takes time."

Farah nods, licking her teeth. A moment of silence, Farah shuffling her feet. "Did you want any help cleaning those?"

"No," I say. "It's okay. If you're running out of stuff to do, feel free to mess around on the computer."

Farah raises her eyebrows and nods understandingly. "Okay."

I widen my lips into a smile. I feel as though I am lying to the both of us. In an unwarranted way, I feel as though I am being pitied. I am getting a paranoid feeling that every time a potential customer walks by the storefront, subconsciously they are growing more and more sorry for the circumstance that my studio even exists. A shopping complex seems to be designed in this way. It is much safer and more comfortable to go where you do not feel the presence of the person behind the store.

The customers undoubtedly keep track of a store's position, even if it has no use to them. So every time they are passing, it is as though they are making an active decision not to enter.

"Hey," says Farah, reappearing. "I think you're a little late with my payment?"

Jean Paul calls ceaselessly after work one evening when I'm in the staff room, eating milk biscuits out of the jar and transferring money to

Farah's bank account. I pick up Jean Paul's fifth call after the payment's gone through, staring at the back of Freddy's head on the couch.

"Sorry, I was closing up."

"That's okay. I got off work early. But I need you to come. Huy's here too."

"Meeting's not tonight, is it? Fuck, is it really Wednesday?"

"No, no, not that," says Jean Paul. "I'll explain in a second. You're still here, no?"

"Yeah."

"Wonderful."

At the pharmacy, Vic is restacking the sunscreen aisle and comes to let me in, opening a gap in the plastic screen doors. He looks exhausted and deadpan when he tells me Jean Paul is out back.

Jean Paul and Huy have surgical masks on. We're in a supermarket storage room that we accessed via an offshoot section of the same concrete hallway used to get to the staff room. Huy had hacked access to documents about the complex's access codes and security numbers.

We're taking from the flour section and the rice sections, in which there are excesses. There is the sound of someone approaching down the hall from a different entrance. Jean Paul is content with taking three bags each, and we exit immediately.

The point is to place the bags under the supermarket branch manager Mary's Ford Fiesta parked in the reserved supermarket loading-zone spot, so that she either drives over them as she leaves—and it looks suspicious to any other staff walking by—*or* she sees them before driving off, becomes humiliated and has to deal with the rice and flour.

A harmless skit, Jean Paul called it. "And we'll film it from the inside of your car, Leen."

I feel sick lingering in a place I know I shouldn't be; the thrill, the sense of gratification only occurs once Jean Paul stops recording and I start the car and drive us all out of the complex, towards Huy's parents' house, into an orange sun.

"That went well," Jean Paul says, a nonchalance in his eyes.

Jean Paul says, "The people here value personal comfort. So the idea, friends, is to pick apart that personal comfort . . . one slice at a time. Loud enough for people to look outside their windows, but not loud enough for people to step outside their doors."

PHARMACEUTICALS

HUY

HUY READS: MIDAZOLAM. "AMNESIA EFFECT?" He looks at the other oral phenobarbital. "Dosage," Huy mutters to himself. He sucks his cheeks in, scrolls down.

Huy remembers sitting on the bathroom floor reading the side effects of a packet of flibanserin, little pink pills.

Huy fucking hates it when his parents walk into his room without knocking. He watches porn a lot, sometimes takes pills and snorts from his *Course Notes on Orbital Mechanics* book. It's enough that he has to live here until he gets himself a day job; on top of that, they always want to come in and talk to him. *Huy, what are you doing?* Through the door, a knock, opening it without waiting for an answer.

When they leave the country, which they often do for their bitch-ass conferences, Huy will invite a guy over who he knows from social media and they'll make love—this has happened twice. He'll walk around with his pants off and rap to A$AP Ferg. He'll punch his father's cushion, which is what he uses to support his bony fucking ass on their cheap-as-shit couch. He'll punch it until he falls over and watches another whole season of that trashy sitcom with the women's nipples exposed through their shirts again.

. . .

After class, for which the time changes every trimester, he has been taking a bus back over to Topic Heights, a fifteen-minute drive, a thirty-five-minute bus ride.

School kids hang around there. People sit and chew gum in the shoe store and outside of it. Huy sneers. He waits until Jean Paul gets off work, then they walk over to the gym, which is not immediately attached to the complex, but is a few blocks behind it within one of the old warehouse buildings. Together they go into the changing rooms to drop their bags off. Jean Paul changes out of his white coat and pants, his shirt. Huy out of his khaki trousers and Palace T-shirt. They wear their wifebeaters; sometimes Jean Paul goes shirtless. You can see veins if Jean Paul is tensing. And actual bulging. Though his frame remains skinny and his muscle is not round or protruding, it's kind of like extra padding or something.

Huy's been deadlifting 180 pounds, squatting 150. He is firming up his back. He does more reps of the deadlifting than he should. He wants a tighter ass too, if he's being completely honest. He watches Jean Paul, who effortlessly bench presses. He wonders what Vic, the manager at the pharmacy, does at the gym—he's been getting fucking ripped.

Huy reckons people do what they look best doing at the gym. So you'll see a guy with fucking huge biceps and skinny chicken legs. Like a triangle or some shit.

In the boxing room, Huy punches and looks at the face he's making in the opposite wall mirror. What's the point of punching if you don't look like you're supposed to be throwing the goddamn punch?

There's someone looking at him from outside the boxing room. Huy wipes himself down.

Jean Paul shares the books he's been reading about psychology and human experimentations. Huy admires it, how Jean Paul writes notes and generously shares them with the forum. He turned in a few vandals by sending pictures of them to Aden. This, and the fact that he's recruited two new Asians, has really placed Jean Paul in a high position of trust within the community group, and Aden's been looking at him differently since. He used to roll his eyes at Jean Paul as he went on and on during meetings, but now Aden is realizing he isn't just all talk.

They've performed three pranks now. Huy both loves and obsesses over Jean Paul, yet simultaneously wants him to be something smaller, something wrong.

11 **SUNDAY. THEY HAVE SO MANY** words in Japanese for feelings, things we don't know how to describe in English—my mother tells me this over the phone.

I call her at a time I know she'll be back in her office. After a full day of ear cleaning, when she's sitting reading the news, doing some administration. I imagine her in a grid-check business shirt and plastic slippers, using her Disneyland pen to write down numbers and dates, times, and codes. I'm on speaker.

I sometimes imagine her walking home and stopping by the corner store to get ga li yu dan. I imagine her walking with her glasses halfway down her face, around the apartment blocks, down the road, passing schoolchildren and mothers. She'll swing her arms around for blood circulation without thinking about it. She'll think of something she needs to do for the apartment, like buying new curtains to install, or repairing the bookshelf in the living room. It'll distract her from falling into a certain type of feeling.

"What words?" I ask.

"Irusu," she says in a perfect accent.

I hear her penning something down on a notepad, then typing on her keyboard. I wait for her to continue. My phone is pressed between the pillow, my ear reddening from the screen heat.

"Is the act of pretending you're not at home when someone's at your door."

"Gad," I say. I've never said *God* like *gad* before. My mouth is tired and my temporomandibular joint is loosening. "That'd be so useful."

When she doesn't reply, I ask, "How do you know about these words? Are you learning? You don't have time, do you?"

"Of course no time . . . I was on Facebook," she says after a little while. I hear her sniffing and she turns her desk fan off.

"You're getting a cold? Siu sum doong *tsun*-la."

"No, no," she says slowly. "My nose doesn't do well with the air-conditioning in this building."

I hear the remote scrape the table softly. I imagine the air conditioner closing up like the mouth of a fish.

I want to tell her about the last few weeks: about the lack of business, about my new friends and what we did to the supermarket manager, Mary. Instead I say, "The shopping complex seems really small and funny lately. It's feeling like there're no more people to convince, that it's just a cycle from here, of waiting for no one."

"How do you mean?" she asks.

"In the staffroom you always see the same people, there're only so many people who would visit the same shopping complex in a week . . . I saw a sign the other day when I was making coffee. The CEO is having a Chateau party for all store tenants."

"*Chateau?*" My mother scoffs. "Silly."

"I think she's trying to socialize everyone."

"*Chateau?* French?"

"*Chateau Marmont party,* she called it. Like the Hollywood hotel."

"No relation?"

"Maybe a dress-up party . . . Maybe the house is earthquake-proof. You know the real hotel is earthquake-proof? You know, Ma, John Belushi? John Belushi died of an overdose in Bungalow 3."

"What better place to die than a nice hotel."

My mother's favorite kind of music is strings, when they're crescendoing. Her favorite hotel in Hong Kong Island provided a string quartet to play on the balcony over the staircase the night of her wedding. She's a true lover of strings, will listen anytime and anywhere.

As long as they are the pitch between the extremes of brooding and piercing, typically a Henry Mancini composition.

I play a disc on the portable radio under my fold-out bed. She is able to hear it too; our connection is rich. The internet is thriving in our neighborhood today.

I tell her I am concerned that if I don't get more customers soon, maybe my father will stop supporting me financially, he'll tell me to try something else instead.

She says, "I'm sure your father understands. A business takes time to start up."

As I begin to feel the bottom of my eyelids wilting, I ask if I can fall asleep while on the phone with her. If I can hear her typing, my mind will be less prone to its habit of recycling old thoughts. Trying to fall asleep in silence is like collapsing into an orbit of searching for noise, elsewhere.

She says, "Yes, of course."

I imagine her listening to the strings in her headset when I close my eyes.

"*I miss you, Leen.* Don't be scared to go out and meet different kinds of people. Don't take your job too seriously. It's just a job, remember. And don't worry so much. I'm sure your father would love to help you with rent. Sleep well."

12 "IF SOMEONE COMES IN, ASK for their name and if they have an appointment, even if you know they don't."

Farah pulls out a notepad she bought from K.A.G.

I wonder if hating to work somewhere diminishes the appeal of the products sold there. Farah tells me K.A.G. has started stocking notebooks, binders, and stationery in the last week, and now the other stationery store, PaperX, is losing customers.

She peels the plastic back off her new notebook and writes down my instructions. "So, remember Big Red Boss, right? When I walked in to grab this, she went to an employee and started to freak out. I heard her saying, like, *No, no, I can't be around that girl.*"

I let out a laugh. Farah looks pleased.

I'm still thinking about how to obtain potential customers. Robert Greene suggests to plan all the way to the end. Even if the process is meant to be natural, it is always somehow constructed. Perhaps this is what I've been missing the first few weeks the studio's been open.

I tell Farah that the next step is to assume they want an appointment. "Make sure you look like you're having difficulty finding an opening—it'll keep them wanting it."

Robert Greene suggests: *To be royal in your own fashion—act like a king to be treated like one.*

After an hour of reading through articles that've been linked on the forum, I hear the chimes as somebody walks in. The music playing in here is Mikado Koko. The pinewood diffuser is trickling out of my main studio. The smell is clean and reminds you of your lungs.

In 2006, a study looking at scent control was conducted in a Las Vegas casino. An increase of attendees was found only in the casino that offered a pleasurable scent. Olfactory memory. The scent triggers the memory association of odors, perhaps a feeling of nostalgia, perhaps a familiarity and an attachment to an autobiographical memory of consuming a successful product, consuming a successful experience. Aromas can put you in a state of flow. Flow sounds like money.

So I had specifically chosen the pinewood to remind the customer of freshness, openness. That although this studio has little space to move around, which may be stress-inducing, the energy is *abundant*.

"Sorry," I hear the potential customer say to Farah.

I listen carefully against the wall of my studio, hope that Farah will remember all her steps without needing to look at her notes.

"I've never been to a Chinese health clinic before. Do you have a set list? Like a list of services?"

Silence, just Mikado Koko's *Reconstructions* and the subtle sound of coiling mist.

"This one," says the woman. "What's this do? Does it clear your hearing?"

Silence from Farah. Then she says, "Yes. That's a popular choice, that one." She sounds shaky. "What it does," Farah tells her, "is it makes you feel really relaxed."

I let out a breath. This will have to be good enough, and I'll have to play to it. A client never likes mismatched information from voices within the same business.

"Would you like me to book you in?" asks Farah. "You just have to sign a form and I can tell you when we have an available time."

"Yes, yes, of course. A massage as well, please." A bag rustling around.

One thing we've forgotten is pens. We'll have to go down to K.A.G. to get some.

"Uh, pen? Sorry, I don't have one," says the woman.

Farah's typing hands stop.

"Oh, whoops."

I hear Farah digging around the drawers. "Sorry," she says breathily.

"So where are you from?" asks the woman politely.

"Malaysia."

"Malaysia?"

"We migrated there from India, from there to here . . . my parents did. Before I was born," Farah says very courteously. Though I still sense her frustration. She knows this woman just wants an answer she can fully digest and nod her head to.

Farah starts to type loudly again.

"So we can give you an appointment now, because our master is in and she doesn't have her next appointment 'til an hour and a half from now."

I find myself impressed with Farah's response. I decide she must work well with resistance.

"Yes, now is perfect," says the woman.

I try to map out what she looks like. Farah knocks on the door.

"A client is here for an ear treatment and massage. Are you okay for her to come in now?" There is a hint of a smile.

"Yes, send her in."

Farah opens the door fully and the woman steps in.

She is younger than I imagined: late thirties. Her voice sounded slightly more mature from the other room.

I read people's bodies quickly; it's what I imagine will make me proficient in this industry.

"Nice to meet you." I shake her hand. "I'm Leen."

"I'm Andrea. Lovely to meet you."

Farah disappears back to reception.

I welcome Andrea through to the center of the room, where the table is. The diffuser is huffing white silky trails. Andrea admires the shan shui.

"I love this type of art," she says, removing her shoes.

"So we'll perform the massage first, if you'd like to use the divider to remove your clothing. Just put this on." I pull one of the disposable underwear out of the box and hand it to her. "When you're finished just lie down on the massage table and I'll be right with you."

She disappears behind the divider and comes back quickly to lie on the table. I turn to the bench, gathering little bottles of oil and warming my hands with hot water. I hear her say, "Done."

I notice she's left her track pants behind the divider as I approach the bed.

"How are you?" If I get too carried away with small talk, I find I can't stop. So I am brief.

"*Okay*, thank you." She returns the question.

I wish she hadn't. I try to detach from those I do treatments on, as though I am behind a one-way glass screen. I smooth her shoulder blades.

I feel for where the tension is located and tell her she should have a deep tissue massage.

"Oh, yes. I've been feeling fairly tight up the top."

I take the oil and begin kneading it through, preparing the muscles. Then I glide my fingers along the muscle fibers. A bit of friction, like preparing meat. I close my eyes. I'm moving too quickly. I feel out of practice. I take a deep breath and decide to locate the power of Andrea's discomfort. I know I've found it when she makes a gruff noise. I've found a knot. I dig my energy into it with both passion and stillness at once. Tenderly pushing it, I ask her how it feels. I imagine the taut band compressing. I apply this to several spots until I feel her relax. After it's done I ask her to please get dressed and return to a sitting position on the table.

Meanwhile, I turn and grab my fabric case of utensils. Lay it out on the bamboo table. I smell the pinewood scent. I remind myself to take it slowly. I can't puncture her canal if I take the process slowly. I pull the bamboo table over. I stand. There are cotton buds. The smell of the antiseptic liquid is strong and I wonder if her olfactory memory will associate this with more of a clinical treatment, or surgery.

She comes out fully dressed, smoothing down her T-shirt. "Okay."

"This one's a popular choice," I say, then ask her to take a seat on the massage table. I pick up the wire tool. "Relax your arms and focus on breathing," I instruct.

She seems to struggle, her shoulders already locked back in.

I count her through. "Four counts in, seven counts hold, eight counts out."

I look at my tools. The wooden scoop is the one I feel most comfortable with. Maybe I should begin with that one. I fix the headlamp tight around my skull, turn the light on. Swap the wire tool for the wooden scoop.

I go to turn the music up just slightly and drip a few more drops of pinewood oil into the diffuser. On the massage table, Andrea looks thrilled.

"Turn your head up a little and relax," I tell her. A little too bluntly. I'm impatient for things to happen. A habit I still have. Business is a performance as well as a skill.

Robert Greene says master the art of timing: *Never seem to be in a hurry.* This communicates control.

She does as I say, though I feel that I've rushed her. I insert the wooden scoop into her ear, feel around briefly.

She lets out a half snort, half laugh and apologizes, says it feels ticklish.

"First time?" I ask her.

"Yes!"

There is a bit of wax coming loose. I switch to the wire scoop. The rest happens naturally. I finish with an ear rub, tugging at the lobe, pushing with the thumb and pulling with the index.

"What does this do?" she asks.

I tell her that the ears are connected to the kidneys, that doing this exercise will activate it. "Do you feel the connection?"

"Yes," she says.

That afternoon I tell Farah she works well with resistance. We're eating meatballs her mother made out of a plastic tub on the floor of my studio. Doms had come in this afternoon with Vic. The pharmacy had a staff meeting, which he conducted every month. Doms tried to work on some candles in the small studio but ended up going back down to the pharmacy. She hasn't been waking up on time to get a lift with me in the mornings.

Driving Doms and Vic home that night, I think of strategies to pull in clientele. Word of mouth. People are friends with similar people with similar habits and routines—it's what keeps them safe. It's what makes it so easy to relate to pools of people at once, once you recognize the language that will appeal to them.

I ended up liking Andrea. At the end of our session, I told her, "Tell your friends about us."

She said, "I definitely will." She paid us $150 for our services. Before she left the studio, she asked, "How often do people get their ears cleaned?"

At the time, Farah and I, both high off the experience, agreed it shouldn't be done very often, maybe once a month. Later, as the excitement faded, we decided we wouldn't recommend this to anyone again. Instead, we'd say every *fortnight*—a week wasn't believable and wouldn't be healthy for the customers.

In business, you have to find information that balances. The truth, but not quite.

On the radio now: *... rise of vandalism ... don't kids have anything better ... and two police officers wounded when entering private property ... however much ...*

I'm driving us through a McDonald's drive-thru as if the shape of it is automatically programmed into my hands. Doms and Vic stop the conversation they're having and cheer. I order a Filet-O-Fish. I'm becoming my mother. We take the meals home and eat together around the table. They've been talking about something this entire time and I haven't been able to concentrate at all. Vic is saying something about the economy in Nigeria, and his uncle's farm.

Later, I try to finish *2001*.

I'm afraid ... I'm afraid ... my mind is going ... I'm a ... fraid.

13 **IT'S SEEMING AS THOUGH JEAN** Paul's forgotten about the discussion group this week. He hasn't texted or called in a few days, but posted on the forum earlier in the week, something about another thing he and Huy did to Mary, the supermarket branch manager.

· · ·

It's morning. I'm drinking coffee with my feet diagonally angled up on our coffee table. Doms is leaning against Vic; they're standing in the kitchen talking so quietly I can't hear them.

"What happened?" I say.

They look up like cats. It makes me feel moronic.

"Have you seen Jean Paul around?" Vic asks. "He hasn't been at work. Pulls out of every shift last minute. I've stayed back late doing his prescriptions every night. Working has been making me feel . . . anxious and shit, and I need my staff. Especially behind the desk."

"No," I say, and screw my mouth to the side.

I offer to drive him home after work if it's about the incident and being afraid to walk in the streets. But he quickly says that he likes to go to the gym after work now anyway. Doms has seemed better about him lately—perhaps it's the body he's obtained over this time. Often it takes a few months to show results if it is muscle you are building. She is always holding on to him recently; if he's not at work or the gym, they are, at all other times, attached.

"There are two bookings," Farah says.

We're making coffee in the staff room the next morning. I'm hoping there will be more walk-ins. I wonder why my mother receives so many *Western* customers in a day, but everybody here is *Western* and doesn't want to book a session.

I smell the milk and it's off. There are three boy-looking men playing hacky sack. And Freddy, who has not talked to me since I gave him the flyer. He avoids eye contact, with an inconsistent rhythm about it. He is probably dreaming of sexual favors. It's the way he looks and then looks away when I display any particular sign of agency.

I sit on the couch across from him and place the mug on the coffee table, hoping he'll bring it up; I promise I won't speak first.

The pocket of my white lab coat is full of the leftover flyers.

People don't like that I look like a dentist when I walk around the center, so I take the headlamp off and leave it in the main studio. Still, the lab coat provides a social barrier. I take it off now. Underneath, I'm wearing an old, ordinary pink blouse and trousers from Mee & Gee. I lay the coat over the arm of the couch.

Freddy looks up from his phone. "You look lovely."

His breath smells like mothballs. He's wearing a maroon jumper. The downlight in the farthest corner of the room is flickering. I pick up a magazine—it's a horse one.

I pretend to flick through it. "When are you going to use your discount pamphlet?" I lean over and stir the coffee.

He looks at my chest. "Tomorrow."

"Make a booking, please," I instruct, as he's still looking at my chest.

The first customer arrives at the studio today around half past eleven. His name's Philip. He comes in wearing a short cowboy hat. I'm leaning against the reception desk and I don't know where to go because he's already seen me.

"I think I'm getting a call." I put on my white coat and disappear into the studio.

I hear Farah asking if he's booked an appointment. She asks him to fill out the registration form and they don't speak. A few minutes later, Farah knocks on the door of the studio and I let him in.

He goes straight to the table, sits down. I look at Farah.

"This gentleman is just after the massage," she says.

I ask him, "How about an ear clean?"

"No, what the heck is that?" he says, slightly amused.

I ask him to go behind the divider to remove his shirt, then to lie on the massage table with the sheet over him when he's done.

"Just the shirt off?" he asks, stays sitting there. After a moment, "Pants off?" He says this a bit more aggressively.

"No," I tell him quickly, motioning toward the divider.

"I'm not getting a full body massage?"

"Okay, you can. I'll give you a second to undress and get under the sheet."

I slip outside the door, and my breath is difficult. Farah looks over at me with a puzzled face.

Doms is coming through the glass door, and the chimes we'd bought from the dollar store go off. The sound has already become tiresome. Doms is wearing a hoodie and drinking from a McDonald's cup. She's carrying a box.

"I'm gonna promote this place at the craft markets. Should I bring flyers?"

I take a few from my pocket.

"Good, good," I say. "Shh, I've got a client."

When I'm nervous I start to half whisper, half yell. I hear Philip call out and I enter the studio again. He's sitting on the massage table, his legs shoulder-width apart, a little dick furrowed between his thin thighs, under minimal hair.

He looks at me, eyebrows raised, nearly smiling. "Let's begin," he says. He seems cheerier.

I remember the disposable underwear and pull one out from the box, flustered. Pass it to him.

"No, thank you. I'm fine," he says, looking me right in the eyes.

I tell him he must and he reluctantly pulls them over his genitals. He attempts to move himself closer to me as I arrange things on the bamboo table unnecessarily.

I say without looking, "On your front."

He does as I say and I grab the drape, shaking, trying to unfold it. The art of draping a client is a learned skill, a felt skill. This is something I had forgotten to do with Andrea.

Best not to initiate the art of draping if one cannot sustain the art of draping. It is a state of flow in itself.

This white towel—the dignity of the client. The physical, emotional, and spiritual boundary between master and client.

Prone, face down. Glute draping. Spread the drape out, roll it down the body, not too far so as to expose the client's crack. No fussing.

I pull the towel back so that it's higher above the crack, slightly brushing it, and he says, "Oh, I don't mind." He tilts his head up, his pupils as close to the corners of his eye skin as they can be.

I don't respond. The diffuser continues to steam. Laraaji is playing softly in the background.

His whole body is smiling a shit-eating grin as I press my palms into his upper back. The skin is moldable. Ten minutes of loosening the patient's back. Spreading his wings out.

I find myself remembering the lecture videos I watched when I missed classes. What did they say? I feel detached from this body; it feels different from the way I had felt toward Andrea's. His back, although full of bodily essence, reminds me of soullessness, a disfigurement of his own physical intention. Like quick, unimpassioned sex or sugar rushes.

Don't go in too deep too quick.

I rub all down his back, then decide to use my shakiness, the tension in my fist to do a compression massage. Then, using the fores of my arms, I flatten out his posture over the mid-back, my stance shifting. *Sink* and then glide, I remember.

He grunts sexually. The tattoo on his shoulder blade is a picture of John Lennon. On his other shoulder is an image of a skull smoking a cigar.

After the session, he returns his hat onto his head and leaves, paying in cash. He looks upset again.

I go down to the staff room without looking at anyone on the way, down the escalators, past K.A.G., past the dollar store. Farah will text me if there are more clients.

No one's in the staff room. I stir a sachet of OldTown coffee into boiling water. I look at the little bulb, the security camera, and I think I see it blinking at me.

Keep them in suspended terror, says Robert Greene.

When I get back, Doms is still in her studio and I wonder if her presence is entirely necessary here. A space, particularly a healing space, is designed to be open and growing. Each energy introduced drops into the flow of the dynamic, forever altering it.

I go to knock on the second studio door but decide against it. When I think about Doms, it is always about favors and repayments, and somehow always being slightly afraid of her, even here in the space I've given back to her.

After a moment of standing in my studio, I decide to go to the food court for a break, walking the other way around, distracting myself with the mannequins in the shopfronts. I go to the Asian grocers and get some snacks in a plastic bag.

When I arrive at the food court, I scratch my arm for a few minutes and go to buy a pea-and-ham sandwich.

I eat it with my phone beside me in case Farah calls. I scroll through the forum, and when I finish the sandwich I open the pack of Crown Choco Heim wafers I got from the Asian grocers. I read through some of Aden's threads about city planning and then a new thread that Jean Paul has posted this afternoon discussing the use of recreational drugs in times of revolution. I watch the escalator ascending to the next floor and the other traveling back down to this one. A mother rides up the escalator as if it is the first time she is doing it with a baby carriage. A new accessory to show the nail technician who does her shellac on the first Wednesday of every month. Gary Bartz is playing throughout the center—that's how you feel Peggy's presence without seeing her.

Peggy appears suddenly, at the top of the escalator. When she sees me over the handrail, her face beams. She is shaking a water bottle in her hand.

Halfway down the escalator she mouths to me, *How is the sandwich?* I tilt my head from side to side, a little taken aback by her enthusiasm.

Peggy comes and sits herself down on the other side of the table, drinking something from the water bottle that is not water or juice. Noticing me stare at it, she lifts the bottle up. "I just drink protein shakes." She bursts out laughing. "It's *not* shit!" She coughs something up. "Ling," she says under her breath. "Ling, tell me how it's going at the massage parlor?"

"It's going okay."

"Is that so? A few more customers now?"

"Yeah, a few. Mostly for me. My business partner isn't getting much business."

"You have to be audacious!" offers Peggy. "In other news, I wanted to ask if you've noticed any odd behavior. I see you're using the staff room a lot. Are all the facilities being used correctly?"

"Everything looks fine."

Peggy is big money. She takes down notes on her phone, but doesn't tell me what she's asking for.

When she stands up to leave, she says, "Come to my get-together this Saturday. All the tenants are invited. You've seen the poster, it's up on the pinboard. You and your cool friends."

She points a finger at me, winks, points, shoots.

That same afternoon is the first time I notice something off.

In the hallway leading to the staff room, someone has pinned up a sign on the community board with a picture of a self-serve cash register from the supermarket. Written underneath: *Are you worth more than this?*

I am exhausted by now. I scan in to the staff room and take four milk biscuits, putting three in my pocket before chewing softly at the first. I open my phone to Jean Paul's new thread, and I scroll through, an aggressive feeling in my thumb. Something about LSD for the purpose of computer research. My thumb is twitching. Energy I need to relocate.

14 **FRIDAY MORNING. CUPPING ACHIEVES THREE** things for the body: weight loss, release of toxins, and clearance of respiratory conditions. The blocking of qi changes vital energies, fluids, phlegm, lymph, and blood as human functions. Cupping breaks the blockage of routine in modern human cycles. Energy is restored.

Following the lines of the meridians. The cups are placed on each of them.

Doms is lying down. I tell her, "We're opening the channels."

Ge Hong was the pioneer alchemist in 283 AD, providing methodology for walking on water and raising the dead.

I say, "This'll look weird after."

15 **WE ARRIVE AT PEGGY'S HOUSE** on the Saturday night and I'm wearing '94 cargo pants from M.N.G and an army salute hat over fake furs.

Peggy's house looks like a powder puff sitting on top of a hill at the end of a court on the coastal side. It overlooks rows of palm trees on one side and a train line on the other.

Doms and Vic ended up flaking and usually I would've stayed at home too. But now I've got Farah, who decided to come last-minute. She seems to be spontaneous like this, which I both like and admire.

We get off the bus, and the ground mumbles under our heels as the bus accelerates off again. Just three people waiting to be dropped somewhere. Only a few stops until the end of the route.

"*Fuck,*" Farah says as we stand at the foot of the hill.

She had rolled her ankle at futsal practice a couple of days ago and the muscle is still stiff.

The sun is big red behind the rooftop, where people stand scattered around the balcony area, like a garden party. It looks something like a three-story farmhouse. As we get closer, an irregular, booming rhythm becomes apparent.

"It's one of *those* parties," Farah says. "We're in for a night and a half. You know what people say about Peggy, right?"

"What?"

"It's like a swinger's *hub*, her house."

"*Wow . . . what?*"

"People really talk, they really talk in Par Mars," she laughs.

There's a naked man in shoe-laced suit shoes and no socks running down the hill.

"Whenever anybody's naked, it's important," I tell Farah.

"Sexually? Like, physically?"

"Mmm . . . emotionally," I say matter-of-factly. "It's all they have."

"Whatever. No business tonight, please. You think they have food? My foot hurts."

I'm laughing. I'm happy to be here.

Inside the house, there are popcorn ceilings and oil paintings hanging around every corner. The sound of a saxophone hovers in the long front hallway.

A man takes our names, phone numbers, and identities. There are two identities to choose from: *Topic Heights tenants* or *house guests*.

We choose *Topic Heights tenants* and are given an opportunity to use a makeshift cloakroom.

When we come into the hallway we notice there are almost three different songs playing. One from outside upstairs, one from inside down here, and one from somebody's real saxophone playing along to someone else's playing of the grand piano in the next room.

As we continue walking, we notice that the second room has some chairs arranged in the center. There are two people in there talking, pointing at artworks hanging along the circumference, as if a small art gallery.

A staircase to the right if you continue down the hall. There are yellow lampshades, and two or three stained-glass windows with Mother Mary on them at the end, the entertaining space opening up to a kitchen. Most people are in there.

Peggy welcomes us as we approach the kitchen and Farah asks if she has anything for her foot, which is inflamed, and Peggy leads us back toward the staircase, taking us up to her bedroom. She's going to get a heat pad for Farah.

Peggy's room seems particularly small. Seemingly smaller than any of the other rooms. There are bowling trophies on the dresser, workout clothes hanging over a chair.

Farah widens her eyes, nudging me. There's a frame of two men on her bedside table.

I ask Peggy who they are.

"Bob Dylan and Johnny Cash," Peggy says.

Farah looks at me with a smirk.

"They're my parents," says Peggy. She's drunk; she smells of it.

Peggy adjusts her impressive, muscly cleavage. She has big breasts from chest workouts; there's a way you can tell, how the chest sits. I feel tiny and insubstantial standing beside her. She is strong yet shapely in a way that makes her body seem like all actual muscle. It is her lips and cheeks that've been aggressively injected into over time. The look suits the platinum of her hair and is currently fashionable.

"We sleep in separate bedrooms," she says, without either of us asking. Then, promptly, "You two go down first, I'm sweating like a bull hog."

When we leave the room, Farah asks, "What's a bull hog? Is she confused?"

There's a man standing in the corner filming us.

She directs the question at him. "What's a bull hog?"

He shrugs and we watch the lens zoom in on Farah's face.

The man follows us down the stairs and he trips and clutches the banister.

Farah turns around, her nose in his lens. "You okay, Tarantino?"

"Tarantino doesn't film documentary."

She rolls her eyes, the best I've seen anybody roll them.

Downstairs, Big Red Boss from K.A.G. is drunk and tomato-like on the white leather lounge. Farah sees her and disappears into the kitchen.

I watch as she reclines with one leg propped up and the other dangling. She yells to the man sitting on the opposite lounge, "The things we do for attention!" Her voice is shaking. She appears to be sulking. Mascara trickles down her cheeks and she wipes them with a hostility. We meet eyes. She waits a moment, then yells, "Take a picture, it'll last longer!"

I think about where Big Red Boss will be after the party tonight. Wonder what street she lives on, what sector of Par Mars.

I sit on the arm of the couch she's on; her leg has sweat beads rolling down them. I imagine tears and sweat like a waterslide down her body. I feel bad about the Farah incident. But people steal friends all the time and it's okay.

She looks at me and something in her cheek flinches. She starts to lift her arms as if they are being controlled by something else, tightens her fingers before grabbing my neck and squeezing. Her fingers are insubstantial and don't make much of an impact. Nobody else is looking.

"What are you doing?" My voice cuts off, my chin scrunching at the bottom. I look her straight in the eyes. One of them is looking just off from me.

"I'm just seeing." She grits her teeth, squeezes harder. "Seeing, seeing, seeing," she hums.

· · ·

Later in the night I'm sitting with a guy called Luis, who's quite tall, tall enough. Everybody has been asked to wear the name badges they've been given for their workplaces, so although he's told me his name is Luis, his K.A.G. name badge reads: ANTONIO.

He looks at me looking at it. "It's one of my middle names."

I say, "Come upstairs with me?"

He nods and we relocate. He follows me up each step like a puppy. "Do you go to Boneyard's ever? Have I seen you there before?"

When he talks his eyes smile, it feels attractive.

"No."

I'm in a strange, confident mood. I don't have to look at him to know he's connected to me. And that we've attached ourselves to one another for the remainder of the night. I don't have to look back to see if he's still following, I know he is.

Energy never depletes; it is only transferred.

I open the door with a golden nameplate reading BUNGALOW 3 and notice how the lights are romantically low, glowing like cherry reflections. It's a gray room with dial lighting behind the headboard of the bed. The sheets are white and cotton. There are blue-framed mirrors hanging over a dormant fireplace. White, unidentifiable flowers on either side of the bed. Reminds me of a Beijing hotel room.

"There's an app to find out flower species," I say.

He smiles and sits on the bed, rubbing his thighs. "Oh?"

Staring at the detail of the blue frames, I think about the obvious homeliness of the place—how it should feel comfortable, but somehow still doesn't. Like when people don't use their houses for homes. I imagine having enough space to make a house not a home.

"They're nice," says Luis. He is leaning over, touching the white flowers, his shirt lifting up a bit. "They're real."

Peggy wants people to fuck, maybe. Rilke says art and sex emerge from a similar location. Peggy is making a container for both. The sacral chakra, orange chakra, deals with both sex and artistic impulses.

Luis has brought a red wine with him. He's wearing Tommy Hilfiger cargo pants and a Bruce Willis disco top. I'm looking at his pants too much now and he lets out a laugh. Looks down at his pants too.

"Did you dress up for this or are you usually dressed like this?" I ask.

"I could dress like this every day if I wanted to."

I've lost all track of time as we pour a second glass of wine together. His round brown eyes. I start to feel warm about him.

He's standing in the room, pulling the books half out from the shelf, looking for something he recognizes. It looks very humble.

He swabs his upper lip with his tongue. "I wonder if Peggy's read these books."

The sheets feel cold and un-slept on. I lie across them.

I tell him I've been trying to read about ancient healing.

He turns and looks at me, distracted. He asks me what it is I'm reading and I say reflexology.

"The hands can be explored using reflexology," I explain. "The inner part of the thumb connects to the meridian connected with the lung, and when pressure is placed there, you can access almost everything from the hands. Flush energy, restore circulation."

I press my thumb into the hollow between my opposite thumb and first finger, a gentle, circular motion.

He does the same with his own, then offers his hand forward so I can do it for him.

"Does this throw something else off, though? If I press here? In terms of energy," he asks.

I take a moment to think about it, pressing into his skin.

He smiles. "Is that a stupid question?"

I shake my head. "The measurement of energy is a measurement of interaction and relationship. More than this, it is the measurement of how much energy is located in one spot. So the pressure is a measure-ment of the meridian, rather than the past or previous location of it. Does that make sense? I must be drunk."

He tells me he honestly had no better thing to say or question to ask and settled for the one he had asked purely out of an inherited tendency from his father: to obstruct and adopt contrarianism. He comes back over to sit on the bed beside me.

"Your energy can get stuck." I yawn, my cheek in the pillow.

He brings out a pair of earphones from his pocket and begins untangling them. They're the kind that plug tight all the way into your ear. He tells me, "If you push a certain way—too far in—you stop hear-ing anything."

"Ears are so important," I say.

"Yeah, yeah right. They're a . . . passage to the soul."

"To the kidneys."

He hands me one bud and lies down beside me. He begins playing something. I look over and he shows me on his screen, "Violets for Your Furs." We lie on the bed and listen to it five times on repeat accidentally.

When I start to fall asleep, I feel Luis moving over and brushing my cheek. I flutter my eyes open and look at his lips.

"Hi."

"Hi."

Then he pashes my neck for ten minutes. I hold his temple while he's against me and stare at the way the delicately formed plaster on the ceiling meets itself in the center to create a bulbous estuary. When I roll to my side to face him, he blinks slowly.

He tells me his father had been the head of philosophy at the University of Rio de Janeiro for most of his life. Then he tells me he's interested in every-thing, though his heart tells him he should also be interested in philosophy. For now, he likes K.A.G. because of its focus on consumption culture and how it utilizes theory on late capitalist philosophy. Everywhere tells you to focus on your career or living in order to earn. But K.A.G. talks about how the career is a minuscule part of living. Living is how you prepare your food, how you dress in the mornings, take the clothes from your cupboards, how you wear a T-shirt, how you store your shoes. They are enough.

Luis opens his eyes and rolls over, wrapping his arms around my tummy. I wonder if he'll try to have sex. I shift to my side. He nestles his nose into my neck. We lie there and I try not to breathe, so I don't disturb him. I press my nose into the pillow and it smells like how my mother's old bedroom smelled. Like comfort, some kind of flower I don't know how to identify.

I remember what I said before about ears being important. I wish I hadn't said that because maybe that's why he's decided to sleep.

I think about getting up and maybe he'll want to fuck tomorrow.

Police arrive, blues, reds on the wall, making the room a sort of purple. I stand by the window. A man in a leopard-print tuxedo and fedora hat is being arrested at the top of the hill.

Half-asleep, Luis says, "Don't draw any attention up here." He turns his body to the opposite side.

I go downstairs and follow the string music projecting from a room down the hall, closer to the front door. By the time I reach the front hallway to peer out the windows, the police car has driven off and it's as though nothing has happened.

The room closest to the front is the gallery room, and it's filled with around a dozen people, some sitting and some standing to observe the art on the wall. It reminds me of reality television: the people are trapped but enjoy the contractual standardizing of it; they have signed up only to compete with a certain amount of people, the amount that can fit in the house, in the room.

One of the art viewers is looking at me. "Coming in to see the art?"

Who has come to see the art most?

I wonder if I'm drunk.

One of them is touching a painting. I think he works at the shoe store near the dry cleaners, a Payless. "Flamenco Sketches" comes on the stereo. One of them leaves the room and stands outside. "When are you going to put the goddamn fucking Bob Dylan on?"

I take a seat on a velvet chair and cross my legs.

An older woman in real furs says to me, "I'm loving the diversity at this party. So fascinating."

Peggy walks in and the woman sits up in her chair properly, folds a leg over. Everybody adjusts themselves to face Peggy now, who looks pleased and slightly nervous.

"Everybody enjoying?" says Peggy. "Remember to ask Ramon if you need anything. He is very friendly."

She points out the door to the small man at the front. He wears an understanding smile and tickles his fingers in the air. Some people wave back.

I shift in my chair.

The person sitting next to me, a middle-aged man with thick black hair and a Nike T-shirt on, leans over. "Is this a swingers' party?"

Peggy shuts the door of the gallery room. Without question, this happens, and we are all encased in here now. Then she announces, "In the meantime, I'm going to give that reading I promised."

She pulls out a curled piece of paper. There are murmurs around the room and everybody readjusts themselves in their seats. Peggy centers herself between the couches and chairs. She wipes some lipstick from the corners of her lips. Parts them romantically, her lips like the lips of a clam. She is sweating nervously, the paper quivering in her hands.

She reads: "I am a golden star sitting in a beautiful shell. The sea is part of my stomach, my eyes, my brain. I am a golden star sitting in a beautiful shell. This is the sky that tries to swallow me with blackness. This is the sky that tries to swallow me with the sun the next morning. I am a golden star sitting in a beautiful shell."

Peggy sniffs, as if she is about to cry. She rubs the side of her bottom lip, checks her finger for lipstick. She mutters, "I'm so nervous, excuse me."

People start to put their hands together, but she begins again: "I am a golden star sitting in a beautiful shell! I watch the people walking on the electronic highways. I am highly aware of their forms, I make them aware of their forms. We keep straight lines and curvy asides to keep from insanity. I am a golden star sitting in a beautiful shell. I read a Bible Genesis and watch the wet faces that read it. I am a golden star in a beautiful shell. I see the empty rooms and the faithful believers with their props. I watch through a lens. I keep the empty rooms light and watch them believe. I am a golden star in a beautiful shell."

Someone shifts again in their seat. Makes embarrassing eye contact with me.

People want to leave the room. Someone bends their fingers into the ottoman they're sitting on. I see beads of sweat developing on Peggy's face, one rolling moonily down her cheek.

She takes a small bow, as if attempting to curtsy, and then laughs. "Okay," she says, and slowly leaves the room. Everybody follows, discarding their chairs.

When I'm back out in the foyer, I don't know how I got there. I look around and don't remember who was in the room with me, can't talk about it with anybody. I go back upstairs to Bungalow 3.

Luis is still asleep there on the large bed. He doesn't wake when I open the door but turns as I close it.

"Hey, where'd you go?"

I say I went downstairs.

I can't remember what time I left and it's now 2:40 in the morning. I've started convincing myself recently that the worst time for the susceptible brain is somewhere between 2:00 a.m. and 3.30 a.m. The hour of the liver in the Chinese body clock of organs. This is a time when deep sleep and subconscious planning occur. The blood is detoxing. This time is worse too because it can still consolidate to "the night before," not near enough to sunrise to forget about the day before. Not close enough to the previous sunset to change the way you feel about it in any significant way.

"What's happening down there?" he asks.

He opens his arm for me to rest in. I go to the bed and lie down. I don't know what to do with my hands. His smell is familiar.

I put one of the earphones back in. I slowly start to recognize the shape of "Violets for Your Furs" still playing. I recognize the smell of sweat. I realize the bed does not feel as it did before, that perhaps the sheets are not clean. The pillow has been recently slept on and I start to fidget.

"A performance, a poetry reading," I say.

Luis frowns, surprised. He props his head so that it's resting closer to mine. I'm lying on my back, my hands on my stomach. I try to ignore the sweat smell.

"You can learn so much about people from what they make," says Luis. "Or, better yet, how they go about sharing or making it. Sometimes like a call for help."

I shake my head, rub my fingers down my face so I'm melting.

He says, "You know, I've done a poem before."

I keep my eyes closed. My hands back on my stomach.

Churning, like I'm about to throw up.

"Astrology," he says.

When I get out to the front, Farah is sitting on a brick step, looking out beyond the hill to the horizon. A man is smoking on the porch behind her. There is a bit of sun coming up.

I throw up around the corner.

Farah appears behind me. I look at her. She's staring into the distance, her nostrils flaring.

"Too much to drink?" she asks, patting my back.

The strangest time of the day, I think. I stand up properly and turn around, stare at the dark blue sky, a hint of pink. "Where were you all night?" I ask. "Did you have a good time?"

"Too many people," she says, and shrugs.

When we come back around to the front, a woman has assumed Farah's spot on the top brick step. She appears to be crying, her lanky, cardigan-clad body folded over itself.

Farah looks at me and goes to sit beside her. "Are you okay, ma'am?" She gently hovers her hand over her back.

It's Mary. Mary who runs the supermarket and who Jean Paul has been pranking.

Mary sits up and exhales open-mouthed. Her bob is cut very particularly, her hair dyed a color between red and black.

"If I'm honest, I've wasted my time here," she says, shaking her head. "And men are *just so darn rude.*"

I notice she has a very proper accent. It would align most with a transatlantic accent. The accent that was once used to signify a sort of class distinction—a universally recognized class distinction, something learned rather than absorbed.

"Your life goes very quickly, dear," she says to Farah. I am standing at the bottom of the stairs and she looks to me. "Life goes very quickly."

Farah pats her back. "Hey, it's going to be all right."

I don't say anything.

Mary is picking her fingers. "The real problem is that I keep resigning from good jobs because I don't feel all that attractive when I'm successful. I feel rather lonely. My daughter, I never see her anymore. But as soon as I resign, I have to settle for less for *myself* as well as for her."

She's lighting a Marlboro. She offers one to us. She has dainty hands accustomed to the cigarette and its lighter. She looks out to the sun. "The problem is, you should decide what you want in this life. Decide now."

Farah nods. I try to imagine Mary much younger than she is now and find that I can't.

"I worked for a security company straight after my degree, then for the airport. Now those were great jobs. Then Beatrice, the divorce. And now I've quit a good job, one that kept me close to Beatrice, but I feel like I have to get married again. My husband, he was a God-fearing man, but even then . . ." She lets out a laugh, the kind that encourages you to laugh too.

Farah and I try to smile.

"You young people." She almost has a look of tenderness in her eyes. She stands up, pushing her knees for leverage, and laughs again. Dabs at the dampness around her eyes. "You know, I was a blonde. Before I dyed it all."

Farah just looks at me.

Mary goes to open the front door but before she does, she glances at the man. The one seated on the porch, now asleep.

We walk down the hill and take a bus. I've got my 900 parked at Farah's. We sleep in her bed, which is an uncomfortable double. At noon we wake up and her parents are out somewhere. Her siblings are up, one watching television and the other practicing violin proficiently.

I drive home.

16 JEAN PAUL'S BACK FROM A workshop or something, and he won't say much else about it except that it has changed his idea on passivity.

"I'm more inspired than ever before," he says.

I'm giving him an ear clean.

Ear cleanings something you have to practice often if you don't want to lose the skill. Your hand starts to form a shape about it.

For the customer, it is good to do once in a while: you don't want butter to start consolidating, but you also don't want to disrupt the natural lining of the ear, which your body works to fabricate.

Jean Paul orders crab soup to come to Doms's condo. But I can't stop thinking about Luis.

"Mmm," says Jean Paul. He keeps shivering. "I've never had anyone put anything in my ear before."

He decides in a moment that he needs to take his Moncler off.

I find the mound behind his ear and massage it. The inside of Jean Paul's ear is shaped like a vase. I lower the scoop in and reach around diagonally, scrape a bit. Pull it out, just more oil.

"Your ears are pretty clean already," I say.

"Except for all the voices in there." He laughs, the outer corners of his eyes almost drooping, for comedic purposes, it seems. He is pleased and smiles. "Yeah, anyway, I cleaned them before I came. I get embarrassed."

"What?"

Jean Paul says, looking at the status of the order on his phone, "The soup's here." There's a knock on the door.

I pull myself up off the ground and Jean Paul stays sitting on the cushion. The delivery person hands me a paper bag with two foam containers inside. When I come back, a cockroach runs out from under the television console and under the couch near Jean Paul. I say nothing.

"We're not animals," says Jean Paul. I can't decide whether he's being facetious when he gets in these moods. "Get us ceramic bowls!"

"Lotus Collage" is playing.

Jean Paul says, "You, me, and Huy make a well-balanced team. We have the leader, the driver, and the tricks man. I think we need to be more active. Instead of just sitting around talking all day. What does that do except make us more *annoyed* about everything?"

I spoon some of the chowder into my mouth. I look at him inquiringly. "The leader, the driver, and the tricks man?"

Jean Paul's quiet for a moment. Under his breath, he says in a certain silly voice, "*That's all you need.*"

I pass him a ceramic bowl, now full of crab soup, and he leans against the television console.

"*Bisque*," he says. Then, "There always needs to be a tricks man. He's almost the brains, just no sense of purpose." He shakes his spoon and the soup on it wobbles. "And I swear to God if Huy wears that college logo jumper one more time, I'll slice a bitch." He laughs.

We finish the soup and Jean Paul is wearing only his white underwear and lying on the dining table. I've draped him so that his left leg is showing. The bodily condiments are in the back part of the couch. The bottle of jojoba oil is available beside me.

While I smooth out his skin, he tells me that fashion is very important in a revolution. In New China, the idea of modern fashion was far too individualistic. They thought about everything, the superficial desire and the promotion of women as visual objects, and so everything they wore was masculinized. The same thing happened in Russia. No need for lace and corsets. Just textile, linen. The woman bodysuit and the man bodysuit not much different.

He says, "It's almost like the stuff they sell at that K.A.G."

A few days ago, K.A.G. started selling chairs and humidifiers.

Jean Paul is sitting up again, cracking his neck side to side. "That was fantastic," he says.

I'm going to try fire cupping. Shanhuofa. Watching a video tutorial.

Jean Paul puts his legs up on the dining table, still wearing only his underwear.

I have cups on the table. I pick them up one at a time, rub isopropyl alcohol on the inside. I gently prod his legs off the table, not because it's rude but because he will need to lie down again once I am ready.

He takes his legs down and continues talking. He tells me his father was always buying and swapping cars, that it was his entire passion. He would have been buried in his car or had his ashes stored in his Audi if he could. Jean Paul says that transport is important and its style implies something about the passenger.

I invite him to lie down on the table. The cotton ball's a little wet. I clamp it securely into the plier. Fire it with a lighter. Hold it briefly inside the globe of the cup. Remove it quickly. Put out the fire and let the rim of the cup suction onto the skin of the back.

Jean Paul jerks slightly but continues to talk. His skin is being pulled tight.

A red bulb is enlarging. I pull the cup up and it makes a choking noise.

"Oh," he says.

The red welt is perfectly round. My lips contort about it. I try not to let Jean Paul see the face that is naturally forming on me. It's not so professional. But I think he's distracted, saying something about: imagine twenty of us all wearing the beige collection from K.A.G.

"See, aesthetic outerwear is very interesting. People trust you and leave you alone if you are outwardly indicating a certain criteria," he says.

I give Jean Paul four cuppings. Eventually he starts grunting and wincing more.

"This feels sexual," he says.

A massage therapy forum said to practice this type of silence.

Not responding to any conversation outside of the service.

I think about doing themed months for the studio. Maybe a cinnamon month where Doms will sell cinnamon-flavored candles and soaps, and I will diffuse cinnamon-smelling aromas and have cinnamon-colored decor.

When Doms and Vic get home they go straight to run a bath. Vic looks as if he's been crying, like he hasn't slept properly in a long time. He barely says hi to Jean Paul.

I wonder if Luis is a bath man.

"Do you clean noses?" asks Jean Paul.

I tell him no.

We put the bottles back on the table and I clean up the oil I spilled. Doms comes from the bathroom in a towel and gives me a look. "*Okay*... but don't use our oil," she says, and takes the bottle from the dining table.

I tell her I have my own oil. Mine is considered to be the community's oil, the universal oil, *the oil that connects*.

Later, Jean Paul and I are on our way to pick up Huy from his parents' house. We're listening to Los Indios Tabajaras on the radio as I drive.

When I touch the hot steering wheel it stings a long paper cut across my hand. I'm not sure when it got there. The windows are down. There's a red streak across the sky and a dead animal on the road, which I swerve around smoothly. It looks like a bear, a chunky little thing. The mega gas station is lit up with white lights, flickering like a mirage. I remember to breathe in my nose and out my mouth.

Jean Paul is fully out the window. There's enough wax in his hair to hold it from blowing. His eyelids must be flapping.

"Milonga del Angel" now.

The radio says: *It conveys a sad, tropical mood.*

We come off the highway. We're at the big windowless shopping complex, the Galleria. Topic Heights' main competition, and they're doing late-night shopping every weekday now. There are cars queuing to go in. Inside, it always looks like the light you get in the morning at around seven. It always smells neutral; there are always "sensible" people.

We turn down a hill and come up again and all the houses are spread out. The property is a long redbrick house. Huy is waiting in the driveway and runs over with a backpack, one strap snapped and the other looped around his shoulder.

"Nice house," I say when Huy gets in the back.

"Thanks."

We're driving now. "Are you French, Jean Paul?" Huy asks from the back.

"Kind of," says Jean Paul. He pulls his window down again and drips himself out of it.

We are on our way to Big Red Boss's house now. A complaint came in against her, accusing her of being verbally abusive and on the cusp of becoming physical with a sixteen-year-old employee. Jean Paul had been in contact with three people from K.A.G. who all agreed that her behavior was consistently like this. Then Huy did research on her. He often tells us, "I could hack into your messages, probably. Actually, easily. Don't keep anything you wouldn't want *me* to know." Sounds like something he says to everyone he meets for the first time.

The plan is to commit a similar prank on Big Red Boss, only over a longer period of time. After what we had done to Mary, Jean Paul had posted the video of her to the forum. It had been a brilliant success with the forum members. Then he'd disappeared for that workshop.

"There are many ideas," he'd said when he came back. "There's much more where that came from."

Big Red Boss's house is nearly twenty minutes away from Topic Heights. Huy's navigating.

"What if it's not the right house?"

"Everyone's address," Huy explains defensively, "is on the Topic Heights database. It's a prerequisite for managers, employees, and business owners to upload it. They get you to update it if you move. Her name is *Berta Girardi*, isn't it? As long as that's her name, it's her address."

The highway goes on for ages and Jean Paul sits in the front rubbing his hair. "I've given myself a headache," he mutters.

"It's semisynthetic," Huy says, leaning in between us. "Ten times more powerful than morphine, so you need to take it every four hours instead of two."

Jean Paul picks his teeth.

Huy says, "But it's cheaper than heroin. It makes scales on your skin where you've injected it. You can make it at home. I have suspicions about which of my codeine buyers are cooking it."

He tell us that if you miss a vein you end up with dead flesh that looks a bit like crocodile scales.

"So if you mix codeine with gasoline," Jean Paul says, "then mix it with lye. Hydrochloric acid, which you can get from the hardware store, is mixed in too and then you get the codeine salts. Then you've got to mix them into another mixture with red phosphorus, which you need to get ordered in from overseas. This is the element that makes it chancy."

"Yeah," says Huy.

"Limbs amputated and life span limited to two more years if you're an addict."

"Yeah."

I think about a picture I saw in a book on the A-bomb called *Little Boy, Fat Man*. Children with what people would consider to be abnormally small heads. I read that these children had been fed a large neutron output, a biologically significant radiation dose. My nose fills up with cold air.

"Just here," says Jean Paul.

I pull up in front of the driveway.

"Double story," observes Huy.

"How are you going to be inconspicuous with those chains on?" Jean Paul says, turning around to look at Huy.

Huy starts undoing them. He's got three on, different widths and lengths.

They put disposable surgical masks on and rubber gloves dispensed from boxes like tissues, which Jean Paul has started to keep in my car. As he gets out, Jean Paul tells me to drive around the whole block five times. They'll be about ten minutes.

I take the drive around the block. Neither of them have told me what they're doing because I've told them not to. If I'm oblivious, I may as well be their Uber; this gives them a better chance of doing things discreetly. When the person driving a car is guilty, the behavior of the car changes the way it appears from the outside. As if the vehicle itself is holding its breath while it takes its three-point turn.

It's nice to know you're doing something other than living the way you are expected to. It feels nice to be contributing to the construction of a bigger picture by dismantling the one which is disproportionate. But to get to the point where the bigger picture is visible, and real, and important—you have to get through the early and unpredictable versions of it. Before everybody feels like they're supposed to be doing it, the pioneers have to feel like they're *not* supposed to be doing it.

To interrupt the violence of routine, I guess.

I've never lived in a farmhouse, I realize.

Endless apartments, our suburban condo. All of a sudden I feel like I'm missing out.

I think about if you lived in a farmhouse during an A-bomb. Beam of cancer scintillating across broken crops. If the plants are visibly dying, why doesn't your skin show a visible reaction, still the baby in your womb is affected?

There is a glumness to the street I'm driving on. A man in an all-gray tracksuit is walking his two pit bulls, talking on the phone. He darts his eyes at me but doesn't turn his head as I drive past. I realize how slowly I'm driving. He starts to yell after my car as I speed up. Though he is on foot, and seemingly harmless, I suppose I better stop. He speed-walks over to my 900, dragging his pit bulls behind. They begin to bark.

"Excuse me, excuse me," he says. *"Did you want something?"*

"You're the one yelling, I stopped to see what you want."

"I'm neighborhood watch." He grabs a little badge out of his pocket to show me, sticks it through my window. "I keep an eye on suspicious vehicles in my zone. You were lingering. What's that all about?"

"You can't just self-assign the authority to ask such personal questions," I say.

"Look. You just politely tell me what your business is, and I'll let you go."

I find myself panicking. "I dropped some friends off who are picking something up."

"*That's all you needed to say.*" He pulses his head from side to side, his teeth spreading and mustache lifting from his lip.

As he walks away from the car, I feel like slamming the horn to frighten him but I consider the dogs.

He continues walking his pit bulls. I see him start to move his mouth again. I wonder if he had ever been on the phone at all.

I'm parked down the street just scrolling through the forum, only for a few minutes before Jean Paul gives me the go with a quick-ring-and-hang-up. I pull up again in the same spot across the driveway. They're half jogging towards me.

I say, "I hope no one was killed."

Jean Paul straps his seatbelt in.

"Rebels," Huy says. "That was exhilarating."

Jean Paul doesn't respond to this.

They don't acknowledge me and I drive off, looking in the rearview at Huy, who is panting with a smile on his face, and Jean Paul, who is lighting a cigarette. "You guys did it?"

"Yeah," says Jean Paul. A pleased smile forms on his face and he turns around to Huy and offers him a high-five against his flat palm.

"That was kinda badass," says Huy under his breath.

I decide not to ask for specifics anyway. Perhaps the point is to see how this action will ring out and surface between work hours, when everything is ordinary and everything seems expected again. To see how Berta's mannerisms have changed, to feel the environment shift. This is the point, Jean Paul always indicates in his forum posts, in his long spiels.

We drive down the highway. I wind my window down, my short hair bristling in the whisk of simulated wind created by the calm air and the speed of this car on the highway. With every kilometer we travel, there is a renourished fluency of breath. A bit like how a high feels. Passing the petrol mirage, I think I see scorching, and I sort of smile.

17

A GROUP OF KIDS, STILL in their uniforms, have come to try the ear cleaning. They're filming it. I put on a surgeon's mask from the pharmacy. I feel decrepit. Farah wisely asked them to pay before entering. Farah is spontaneous and so full of initiative.

The first kid is seated on the bed. I turn the headlamp on. "Don't look directly in the light," I advise.

The rest are chuckling on the chairs in the corner. I hear one of them making a comment about the diffuser. "I heard it's supposed to get you a bit high." The other one says, "That's cool, sometimes I don't always feel like *actually* smoking, you know? I should ask Jodie to buy me one of them for Christmas."

They're filming as I go in with the wire. This ear is small and bunched up. I put the wire down. My hand is shaking, I don't know why. There's a bandage still wrapped around my paper cut.

The other two start giggling. "What does it feel like?"

"I don't know." All of them laugh and the kid moves his head suddenly.

I'm infuriated. "Don't move," I instruct. "It's dangerous."

He sucks his mouth down to his chin.

"Ooh," say the others.

"It feels tingly," the kid says, when I go back in with the wire, and then with the feather. "Like you're, you know, letting out piss."

The other two burst out laughing.

I wash my hands and they swap. Eventually the laughter subsides, and the two who aren't getting the ear clean are on their phones, silent.

As they leave and say, "Yeah, thank you."

"Come again," Farah says, and they all give each other a look.

Farah grabs her lunch box and asks if I want to go down to the staff room for our lunch break.

"Is Doms in today?" I ask, massaging the side of my neck.

She purses her lips and shakes her head. "Nup."

I consider this. I hang up the BE BACK SOON sign. "You know they should get a table tennis table down there."

Farah says that she's quite bad at table tennis. She plays a version where you have to keep it off the table instead of on. Bounce it off objects around the room and run around to keep it in the air.

I lock the door and shove the keys in my white coat pocket. Across the floor from us is a B-grade card store that has relocated here after they were finally extracted from the Galleria. The Galleria is rumored to have over fifty commercial businesses on their waiting list and paper cards are becoming out of fashion. The owner of the card store is here every day, standing out the front, fraternizing with the shoppers walking by.

On the escalator, I yawn and ask Farah, "Why futsal, of all sports?"

She says she likes team sports. She isn't trying to get fit or anything; she just likes the team environment. It's where she thrives. She tells me the first sport she ever did was synchronized swimming.

I try to imagine her doing this and can't. I imagine it'd be like ballet but in water. The banner hanging under the skylight near the food court is an ad for lingerie.

"For it to work, you had to look the same as everybody else. I didn't get it." Farah smirks, her hands referencing her body.

"How old were you?"

"About twelve. I stopped a year later. There were less brown kids in my area back then. All the kids I went to school with had a different bone structure to me, our bodies just looked different. So it started to make me feel . . . I don't know."

I elbow open the double fire doors and we walk down the dimly lit white hallway. The funny thing about this hallway is how it's shaped so that when you hear an echo, you can't tell if the person is behind you, in front, down the left-hand side, or down the right-hand side where the staff room is. The bulletin board hanging on the cement wall right before the staff room usually has newsletters, business cards, and motivational or work-safety posters.

Today, pinned in front of them all is a poster of a bloody face. Underneath it says: *Don't pretend you don't feel like this.*

I point it out to Farah and she rolls her eyes, her voice monotone. "God, people do whatever they can to stop you in your tracks. It's all shock factor."

She continues, "You lose a lot of oxygen when you do it. I started to pass out because my brain was thinking too quickly, all the inversions underwater. And the makeup mixing with chlorine ruined my skin for my teenage years."

I look at her skin, some bumps but not too many, slight inflammation, the little dints gathering on the edges of her cheeks.

"You have to smile and keep your mouth open," she says, sticking her container into the microwave.

"It was strange"—she presses in three minutes—"our coach made us watch our videos back and imitate each other's movements and facial expressions. The more I watched them and obsessed over them, the more I found myself taking on my other teammates' expressions and mannerisms even when we weren't swimming. We had to all look the same. Except I was the only brown girl and there was one other mixed Japanese girl. I was a little chubbier and she was a little shorter, so I felt like we were always trying harder. But, man, if you saw it, watched it back, it's so terrifying the way our eyes were when we came up out of the water."

I watch the container spinning. I imagine Farah's eyes open all the way. They're now hooded with a coolness, as if they've grown tired of being stretched.

I ask if her teammates were nice or if everyone sort of hated each other. I take three milk biscuits from the jar and eat them each in two bites.

"They were all a little older than me, so none of them bullied me or disliked me. It was something unspoken, you know?" Licking across her top row of teeth, she says, "We all had hollow eyes."

I ask if it was at all competitive between them, or if they were just separate vessels carrying the routines and muscle.

She thinks for a moment. "We were way too young to think about it like that. And the coach was . . . very team-oriented." She scratches her fork against the plastic countertop. "A girl did die, I remember. I forget her name. She was on the team for a month and then she died after that."

Behind us the door slams.

Big Red Boss is standing there, looking down at something on her phone before continuing toward the row of lockers.

"Hi, ladies," she says, still without direct eye contact.

I swallow another milk biscuit, trying not to watch her. I tell myself I don't know what happened to her last night.

"Hi, Berta," says Farah, completely calm.

Farah continues, "A few days before it, she was alive and fine and she swam with us. Only thing I noticed was that she had her period as soon as we came out of the water. There was blood down her leg which her friend noticed. Then she ran to the change rooms and the blood was dripping behind her. In the change rooms, I overheard her telling one of the others that she wouldn't have come today if she'd known. Then our coach took her outside and said that it's never regular at our age, and . . . and don't worry. She seemed fine. Then, that Thursday, the coach was late and when she did arrive, we were all in the water and she stood in front of us and told us that the girl had died overnight in the hospital. None of us ever found out how." Farah swallows. "Or, hmm, maybe it was that no one ever wanted to tell anyone else. Or me, the youngest." She takes her food from the microwave before it dings, to do something with her hands, I suppose. I take two more milk biscuits and put one in my coat pocket, begin to eat the other.

Berta is becoming visibly upset at her locker, hyperventilating to herself.

Farah looks at me with wide eyes.

She mouths, *Let's go back up*. Farah carries her container using the sleeves of her cardigan. We shuffle out the staff room door.

Look at the poster of the bloody face again. The eyes popping out.

"*Nice*," says Farah. "Hey, did you hear the weed going around at Peggy's was laced?"

18 I KNEW SOMEBODY WITH ANOPHTHALMIA when I was small— where the baby is born with one eye. A person I attended school with. They wore an eye patch every day and peeled it off behind the school gymnasium for me to see.

My mother, when I told her about this, said that Auntie was born with a missing limb, without an arm. They attached one, she told me. *What you can't see is the underdeveloped heart she still has*. When I asked her what had caused it, she said it might have been a drug their mother had taken to induce pregnancy. However, nobody had really known, and it had not occurred to anyone to ever ask or wonder. It was just the case of the matter. But the more my mother mingled with other cultures, receiving a scholarship to an international Canadian school, the more she began to question. Eventually she finished with a degree in medicine. She was passionate about it and became a GP at the same age she was permitted to gamble in Macau. As her practice grew into her personality, she scolded her mother and sister for their ways of life, which were incompatible with the Western version of medicine she had spent many years studying. But over time, she began to unravel from it herself, finding spaces in her own arguments, which had become mere reflex, an imitation of textbooks. Secretly, she was becoming anxious toward the scientific, toward anything that was designed to give an immediate sense of relief.

She stopped her practice when I was around eight, when my father started traveling for work more often, and in a year's time we were jumping between continents as a family unit. *There were many reasons to stop practicing*, she told me. It was not just that I was born or for my father's work. She said she could not ignore the intense, almost voyeuristic curiosity she had developed for the ways the body worked with qi. She had always assumed Popo was speaking in riddles when she described the way we ate, the way we flared up with redness, the way our feet would become cold. Pressure points, her practice of movements seemingly performed to "relocate energy." She says now that it had not been a riddle; it was an intuition, a closeness to her personal anatomy that she had conditioned herself in, even if it may have been placebo. To live until the age at which Popo passed away, but happy to, and at peace with it; thankful for your body rather than resenting it.

My mother did not give Tylenol. Avoided medicated creams. The remedy was to be ingrained, instinctive. We took ginseng or ginger if we had anything mild, to enrich the fire in us. Abalone for the lungs, shiitake to dissolve mucus. No cold foods or drinks during the menstrual cycle; irregular cycles were due to dampness. When I asked for chewing gum, I was given the ends of dried sea animal to chew. Dried fish maw or fish bladder for hair, skin, and nails. Pei Pa Koa to soothe something in the throat, a change of diet to dissolve the symptoms.

As a result, I am usually conscious of what I take.

I'm unsure then, of the drug that Jean Paul is offering. We're sitting in the pharmacy. It's a Sunday and the studio is closed. I'm preoccupied. I can count all the clients I've had on my fingers, for fuck's sake.

"It's just a diet pill," says Jean Paul, sighing. I put it in my hand.

"This has just got bitter orange in it, a little bit. Which is synephrine, supposed to give you a buzz. Fix that fatigue and appetite of yours. *C'mon, seriously, you people.* Rather complain than accept the solution!"

Vic catches my eye across the room. He calls over in a flat, general tone, "Don't take anything you don't want to take, Leen." He buttons his white coat and comes out from behind the counter.

"What's wrong?"

I tell him I keep eating when no one comes into the studio. "Poor friend," says Jean Paul.

All day long I eat the Crown Choco Heim wafers from the Asian grocers. The milk biscuits have been getting boring and the Crown Choco Heim wafers keep being on sale and people keep not coming into the studio for the appointments they've booked—so there's time and there's food. Doms hasn't been in the studio for the past couple of days. Farah is at the front typing away on the computer, holding up the dignity of the place to the public eye.

"And the people that've booked just *forget*," I say. "People just forget about the time I've reserved for them."

Jean Paul is going through the pill bottles in the bottom cabinet. Reading them softly to himself.

The lights in here are making my eyes want to close. I can never be in here too long.

Vic sighs. "Have you tried drinking tea instead of eating? We have peppermint at the house. I bought it last week. Just take some of the teabags to work."

"I'll bring some tomorrow," I tell him.

The lights are dim, almost quivering.

. . .

I am moving, relocating pity. All Sunday I'm moving between the people I know and complaining about my fatigue and addiction to food. An oppressive headache stuck between my temples has been circling in and out all weekend and the only time I don't feel it is when I drive. And when I sit in my car reading through the amusing posts on Jean Paul's forum thread, watching linked videos of different pranks happening around the world, to different managers.

My 900 is parked a few houses down from Farah's. She lives in one of the young-family estates. Not Beverley or the Sunshine Estate, or Glenvale, the one closest to us, but one of the older ones. One that has become less associated with its marketing package and is slowly becoming just another faction of Par Mars, a smaller suburb with less police presence, more affordable in price for anyone with a family who isn't imploding with money. She warns me on the phone that her parents may seem hostile because they're often busy at work and don't get much sleep.

The sound of violin practice can be heard from outside the front gate. I open it after waiting a moment. The wooden door is casually open when I get there, but there's a screen door, which I hesitantly try to push open. I decide to shut it again softly. I ring the doorbell. Inside the house, I can hear one of Farah's siblings singing along to a TV show tune.

I notice this time that the walls are beige and gray.

Farah is walking towards the door. She says hi before opening the screen door.

She's wearing school socks. Not the same school I had gone to, but I recognize the logo and color combination.

She lets me in. The floorboards are slick.

The corridor that opens to a big kitchen and dining area has plastic toys everywhere. It feels like a display home but with little drawings scribbled on some of the walls and with too many mismatches in color throughout the furniture.

Farah gets me a glass of water and a snack from the fridge.

I tell her, regarding the snack: "No thanks. Not today." And take the glass of water, scull half of it immediately.

She gets herself a bar of some sort. It's a protein bar with rich sources of aminos and calcium in it.

"Good for energy."

"I have enough today."

"Doesn't look it."

Upstairs in her bedroom, this time I notice she has a *Pink Floyd— The Wall* poster up and a bookshelf with some old Shel Silverstein and various versions of Sims disc cases on it. There are posters, too, of films I am not aware of.

Farah wants to go back and study film but can't afford it right now. She graduated from her undergrad program in politics a year ago and says it's harder to go back. She had been unsure of what it meant to study politics, but it interested her. She says mostly everything interests her if she gives it a second.

We're seated on her bedroom floor, propped up against her bed.

"So with the business, we have to look at the bigger picture," I tell her. "Right now, it's not just about me. It's about why people aren't convinced they want to heal."

"Maybe we need to think about ways to advertise it better," says Farah.

We sit in silence.

It's started to rain outside. Droplets hitting the windows sideways. I notice the dreamcatcher Farah has hanging over her window.

Her laundry basket has a bottle of wine in it underneath all the clothes.

Farah laughs. "You're looking at everything."

What's uncomfortable about it is that she seems to be very insecure about living at her parents' house. She's twenty-two and most of her friends have moved into apartments farther into the city, or gone overseas to study or work.

I tell her, "I understand. If my parents lived in the same country as me, I'd be living with them too."

"It's more about not having enough space to do your own thing. I can't lie down on the couch without my parents being like, *Are you sick?*" she says.

Curiously, I feel the same way about living at Doms's. I find I sometimes crave to be inconsequential physically, but simultaneously appreciated in energy. It is the Buddhist belief, anatman, or anattā, which speaks about the "non-self." It suggests that the more the perception of self is rooted in the material, "solid" objects—the name, the body, the interaction, the memory—the more we are entrapped in the relaying of impermanence. The more we become no-thing, the more we are able to experience life firsthand, unbiasedly. We stop relying on our exteriors to divulge to us, how we should treat ourselves.

I think about the moment Doms started to introduce herself as Doms rather than her full given name, or the moment her chin started to look different from the chin I had known when I had first met her, when the twenty pounds she'd gained began to manifest on her exterior. When had these physical things changed, and why hadn't I noticed the physical transition, only the energetic one?

I wonder when Doms's warm smile and the *Of course you can stay here, as long as you want ... it'll be fun* shifted into the boredom and dissatisfaction of our current state. I get paranoid that Doms and Vic remember these moments differently.

"Does it concern you," I say to Farah, "that the studio is being viewed differently by those who've never been inside compared with people who *have*? It's frustrating to think about how we can translate the experience."

"Well, of course," says Farah, chewing the bar on one side of her mouth. "It's decorated nice but people are unsure when it's ... well, they have to offer *themselves* rather than be offered something, right?" After a pause, she says, "I know someone who went to get their hair washed every day by someone else for months just because they were so lonely."

"So I guess these kinds of services have to be found by the customers, not just passed to them. It's the finding that makes it seem special and a novelty."

Farah's father appears at her bedroom door.

"Pa," she says.

Her father looks indifferent about my being here.

"The laundry," says her father. He's about to leave the house.

"Ya, yeah," Farah says.

I say hi.

Her father looks at me and smiles. "Hello, I'm Farah's dad. It's lovely to meet you."

He looks at Farah. "*Before you go out with your friends tonight.*" He leaves and pulls the door halfway shut.

She tells me he's got his rounds. Farah huffs with her legs up on the wall. "*I'm an adult child.*"

Lying on her back, she turns her head to me. "By the way, do you have the payment for last month yet? I think it's a bit late."

For the last hour and a half I'm at Farah's, I write a buyer persona profile. This is a marketing term I learned about on the internet. As the image of the buyer forms in my head, the sight of Mary at Peggy's the other night materializes.

I say to Farah, "I have this friend, and we're always talking about managerial staff and franchises. How there's so much frustration, boredom. After working so hard to achieve a respectable role, they're still in the same cycle they were in before, only they've worked harder to get a different badge. It's as if they've hit some sort of ceiling in the middle of a prism of power."

"Sounds like Big Red Boss," sneers Farah.

"Yes," I say. "We need to target our services to people like Berta. Remember Berta crying in her locker the other day?"

"That was a tragedy."

"We need to target those, those who need to catch up to their bodies."

I'm driving Huy and Jean Paul to Berta's again. This time I ask them what the prank will be.

They correct me: "It's called a Resisting Act."

They tell me they've been leaving rocks in a compartment of her backpack which they made by slitting a bit of the inside cloth, creating enough space for two stones to fit through, sewing it up again each time. They do this at her locker in the staffroom, then they take one out again at her home. Over time, it's assumed that she'll continue to gaslight herself. Every time she goes to the complex and every time she leaves. Eventually her brain will become so hardwired to this pattern that she will begin to distrust herself. This imagination will manifest into a mindfulness, urging her to consider herself merely human, to consider the fragility of others' humanness. Or it will slowly humiliate her, making her less inclined to any aggression or antagonism.

I only ask this time because I feel slightly bad for Berta today; I am sort of starting to empathize with her. "I hope it's not too physical, or heavy or anything. She has a thing with her leg."

Both of them look confused, even at the slight suggestion that they would put her through any serious physical trauma.

"We'd feel a lot more *remorseful*," Huy says at a random moment.

Jean Paul picks his teeth carefully, holding one hand up to cover himself, as if to be polite. Huy takes out two stones from his backpack and slips them in his pocket as I pull up across the driveway.

Jean Paul puts his toothpick in the side compartment. "Now, go on, *git*."

I drive around the blocks in a figure eight. I turn up the radio, two men speaking. Sound of saliva smacking, so close to the microphone, so close to me. *They call "going green" a collective priority but I bet if we did a vote right now, a, um . . . what is it, a census . . . 80 percent of us are just trying to get by . . . Why change the rules now, all of a sudden? . . . Fifty-year farm bill—that's a load of rubbish . . . People are going to lose their jobs . . . Mmm, mmm, yes . . . that's correct.*

Drive the corner and see the same gray-tracksuit man walking one of the pit bulls. I speed up and try to avoid him seeing, but it seems he has made himself available to *see everything* and he's already pulled his phone out, filming as I drive off into a semiblackness. The sky is the blue in between night and day. I turn the headlights off.

It gets dark in these streets quicker. The streetlights more dim.

I park a few houses down from Berta's. There are two kids still playing in the sprinklers outside their house. They haven't noticed my car yet. It makes me, for a moment, feel queasy.

Jean Paul rings, then hangs up, and I quickly drive up to the front of the house.

"Absolutely seamless," says Huy, panting, bouncing in the back seat.

Jean Paul retrieves his toothpick from the compartment and begins picking, covering his mouth with his hand again. "Thanks, Leen."

We pass the same mega gas station and I realize now it must be designed for trucks and large transporters. I think I see a tractor parked at one of the dispensers. The light from it becomes unbearable to look at. My fatigue drags my eyes down so that more light hits the red gummy bit under the eyeball, stinging and straining outwards, feeling like it's pulling the balls from the sockets.

Jean Paul asks, "Leen, are you okay?"

19 JEAN PAUL IS TREATING MY faintness with pills. Doms and Vic are sitting at the table looking at me.

"You completely passed out," Jean Paul says. "I had to do the hazard lights and pull the hand brake. I've never seen anything like it, but no one stopped to question it or anything." Jean Paul gives a warm, charismatic laugh.

Doms comes over and feels my head with her lips. "Leen, you need to take more vitamin C."

I swallow whatever Jean Paul is giving me.

"That's not vitamin C," Doms says in a shrill voice.

"Fludrocortisone acetate," Vic's voice.

"Where's my car? Is it okay?"

"It's fine. Huy drove it cause I couldn't figure it out. Fuck that."

I'm falling asleep.

"Where's Huy, then?" I ask.

"He's in the bathroom. Taking a shit."

Doms' soaps are boiling. The familiar smell of it. She disappears into the kitchen.

Vic comes over, looking concerned. "Leen," he sighs.

It feels nice to be touched on the head. I think about the feeling of a lover touching me around my ears and through my hair and how it becomes a language you don't remember learning. I think about Luis and as each of them take turns touching my forehead to check for fever, patting me on my shoulder or knee, I feel almost a sadness.

Doms comes out with a bowl of what looks like mashed potatoes. This is what her soaps look like pre-mold. Strange what the mind does to readapt an idea to a shape, same with the hands.

I look at my hands.

Huy appears at the archway then fits himself at the farthest possible corner of the dining table. He casually pulls his legs up and crosses them, checking through his phone.

In the morning I'm feeling better and there is nice sun coming through the window, warming where I am on the couch. Doms has left a mug steaming beside me on the coffee table. I notice I have a blocked nose as I sit up. There is the noise of Doms or Vic in the bathroom, getting ready, the sound of the tap running. I'm comforted by it in a way. I pull on my professional clothes.

I check my work email. Dating, Viagra, and catalogs.

At least without any traction, without customers, I am not concerned about losing them. Who said deprivation makes the mind grow stronger and the spirit hold longer?

I take the mug, sit it in the cup holder in my 900. Before starting the car, I take one of the diet pills Jean Paul introduced. Eating less is eating more.

When I get to the complex, I throw up bile. I'm feeling good, and I don't feel like eating, but maybe drinking a juice that's green.

Farah looks at me strangely when I walk in and the door chimes. "Are you tired or something?"

"No," I reply.

"Good news," says Farah. "One client already booked today."

"Who?"

"He says he's been having trouble feeling that his body is connected and absorbing what people are saying around him."

"Any injuries or preexisting health problems?"

"Not that he mentioned."

"Okay, what time?"

"Midday." Farah lets out a squeal and raises two thumbs up. I rub my eye in.

I sit in the main studio waiting for midday.

At one point, the chimes ring and I hear Doms's sneakers treading slowly. She says hello to Farah. I think about her room, probably just full of soap.

I open the door out into the hallway. "Hey, thanks for the coffee."

She's standing at the doorway of her studio with an empty box in her hands.

"No worries." An overly kind smile is resting on Doms's face.

I nod my head and smile too.

"Hey, look," I hear as I turn to go back into the studio. "Leen, look, to be honest, I *just* don't think this studio is serving my soap and candle business." She twiddles her thumbs against her stomach. "I actually think the best way to do this is to split ways early."

I'm silent, blinking at her, seeing if she'll say something next. She puts the box down and says, "I think I'm just gonna go back to farmers markets and craft sales."

The hurt in her eyes makes the whole thing worse. We're at a standstill with this conversation. We don't know what to do with our hands. I itch my arm through my white coat.

"That's fine," I say, almost attempting to shrug.

Doms nods and looks half-heartedly pitiful, the way her eyebrows are arched.

She doesn't think this is enough and continues, "I just *feel* like I can focus more when I'm at home."

We're at another standstill. I urge, "It's fine, it's fine."

Doms hugs me, which feels inane, almost belittling, all of which I know it shouldn't feel. "Well," says Doms. "I'll see you at home."

I half smile. "Okay, see you."

She kneels and begins to put some candles and soaps in the box, then says, "Plus, Leen, I'm saying this as a friend, okay. You might want to consider changing the name. Maybe Lotus Fusion Studio doesn't say *enough* about the services, you know?"

It's been about two months since opening the studio, and after one or two more, my father will stop helping with the rent and the business will inevitably close.

I wash my face in the public restroom, WhatsApp my father about my concern, and wait for his reply, checking the time difference between us.

I look in the mirror. Acne is flaring on my jawline again, my hormones showing.

A woman emerges from a toilet stall. "You know, they're really not that bad."

"Thanks," I say.

She nods politely, smiling. "They're not, okay? No one can even notice them."

A moment of silence. She runs the water into the basin.

"I run a healing studio," I say, before we lose momentum.

Two squirts of soap, two spritzes of tap water. She has her lips pursed. "Oh, *okay*." She is checking under her eye for residue. "Good to know."

"Here," I say under my breath. Take a flyer from the pocket of my white coat.

"Pardon?"

"A pamphlet for the studio. I'm located on level one above the ... you know where the K.A.G. store is?"

"Oh, *okay*." She is scratching black kohl eyeliner into the corners of her eyes and on the waterline.

"You know, the stuff used for eyeliner is absorbed into your system and stored as toxins."

She looks at me, blinks all of a sudden. "Ah, is that so?"

"Yes, I learned that because of my acne. See all this acne, it's made up of toxins. This pus is all toxins from my cosmetics."

I tell her I got into this industry because I wanted to know about the release of toxins, the cleansing of the body, how cleaning even your strangest parts makes a difference to your everyday performance.

I look at her in the mirror.Without sounding too panicked, I say that I would like to begin a holistic journey with her. Perhaps we can start exploring her capacity for healing this afternoon.

She has a frown on her face, her lips now twisted into a big knot. My next step is to talk about the tension she seems to hold in her face and suggest to her: *Let's release that.*

Before I do, she scratches her temple and says, "Yeah. All right. You know what, let's give it a go." She goes back to the mirror. "Maybe after I finish the groceries?"

"Of course, come in and we can see if we've got a spot."

She smiles, though her lips are somehow still knotted, and she nods.

When I hear the door chime half an hour later, I have the water boiled and I'm stirring ginseng tea in a white ceramic mug.

The diffuser is on, puffing cold lavender.

Laraaji is playing "I Am Sky."

It's eleven. The next client will be coming in an hour so I decide to hurry things up. I emerge from the studio and tell Farah that perhaps this lady would like to sign the registration form after the session.

Farah nods. "Good idea."

I bring her in. She still has a knotted lip, though her groceries are done. I find out her name is Kerry.

I decide against telling her that she has a tense face and instead ask her to sit on the massage table. She puts her grocery bags on the chairs by the door. Then we talk about her health history. She says she's never broken a bone or had any issues with health and that she visits the doctor's annually and every time it seems she is perfectly fine.

I ask if she's ever dieted before.

"That's *definitely* something I do," she replies.

I pass her the ceramic cup. "Ginseng," I say. "I made it for you but don't feel like you have to drink it. It can be a bit unbearable." She takes the cup and smells it, makes a face.

"Yeah, all right. Thank you."

"Now tell me, what are your major concerns then . . . for your body?"

She tells me that no matter how much she exercises, she always has this bit just above her hips, what they call love handles. She tells me she takes diet pills.

I smile understandingly.

"I work at a *bank* three days a week. My mother takes care of my kid on those days, picks him up from school and everything. Same day I go to a gym. I don't really know how I got to this point alive, honestly. I live in a *beautiful* home. I try to do Pilates." She taps her acrylic fingernails against the padding, her eyebrows raised naturally. There is something beautiful about that. "I don't know what else to say." She scrunches her nose like a pixie and touches her finger against her eye as if she's got a tear there. It seems like allergies.

"No. That's perfect," I say.

"Did I say too much?"

"Everything sounded lovely. Pilates is good for relaxation."

There's a silence. Unprofessionalism. Silence can only be unprofessionalism or extreme professionalism. It cannot be anywhere in the middle.

I try to let it pass as extreme professionalism.

"I think you would really benefit from a traditional ear clean."

I figure placing *traditional* in front of anything will provide a portion of the money's worth.

She says, "Sure."

"We do it for the clarity of the mind, cleanliness to receive. And it's great for relaxation."

When I begin, I look down the dark hole. Begin to let the rod find the shape of the canal.

She shivers and begins to shake her head.

"Don't!" I say. "Don't move."

"Shit . . . oops."

After the rest of the ear clean, which she managed to endure without giggling or physically reacting again, I decide that she needs an upper-body massage for stimulation.

She goes to lie on her bare stomach. I ask her to unclip her bra.

She tells me she has hacky-sack breasts.

I say, "It's okay. Mine are shaped like noses."

I see her trying to imagine it. I turn to the table and fidget with the diffuser.

"I wish I were more comfortable doing things like this. It's so *relaxing*." She is uncomfortable with the silence. "Here we go," she grunts.

I turn and she is nestling herself back against the toweled table.

She says, "I need a new bra. You know, buying yourself something when yours isn't broken is something to be proud of in this day and age."

It is a type of knowing-what-you're-doing.

"That's true. Only we're kind of made to think that if we can't afford it, we are out of control and that's where the problem is," I say.

"Those people should just find a job," says Kerry.

We're standing at the door of my studio.

"Well, that was good," says Kerry. "Very soothing, just what I needed. What a great morning it's been." She lets out a polite laugh.

It's 11:58 and there's no middle-aged man in the reception area.

I catch my breath.

I nod. "Yeah, thank you."

She stops at the door, turning back to the two of us. "How often do you recommend I come?"

I look at Kerry. There's something in her eyes that wasn't there before. She looks modest, though her voice still staccatos in a way where it seems she is constantly presuming.

"I'm reading a good energy from you," I say. "So maybe come back in a week."

She nods. "Alright, okay."

Waiting for the man.

I stand at the corner, where the corridor to the studios begins. Farah is reading a website. She's humming to the music she's got playing in the reception.

"Do we need to paint the place?" I say.

Farah turns her head to me. Pursing her lips. "No, I like the off-yellow."

"Hmm."

"It's a vibe."

"Mmm."

Farah sighs. She tells me she's reading about essential oils used in Ancient Egypt. "They were the first to invent perfume."

I come to her shoulder and start to read. I feel like holding a cigarette. It would look fitting. I'm tapping my foot. Every middle-aged man is walking past without considering.

Animal fats and pastes used to extract the essence of jasmine. It began with wanting to search for immortality and the act of preservation of corpses. Beauty regime of the dead.

Farah reads aloud: "This furniture displayed the pharaoh's wife wrapping his body using lotus oil . . . the endocrine system, pineal gland, thyroid, thymus, spleen, testes . . . testes and ovaries . . . and pit . . . pituitary gland. The energies center here."

A man comes in. The chimes screech. Farah darts her eyes up.

"Sorry, give me a moment," says Farah. "I'm just logging some details in about another client."

Across the desk the man looks very understanding and has his hands folded in front of him.

I look at the man. "Hello," I say softly.

When I get back to the condo, I wash my face and notice that my skin has gone a bumpy texture. Textured texture. I ignore it. Doms is preparing dal in the kitchen. I open a pack of Crown Choco Heim wafers at the dining table. Vic is on the couch on his phone. We haven't spoken the way we used to for a long time. It feels like something I need right now.

I have often complained about men, men in cars, men on the footpath, men at the complex, and Doms would often chime in about experiences of her own, and though she would, it never felt like she could entirely relate. The sort of belittling was slightly different between us, neither more nor less but it felt like my experience was always somewhere between Doms's and Vic's. I watch Vic, who seems bored, heavily exhaling on the couch and rubbing his eye in.

This is how it went:

When I turned from the bench he was naked and standing up with one foot behind the other. He started to move toward me. I let out a short, high-pitched gasp.

He stopped. "You want me on the mattress then, presumably?"

"It's a massage table."

There had been a question about this in the short course I did a year ago. *What if somebody presents themselves to you fully nude without being asked?* The teacher said: *Remain professional and ask them* politely *to drape themselves.*

I tried to pass him a sheet. But he didn't take it, just smiled, his breath under his pressed lips. His body lurched, tilting a bit forward. A foully carnal exhale coming through his nostrils. You can see on the face.

"Take," I'd said. Basic English, no emotive words.

He performed a sort of sneer and went over to the massage table, leaned up against it. He looked down. His body looked like a pouch compared to it.

"You *take*," he said, this time using a slight accent. He had a ten-dollar bill scrunched between his fists. "You *take*."

I went over to my diffuser, the farthest possible corner of the room. The cold air felt delicate on the back of my hand. I pretended to play with some papers, which were just receipts and invoices for the furniture and rent.

He sat on the massage table. "What did I pay for?"

He said it again louder, could have been a yell, "What did I pay for?"

. . .

Half-mast, the flag outside the community library.

I wonder why without thinking too much and go inside the library, needing to be anywhere but at home where Vic and Doms are keeping conversation between themselves on the couch. I go to a trolley and open up a random novel. The book is described as being a romantic escapade between a London man and woman. I go to the section about architecture, just something I'm vaguely interested in.

20

APPARENTLY THERE HAD BEEN A raid at the community pottery center. A gang of middle-aged flight-jacket skinheads had barged in on a Pottery of the World class, a specialized class which happens every Monday evening around five.

They entered the premises from different points of the school. One came in through the window, another through the door, another through the back way, where the kiln's located.

The witness is filmed in front of the pottery school, suggesting the perpetrators had expected the participants of the class to be ethnic, non-white, but found only three of them were.

The authorities declared it may have been a racial incident only after they found two of these three had been beaten, and the third severely burnt all over the arms and chest. The photo shows one of the victims, a blurred-out red mushy face. But others had received a beating too and the final pronouncement was that it was not racially targeted: *An act of random, unprecedented violence.*

The pictures of the gang make them look like a punk band. Black jeans and khaki or navy jackets, pink skin, combat boots. The newsreader comments that it appears to be a uniform; the other notes that it is *actually* a clothing brand which has over the years become very popular among these "types" of gangs.

Vic murmurs softly, musing to himself, "Combat boots."

IMAGINE YOU ARE FINISHING IN the storeroom. You exit into the customer area of the K.A.G. store. The other day, you overheard the seventeen-year-old call you *Big Red Boss* during a conversation they were having by the children's wear. You walk all the way around the children's wear now to avoid the stress. Something your psychiatrist told you to do when you were trying the whole *therapy thing* in your thirties. You paid too much. Anything costs too much. Everything is absolutely inaccessible these days.

You've been attending a chiropractor for almost a year now at odd intervals, but frequently these last few weeks. Yes, your back has been quite sore when you wake up. Should this be happening? Is it common to be uncomfortable while you sleep? God knows, you've felt it longer than your children have been alive. Maybe you never sleep the same after pregnancy. You have plans to see a specialist about it soon, and you're taking magnesium and melatonin; sometimes a good Restoril doesn't hurt. The waitlist for an appointment is three months and there is no rebate on it.

The dim downlights flicker on and off.

There is the quiet boy Antonio—or was it Luis, folding up the collection of fleece jumpers, keeping to himself as usual. He says, "Bye, Berta!" You flash him a smile, wondering if he calls you that awful name. Neither of you acknowledge the lights. That is all for today, no time to sort it out. You're already out of breath. You're leaving half an hour early and you'd like to enjoy it. Besides, it must be the complex's problem. Topic Heights has been the same since you were in your twenties. Antonio (or Luis) is already back to work, so particular about how each piece is folded.

You make your way down the emptying hallway of the complex, looking up at the banisters above you. There is a kid waving at you. You huff and feel a frown forming on your face, ignore them.

It's your left leg that hurts.

Kids taunt you. You hated them growing up. They bully recklessly. They don't like your Roman nose.

You look straight ahead. *Don't give in to anyone*, your mother used to say.

She needs magazines and the people at the old folks home won't buy them for her. Magazines. You need to get them before leaving the complex today.

Push the fire doors open. These corridors make you sick. You've been throwing up every night this week, but you're not pregnant. You haven't been eating well. But you haven't eaten well for eight years since the kids were old enough to pull themselves things from the cupboards. You won't skip work because it'll look bad. Besides, you always feel slightly better in the morning.

Down the hall, someone is standing against the cement wall. You only half recognize them. A dark-skinned Chinese girl, short hair, wearing what could be a nail technician's uniform, or she could be the janitor. Had you gone to her nail salon? A dentist? You had met briefly at Peggy's, perhaps? You threw up a couple of times that night and passed out, it was so hot. You ate something bad. Perhaps it was the cannabis, you hadn't done that in a while. Not since the kids could detect the smell. The mixing of alcohol never did you well.

You catch yourself watching the girl. Your children tell you all the time not to stereotype or pigeonhole people. *You always assume! You're so rude!* They are only seventeen and fifteen. Your children never had bullying problems at school; in fact, both are very popular boys.

You try to see if the Japanese girl's nails are painted.

She looks at you in the eye and then immediately tries not to look at you. You notice this sort of behavior; there are odd moments like this all the time. You shake your head, nearly out of breath as your anxiety influxes again. She has a pair of keys in her hand and is fiddling with the silver ring. You spend too long looking and worry she might think you're being rude. You say, "Afternoon!" in a short, panting tone. Sometimes you don't think you'll ever understand people. Or how they see you. How you see yourself.

You scan open the staff-room door. You realize, as the door shuts behind you, that it's completely dark in here. Then you reach for the light switch. Are there automatic lights now? You wave your hands around, which feels silly in the dark. "Hello," you say. "Turn back on." You laugh but are a bit annoyed. You find the light switch, sensing somebody there. The lights blink stickily and then all of them turn on, though still dim.

Why were the lights off!

All of the things you notice when one of your senses is taken away.

There is a man standing at the fire escape door about to open it. He looks at you.

"Why were the lights off?" you say.

"I'm . . . I'm unsure." He is opening the latch of the emergency door.

It is your responsibility to ask for answers, Berta. Nobody will ever give them to you and everything always falls onto you. Why must everything always fall to you: the children, the cooking, the magazines.

You go to your locker and you realize it's wide open.

You look to the door and he is slipping out.

"*No*, excuse me," you say, and march over. He's out the door, and wimpish. You grab his shoulder with your hand, which fits over the skinny thing dexterously. "Excuse me, what's happened in the staff room? Were you aware?"

An odd smell. You feel like throwing up, but there is no cavity.

"My locker is open. Were you aware?"

He tries to slide out of your grip, but you dig the tops of your nails into him. "*No*, explain please," you order. You hit him, there is anger already in your fists. It is a problem.

A ridiculous, cowardly look is on his puny face.

"Give it," you say, when he won't say anything in return. "*Give* it." He shoves you back.

You are in absolute disbelief. "Give it!" you yell, mucus in your throat. Your stomach is sick.

He is so *wimpish* and will not look at you.

"Give it." You push him and push him and push him.

Another hand from behind you, feeling around your face for your mouth, covering it. You will throw up in his hand. It smells like Lynx.

"For Christ's sake!" you yell into the palm. A few more fingers of a hand wiggling to grab you around the jaw and in the opening of your mouth, feeling for your nose with the other two fingers. You are conscious of your nose. You use it to resist the palm. A bag over your head now. Walking you to the left.

"*Give* it," you try once more, a spit. "*Give*. Give, give. *Give, wimp*," you growl.

Magazines, you think. Need to get magazines. Soon they will realize that you just want whatever they took back and you will leave them alone and go get the magazines. You will not hit them again. You will try not to hit them. Perhaps you will get some cigarettes after this tiresome act.

At some point, you say, "Excuse me, excuse me. *Berta*." You say your own name. "Berta. I'm *Berta*. *I just work here. I'm Berta*." There is a vein in your head. Not this feeling again, where you might pass out, where you yell, *Help*. Even if for no apparent reason, you are always dreaming, and they are always nightmares.

THE BUSINESS

21 **IT'S A SUCCESSFUL BUSINESS IF** you count the quality. The key is to have a good relationship with your customer.

They're not just a customer, they're a person.

I mean, they're not just a customer, a resource, a person—they are dying. What distracts them most from that?

It's a 20 to 80 ratio of female versus male.

I've had children who want to film and laugh at me looking in ears, opening them, and reaching inside. Men in business suits who get naked, then put their clothes back on while looking at you as each item covers up their skin again. People who come in hopes that the practice of it will cure a loneliness or a lower-back ache. People who come for conversation. People who come as a gift to themselves. Sometimes people need you once and that's it.

On the phone, my mother says to me, "It is unnatural: addiction. Addiction only happens when someone assumes that everything is available without growth. Addiction only happens in a quick-moving culture and a quick culture happens only when something is not right, the growth is not natural."

A week after Big Red Boss disappears, I find Luis crying on the step of the staff-room emergency exit.

The door had been ajar and I'd heard sounds of sobbing. He turned and said, "Oh, it's you."

It's sunset. The sky is being torn open with orange. He's smoking, hasn't got a shirt on.

"Do you know what it's like, guilt?" he says.

I find myself becoming annoyed by the way he talks, this raspy breathiness. The way it seems as if he believes that nobody has ever experienced the thoughts he's thinking. He has these back muscles, though.

"No," I say.

I had not wanted to know what happened to Berta after dropping them all off the other night. What's more secure than obliviousness is resisting the source of knowledge and the source of knowledge agreeing to resist you too. A most healthy dynamic, the most common.

What they write in stories: knowledge makes you a dead man walking; the hero is the one who doesn't tell, who holds their integrity.

Luis drops his cigarette as if by accident, as if it's just fallen from his fingertips. Then he shuffles his foot over to stamp it out. I notice a tattoo of something in a different language, symbols, maybe Sanskrit, perhaps something entirely different. I always pretend to know such things so I don't have to ask. These words seem to mean something to him because they are on the side of his chest, something only he would see while facing sideways in a mirror, deliberately looking at himself, looking for something.

I sit beside him. Run my fingers down his back. Feel how his spine is put together.

"So what happened?"

He sobs. "Do you know Berta from K.A.G.—the manager? She was at that party." His voice is round the way a voice becomes circular in sobs.

I say, "I don't think so."

"She was my boss there," says Luis. He's sniffing now, sitting up straight and stretching his spine long. My palm slowly falls back to rest on the scratchy concrete behind him. "She disappeared last week. The day we closed together."

I nod. "Oh."

"My demons are taunting me." His voice lathers and there's a bubble in his throat. He clears it and starts crying again. "I can't stop thinking about it. She has children, you know."

He puts his hand on my knee suddenly. He looks down at my legs, then out to the sky. "I'm gonna go visit them."

I swallow. "It's not your responsibility."

"Come with me," he suggests.

"You want me to?"

His expression changes, he looks surprised. "Oh, sure."

I want to pull him into my chest so he feels comfortable.

He has this awful look of pain, it rests in the curl of his lip.

"Where's your car?" I ask him.

"I don't really have a car," he says.

Luis and I are driving in the dark. I ask him to navigate, though I know the route well enough.

We drive the back way. Toward the man with the two pit bulls. He's wearing a different-colored tracksuit today, a muted maroon.

The radio says something about diehard Stalinists. I look down at the FM button.

When I look up again, the tracksuit man is sticking his head forward pointedly, looking at us rolling towards him, my headlight scanning the length of his body. Hand shielding his eyes to see closer.

I speed up and turn the corner. To Berta's house. It's a talent of mine: if I drive somewhere once, I know how to get there forever.

"Oh yeah, you turned the right way. Sorry, I'm a bit slow," says Luis. "Actually, I'm really out of it."

Is your boss still your boss if they disappear on the job? I park right outside her house this time.

We get out. Luis puts some gum into his mouth to chew, he observes me staring at his lips and smiles, holding the pack of gum to me. I shake my head. He comes around and squeezes my shoulders before leading us over the untrimmed lawn. Berta's is a redbrick house with barred windows. From the outside it's not very big-looking, but when the man opens the front door, I notice how long the house is on the inside.

"Yep?" he says, his cheeks gaunt and his eyes uninterested. It looks like a vein is popping out of his head. It looks green. He's rubbing it distractedly. "Sorry, I assumed you were the cops . . . What would you guys like?"

I can hear the television.

"We're here to visit the kids, give our condolences," says Luis.

"What?"

"About Berta. I was her coworker."

"Her employee?"

"Right."

"Do you know the kids or something?"

"No, I just wanted to check up on everyone."

"Oh," says the man. He's wearing a Lonsdale shirt. He looks at me. I realize I'm wearing my white shirt and business trousers.

"So *you* are?" he says. "His therapist, or . . . ?"

"No," I say. "I'm his ear cleaner."

The man has a bruise on his neck. He's the kind of man where you can't tell if he's aggressive or passive. The fact that he's either is what he is.

"She's not dead," says the man, folding his arms.

"Are you their father?" asks Luis.

"Berta's boyfriend."

"They're staying with you?"

"I'm staying here," he says.

Luis is politely confused. "Yeah, yeah right. Where is their dad?"

"Dunno."

We're all standing there.

"Yeah right, um." Luis pauses. "So can I speak to the kids?" The partner is looking past us, not at us.

"Um, sure," he says, using just the lips of his mouth.

Luis and I follow him down the hallway. The house is decorated quite nicely. It isn't what I expected. The walls are painted a warm, deep red. There are paintings that take oriental shape but aren't by any traditional artist. I recognize some of the furniture from Pottery Barn, midrange expensive-looking things that match only in value, not in style.

I follow closely behind Luis. On the back of his T-shirt it says: PEACEFUL CORRUPTION. Band merchandise, the tour dates listed underneath.

Two teenagers are watching a TV serial, sitting on separate velvet couches. Someone on the screen is being killed nimbly with a knife. The character looks at the knife in their stomach and then at the killer. *Suspenseful music*, says the subtitle, and the music sweeps in slowly.

The kids look a lot older than I imagined. They're watching the television, dissatisfied, mildly bored by it.

Luis sits on one side of the velvet couch and I stay standing.

The partner is beside me.

Luis says to the younger son, "I'm sorry about your mother. I was the last one who saw her. I was her colleague."

"One of her employees, boys," corrects her partner. He's watching the television screen with hands in his pockets.

Luis hovers his hand over the younger son's shoulder. "She was really peaceful that day. Quieter than usual. She spent the whole day refolding the business pants. She was a very hard worker."

"Is," says her partner.

After a bit, Luis manages to get the younger one to cry. He holds him under his armpit and into his chest.

Her partner keeps saying, "She's not *gone*, you know. She'll be back." He's looking straight at the television, drinking a can of beer. "She'll be back, boys."

The younger one then snaps, "*How do you know?*"

And then the partner quietly starts weeping, holding his forehead to his hand. The only ones not crying are me and the older one, his eyes still on the TV.

I itch the acne on my cheek using the back of my hand. I wonder how long Luis wants us to stay for. He's passing the tissues from the coffee table. The older one glances over at one point, doesn't react. The two kids look nothing alike.

The older one soon gets up and goes down the hallway into one of the rooms. Slams the door shut.

"*Luis*," I say. "We should go."

We leave the house, the younger one still sobbing on the couch in front of the television. The partner walks us to the front door and doesn't say anything. Soon all of this oddness will be over and Berta will be here and her kids will be fine, he probably expects.

"Feel better?" I ask when we get in the car.

Luis side-eyes me. "I didn't know we'd be there for half an hour, that's my bad."

I start the car and he begins to direct me to his house. When we get onto the ramp for the highway, he says, "Maybe I need to go pray."

"You're religious?"

"Catholic. My family." There's a silence. "I want to pray . . . for them."

I bite at my lips. He is unexpected, and I suppose I must be making some sort of face about it because he says softly, "We don't have to, obviously."

"No, no," I say. I pull out onto the highway and look in my rearview mirror for a moment. Almost empty roads.

We stop and buy Coronas from the twenty-four-hour mega-mart.

.   .   .

Luis has red eyes. "I know it sounds stupid but maybe I could've done something. I guess I could *still* do something. I could go looking."

We're sitting now in the car in the parking lot. Big white lights shining through, reflecting off the dashboard. I've got the engine off and the only sound is cicadas and other engines starting up.

Quiet cars at this time of night.

One motorcycle speeding.

"No one can fully protect anybody," I tell him. "If someone wanted to get her, they'd get her. They know where she is. She's either at the complex, at home, or with the people she knows. If she wanted to disappear . . . I think that's what is most depressing. Do you think she just wanted to go?"

Luis says, "Whoa."

"No, I don't mean to sound mundane, but . . . you never know. Do I sound defensive or . . . ?"

"No, you're making absolute sense," says Luis. "I think it's just that . . . when people are gone and you didn't really like them, you tend to forget why you didn't like them."

"Like with . . . being dead, they're absolved from any of the harm they did?"

"Yeah, yeah. Like it had all been dumb, now that they don't exist. A waste of energy. Kind of like . . . you feel sorry for them. As if not being here, they're somehow worse off."

I prop my arm up on the window to look at him. He looks down to his lap and shakes his head, lets out a loud exhale.

He says, "And with someone like *Berta*, she was the worst employer I've ever had. I mean, a really emotionally manipulative woman. In a really strange, grooming sort of way. But all of that doesn't seem to matter against the guilt I still have. Like, if she died as what she was in the world—just an abusive retail manager—we're still able to see her skin and bones more than we see what she did with them. Because if you told that story, it would feel so inconsequential. You know what I mean?"

"Right. But regardless, she's still a little molecule of a larger problem. Like the domino effect."

"Yeah, mmm. I don't know. Maybe I just feel weird because, deep down, people always want to see someone change, overcome."

"She might come back. It might not be that bad. And is it so bad that for a little while at least, you don't have an abusive manager?"

"I guess. I think I feel selfish thinking of it that way."

"I understand."

I feel nice, driving with one hand on the wheel and the other pouring beer down my throat. It's cold out now, finally a crisp wind. Luis is singing along to a modern flamenco song playing on 91.2. I just focus on breathing and the lines on the road.

We get to the church. He tells me this is the local one he'd grown up going to, just him and his mother; his brothers were old enough not to have to follow along.

I pull up in a parking spot, the headlights dim along the gravel, making it somehow appear illicit.

Engraved in big letters on the white arch over the entrance: MAGNI-FICAT ANIMA MEA DOMINUM.

We stand outside for a moment while Luis smokes. "What does it say?" I ask.

He says he doesn't know.

He drops the butt on the bricks and presses it in. We walk towards the door. It's not much warmer. I wrap my white thing over my chest. In a moment, an old woman wearing a headscarf walks up behind us and taps Luis on the shoulder. She passes him the tiny remainder of the butt he dropped.

He takes it. When she goes inside, he throws it over the stair rail. We enter the nave. It's more beautiful inside than it is out. And it feels warm, in an odd way.

There are a few people inside. People in work suits. An elderly woman in an off-red-more-pink tracksuit.

"Contrition," says Luis. "Prayer of contrition." We slide into one of the pews.

In prayer, he looks peaceful, almost like he's nothing. But his mouth is moving very slightly. I fall in love with him while he's in prayer.

Then we're standing by the candles, looking at the crucifix.

"The craftsmanship," says Luis. "I was raised to be a carpenter or a builder like my brothers, but I went to a psychic reading and she told me that I shouldn't pursue it any longer, she said *building* would doom me, the collapsing of a structure would kill me."

I tell him about something my father told me about the Lu Ban Jing. Carpenters have the potential to deliver a curse, which, if done correctly, results in a person perishing in a river or in a water well. Using a wooden boat that is designed to seduce a common person.

Luis looks at me. He's immediately obsessed with the idea, I can see it in his face.

"*Yeah*, right, cool," he says. When he can't think of anything else to say, he offers in the same tone, "How about this, how about we go to my house and we just sleep together. See how it feels."

I'm only slightly looking at him; he looks a little puffy from the beer.

"No," I say, hoping he might ask again. But he doesn't.

We're in the car. I'm driving him home, following the GPS he set on my phone. I wait for him to ask again.

We pull up to his house.

"Do you really want to?" I say.

"Yeah."

He's falling asleep, though, and he's got half his beer left. I ask him if he's a lightweight and he shakes his head. I take him to the door, holding the lower part of his back, help him open it with his keys. His house is number ten in a set of double-story units. He lives close to Huy's community college. It looks as though they might use this block for cheap student housing.

His pale roommate with a shaved head is sitting in front of the television, his back falling into the couch. He doesn't say anything, just smiles at me.

There are some flowers on the dining table that look fresh.

"They're for the funeral when it happens, because she's *dead*, I just know it," says Luis miserably. He gets two glasses and fills them with tap water. He looks welled up with tears.

People who take other people's sadness. I think about this for a second.

"She didn't *have* to be," he says.

I ask him if anyone has ever died in his family. I notice that I ask this condescendingly.

He says his father left them to go back to work in Brazil so often it felt like that. But nobody has *died*, no.

We take the glasses into his bedroom.

"It's usually just me, my older brothers, and my mother for as long as I can remember. He's here sometimes. He's here now but I don't want to see him," he says.

We sit on the bed; he falls asleep obnoxiously after ten minutes and I slip out of the bedroom, shut the door behind me. His roommate is looking at me. "Hey, you have plans tonight?"

I tell him I'll probably just go home.

He says, "You know if you're tired you can sleep in my bed."

22 **I SLEPT WITH THE ROOMMATE,** Dmitri. Snuck out while Luis's bedroom door was still shut at half past five.

Now I'm watching the sun come up from my 900, on top of a lookout at the end of a nearby street. "My Love" is playing. I have a 7-Eleven coffee too.

This is so peaceful and it's so nice; the smell, how it feels to absorb the cool texture of the car that comes with morning air. My clothes smell of the sweat from Dmitri, but with the windows down it hardly matters. The polite frostiness seeps through.

I have an image in my head of Luis praying the night before. In low, orange light. I hold that here for a while.

23 I AM THINKING AGAIN ABOUT atomic bombs and nuclear weapons. There is a cloud in the sky that looks like the pictures.

If the clouds just happened to look like this every day I wonder whether we'd consider photographs of "mushroom clouds" to be beautiful. I wonder if by now, the magnitude of these images amplifies the amount of empathy and grief we feel, or whether it pacifies it, numbs it. I think about how we develop feelings by associating shapes; how we have to continually find new shapes to resemble them.

Farah is drawing the shape of a dress, but different.

We're standing at the reception desk, watching on my phone, a film analysis video about the movie *American History X* and how film can show the transformation of irrational psychology.

Someone walks in. I press pause. She has short hair and tattoos on her neck, one under the eye.

"Can I book an appointment? I tried to ring earlier but no one picked up."

I look at the phone and it's disconnected from the power board.

Farah apologizes and I return to my studio, confident they're booking an appointment for a later time today. When I hear the chimes, I come back out.

Farah says, "I booked her in for tomorrow at three."

"Why not today?" I ask, massaging my palms.

"Look busy, right?"

Imagine if we're always trying to look so busy that we never actually end up doing anything. I wait for the client that we have today at two. His name is Oren.

I'm playing with the diffuser. Pouring oils in. Mist that smells like mint. The gum that Luis had in his mouth.

Oren comes ten minutes early and I hear Farah saying, "She'll just be a minute."

I wait two minutes, then come out.

"Oren?" I shake his hand. He follows me into the studio.

He tells me about his shoulder problem. I decide to give him an upper-body massage and instruct that he remove his shirt only.

He says he can't stop ordering fast food on the way home from work. He chuckles. "It's much too easy nowadays, isn't it?"

He feels all over the place. His partner is always out doing things. His partner is a spin class advocate. He's never home when he's home. Oren works all hours during the day and his partner is out in the morning and at night.

He says he wants to stop thinking about what his partner is doing all the time. And he also wants to stop the ache in his shoulders. He wants to stop his addictive personality. Most of all, he wants to stop looking at his phone all the goddamn time, as it might be the root cause of it all.

The trick is to make your client feel as though you have taken responsibility for all these issues. The same way the medicine in a sugar pill is for the purpose of lifting anxiety from the patient. The feeling when a doctor assures you there is nothing particular about your blood. It may seem as though I've taken a soreness from their back, but the reality is that I have just given it a touch, a whisper to the fibers they may loosen. In response, the brain will become less concerned about sending the signal of inflammation to it. And it may focus on the more important, more emotional residue located in the subconscious.

Just breathing.

"So," I say, "there is something powerful about being in between, not just one extreme or the other. And it's difficult to do this. But if you don't look at your phone, your partner both has and has not texted you. If you don't look at your phone, you are exerting less energy so there is more energy available to you for other things, for your body to begin to heal. The best way to stop looking is to literally stop as you are about to. And you don't have to choose any reality."

"Right," he mumbles. His body softens under my hands.

"If you exist in all the possibilities available to you at the same time, your body then begins to realize it does not have to resort to the action it would if it were on autopilot, changing your brain's chemical release, sending signals to your body to react and justify the chemicals via your emotions."

"I understand, I guess. So naturally the mind will grow out of the habit because your body will have?"

"They seem to work hand in hand, yes."

"I guess that's a bit like what I've heard about meditating."

He lets out an unembarrassed moan, indicating an absolute peace and comfort, as if the ego had just become unattached.

I tell him, "Well, with me, I can help you relieve the tensions which build onto that physical routine, the one you associate with your obsessive behaviors."

He seems convinced, but the best thing about massaging is not having to make any eye contact. My eyes are currently distracted and probably unconvincing. It is as though, when massaging clients, the mouth is one thing, the hands are another, and my mind is on a separate plane.

If the body is also larger than my own, it requires much more effort, much more concentration, and so my face will be contorted in such exertion. Massaging a body that is heavier than mine, I am able to push into them. What could be a violence is then transferred into an almost compassionate energy; it takes focus to do this. Aggression is never depleted, it is only ever transferred, depending on the roots of one's intention.

Oren pays and makes his next appointment for the same time next week. When he leaves, the chimes shimmer.

Farah cracks a grin. "Lunch break?"

We hang up the BE BACK SOON sign and plod down the escalator, passing K.A.G. and the dollar store leading to the food court. Today the banner overhead has a man holding a shoe to his ear. I push open the double fire doors, down the concrete hall.

I think about the curb-stomp scene. Teeth. Passing the bulletin board without looking.

Farah scans her card.

Freddy is in the staff room.

Farah's trying to show me something on her phone, someone's photo. "Look, someone's in the window—do you think they knew he was there?"

I look at the photo, a vague figure hovering outside the dark window in the flash.

Freddy says, "Let me see."

"No," Farah darts her eyes up and flickers them into an eye roll.

Freddy gets up, his hands on his hips over his woolen jumper and black trousers. He comes over and looks from behind Farah's shoulder.

"Stop," she says.

He's laughing. He thinks we're all laughing. That seems to be the tragedy here.

"Oh, is that an iPhone ten? Trendy, very trendy."

In Farah's hand is a palm-sized, rose-gold sixth-edition iPhone.

"Fuck off," groans Farah.

"Well, *excuse me* for trying to bring some fun to the office!" He's still laughing. His breath smells like dusty grapes.

He goes back to the couch, throwing a scrunched-up tea towel in the air and catching it again with both hands; he begins to sing softly to himself, a waltz rhythm.

Farah heats up her lunch. We wait.

She's telling me about the date she went on the night before. She'd met him through a mutual friend. She tells me how she thinks his pheromones speak directly to hers. There was something specific about him that she couldn't resist; she needed to touch his skin. She says that afterward, at home, she'd googled pheromones and female response, and the first link that came up was in the shopping tab: an elixir on Amazon designed to attract "females." The product contained an eighteen-milligram blend of androstadiene, androstanol, and aldosterone.

She shows me a screenshot of a customer review: *We went out to a bar and then to the club and not one female turned their head at us. So me and my friend poured the bottle over our heads and hair and it still made no difference, no girls looked at us.*

Freddy stops singing softly in his mouth and says, "Mmm, I smell butter chicken. Is that butter chicken?"

Farah says, "It's vegetarian spaghetti."

Vic and I are eating a salad out of a plastic carton we bought from Costco. Sitting in the parking lot near the trolley bay. There's a baby crying. I'm telling him about Farah's pheromone story. Talking about which is better: permanent manipulation or the placebo effect.

"Actually, making artificial pheromones," I tell him. "You know when you get your hair cut or dyed, and you start to dress yourself around it? It'd be like that. It depends on who you are."

"You know you can fake urine," Vic says.

He shows me on his phone. He has it written down, deep in his notes: hydrochloric acid solution, ammonia solution, sodium chloride, which can also be swapped for table salt, potassium chloride, urea, calcium chloride, magnesium sulphate.

"But the most important part is how specific you are with portions," he says.

"You could probably make a business selling synthetic urine."

"*Synthetic* urine," he repeats.

We finish the salad. He drops his fork into the container.

"I faked my piss for the pharmacy drug test," Vic says, as if he wanted me to ask him before. He lights himself a cigarette.

I ask if he's still been going to the gym as much. There was a stage when he was going every night, but recently he's been home before me, usually in front of the television.

He says a little, but mostly he's been too anxious. "Too busy," he adds.

He's been like this since the attack, one extreme to the other. He would never admit it. It's too easy to be unconcerned about him. The way he indicates his anxiety is to retreat into what appears to be a sort of frustration with routine, moments of relentless boredom, then moments of absolute spontaneity.

He's pulling his scrubs on over his Adidas, off again, on again, then off, scratching at them. Then he sighs, collapses his hands over his knees. "Everything's so quick. Everything happens so quickly. I don't have time to think about what I want to do or want to be, I just keep doing this because it's what I'm doing."

I notice the sky. It's Voss gray, clouds simmering right above the horizon of green ranges. There are bloated birds walking under the cars and back out again. They look like pigeons but aren't. It's kind of warm.

These are the moments that feel relieving, I think. This is the best it's going to get. *Relief.* Spoken word communication. A feeling of infinite possibility, having spoken it.

Vic takes his Valium. It's been helping him at work in the later part of the day.

"You should do whatever you want," I say, shrugging.

"Yeah, I know." Vic puts out his cigarette.

A breath of fresh air, a piece of plastic blows skyward near the fencing.

24 **NEXT THING I KNOW, DOMS** is telling me how she and Vic have started selling elixirs of artificial pheromones, saliva, sweat, and urine on social media. She's also selling her candles, soaps, and oils on the same platform.

We're standing at the escalators of the complex. She's come to shop for plastic bottles and containers.

"Daiso," I recommend.

It's where I get my goods, particularly containers for health goods. I make a point of walking her up to the Daiso.

"Actually, have you tried K.A.G.?" Doms asks me while we're browsing.

It's a Wednesday and I can't afford the lease payment for the studio. I've just bought new door chimes from K.A.G. that apparently ring on 432 Hz. They sound the way entering heaven would.

The leasing team comes to the door once I've put them up. They say we can move to the hair salon. It's just the one room, so everything—the cupping, the nudity—would be done in the open. But it'll be about three hundred dollars cheaper.

I look at Farah, who has her arms crossed.

"How long do we have?" I ask them.

The woman says, "Well, ideally, a day and a half. You need to be out by the end of the month. Two days."

We tell them we'll come to their office or give them a call.

Later, Peggy comes to the door, right before our client at three. She knocks and enters without waiting for a response. The chimes go off, absolute bliss. I'm sitting in one of the waiting chairs, sorting magazines. *Harper's*, a copy of the most recent *Gardener's Gazette*.

"Ling," she says. "The leasing team needs you to make this decision quickly." She crosses her arms.

I tell her I'll give them a call as soon as I finish with the client.

Peggy says, "You shouldn't be having clients." Then she leaves and our client arrives a few moments later.

The face-tatted woman's name is Sarah. I shake her hand and we go into the studio. She takes a seat on the massage table.

I've started noticing small things, like the kinds of people who'll go sit on the massage table in the center of the room, those who'll wait to be asked, or those who'll stand as close to any corner as possible.

I make up my mind about these types of people, but I don't express it. I merely pull the assumptions of them through the meridians of my body to treat them, through my throat and eyes in order to communicate with them. I realize they will never know the weight of this, they will not be able to compare or know the distinctions I make per body.

Sarah is interested in the ear-cleaning service. "It sounds cool." She shrugs.

She says she is into aromatherapy and alternative healing. She has just begun a Chinese medicine course and is curious about traditional forms of healing available locally.

I say she's come to the right place.

I look at her. She's wearing a Mickey Mouse jumper. She looks at me.

"I started my course on Monday." She has a calm, steady voice. "It's really *fascinating*."

We tie her hair back together and I put a sheet over her. Open my cleaning set. I choose the scoop first.

"This might feel a little ticklish, so try not to jolt or stop breathing."

Even if you can see right through somebody else's spirituality, there is always something that makes you take it as seriously as they do, reflecting their energy.

I swap my scoop for a lighter scraping stick and hold it like a pencil. Her ear has a giant helix, which is obstructing the process drastically. The shape of a shell, her ear is reminding me.

I remember holding rolled-up shells to my ear, imagining that the shell and I were both listening to each other. This is what it feels like.

She says, "Can you see inside?"

"Barely. It looks like a tunnel. But there are a lot more intricacies than that, than seeing. And that's the trick of it."

"So your profession must be so much about prediction?"

"Yes, being able to read people and shapes quickly."

Shapes. I think about it, while reaching into her ear with a feather. A big mushroom cloud.

I tell the leasing team that we'll move into the hair salon.

Farah and I go to the mega Chinese supermarket on the way home. We stand in the aisles. I buy a pack of imported dried mushrooms. Some anchovies, also imported. Farah gets a pack of Crown Choco Heims and lemon cream 2 + 1 biscuits.

We park out the front of hers, sit in the 900, and open the 2 + 1 biscuits. I have a half hour before I have to pick up Jean Paul and Huy for the discussion group. The sky is burning up red, almost like there are two separate, more gentle tones colliding and creating it. There is the residue of clouds in the west, breaking off like crumbs. Farah is exhaling out the window, looking up to the sky. Here as in limbo.

I'm a practical person. Though when nature gives a sign, I take it. It looks to me that there is evolving to be had.

SURVEILLANCE

PEGGY

Login: Peggy Marie Alden, Center Management Office IP Address
(http://194.178.1.134) Model: CheckVideo_ checkvideo
_M50288 Canon
User: admin

Switch-to: North_Escalator GroundLevel_ 9:04:05AM
Young mother of South Asian appearance, shopping with preschool-
aged child. Child is pulling at mother's top. Mother looks to be
pregnant with another child. The bottom of her shirt is lifted. At the
bottom of the escalator, the mother moves to the side of the handrail
and un-velcros her shoulder bag. She tugs at something. It does not pull
out easily. It is a ziplock bag. Inside is a teething biscuit. She breaks it in
half and drops one half back into the plastic bag and passes the other to
the child who reaches up with both arms to take it.

Switch-to: North_store_152_exterior_(KAGext.)_GroundLevel
_9:05:01AM
Young mother enters K.A.G. Takes a basket from the male welcomer.
Male welcomer is medium-sized, Mexican or Puerto Rican, Latin
American descent, with piercings. Male welcomer smiles. As the
young mother proceeds inside, the smile from his face softens into a
neutral face.

Note: piercings.

Caucasian male walks in. Does not take basket from male welcomer. Male welcomer nods after him. Male welcomer swaps with female welcomer.

Switch-to: Central_East_foodcourtcam_Ground Level_ 9:10:43AM
Man eating meatball sub sandwich from Sub'd! and sushi from Tosai. Center table beside the section of plant/greenery. Man looks toward a plant while taking two bites from his sandwich, puts it down, and reaches for the sushi roll. He eats the other sushi and holds the plastic tub the sushi came in. Man looks around and brings the tub under the table, reaching across to put it on the chair opposite him. Man wipes his hands on his trousers and picks up the meatball sub.

Note: litter

Switch-to: Central_North_foodcourtcam_Ground Level_ 9:17:03AM
Lotus Fusion Studio owner, Ling, entering fire doors.

Switch-to: staffroom_cam Ground Level_ 9:19:00AM
Takes a moment to load. Screen glitches. Something wrong with the server.

Refresh

Switch-to: staffroom_cam Ground Level_ 9:19:21AM
Then, Ling is leaving a flyer on the magazine table. Waits a moment, then leaves another. Slides it under a magazine.

Email notification: Galleria Quote . . . Hi Peggy, Daniel just passed me your email. I was wondering if you've had any further thoughts on providing a short . . .

Open: Inbox

Mindy Lim: Galleria Quote

customer.alert: Your receipt for MegaSports is available . . . Meal
Replacement Powder Bulk OxyWhey 930g

Hubby: John and Angie. Possible . . . attached Facebook profiles . . .
thoughts?

Hubby: Invoice "LushIndoor" plant retail-landscaping job.
Please pay ASAP!

Close: Inbox

**Enlarge: IP Address (http://194.178.1.134) Model: CheckVideo
_checkvideo_M50288 Canon**

Switch-to: staffroom_cam Ground Level_ 9:25:00AM Glitch.

Refresh

Switch-to: staffroom_cam Ground Level_ 9:25:27AM
Man of African appearance enters, seemingly the manager of Big A
Pharmacy. He opens a tea tin. Speaks to Ling across the room, who is
eating something on the couch. Man approaches her and passes her a
tea bag. Sits on opposite couch.

Open: New browser Type: Glitching IP ad . . . Backspace

Type: Jan . . .

Auto-spell: Jann's Marriage Fiasco Blog

Question of the day: How to deal with your husband watching porn . . . without you?!

Alarm: 10AM! GET UP, 10 LUNGES W. 10KG WEIGHTS, 10 SIT-UPS, 10 BICEP CURLS!

25 **THE RELATIONSHIP BETWEEN MY MOTHER** and me would have deteriorated a long time ago had we never found a place to rest. During my early childhood, before age eight, I had already slowly begun to withdraw more into myself. My mother was, at the same time, feeling lost, having just quit her medical practice. Her new routine was to keep busy, to understand why it was that every time she set up a new life, my father was ready to jump ahead again. Every flat we lived in had the smell of a different sort of lotion we would buy to massage into the coarseness of our feet. How tired they would get, moving around.

When we found Par Mars, it was not the look or feel of it—but the tiredness of it, the bored unattractiveness of it, the lonely, antisocial nature of it, that made us both look inward. To look inward and to the sky. *If there was nothing to look at in front of you, why not look up at the sky?* my mother would say. She'd say this every time I bowed to scroll on my phone. She would urge me to read a new book every vacation period. And would ask me to recount the contents in fine detail after every chapter.

From the telephone there is never true rest, she would say. It is not in its design. There is always the possibility for communication whether or not you choose to take part in it. But the telephone is designed to taunt you in your most inactive hours. To remind you, as your television does, that there is much to "seek" outside before you heal inward. Much to compare yourself with, much to be sold, much to do before sitting down and realizing, with a full stomach and a quenched tongue, that you have everything you need in the lungs.

Still, when I think of rest now, even when attempting to put into practice the theories my mother often preached, I imagine that while I am sleeping, while I am wrapped in a private casing, there is something going on outside, something always on the other side that I have missed.

.   .   .

The complex is playing the Colbie Caillat song. If you walk into the shoe store, they're playing "Get Right Witcha." Walk past the supermarket, they're playing Julian Lennon. My head is hurting, just where the right temple is.

Interesting then, as I walk past Luis near the dollar store, how we look at each other. It's almost as if he is afraid of me, how he pulls his eyes back down to the ground. And my imagination of why he hasn't called makes me paranoid and feel estranged from my limbs.

I try to forget about Luis. I don't like the slowness. I don't like indecisiveness. This is why I've decided to make it work in the hair salon. Strong decision-making, action-based thought.

Farah says this move is beneficial because it gives us an excuse to call every customer we've had and remind them that we are here, waiting for them. So we start by calling our eight loyal clients to tell them we'll be closed for a week. We'll be right back with them soon.

Oren tells Farah on the phone that he told his friend, who is a swimmer, to come for the ear-cleaning service.

We book Oren in for an appointment in two weeks.

Clearing out the drawers of the reception desk in the afternoon, I find a bottle of rum that had rolled to the back. Farah has gone down to the staff room to heat up our lunches. When I look inside and shake it, there's just enough for one sip left.

I take everything out of the drawer but leave the bottle in the back. Truth makes you brutal.

Today a visitor comes in as we begin packing, though our OPEN sign is not flashing.

This is the first sign of hyper-confidence in someone.

He introduces himself to Farah as Lonnie Luther in an emotionless voice.

He says he needs weekly therapy. He swims every morning at six a.m. before returning to the desk he has on his apartment balcony and writing his screenplay up until about eleven a.m. This is when he grabs a coffee and a pack of peanuts at the gas station and returns to his desk until one p.m. He needs something to do between one p.m. and three p.m. This is when he has to pick his niece up from school. He gets paid ten bucks from his sister when he drops his niece off at home. Then he goes back home and writes emails or responds to them. He says he often just walks around the complex looking for people to look at, looking for things he might need to buy for around the home.

"Being a creative, you can't always create," he says. "What services do you offer?" He has been scratching his thigh this entire time.

Farah taps her pen against her lip. "We specialize in ear cleaning."

"Okay, so ear cleaning, what is that?" He props his gold-framed glasses up so that they sit properly. Relying on Farah, hanging on each of her words now.

"Well, you say you swim. It can help clear the buildup that's in your ear. It is a meditative experience and helps you relax and breathe."

He turns to me on the waiting seats. I rest the stack of magazines on my thighs. "Are you a doctor?" he asks.

I tell him I'm the master.

"The ear master?"

"The healing master."

"All right, no harm in trying something new. I like to do that every now and again."

He passes us his business card with his number on it. It reads:

> **LONNIE LUTHER**
> *Movie entrepreneur, emerging film*
> *director and Junior JavaScript*
> *Developer at TechPort*

"My father worked at TechPort," I say.

"Would I know him?"

"He left a while ago."

"I just got to Par Mars about a year ago."

A natural silence. He says he'll call to see if we can arrange a time. We agree to this and he performs a sort of bowing motion.

When I get back, Doms has rearranged the condo. The fold-out bed is in the smaller corner, right beside the entrance to the kitchen. There is a large air-humidifying thing where it had been.

"What's this?" I say.

She says calmly, "It's my house, Leen. I can do whatever I need to do."

Tonight I sleep in the corner where the dust is. Because they are starting their new business, they need the space for experimentation. I sleep among the artificial urine and blood.

They are planning to target sales to competitive athletes and their PR teams, schoolteachers, moviemakers, and employees who do drugs recreationally. On the coffee table and in shallow boxes all over the living room there are beakers with their own saliva, other people's saliva, and urine. It's mostly test urine, thick urine smell everywhere.

The rhythmic vibrations of my phone feel violent. It's a text flood from Jean Paul about the manager of the art store. Two of the store's employees, who've joined Jean Paul's forum thread, have said that the manager has been following one of their younger colleagues around. He follows her to the parking lot and then tails her home, waiting outside her house for maybe half an hour, before driving off again. The young employee is too afraid to tell anyone about it, even her parents.

Jean Paul is typing. *Preposterous. Disgusting. Perverse.*

My phone continues buzzing as I fall asleep. A headache begins to develop. The bodily smells pulsating.

26 **JEAN PAUL IS DRIPPING WATER** on the manager's forehead using a dropper. Holding it right above the third eye so that each bead of water developing on the end of it creates a moment of this distressing limbo. This form of torture is something Huy has done a class assignment on.

"Common misconception," Huy had said before the Resisting Act. "Though it's called Chinese water torture, it doesn't actually come from China, it's from Italy."

It re-creates the disturbing feeling of waiting, of trying to comprehend narrowness. The brain: obsessively attempting to locate comfort again.

The man has his hands tied together behind his back, lying crookedly on top of them. He has Jean Paul's brown tie wrapped around his mouth. Huy and Jean Paul have these new balaclavas on.

We're sitting in a storeroom that has nothing much in it—one of the storerooms of a company that had recently moved its business to the Galleria. Jean Paul says, "It's neighborhood Watch, *bitch*."

I worry that Jean Paul and Huy are too impulsive, *juvenile* at heart.

"Is this a threat?" barks the man. The empty storeroom has just one lightbulb on near the exit. Jean Paul takes a quick photograph of the scene using the flash. Huy is present in the picture, standing to the side. Then Jean Paul throws a few heavy hook punches to the man's head so that as his jaw slackens, Jean Paul is able to force-feed a powdered pill down his throat. In a moment the man appears weaker, his cheek melting into his neck, and after another few minutes his muscles entirely lose momentum. Then Huy unwraps the tie, letting his arms go.

Jean Paul looks appalled at himself; his face has never looked so feeble. Huy is shuffling toward the exit. Without saying anything we leave out a back exit to the far end of the parking lot where my 900 is parked.

In the pit of my stomach I feel different, how we've done this.

.   .   .

I've read Freud's trusted partner Fliess's theory about a person's sexual problems being linked to the nasal activity and the function of the nose.

Jean Paul and Huy are snorting crushed-up tablets of OxyContin from the pharmacy on Huy's parents' coffee table. This has a different effect to the Rohypnol Huy stores under his bed. OxyContin is an opioid, intended to induce a nice "elated" emptiness.

Sitting here I notice we never gather at Jean Paul's house. He says his girlfriend is always working there. I'm reading the comments on Jean Paul's latest post.

I exit and above Jean Paul's thread a new thread has just appeared, titled: *How to recruit more diverse members*. I sniff, rubbing my nose.

"Crushing the tablets breaks the time-release mechanism," says Huy.

Freud excessively snorted cocaine. This is how he met Fliess. They experimented on other people *together* for friendship's sake.

Huy and Jean Paul laugh about nothing. Huy has his arm around Jean Paul, both of them giggling to the point of boiling until a laugh spills out of their mouths. I think they might be whispering about me. I look down and read that one of the tips in the new thread is to *relate to them on a deeper level*.

The high soon wears off. Then Jean Paul says something about the community group facilitator, Aden. "He just removed me from being an administrator in the forum. Just now, just after I posted the picture. I think he's hiding something. He was all on board with what I was doing a few weeks ago. He's got to be hiding something."

"Do you think there's someone controlling his actions? Someone who wants all the changes to be ineffective. Like all talk, or something?" asks Huy.

"No. I think *he's* ineffective. I think he's the faulty part. I think his philosophy is confused."

Jean Paul keeps scrolling up as if to refresh the browser.

"All I wanted was to share opinions on ways we could be more proactive," he says. "But it seems people become intimidated too easily. And what's the point of always just talking about things, never trying to change anything."

"I think he must be intimidated by your access to supplies, to the drugs," suggests Huy.

"If we all did our part, using our skills . . ."

"Things would change."

"Correct."

"Do you think his decision is a sign to tone it down a bit?" I ask.

The two of them look at me, contemplative.

"I was wrong to take out my physical anger on Rick today," says Jean Paul. "But there is no harm in the delusory techniques. If Aden practiced what he promotes, he would know that the only way to enforce change is to disrupt a routine. Delusion is the least violent way we can do that. And these people, they're taking the same thing in different packaging anyway."

"That's true," says Huy. He's scribbling in a notebook, on a page that looks as though it's been used a thousand times. Huy bangs his hand on the coffee table all of a sudden. My head reacts in the form of a sharp shooting pain and I press the heel of my hand into my eye.

"Look, friends. I personally think we did something good today, even if we had to do something bad. We're learning as we go," says Jean Paul. He clasps his hands together.

He's said something along these lines a few times now. I believe him.

"There's no growth in comfort," I say quietly, as if to myself.

Jean Paul says, "What?"

I repeat a little louder. Both nod, hum and Jean Paul smiles. "That's right." A silence.

Huy goes to heat up a container of food his parents left him and eats in front of us quickly with chopsticks and a big spoon.

"Okay, I have to write my essay now, guys, and I've got other stuff I need to do later. Do you mind going?"

27 **THE SAD STREETS DRIVING BACK** home to Doms's, the round-abouts, stopping for cars coming from the right. Windows down, summer darkness feeling the same as summer morning: just itself, unconcerned with its dwellers.

"Physical, potential energy," Jean Paul said as I dropped him home, "is in the way the jaw tenses. I had to knock it out of him."

I drove home in silence.

At the condo, Vic is sitting on the front step, smoking a cigarette.

"Everything okay?" I ask him.

He gives a pressed smile, looks embarrassed. "Ah. Come here." Offers me a hug. "I know you've already had a lot of moving around to do, but we need to talk."

I fall asleep at night, sometimes worrying, sometimes saddened by the things out of my control. Tonight I am too tired and have too much pain in the corner of my head to do either, and I watch as the moths land on the window and come loose from it again.

CHILDREN

MARY

IT WAS A LOVELY SUNDAY afternoon when Jean Paul had first introduced himself to her. Madonna had been playing over the PA system of the supermarket while she was finishing up at the cash registers.

He approached her with such outrageous confidence. Uncommon for young men these days who usually answer in low, uncommitted tones.

He asked her how the new job was going.

She had been doubtful of him at first. She assumed he was a Mormon missionary.

But the more he explained himself and why he had chosen to approach her, the more she understood it to be a sign of the life she had always longed for.

A life of purpose. Not one path or the other. But a long *road*, one which could stop her at many things, many prosperous things.

Social, spiritual, *political*.

He spoke of his keenness to work with her, how she seemed to have a meticulous understanding of the anatomy of structures "like this." Big corporations, what they do to good, fair workers.

Online Registration Form:

Name: Mary Dunn
Age: 52
Ethnicity: white, Irish

Place of birth: Par Mars
Address: 89 Violet Cr. Par Mars East
Relationship status: Widowed/Single
Dependents: 1 child

How did you find out about us?
Jean Paul approached me.

What is your reason for joining?
I have been searching for purpose for a long time. Ever since I had
my beautiful daughter, I have felt my only purpose is to protect her.
As she grows into a young woman, I cannot help but wonder what
else is out there for me. I am a caring person, some friends would
say I am the definition of motherly! But often my caring is unseen. I
am attracted to the learning aspects which Jean Paul described to
me. I am fascinated by the community aspect as I am quite a hermit
outside of church.

*Have you ever been part of any prior neighborhood Watch/community
group/organization?*
I have attended the same Bible study group for six years.

List any skills you have which might be of interest.
I can fix up cars and broken tap systems. I am a very hands-on person,
good at sewing. I have built planter boxes for my garden from scratch.
I can measure things and cut very well. I may be cut a dainty figure
but I can put together a fence! Having worked in airport security, I
have a proficient understanding of those technology systems. I have a
proficient understanding and am also keen on—

"What are you doing?" Beatrice is at the front door. She drops her bag,
sliding her shoes off without undoing the shoelaces.

Mary minimizes the window.

"What?" Beatrice comes over. "You're on a dating site?"

Mary stands up and returns to the kitchen. Beatrice hovers by the desktop computer.

Mary hesitates, then says, "Yes."

"Mom!" Beatrice grabs Mary's tiny shoulders. "That makes me so happy!"

Beatrice goes to the fridge. She takes out the leftover pork fillet and begins eating it cold with her fingers.

"Fingers! Please, Bea. Germs." She takes a fork from the drawer and hands it to her silly girl.

"Maybe now you'll stop spying on me all the time."

Mary wrinkles her nose. "I don't know *what* you're talking about." She takes another fork from the drawer and starts at the pork too. Bea is becoming very rebellious for fifteen.

Prior to the job at the supermarket, Mary had a desire to work at Topic Heights to be closer to Beatrice. The airport had been an hour's drive in peak-hour traffic. She knew that Beatrice, in all her youth, would go to the complex to be free. All those teenagers after school, they only wanted to be free even if just for two hours before dinner.

When she was promoted to the managerial position at the super-market, she was able to access the security cameras in the loading zone. From the camera's angle, you were able to see a group of teenagers who would sit there smoking and drinking. She checked obsessively to see if Bea and her blue hair were there too. There was no way that Beatrice would not one day appear, snorting cocaine or something awful.

Mary grew concerned that it was she, herself, who was manifesting all of this. That she was growing tirelessly, unnecessarily paranoid. There had been so many incidences—incidents which she trusted God had planted right before her to show that her desire for control was get-ting out of hand. Strange accidents. Strange, telling moments of her fate. Her gospel community group told her she had nothing to worry about. The incident with the bags of flour, the graffiti on her car. And still, Mary could not help but feel she was bringing all of this upon herself, that God was urging her to back down.

She resigned, went into a casual cashier position, which gave her more time to wait downstairs for Beatrice, to want to hang out with her. Cutting off her access to the loading-zone footage. Along with the addiction to the footage came the constant obsession for something to be wrong. She would deliberately look for people stealing things, keeping items in their "environmentally friendly shopper bags" without scanning, putting things in their pocket, peeling stickers off, swapping products.

This became unhealthy too, the negativity.

"Anyway, we don't even *need* dinner now," says Bea, eating the last bit of pork.

"Hmm?"

Bea sighs, laughs exasperatedly. "Oh my God, you weren't listening that entire time, were you? You never listen to my stories."

"Lord's name in vain," Mary accidentally murmurs.

Bea shakes her head. "Yeah, okay, got it."

She goes upstairs, leaving Mary to put the empty Tupperware container in the sink.

28 **THE BUGS ON THE CEILING** zap and fall on the minibar fridge. Luis is asleep on the mattress.

"Where are you now, Leen?" asks my mother on the phone.

"I'm staying at a new friend's."

"How is it there?"

"There's no pool . . . like at Doms', but I barely used it anyway. It was starting to give me acne. It's getting colder."

"What's your friend like?"

"He likes poetry. He's interesting."

"That must be nice."

"He cooks his own meals, but he only knows how to cook three things."

"I hope you cook for him."

"Yes, in the last week, I've cooked twice."

"That's a good girl. You have to pay people back when they do you favors."

"I know."

"You have to appreciate people when they help you for no reason."

"Isn't it the same if people help you because they want to feel like they're the kind of person that deserves something?"

"Too clever for me."

Staring at Luis sleeping. He sleeps like a cocoon holds him. The television is still playing outside the bedroom. I lie down and curl up too. He is sometimes out at his other job late at night, or in the early hours of the morning. He says it's a small cleaning job with a friend—moving around boxes and furniture, cleaning out houses or studios or warehouses for people who need to use the space the next day.

In the morning I'm alone on the mattress and there's this sunlight coming through panels of blinds, yellow onto yellow. The soles of my feet against concrete tiling. I come out and notice the television still playing softly. A black-and-white film has just started. A screaming woman with mascara drooling from her eyes. A man holding onto her shoulders when he kisses her, freeing her from the people who are "wild." I wonder why they play these old films first thing every morning—softly urging some sort of frame of mind.

Luis comes through the door as I step out of the shower.

His roommate hasn't been around. I feel anxious about it, wonder if it's deliberate. I've forgotten his name. Forgotten what type of belly button he has. It feels embarrassing between the three of us, and when I shower here, in their house, the home they made of this place, I feel a peculiar shame looking at my own body in it. Placeless, my things all packed in one suitcase. Feeling just like my mother, feeling just like the way we'd been—nowhere and everywhere at once.

There is a new line of K.A.G. foam wash on the bathroom counter. This time it is scented. It claims it is a natural scent enhancer. There is a pack of K.A.G. sanitary wipes. A K.A.G. diffuser. I stare at my body and want to wipe it down with a coolness.

Back in the living room, Luis has this pouty look on his face when he comes in and collapses on the old cat-ripped sofa. He stares at the television and comments on the way the white man who saves the heroine is dressed in animal skins. I come over and touch his cheek. He wraps his fingers over mine. He looks at me, softening his eyebrows. I melt and overflow.

"Was the job difficult last night?"

"Not too bad." He kisses the back of my hand.

We're both whispering. He's letting his hair grow out a bit. I run my hands through it, bristling my fingers. He shivers a little. Someone told me in primary school that if you shiver and it's not cold out, a ghost has walked by you.

He tells me the job last night was at a display home, and it made him think about where his life was going. He's been interested in design elements lately, how they have a power to change your mind.

The K.A.G. outlay, for example: so *addictive*. The genius behind the design of something beautiful is that it can stand alone. We live in an age where we would like things to stand alone, to be one with itself, so that we can, as its consumer, become the one to define it, the one to understand it and its purpose, then curate it alongside other things. We are less the type to fall for branding. We see ourselves now, before we see the brand.

I've been learning how Luis loves to speak and rarely wishes to be silent; he is silent only if he is tired, and even then he could ramble in half sentences. I can tell he is accustomed to speaking with people who grow tired of his voice by the way he looks at me with his eyes when I respond and counter-comment in a way that begs for him to continue. I seem to be accustomed to the sorts of men who conclude a moment of speaking together once I begin to speak. But Luis loves to speak in response to how I do, so on and so forth.

Though he seems to switch in mood often. Sometimes very physical and sometimes not. When I ask him, over a microwave meal the following night, if he let me stay only because he thought that I'd let him sleep with me, he ignores the question. A cigarette in his sturdy hand and a glass of tomato juice in the other.

I say to him, "Your cigarette is such an attitude right now." And then he puts the glass down and blunts the cigarette in the ashtray, his hands become full of me. Lurching at my underarms, wrestling me over the couch arm; him softly laughing, "You're a fucking little punk!"

I'm laughing too, we get drunk, he has no weed. There's no growth of it, but he does keep alcohol in the fridge. Run through his blue front door, sprint to the 7-Eleven for the good brand of jerky and instant noodles; they've started stocking Ramyun usually only available from specific stores. We eat it all lying on the tattered sofa.

And now we're preparing a Thai green curry for Berta's family because the investigation is closed for the time being. The two children have said they enjoy Thai green curry, but Berta's partner doesn't want the children eating the MSG-filled tubs they sell at Costco, and it's too expensive to get it from the local Thai place every night. It was our idea to do the casseroles thing. Nobody else in the community has initiated it. Either they've forgotten about the incident, or they do not want to believe she is really gone. And so no one has been doing the casseroles thing.

We're having discussions while preparing the curry. Luis leaves the pot simmering too long and the coconut milk boils over. I clean it up and we continue chopping vegetables on either side of his kitchen. We talk about his parents and the neighborhood he grew up in. He tells me how kids would steal another's mobile phone and texted everyone from it, provocative things, so that the kid would get beat up by their parents or their peers. There's a ticking sound coming from the oven. He tells me he hasn't used it for two years. My fingers across his forehead, I fidget the silver thing in his eyebrow. Draw down his face, put my hand over his mouth. He yells into my palm and bites the skin.

We fall asleep for the rest of the night.

29 I HAVEN'T SPOKEN PROPERLY TO Doms in almost a month. It's been about three weeks since I moved out of her condo and into Luis's house.

When my mother asked me why Doms told me to move out, I told her I considered her reason of needing "more room" for the elixirs to be very petty and sudden, seeing as I had offered Doms a space at the studio. It occurred to me that the interactions between the three of us had become stale, their mannerisms now so strange, foreign.

And when Vic sat me down that warm evening, he was gentle and open, but he gave a different reason from what Doms would. Telling me how he's now only doing a casual position as a pharmacist. His hands were shaking. He said there was going to be a lot less money coming in and that they couldn't afford to have another person with them anymore.

I see Doms across the other end of the aisle in K.A.G. We're in the kitchen section—which has opened up in the last week—an expansion that swallowed the small dry-cleaning business beside it. But everything in this new section is too lovely to resist.

I'm here to bottle my new oils; she seems to be here to bottle her artificial excretion elixirs.

"Hey," I say, walking toward her.

I'm listening to a podcast about Stanley Kubrick's *Eyes Wide Shut*. The podcasters are talking about the overdosing woman. A sound clip from the film, the doctor: *Just move your head if you can hear me*. I pause it, take my earphones out.

"*Hey!* How's it going?" She props her head up, looking slightly distracted, but reaches her hand out to my shoulder and rubs it.

"Good," I say. "The studio's about to reopen, just a week now."

"I was wondering how long that'd take. I thought for a second you guys were going to have to shut down."

I tell her it took longer than expected, then I ask about the elixirs business and she seems enthusiastic, telling me which bodily fluid is most popular. Urine is hot right now.

"Everybody's inquiring about prices for the workplace tests," she whispers, "which usually happen around this time, in the next few weeks or something. It's usually a blood and a urine. Most likely just urine."

There's not much else to ask about. I still see Vic at the pharmacy every so often. He's now reduced his hours to just the one day. He's stopped gymming for good, decided to focus most of his energy on the elixir company.

"Um, yeah, it's awesome working with Vic," she says. "We see each other lots now. I think that was always the problem. We never *saw* each other, you know?"

I realize then that she has no idea about Luis, and it's bizarre to me. I don't even know how to mention him and by the time I think of a way to bring him up, Doms is giving me a hug, squeezing me again around the shoulders. "We'll catch up properly soon." Another shoulder rub. And then she proceeds down the aisle with a basket full of glass bottles and cylinders.

The K.A.G. shopping baskets are in the style of a canvas basket with a bamboo ring holder, making shoppers feel as though they're picking fruit from a tree.

A month has moved quickly and has morphed things exquisitely.

Seven more have joined Jean Paul's private, separate community, including Mary and the two kids from the art store. Huy has created a separate forum page hosted on a site independent from Aden's. Jean Paul and Huy are both the only administrators, posting at least three times a week. Garnering aesthetic interest via design choices Jean Paul has personally curated: a simple, sans-serif layout communicating humility, yet urgency.

I notice over the course of this month that the void those initial community meetings and the Resisting Acts once filled is now being filled by my living with Luis. Not in the sense that it is as exciting or purposeful, but in the sense that we are *being* differently. I convince myself the stagnancy at Doms's was the reason for there being any void at all; the staying long outlived its expiry. The idea the lifestyle offered was far more attractive than living it, if we were waking up early to commute to the complex, if we were coming home after six with tired hands and thinned-out brains.

It was a Monday when Jean Paul decided to message the forum informing us of the first in-person meeting to be held at the East Par Mars Community Center.

Five of the seven showed up on the Wednesday and Jean Paul stood at the front of the room, explaining which philosophies he preferred to identify his process with. Nothing was said about the Resisting Acts he and Huy had been partaking in. Huy stood in the back filming this.

After the first meeting, Jean Paul checked the footage and told me, *"Huy can't stable a fucking camcorder."*

Jean Paul has been obsessed with the idea of filming everything recently. He says we need to preserve moments no matter how mundane. We cannot look properly if we cannot look from the outside.

So I told him about Lonnie Luther, the kind client who'd come in before we shut down, who visited me at Luis's and had a personal ear clean, paying in cash. "But I don't want no asshole," said Jean Paul in response. "You have to promise me he's not an asshole."

Then I told Lonnie Luther, "They'll pay twenty dollars for the filming of the hour-long community meeting." But he seemed to find the idea exciting anyway, and Jean Paul will always take advantage of that. Jean Paul's been talking about a large three-part documentary and wants a dash cam. Along with the meetings, he's already asked Lonnie Luther to join us for some of the Resisting Acts in future.

The first time Lonnie Luther attended a meeting, he and Huy got into a rhythm, talking about coding and some of the traveling they've done. "I like Singapore," I overheard Lonnie Luther saying. "It interests me."

Jean Paul listened without saying anything, a rare occasion. But he listened like his ear alone was doing the listening, folded arms, tilting his head.

Tonight, during our third in-person meeting, the group is asked to leave the community center.

The receptionist, standing in the doorway, explains that an important council meeting is taking our time slot. When Jean Paul asks why the council meeting can't reschedule until next week, she says it is about the delinquencies going on around the neighborhood and the state of Par Mars's police presence. She apologizes profusely and shuts the door quietly.

Jean Paul, prior to the interruption, had been getting us all to speak about our routines, and the frustrations behind them, analyzing our own personal habitats, our own personal routines of chemical release. When the receptionist is gone he says he'd like us to take pictures of the insides of our homes every day this week and post them all in the forum. Everybody stands at their own pace and we all trickle out of the room.

I'm heading to my 900 when a loud, rotund sound comes from one of the cars. Part of it bursts into flames; there's a shadow, a hotness. People look a little shocked but not with gusto. As if it was meant to happen all along and nobody wants to look like they weren't ready for it. Everyone thinks, or I think, that Jean Paul has set this up. And on the ride home he doesn't say anything to curb this opinion. He actually doesn't bring it up at all.

After dropping Huy and Jean Paul off, I take a bath at Luis's. I'm watching an Eddie Murphy movie, I think *Beverly Hills Cop*. My thumbs and wrists often ache. I just bend the thumbs back. The ceiling light is flickering. Eventually I get out of the bath and turn it off completely. Now only the light from my laptop. I find myself missing the comfort of Doms's television setup. Also missing Doms's Bodum coffee press.

In my massage therapy course they taught human anatomy, the perception of touch. The skin gathering information about contact and sending it to the brain.

I test the hot water, running the faucet over my naked leg.

Little bubble cases called nerves, from the receptor to the spine, up into the brain. The physical and mental ailment often connected. I massage my own foot; I try to breathe.

The skin might be reddening but I can't see it. The skin might be scorching, taut, tensing up.

We've forgotten the power of touch.

Eddie Murphy says: *Where I'm from, cops don't file charges against other cops.*

In Beverly Hills, they go by the book.

The light from the screen is dawdling through the veins of the water.

Luis knocks on the door.

Luis or the roommate.

"Hello?" I say.

"Need anything?" It's the voice of the roommate. I tell him no, then change my mind and ask for a bag of cheddar popcorn, which should be sitting at the bottom of the cupboard, and a glass of K.A.G. soy milk. He says sure. I get up and wrap the towel around myself, the ends of my hair dripping water onto the tiles. I wiggle my arms from a cold shiver and open the door slightly. My breath is difficult. My mother went through a phase where she made us practice qigong. Cultivation of energy. Heat is important, control of the body temperature is breath: relocation of it.

He's pouring the soy milk, the bag of popcorn already on the bench beside him. Glancing over, he grins. "You know there's a light in there?"

I tell him I know, it was flickering, stressing me out.

"Christ, you're fussy."

I ignore him. He comes over and passes me the popcorn and soy milk. My towel starts to slip. I thank him quickly and shut the door tight. The towel drops at my feet.

He says no worries through the door and I hear his smile through his teeth.

Touch is something special we have as humans; I remember this, watching the gunfight in the movie.

30 WE HAVE THE REOPENING OF Lotus Fusion Studio, and Farah and I have arrived early to prepare and disperse new flyers. We've kept the flyer simple this time: just a stock photograph of a lotus and a picture of some foods being provided.

Our new studio was a hair salon before: one big open room with a desk at the front and hair-washing basins in the back. Mirrors along the sides. We've flipped it over the course of the weeks and I've found myself obsessed with home renovation programs. I don't admit this to anyone except Luis, who will sometimes come and sit beside me to watch them.

Shop-fitting. Farah seems to also have a special passion for it. We've covered the mirrors with curtains, bought one more divider, one more massage table. We weren't allowed to get rid of the basins, but my mother said the more access to water, the more qi would become available.

Doms is dropping off candles to sell at the reopening. When she arrives, I open the glass door for her. "I haven't been candle making, so some of these are the same as last time. I ran out of the CBD ones," she says.

She passes a box over and we look at each other.

She sort of smiles. "This is a great spot." There is the glimmer in her eye of somebody who is repressed.

"Thank you," I say. "We have to put the dividers up still. They're in Farah's car. Her dad helped us move them."

Doms looks at Farah, who's mopping in the back. She looks offended by her.

"Still trying the ear-cleaning thing, or are you going to stick to mainstream massage therapy?" Doms asks indifferently.

It's the kind of "indifferent" that reveals she is trying to appear more uninterested than she is.

"I really think the ear-cleaning side of things is going to take off soon. People are becoming interested in the process. There's more word of mouth."

"I read that people shouldn't clean their ears too often."

"Everything in moderation," I agree tactfully.

We look at each other. It shouldn't be awkward, it could almost be loving.

"Gah, well." She hugs me in. "Come around for dinner sometime!" she suggests unseriously, and leaves.

Once the dividers are up, I come to sit on top of a massage table, my legs crossed. Feeling slightly paranoid, reading on my phone about how amazing the ear canal is. Our jaw movement helps move earwax through the canal. Ear cleaning is fine, suggests a doctor. It's only when you go too deep into the canal that you are essentially jamming dead skin and debris and wax farther in. If it comes into contact with the ear drum, it can cause vertigo, hearing loss. Dead skin preventing sound getting through, imagine. I'm moving my jaw, which sometimes clicks, wondering if somebody who talked as much as Jean Paul would have magnificent, pristine ear canals. Everything is good for you until it's not.

I swap tabs to read Jean Paul's forum. People are posting pictures of the insides of their houses. I look through them curiously, sometimes zooming in to see what it is that's on their kitchen bench. There is a slight shape of a pair of nunchucks hanging out of someone's book shelf.

My attention is brought to my teeth; I'm grinding them together, so I stand up and shuffle around the front section. Farah's begun watering the plants next to the desk. She looks up and smiles. She's been awfully quiet this morning.

"You've been awfully quiet," I say to her.

She wipes the back of her hand over her lip. Licks her front two teeth. "I've been feeling funny—sick."

I come over and place my hand on her back.

"Yeah, I started to not be able to sleep. I was taking Imrest or whatever, but one night I started to swell up in my face and my dad drove me to the hospital. Everything seemed fine but since then I've been getting sharp pains up and down my arms, sometimes reaching up to my neck, to my head. It's only been a week. I'll see what happens."

I tell her she should really keep seeing someone. I tell her to lie on the bed face down.

Look with your hands; to use your hands as if they were eyes. This is what our teacher had said. I'm spreading Farah's shoulder blades with flat palms. "Oof," she says.

"How's that?"

"My right side. That's where it feels weird. And the neck."

"It's tight?"

She nods.

I spend some time in the middle of the upper back, using my thumbs. She lies still.

"Thanks, Leen," she mumbles into the fresh sheet.

Circling my thumbs to create the perimeter of an orb, pressing the fat of the skin into itself.

"That's good," she says.

Communicative clients—I without a doubt prefer them. The older clients seem to be the ones to do it best—they will at the very least, be unafraid to grunt if I've hit a tender spot. They respond to their personal pressure points appropriately.

Farah, with a bit of wit, says, "You're pretty good at this." As if filling the unusual silence.

I laugh and the laugh echoes. In fact, anything that moves in the entire space echoes in a way the previous studio hadn't. It creates profound silence when there is only some. And rather than the silence enacting as a sort of peaceful pause, it acts as a gaping, as if an ugly, uncontrolled inhale. The iffy longness.

I try to think of some benefits for this. Reverberation is a natural part of the hearing we do through our ears. Hearing a sound without its reverberation is more obviously manufactured. Reflections vacuumed into the ear. The hearing performed through the skin is the same way. With a larger space, the skin is not constricted in the claustrophobia a room sometimes produces. So the hearing our skin does in this space will be broader, the reflections from other objects hitting differently. Open to more energies.

I often can't stand silence. I want to press play on the Laraaji. But one should never interrupt a session. The humungous perception of touch being snatched away in a moment can diminish the entire purpose; a release of friction, release of the skin, abandonment, distrust.

Farah says, "For someone who only finished half a course . . . pretty good."

"Well, it's all natural touch." My hands are fairly muscular; it's one of the highlights of my anatomy. That, and the amount of force I'm able to drive to my fingers, to my wrists, having played a little bit of piano as a child.

Something a guest speaker had said during the course:

Disassociation with our bodies . . . being in virtual worlds, has given us the opportunity to function purely as the eyes and the mind, hands on our keyboards. It requires nothing else . . . Makes us question, why do we need to drag this body around underneath us? We feel our bodies take up unnecessary space, our shoulders we forget to move them, our legs tucked underneath us.

The science of sitting. Something my mother has always said: *Don't sit too much—sitting is the worst thing you can do with your body.* She says that the region in your brain responsible for forming new memories can wear thin from it. Hip-flexor muscles shorten, discs in the spine compress.

A brand that makes standing desks.

I research standing desks on my phone, waiting for our reopening to begin. I want to buy one for Farah, for the sake of her new soreness. But there's not much money to spare for it. I think about getting one out of my own pocket and then disregard the idea pretty quickly.

Farah is quietly wiping down the back benches now, where the basins are. I would stop her but the standing and movement will be good for her.

Now Jean Paul is at the door, knocking with his pale, skinny knuckles. He's brought doughnuts in a box and a bottle of the bitter orange diet pills. He winks, throws the bottle to me.

"Vegan," he says, opening the box. "The best kind. What did you learn in school? That protein should occupy a certain part of your diet." He waves a hand over the doughnuts like casting a spell. "Well, one of these doughnuts has as much protein as a substantial slice of chicken."

The comparison is odd. Today he looks lacking, his posture oppressed.

"Tired?"

"Long night."

Farah emerges and says hello. They've only met in passing before, in and out of the staff room.

"Leen has spoken of you—I've heard all good things," he says, giving her a modest hug.

You never question what he does with his hands; he always has them exactly where he wants them. Farah has been made nervous by him, by the sort of purity he presents. Her posture becomes shorter.

He tells me it's looking good in here. He takes a moment to walk around.

From across the room, he starts talking about how Huy's parents might not be giving him Vic's old managerial role. That they've been giving him fewer shifts due to his "erratic behavior."

"People are afraid to see change," he says. "They want to eject it from their lives immediately unless, of course, they are also taking alternate routes themselves. Only then do they recognize it, and it becomes a reassurance to their ego."

I'm trying to pay attention to Jean Paul, but a new advertisement concept has materialized in my mind. I realize I've been shy of astrology but it might be a way in.

I think of the way we leave our bodies constantly. Then justify our bodies by looking at horoscope, or at other bodies online or in print. I wonder how to achieve this sort of campaign, how to translate this.

Billboards are not for a business that champions privacy and interior reflection. Newspaper classifieds seem to be associated with promiscuities by the mainstream public. My mind lands on Lonnie Luther's filmmaking career. I think about the role that film has played in the propaganda of *privacy*.

Jean Paul is still talking even while Farah and I are trying to hang up the banner that says GRAND OPENING, which keeps dropping across the storefront window. We consider alternatives to Blu-Tack.

He's talking over our much quieter talking, now expounding on the Nietzsche principle of individualism: "He was much more interested in the productivity of great individuals. And emphasizes that solitude is important. I'm trying to take time for myself to make sure I am being as good of a leader as I can. A leader who doesn't know how to escape the group-mentality hype will be a disillusioned leader. Every society needs one of us. Needs select people that can *reinvent society's values and norms* by successfully constructing ourselves to be followed. That's something Aden could never do, probably not even *think* about."

I get Farah to run down to Parties 'R' Us! to get temporary stick-on hooks.

"The *Dionysian* cult . . . A throng of maenads. Being in the collective, being Dionysus in a cluster of people is associated with intoxication, but also with passion. Apollonian is the individual, is blissfully enlightened. There is order."

I lump all the Blu-Tack together.

"Jean Paul," I say. "Can you find me some scissors? Maybe if the banner's shorter it'll hang up properly."

He goes to Farah's desk, looks through the drawers. "Reinvention," he continues, "is found when you are alone. In those moments of the Resisting Acts, you are forced to be alone, inside your *eyes*, inside your *skin*, to feel the bone where your finger bends. Isolation of pain, like a *muscle* memory, my friend."

He's holding the scissors. I quickly take them off him and snip the ends of the banner. It looks uneven now. I try taking a bit more off the sides.

"Drunk off power," he says. "Power can overcome you when so many people look to you. Resisting Acts remind you of your body."

I believe it—he doesn't have to convince me. But for the time being, our banner is *too short*.

"If you can find a way to find balance in Apollo and Dionysus, it's apparent. If these people in great power don't have the ability, we provide it. A free service."

"Jean Paul," I say.

"I was once in school. There was a lecturer—"

"Jean *Paul*."

He crosses his arms, like he's holding his lungs in. "Yes."

31 **I'M SITTING IN THE BACK** seat of my 900 with the leftover wine from our reopening.

I always start to become what people think of me. That's what I realize, drinking this wine.

I'm waiting for Jean Paul and Huy. The pharmacy closes a little later than everything else most days, depending on whose prescriptions they have to gather. Vic would complain about this. Sometimes a customer has twenty individually prescribed medications to pick up and they come in at 4:45.

I'm listening to a podcast about Hume's philosophy of the imagination. The podcaster's name is Faye. She's talking about the difference between memory and imagination. That they are siblings. Memory functions in order, and imagination functions, possibly, without order. Both take from faint images of a tangible impression, thus forming intangible scenarios, which can be as close or distant to the original subject of the impression. Our brains are like photocopy machines.

Take the idea of a horse. We can separate the single horse's body from its legs, its head, its neck, its torso. Let's take the legs and put it on a bird . . . Hume thinks this is how we form God.

Jean Paul sends me a message saying that the operation is off. He's too tired to become his alter ego today. He's too bummed about the lack of promotion to do anything.

I crawl into the driver's seat, half-annoyed, mostly relieved. I call Lonnie Luther and we decide to meet at the bottle shop on his street. His bachelor pad is themed gray and white. On the fifth level of something like an eight-level, black apartment building on Bell Street. He collects plants, he keeps some in the bathroom, the tropical enduring ones. Some also decorate his bedroom. *His* places. The rest belongs to the guest.

I ask him if he entertains a lot. He says every second day. Keeps him writing screenplays during the mornings. Gym friends, filmmakers' club, reading groups. Keeps him out of the complex buying cuff links and cardholders, which he's addicted to.

"Adult acne," he says.

He's twenty-seven and was going through a period of stress when he was twenty-five, moved around a lot, did an IT degree. Shows me his jawline. Sensitive combination skin from the East Asian side of the family.

"No offense," he laughs.

He tells me his other side of the family is Samoan, that he missed with the gene pool by a mile.

"Though it might be the chlorine that's fucking up my skin."

He's swum since he was eight. He grew up doing competitive swimming. Moving around a lot has made him more competitive too, because he had to prove himself to his peers every time. As you grow older, he says, people get more difficult to please. People like fast swimmers. Especially if you look hot without a shirt on. He tells me he's lived in Liverpool, Singapore, Minneapolis, Sweden, Chicago, Cape Town. He was in New York last. Then he got transferred to the job here at Tech-Port. But what he's really wanted to do all his life is film.

He tells me I came at the perfect time tonight—he's planning to make boiled shrimp. He goes to the fridge and sculls about a quarter of a liter of Fuji water then puts it back in its spot. He swaps it for a green plastic bag full of damp-cold curled bodies.

He tells me he's felt good since the ear clean at Luis's.

"Don't do it at home on your own," I say. "It has to be very precise. Especially for you. The earwax is a lining for your ear and you need it. To get rid of too much might do more harm."

"Don't worry, I'm too scared I'll pierce my eardrum."

He says he's never thought about earwax before. He gets water in his ear, and it's disgusting when the wax and water mix, but he's accepted that the wax lives there, resides there. "But," he explains, "I've never thought about how the water can remove the lining in there."

"It's sebum, a body secretion of fat."

He crumples his face. "That's graphic."

"And your sweat, exterior dirt and skin cells."

"Delicious."

The shrimp is garlic-peppered. The smell takes up the whole flat. Everything thrown into his Precise Heat twenty-liter stockpot, bay leaves and lime floating at the top.

We stand at the stove and watch silently, commenting on the consistency when he mixes.

We talk a bit, just generally. I ask why he was willing to move out here, to Par Mars, and he says the salary at TechPort is pretty good. He was given this apartment. A lot of people in Par Mars were encouraged to move out here with free or cheaper accommodation. There are plenty of estates that've remained empty for years.

He asks me about myself. I tell him the usual, how I've moved between here and other places. He says my English is perfect. I tell him my father is a contractor. My mother is in the healing business and was a doctor beforehand. I miss them. I like the freedom, though. I don't have to marry to be free and that's not what I'd expected growing up. And now, I've done everything once before.

Collapse of silence. Just the sound of bubbles.

"So what was your big idea again?" Lonnie asks.

We're listening to WZRD.

"It's an advertising campaign."

"I'm listening."

"Having had my business for nearly six months now," I say, "I'm starting to realize how our values have changed over time. The emotional perception of touch is important. As our minds close inwards, the radius of our hands and fingers is limited to sex or violence . . . It's uncomfortable for our generation in our culture to touch or be touched without it being these extremes . . . We sit and feel things and we get up and wonder why we have these joints and muscle and fat lugging behind us. We discard them until something's wrong."

I'm not good at speaking until I get into the rhythm of it, and Lonnie Luther is, in fact, very happy to listen. I adjust my T-shirt, pulling the front bit forward and the back of the collar back.

"So, this is how you want to sell a massage?"

"Yeah."

He nods. "Well, we can easily make a video like that."

I tell him maybe in the future we can do massage ASMR videos.

"Yeah, maybe." A moment passes. Then, "How old is Huy? That guy's so smart."

I say I think he's nineteen, or twenty. I say I think that boy has too much to say.

Lonnie Luther coughs up a laugh. "I love that." He suggests that maybe Huy can help us with the video. That Huy seems to be full of ideas.

If philosophy is what sells, perhaps we can incorporate diagrams into my video, I say as we sit on the sofa and eat our food.

32 **SITTING OUT ON THE HOOD** of the car on this cooler morning, I look up and see big chunks of blond hair flying through the air. I think of Jean Paul.

I'm parked in the court of units that Luis's place sits inside of. For a long time no one drives past and then it hits quarter past seven and cars start emerging in a usual fashion. Children can be heard from the other units. Luis's roommate opens the front door, comes down the stairs and passes my 900. He gives me a nod. He walks to the bus stop. I'm tempted to offer him a ride. He continues down the road. He barely has any hair growing on his body, I recall.

I listen to an argument two people are having in the flat I'm parked in front of. There's a throwing of some kind of kitchen item, a silence, and then a huge yell.

There's a radius I can't step inside; I feel a great sense of unproductivity.

Someone leaves the flat. A woman in business attire. She looks at me with a certain distance, but also a sort of solidarity.

"Morning," she says, and gets in the car parked beside mine.

It's a Toyota.

She doesn't linger, just turns the engine on. Bass starts to bark from the vehicle. She doesn't look at me again, though I'm staring.

The sky is white and orange. Mist blanketing a tangerine orb.

Her car rolls onto the road, she overaccelerates at first. She adjusts, then is gone.

I wait for more noise again.

Schoolchildren, high-school-aged, are beginning to emerge. They have a twenty-minute bus ride to the other side of Par Mars to get to the closest public school. A girl takes a few attempts to light her cigarette on the way down the stairs—this happens as soon as her mother closes the door.

She stares at me blankly, with no intention. Continues down the driveway, onto the road, crossing it, continuing.

33 HUY AND LONNIE LUTHER HAVE started to kiss when greeting each other. Trying to remember when the threshold of physical reactionary habits changes between people confuses me. When did Luis start touching me on the waist when saying something to me? Has Jean Paul ever hugged me?

When Lonnie Luther slides into the back of the car, he shares a short but passionate kiss with Huy. Jean Paul will sit in the passenger seat beside me as usual. The sun is setting quickly. Does so when it's colder. Taking note of the *seasonal* reactionary habits of the sun and the wind makes my head hurt, and my feet too, from the numbness. The weather has been wavy.

Jean Paul just jumps in. He's got an over-the-shoulder bag with the equipment in it. Lonnie Luther winds the window down. Jean Paul's face has flared up. He somehow, despite not looking, has noticed me staring.

"My skin changes tone all the time. It's a blessing and a curse," he says.

He looks at each of us.

Lonnie Luther leans forward. "Show me, man."

Jean Paul twists without saying anything.

Lonnie Luther is telling Jean Paul how to keep his skin a good texture, mostly requiring him to stay out of the sun. Jean Paul keeps saying, "No, incorrect. I've already tried that. It's got nothing to do with the sun."

It occurs to me that Jean Paul wants his skin to be tanned. Lonnie Luther, in a moment, suggests getting a fake tan if it's about the tone of his skin getting paler, and Jean Paul becomes actively annoyed, quiet for the rest of the trip. I am almost positive that if you've just met Jean

Paul, the way he presents himself does not immediately indicate that he is obsessive over his appearance.

We're on our way to a weekly meeting. Lonnie Luther balances out the car. He comments on the radio, which is saying something about fertilizing the sea with iron. "Playing with natural ecosystems," says Lonnie Luther. "Surely that will end poorly."

With sulfur dioxide emissions in China . . . considering they are burning half the global amount of coal used in a year . . . could actually be useful in cooling down the earth . . . mimicking natural gases . . . taxpayers . . . a good day for the beach . . . but when [laughter], when I drove to . . .

Outside the community center before everyone arrives, smoking. Huy and Lonnie Luther are only concerned with one another and Jean Paul, you can see, is glaring about them, if not at them.

"Business should *never* mix with pleasure," Jean Paul whispers to me.

In a moment, he leans over to me again, holding up a canister of pills. "Snorting gives more of an instant shot of the drug's effects."

When we go into the meeting room, Mary from the supermarket is already there. Others come in about five minutes later. Two younger kids, the ones who work in the arts and craft store with Rick, come in for the first time. The rest of the seven here are from the big franchises of the complex.

The thing that differentiates Jean Paul's community group from Aden's is that every week the curriculum seems to change. I wonder whether this is what keeps it marketable.

Jean Paul does this thing where he collages what he needs from texts and films and speeches without sharing the entire context.

Jean Paul first introduces the two new members from the art store, then introduces us all in return as a neighborhood Watch committee.

He then launches into a history of the neighborhood Watch system. Participation in the Watch system has existed from as early as the

Prophet Ezekiel. The duty of the Watchman to blow the horn and sound the alarm in protection of his neighbors—this sort of protection has been prioritized within the last century. Speaking about neighborhood movement and safety, Jean Paul reads an observation by Jane Jacobs in *The Death and Life of Great American Cities: Neighborhoods can absorb a large number of dwellers...But if and when the neighborhood finally becomes them, they will gradually find the streets less secure, they will be vaguely mystified about it, and if things get bad enough they will drift away to another neighborhood which is mysteriously safer.*

This reminds me of Vic's incident. This suburb, supposedly, has become one of the safer ones, costing more to live in now than it did ten years ago. A place where neither Vic nor I had grown up. Why, then, was he not as safe as he was promised he would be?

Jean Paul segues into talking about the "capitalist centrum" within the neighborhood. What Topic Heights or the Galleria is to Par Mars, and how this defines the reputation of the suburb and the kinds of people that might be congregated. The decline of its shopping complex, for example, may explain a shift in the suburban atmosphere.

Jean Paul has a way of speaking like he is speaking diagrams. Verbalizing arrows and emitting his words along vertical lines as blueprint.

I imagine the way a stranger would walk through Topic Heights if they'd first been to the Beverly Center. Or Westfield. The Saturday Grove complex.

The Topic Heights complex has not been renovated since the nineties. There are no self-serve machines, the deli doesn't look plush. It is not going for the colonial, rustic atmosphere. It is stuck somewhere in between.

And Jean Paul is right: there is a vast disgruntlement. There is no compassion or care for its workers. The board can't afford it. Perhaps not only this—it *will not* afford it.

"If Topic Heights is not changing, my dear friends, which is the responsibility of those higher in power, then the customers are not changing. They come every day feeling as if they are becoming closer to us. Not in a positive way, *people*. But in a dysfunctional-marriage way. They consume mindlessly, treat us like machines. And guess what, my friends, our managers are the ones to engineer these situations, allowing us to be used as cogs and gears."

I realize I must be the only manager in the room. I sweat. I think about Farah, who is not disgruntled, but could become so. Perhaps what Jean Paul calls a *cog* or a *gear* is a term he's using to describe the attitude of big franchises. I wonder if I could tell the difference anyway.

By the end of Jean Paul's hour-and-a-half-long speech, there is a great sense of purpose cached in our silences.

Referring to the notes on his phone, Jean Paul says, "We are living in a time where it is not enough to limit the Watch system to the street-by-street communities. Our neighbors are defined by our consumer hubs. With mass production comes mass surveillance. We are engineers simply facilitating a prompt to change. I would like to ask for a few volunteers to run a project that Mary"—he directs his arm out to Mary, who produces a timid wave—"has so kindly helped me with. At the moment, we've only performed one, but we will be planting IP cameras. The cameras record footage twenty-four hours a day, seven days a week. And you can find a direct link for that footage on our forum. This ensures that as a Watch system, we are more efficient. This technique not only accounts for what people do in the public eye, but also what people do when they are not performing for customers, employees. This is what says the most about them. We will need two more volunteers along with Mary, Lonnie, and me to get this up and running."

People leave, feeling a sense of resolve transferred to them by the talkative mood of Jean Paul. It might worry me that his mouth moves before his brain.

On the drive home, I think about engineering someone else's drought, then watching it from afar and saying I can't do anything about it.

I think about wiring, an image of a mushroom cloud in my head again, and footage I've seen of the test on the Marshall Islands, creating a ring like Saturn. I take a bitter orange, synephrine, and feel a headache spawning, expanding, splaying from the center of my head.

When I park downstairs at Luis's, I search for *The Death and Life of Great American Cities*, the Jane Jacobs. I reserve it at the local library to pick up the next day after work.

Luis is home and has made creamy pasta. We hear arguments between children next door. Downstairs there are people playing basketball. We hear the wheeze of a slightly flat ball against concrete. We eat together on the couch waiting for a home renovation show to come on, only expressing ourselves toward the television. There is no intimacy. He's in a quiet mood. It's just that kind of weather.

34 **I HAVE NEVER BEEN MUCH** in the mood for romance unless I'm reading about it. Whenever love has come to me, it's always seemed immoderate, one-sided. It has always been my worst fear, to return home to an anticipative—and, all the more, void—romantic atmosphere. It makes me pick on people.

It's not so much that the energy between Luis and me has depleted; it is more that our relationship status does not accommodate personal exhaustion, hasn't figured its way around it yet. So inevitably, as I often do when I feel this genre of exhaustion, I throw myself into analysis of some other obsession.

It's unimaginable the things you are able to do with a car: I'm driving toward the library after work the next day, and I plan to stay there until it closes at eight. It's a whole other feeling, having hours to access new ideas, new knowledge, where bodies of words and images are building blocks to a new sort of power—whether or not it ends up being productive.

I park out the front of the library, find myself craving to smoke with Vic and Doms. One time a summer ago, by the pool eating imported, non-native fruit Vic had ordered off the internet, grinding buds in a wooden bowl. New experiences. Perhaps it wasn't so much the environment or what we had been participating in; it was more the encouragement of brain plasticity. The ability to reshape our anxieties around scenarios, unlived.

The sun is setting now; I watch from the side mirrors. Slight wind coming through the mandatory palm trees, replanted in the squares of nature strip in this parking lot. Children jumping down from the curbs, their parents carrying school backpacks. I wonder if I had missed anything growing up away from here. Wonder if the circular design of Par Mars allowed for the parent to be closer to the child. I think about the four years my mother spent here with me. Until she had to sell the car, she'd pick me up on time after school everyday, taking us to get extra groceries. I had not grown up long enough in the Territories to have seen much of it, but in primary school the ones who would pick the children up were not usually the parents, particularly among the white kids. They were what was commonly referred to in the city as "domestic helpers," the ones who sat outside on Sundays. I watched them. It had been my popo, my mother's mother, who picked me up, and we'd take the bus. Often I have dreams of those bus rides. Competing for the front seat of the second deck, purple, her lined hands. She would gently graze the back of my head, my neck, massaging tense muscle.

A kid knocks on my back window and I jolt. The parent walks by, shuffles them along, muffled sounds of them scolding the child in a humorous way. My breath is knotty. I press the back of my skull into the headrest, pull my arms out to touch the steering wheel.

The sun is cutting the sky into many quarters. And I realize I don't comprehend my anxiety until I'm alone, in this car.

I step outside and let the last bit of warmth sober me.

Casual public trust, says Jane Jacobs.

I suppose then that the metropolitan city associates its footpaths with "errands," and with errands comes purpose. A casual public trust which allows the assumption that all people walking on footpaths have an unsuspicious purpose. Too distracted by an errand to commit any damage or vandalism to routine.

Jane Jacobs: *All of it metered by the person concerned and not thrust upon him by anyone, is a feeling for the public identity of people, a web of public respect...*

Jane Jacobs goes on to talk about the presence and absence of public trust. In the suburbs, there are clear distinctions. There's a code to it. Because no one has an errand to run which they can't drive to. What are you without a dog, a pram, or your running clothes on. What are you listening to if you don't have earphones in.

Garden privilege.

Vic has talked about a man who's followed him down the street after he walked by his house, taunting him and making him small, as if attempting to make him aggressive back.

Doms often disengages from conversations like these. For her, it's a different kind of "walking-down-the-street"; it was a different kind of conversation, a different visual cue. She seems fixated on her particular experience. Still, I understand everybody has a different way of walking-down-the-street, but more often than not, it is always visual code that is attached to "public trust."

A school student has come to sit beside me. Chomping rice crackers gaudily. I put my earphones in. The student is getting cracker everywhere and somehow I can still hear the crunching.

Window privacy is the easiest commodity in the world to get. You pull down the shades or adjust the blinds.

Said Jane Jacobs. I take the book home after the first row of rice crackers is eaten. I'm back at Luis's a bit after seven, after having stalled at the chicken shop, where I bought a bucket of potato mash to eat in the car. The chef who was simultaneously cooking and manning the register had winked at me and encouraged me breathily to return as soon as possible. Parked out the front, listening to the radio. They're talking about Betty White.

The wind has increased, the sparse spread of trees along the street—they gush. I sit on the staircase leading up to Luis's flat. The lights in the other units are all on, noises of family dinners, pans, cutlery, kids playing, television frequencies.

Eventually I knock.

Luis opens the door, the smell of cooking food flushing into my face, an onion aroma. He grins, a slight look of guilt.

"Missed you," he says, pulling me into his chest.

When Luis sees me reading on the couch, he stops and tilts the book from behind to see its cover.

"Interesting," he says, and continues in the kitchen. "I'll lend you a book after you finish this one. We can swap. I wanna show you this book. It talks about Cicero and the idea of like, property accumulation. You'd like it."

Jane Jacobs said: *You can't make people use streets they have no reason to use. You can't make people watch streets they do not want to watch.*

Luis is preparing food that smells like tomato base for tomorrow. He never does this. It feels like a performance. Unafraid of the noise his tools make: the chopping is loud and the clanging of the pan lid abrasive.

The basic prerequisite for such surveillance is a substantial quantity of stores and other public places sprinkled along the footpaths of a district; enterprises and public places that are used by evening and night must be among them especially.

Jacobs says that this gives residents and visitors concrete reasons to use the footpaths they're using.

I think about the Topic Heights shopping complex, hoarding all the food places, storefronts, and entertainment hubs, which could've been scattered out among the houses and estates. We could've had neighborhoods with lights and shopkeeper surveillance.

Peggy and her husband own the idea of convenience and we've all bought into it.

I tap the book with my short nails, which I cut to the cuticle every few days so there is no potential to scratch a client.

Luis makes noise, slamming a pot down onto the stovetop.

"You're being so loud," I suggest.

He says sorry and pours ingredients into the pot. I look at him for a moment. He doesn't look up.

"How was your day?" I ask him.

He says he was just working at K.A.G. for the regular hours. But there was word of mouth he'd be the one promoted to the vacant managerial position. It's been two months now without Berta with an even more useless sub-in, and with Luis as the model employee. He adds that his sudden excellent workmanship is probably mostly out of guilt, some anxiety.

A few days ago the store received samples of kitchenware and storage items the favored members of the team are supposed to test and report back on. He tilts his head over to the pot boiling on the stove.

"That's what I'm doing. Still working." He gives a laugh, his face softens. "If all's good and they think it's worth it, they want to expand the selection in our store. They're thinking of buying out the the homewares and gift store next door. Build out."

I realize I'm wearing a beige K.A.G. shirt.

Luis is humblebragging. "K.A.G.'s is doing really well. Since Berta disappeared, everyone's been really focused. Our customer base is diversifying. I guess everything you talk about with *energy*, it's actually true. Good energy brings good energy."

"I'm glad."

I tell this to Jean Paul on the phone later, leaning on the hood of my 900. "Do we know where Berta is right now?" I ask him. "I heard the store is doing really well. All the employees feel like they're on an equal level now. I feel like it's worked, everyone's really satisfied."

Jean Paul sighs, "I don't know where she is." I sense a strain in his voice. Whenever anyone mentions K.A.G. or Berta, there is always a sharp wheeziness in the way Jean Paul speaks about it, how he diverges from it almost immediately.

He says, "We should probably meet up. Do you have time tonight? Just you, me, and Huy."

Back inside, Luis is preparing a blunt, sprinkling some tobacco.

"I didn't know you smoked," I say.

He looks up. "Big day. Big things happening."

"That's a shame. I'm about to go meet a friend."

He comes and grabs me tenderly, as I stuff my wallet into my jacket pocket.

"There's a lot you still don't know," he muffles into my jacket.

I smile. He kisses me on the forehead, says goodbye.

I slip out the door and drive to Jean Paul's. Cool air chasing in.

We're sitting in Huy's bedroom, Jean Paul and I on the floor and Huy at his desk finishing an assignment. Huy tells us he has plans later tonight so he's just copying and pasting chunks of text from different documents now. Only the lamp is on. My eyes are hanging. I rub my oily eyelids, check the time and it's nearly ten. "Plans?"

Luis has texted a few times. *Hey let me know that you got there? . . . Which friend's house?*

Jean Paul is discussing the great advantage it is to have Mary on the team. She has done a bit of work with IP cameras in the jobs she had before. She is unassuming and will be able to install them easily without being noticed.

"No one ever checks up on what someone like her is doing."

Huy with his head down and says, as if frustrated by us, "Yeah, so Leen, the camera transmits the footage over to an IP address accessible on a general web browser if you have the log-in details for the camera. The first one she fixed was the one at Rick's two weeks ago. You remember Rick from the art store? Just a tiny outdoor one with awful quality, looking straight into his bedroom window."

Jean Paul is nodding, yes, yes. Waiting for Huy to finish speaking. "Yeah, we're trying to figure out what his home situation looks like, decipher whether he has children or a partner. He's quite a private man, it seems. Doesn't seem to be anybody else with him . . . Mary's done a fantastic job. She's quite precise with her placement. Precision is important. We need someone who's precise. She's got a real talent for it."

"So Jean Paul," Huy says hastily. Huy sort of hates it when Jean Paul compliments others, because he rarely compliments either of us. Huy presents his laptop to me and says, "What do you think our next thing with Rick will be—based on what we've got so far?"

On the laptop I see the lagging footage of Rick pacing around his bedroom. In the corner it says the time. He jumps through the space, as if glitching through it.

"Okay. Outcome of the two Resisting Acts we did with Rick. First was the . . . *Chinese water torture* and then the theft. We haven't heard of any changes in his workplace as of yet."

"Hold on," I say. "When did you do the second one?"

Jean Paul looks at Huy.

"We did it . . . hmm . . . last week? Before the meeting, a day before the meeting," Huy says without looking up.

"Why didn't you tell me?"

"*Incorrect.* We told you in the private group thread."

"No. No one's talked in the private group thread for ages."

Jean Paul looks at the back of Huy's head.

"Oh." Huy turns his head quickly. "Sorry, Leen. We've probably just been messaging only each other by accident."

35 **WE HAVE A LOT OF** customers today. Oren is returning, Sarah the face-tatt woman, and Kerry the banker.

First is Sarah. When she comes in, she says to Farah, "Wow, great lighting. Very feng shui. Very calming." Then, after a moment, "You know this place was once a hairdresser's."

Farah is probably smiling politely.

I come around the divider and Farah is smiling with extreme politeness, her lips almost rounding into one of those unprompted, professional chuckles. Our bodies have learned the physical criteria of running a successful business.

I take Sarah to a massage table in the back. Though we have the dividers, I worry it is not enough to make the client feel comfortable. A divider will never be anything to a solid wall.

We can hear Farah shuffling forms in the front. This space is so open, reflective. I try to maintain focus.

I'm doing an ear clean. Laraaji playing, the diffuser running.

Farah typing lots.

After I finish, I ask Sarah whether she'd also like a massage today.

"How much more is that?" she asks.

"Fifty, but on top of the ear clean, only thirty-five."

She says yes to the offer, says she can't resist a good deal, and we spend another forty minutes focused on her shoulders. Her shoulders are not becoming loose.

Farah's typing is the soundtrack the entire time, despite having the Laraaji on. She's typing so fast. Perhaps this is the source of unconscious stress in Sarah. I turn the Laraaji up, "Sun Gong", and press my hands in deeper.

After Sarah leaves, I massage my own wrists and refresh the forum obsessively, waiting for Oren. I think about engineering someone else's pain. I read a forum post by Mary, who has written about how the first instance of surveillance video was in Nazi Germany. They used it to observe how a V-2 missile struck. IBM had sold it. Similarly, wrote Mary, IBM developed police prediction and area-specific policing devices, which isolate suburbs with crime rate. The crime rate does not differentiate police patrol versus police-requested intervention. She writes her personal thoughts on this. She believes that sometimes you can "turn a bad thing into a good thing". I frown in thought. I scratch under my nose.

I check our private group chat and refresh a few times.

After Oren's appointment I wash my hands in one of the basins at the back. I've been thinking about putting hair scrubs on the menu as well.

Hair scrubs, ear cleans, massages.

Absolving toxic and negative energy, all bacteria, all negatively associated proteins. Self-care, self-love. New marketing strategies.

"Farah," I say.

She looks up from her furious typing.

"What are you typing up?"

She minimizes something on her screen and I see it recoil into the Microsoft icon.

"Open it, please. Is it a new form, a letter to a client?"

"Oh, don't worry."

"Open it, Farah." I cross my arms and hover behind her shoulder.

She opens it. I feel the roll of her eyes, although I am too afraid to look at her face.

The document says it has thirty thousand words in it. I scroll through it, back up to the top, and realize Farah's been writing a novel. Thirty thousand words with separated chapters—she must have been writing it since the beginning, when we first began the business.

I inhale. Trying not to say anything horrible, trying not to pick on her. My hypothalamus.

"This is great," I say.

She's blushing. She looks as though she's about to burst into tears, an alarm clock, inhaling to explode. Her face embodying the same tension in Sarah's spine, transferred from her to me.

I calm my own breath. She closes the document as soon as I take my hand from the mouse.

I come back around to face her. "But—the typing is very loud, Farah. And you can hear everything in this space. The old place, I understand. But we're sharing one room now, one flow of energy. There are no boundaries. We need to share intention because of that."

She doesn't look me in the eyes. It's still for a moment.

"You probably can't write the story while I have a client. It's distracting. Sorry."

She seems to become infuriated all of a sudden. I think it's when I used the word *story* or maybe the way I said the *sorry*.

"Okay," she says, but is boiling with anger.

I return to the back area and sit on one of the stools, just to be somewhere else. We both know that neither of us is doing anything except waiting for our customers. The discomfort, the resentment, is unequivocal. And worse because there are no walls.

I don't hear Farah typing for the rest of the day. She isn't typing when Kerry from the bank comes in and decides to enjoy both a massage and an ear clean.

I finish the ear clean and empty the tray of Kerry's ear particles into the bin at the back. She is standing right behind me, looking at the hair-washing basins.

"Are you washing hair now? Head massages?"

I turn to her. She's looking a bit sheepish.

"Oh, I—"

"I mean, you don't have to today. I just thought I need a hair wash, and that'd be nice, the massage."

I'm staring. I know, because she is only getting more sheepish.

She's picking at the bottom of her fitted brown blazer.

"I can," I tell her. "But it won't exactly be a hair wash. I'll need to use oil."

"That's okay. I heard that's good for the hair, isn't it?"

She sits herself in the black plush chair. I put a towel around her shoulders from the front, to cover her chest. She rests her head back onto the silicone cushion. I realize in that moment I haven't had a chance to clean the inside of the basin, but say nothing. I pull all her hair back. It's thinning, blond. Drooping a little. She's dyed it a few times, bleached it too. Dust comes up as I let her hair splay out into the basin.

I quickly run the water. It's cold at first, but turns warm within a few seconds. I run my fingers through the stream and it unbinds with my palms. Then I turn the dial off.

I go to one of the massage areas and rummage around for the bottle of rosemary oil. I find it in a little brown tester bottle from iHerb. Holding it, I recall the big shipping order I did a few months ago for the studio.

In business, I use things sparingly and exasperatedly, unlike in everyday life. And I use the simpler, cheaper oils for massages. I'm conscious of the droplets in my palm. Note that the benefit is not of the substance, but of the way I use it. I connect with my hands and the barrier of oil between my skin and their skin. Realize the thing they need most is the action: to be touched and to be relaxed into a coma of diversion from their phones, their cars, their businesses.

Kerry has her eyes closed, her hands in her lap, waiting.

I press the gum of the dropper between my fingers, two drops into my palm, and rub through her hair.

The leftover water laps around the mop of thin, blond fibers.

I make a fist around the ends and squeeze in the oil to be absorbed. I take one more drop of the rosemary oil and apply it to my fingertips. My nails follow the parting of her hair. I pull it all back into a tail. I do this a few times and she murmurs. She smiles in a sort of sleep. As if she has left her head, her body to me, has disappeared for a bit.

The appointments have gone well, three additional walk-ins. We close at five, feeling as though it's been successful. Farah is not speaking to me.

I ask if she'd like to come with me to Lonnie Luther's to film our campaign video. I make sure to say *our* campaign video—this technique of "inclusion" is one I've learned from Jean Paul.

I say maybe she can help with the lighting. She agrees, but doesn't speak during the entire ten-minute car ride to Lonnie Luther's, just looks at her phone. On the radio there is something about fires eating up suburbs in the north. I turn it up and she slightly nods her head up. *Is this an act of God . . . there's a mysterious intensity to it . . . now a state of emergency.* I parallel park on the street.

We end up filming the video in three takes, just me speaking to the camera.

"One of them will be good," assures Lonnie Luther, unscrewing his camera off the tripod.

We're relaxing now, sitting at Lonnie's dining table, drinking a new bottle of wine. Ordering some Turkish food from the family-run store at the bottom of the apartment complex. Lonnie Luther's explaining how he's superstitious—adamant about having only a few takes, how it comes across as more natural and natural equals professional these days.

People can feel the authenticity when they watch it. Especially if you're selling something that could be considered a placebo.

"Although," he says, looking at the playback, "you should try putting on some lipstick."

Silence.

He's watching the camera monitor without any sound on. His wine-glass in the other hand. "You ever considered acting?" he says.

"Not since I was thirteen."

"How old're you now, Leen?"

"Twenty-four."

"You look twenty."

"It's just my hair. When it's short, you can see how round my face is."

"Yeah, God. You *do* look young," Lonnie Luther affirms.

Farah says something finally, "We all do. We're all some kind of Asian."

"Mmm, true," says Lonnie Luther. "Farah, you're right."

I read once: high power distance is individualism. Stating some-body's name with confidence is high power. It's something Lonnie Luther does extremely well, in a way that is both endearing and socially intimidating at once, indicating that he has some sort of untouchable, sincere confidence.

In the 900 on the way home, Farah seems even angrier than before. I drop her off and she smiles politely, in the same manner she performs toward our clients. "Thank you."

From Farah's house I drive down the highway and stop to buy a box of hot chips with chili mayo on the side. I eat it in the 900, parked a few meters away from the food truck.

When I get home, Luis is already in bed. Without changing, I fall into the soft mattress and he rolls over to wrap his arms around me.

"No job tonight?" I ask, surprised. Curling my thighs into my chest, squeezing.

"No. I didn't tell you?" He yawns. "I've put that on hold. And guess what, I got the manager position."

I turn to face him. "*See*, hard work pays off."

"Thank you for being here," he says.

He kisses me softly, on my cheeks and then under my chin. Then wraps his legs around me and obsesses over my neck and hair.

36 IN THE MORNING WE'RE NAKED, quickly moving around his room. Blue room, white sunlight overcast, sterilizing the natural curvature of our nude forms. Making us flesh. Goose bumps on my leg. I'm pulling my black suit pants on over it, and Luis is slipping on his beige shirt. He's clipping on a new badge that says: LUIS, GENERAL MANAGER. He says they got his name right this time but it hits different because of the circumstances. I notice there are Chinese characters on it too.

商店经理

"Since when did K.A.G. start using Chinese text?"

"Maybe a few weeks ago. The Chinese here are a huge market. They recognized K.A.G. from overseas."

I'm driving us both into work, which is a rare occasion. Usually Luis takes the bus in right before lunchtime for his five-hour shift until he closes up. Now that he's been promoted he must arrive before everyone else and leave after everyone else at the end of the day.

We talk about the remarkable pay raise.

"Now *this* . . . is a salary," he says.

There's discussion too about accommodation services, which is something they've done in more successful franchises across the world, in larger cities. In the last two months since Berta's disappearance, the forecasting of the Par Mars franchise has been exponentially positive. In fact, it is what has been equalizing the count of shoppers between Topic Heights and the Galleria.

Getting a house would be great, he says. He can't take himself seriously because he hates his current apartment. The drive is long. There are too many negative associations with the house. He and Dmitri have been growing apart. It's a block full of people arguing. He hates loud arguing; it annoys him.

"Sometimes it's better to hear the arguing rather than have thicker walls conceal it," I say. "When you can hear all the arguing, at least you see the full range of people's capacities. In a concealed environment, with more privacy, people are more likely to have scarier extents, because they get away with more too."

Luis considers this. "You're very smart," he says, running his fingers through my moppy hair.

He kisses me when I drop him off at the automatic doors. I turn up the radio and make my way up the ramp to the staff parking lot.

A conference has been held . . . discussing the ban of plastic bagging . . . Another report has been made last night of an attempted burglary in Par Mars, an area surrounding the Glenvale Estate . . . one accident on the 96 . . . however many . . . most likely . . .

Before going into the studio I decide to pick up some bitter orange pills from the pharmacy. The new manager is pacing the aisles. Jean Paul is watching him from behind the pharmacy desk when I walk in.

"So antisocial," he whispers scathingly. "He barely says hi in the morning."

Jean Paul believes he didn't get the managerial position due to workplace gossip, assumes one of the sales assistants badmouthed him to Huy's parents, which he remarked only made *their* jobs harder anyway. "After all, it wasn't a very considerate or sustainable thing to do—to force them to search for somebody completely new."

Jean Paul stares at the new manager a moment too long, as if he hasn't realized his own fixation. Then he disappears to the back and retrieves the bottle of bitter orange for me.

The new manager calls from the aisle, "Jean, could you also grab another box of the hundred-gram heel balms, the green brand?"

Jean Paul reappears to make a face at me. "So where is Vic these days?"

"He's not doing casual?"

"He's been in . . . *once* in the last two weeks. Anyway, Leen, I'll see you later? No pressure. Mary can drive."

In the public restroom, I perform facial exercises, massaging the bloat under my eyes. If I am honest, I don't mind so much that Jean Paul and Huy are relying less and less on me, doing the Resisting Acts without me. I feel happy that Mary is included in some capacity too. She's seemed lighter in spirit as a result.

When I pass her at the supermarket, I am never sure if it's just that she refuses to acknowledge me because she genuinely doesn't remember who I am, or whether we have somehow become bound in a secretive pact, an agreement that in our uniforms we are merely what our customers expect us to be: *at work*, in our separate vehicles, with our separate tasks. In some ways, I consider Mary and I to be very similar. The two of us are lucky that we are not strictly attached to any lawful, marital sort of relationship. We are both no longer convinced by the ecclesiastical communities and the amount of performance they often involve. Though she is spiritual, she expressed in one of her forum posts that she could not stand her local church community anymore, who have treated her with a cruel derisiveness since her divorce.

Yet, the two of us, we still search for that same stability; a constant beyond physical interconnectedness.

VIOLENCE

RICK

THEY DRUG HIM FIRST. "UGH, poor friend," he hears. His hands are tied down so he can't move them, and he can't sit up. "Disgusting, man," says another voice.

They have Rick snort something, threatening him with some kind of heavy, unidentified *thing*, holding it to his head. He obeys and does so without struggle because he is a cocaine enthusiast too. *Fucking coke-head*, his wife had labeled him. This was her immediate attack, the kind of mockery she would use leading up to their divorce. She had always been unpleasant to listen to, even before her crassness towards the end of it. Her voice was so tedious even when they were fucking.

They put him in a vehicle and he begins punching the scrawny one wherever he can. He does this a few times before his own body melts into itself and he feels an awesome, almost comforting *sleepiness*. He falls unconscious. There were four of them that lugged him into this car, if he could count the feeling of hands against him.

He is having an out-of-body experience. He sees himself in the car, but he can't see where the car is heading. In fact, the drive feels forever. He's coming in and out. His body is strong against these kinds of substances; it is used to it and has developed a hard shell for them.

A male voice: *I like Hong Kong. I've been there once.*

Yeah, so she lives and works in Kowloon. You know Kowloon?

A low female voice.

Is that the same thing?

Do Westerners like Hong Kong because they don't feel excluded from it? says the female voice.

Pfft. Of course. *Liberal* types. Rick has thoughts fluctuating in black. He can't bring himself to care right now. He laughs. Liberal types. He feels a slap on his face. Perhaps his own hand. He went to Hong Kong once before on a working holiday, not his own—his ex-wife had been the one attending a large workshop for her business and he had joined her. One night when she had been working late, he had gone to a bar across from a 7-Eleven. He danced on a woman's lap before she pushed him off. A memory of his mother making bread and an image from high school: him eating lunch with his friend. Lovely beach scenery, the holiday with his kid, before his kid hit him. His friend, Allen, driving a little truck and picking him up in it. They're punching a scrawny guy from their lecture behind the truck. With his baseball cap on. His friend pissing on him. The truck is shrinking. They spray the truck later with a hose. He thinks about titty fucking.

When he wakes he's coughing up blood and his phone is gone. The trees are emerald green; the sky gray. There's a chill. Feels like London weather. Leaves crunching underneath him. His arm starts to gain feeling again, gaining the bruising and stinging, slicing through his nerves. Sharp pain in his shoulder. Big bruise in his weak stomach. Circular white waves. He passes out to the sound of several cars driving down the highway nearby, though he can't perceive.

THE GROWTH

37 **WHEN I AM SITTING WITH** my legs stretched out in front of me, I am confident. I sit this way in the staff room. And Jean Paul is heating up a saved half-eaten burrito. There's a smell coming from the fridge. It's about four in the afternoon. I have a wig in my bag.

The day had twelve clients and I am exhausted, my neck beginning to coil, the back of my head falling behind me. I roll my shoulders twice every hour and they return to a clicking each time.

In the last month, the daily average of clients has increased to ten. The video had gotten some good reception in the end. And we paid for it to be sponsored locally, burrowing it into an algorithm. We even had somebody come in from a different state because of it. All you need is one video in this life and from there you can rely on word of mouth and a newfound confidence, a newfound self-worth.

I small-talk in a way that seems like big talk, all the way through the day until night. Then at night I am quietly driving, with no opinion and no apparent agenda.

I'm becoming the product of this last month, a month that has disappeared so quickly under my feet. I've begun texting my mother instead of calling her, I've stopped reading the forum posts intently, only skimming them.

But miraculously, the relationship between Farah and me has pacified to a much less deliberate bitterness. We're both working hard to keep our clients. However, their faces are beginning to blur for the both of us. Farah is forgetting names of loyal customers and I find that I'm forgetting the section of body that needs to be worked on between each individual.

Most people, they tend to have a sickness between the shoulder blades, how they hold their upper back. It's the way we are postured when we work at desks, or drive in cars or sleep on mattresses. And so it is always safe to find the little tangles that've formed there, they will respond almost immediately.

Lately, Jean Paul has been letting the shadow of a beard begin to take shape around his long mouth. He is smiling more infrequently and his mannerisms have begun to take after a dust bird, or a crow. He's been watching Huy with a blank stare, seemingly upset that he is becoming busier, that aside from the assignments and lectures, he is spending the majority of his time with Lonnie Luther.

Leisurely. Jean Paul doesn't seem to believe in leisure. He's been strongly advising against it, in recent forum posts. If it does not involve *work*—or "recompensing," as he's been labeling it—or compassionate care for a dependent, then it is never as urgent as our sole mission.

Mary had come over to me one meeting, a few days after we had driven Rick out. It was the week Huy and Lonnie Luther took a break. Mary told me she'd become quite close with Lonnie Luther, the camera guy, but is he *a homosexual*? She whispered, "I think he is dating Huy." See, she could see herself becoming good friends with Huy too, he seems to have quite a buzzing, youthful energy, but she is wondering whether they are homosexuals. "Not that I have a problem," she'd said, tightening her lips. "They sure do spend a lot of time together, though. Probably not good for the relationship."

Mary has been the one dealing with outreach. If somebody is thinking of leaving—which has happened once or twice now—she will send them gentle but constant messages asking why they aren't contributing to forum threads, where they were this week, whether they need one-on-one time with her to discuss their priorities and situation.

See, after the Resistance Act with Rick, Jean Paul has prioritized the recruitment of new members and the unwavering allegiance of current members.

Rick has not been heard of since that night, and I wonder if Jean Paul wants to keep as many people around as possible in order to keep his paranoia subsided. That night, when Rick had faded into his artificial sleep, his body lying among the drying leaves, Jean Paul knelt down and began to beat the inside of his stomach in. Then he began to weep, clobbering a heavy fist into this sallow art-store manager, who still appeared smug even when unconscious. And Jean Paul continued to punch him until Huy pulled him off. Jean Paul kept weeping for a moment too long.

After that week, I had become more and more useless. I'd missed a period, was experiencing regular migraines, and felt nauseous to the point of having to take a pregnancy test. And I had begun to wear this blond hair. Nobody knew why. Members of the Watch group assumed it was for the sake of anonymity, but it was mostly because my hair had begun falling out in large clumps. Something my mother suffered from the first time we moved away from the Territories.

While I was unwell, Jean Paul asked for more drivers to step forward. He seemed mostly afraid of losing that sense of legitimacy, and the luxury it was: to always have somebody at his disposal. That week, despite his callout for replacement drivers, he was sending me long messages about how valuable he thought I was, how unique my driving is, how wonderful I am to him.

The driving is something that makes me happy. When I'm driving in my 900, I'm just another person going from one place to another, allowing my hands to move without me. Just formulating limbo. Jean Paul calls attention to the way I create a space of limbo, as if it is an art. My 900 and the way I drive it—I am an example to follow, Jean Paul reminds me. I am the idea and my baby 900, the ideal.

I'm driving us to our meeting in the underground level of St. Bernard's Church. This is where the meetings have been relocated. There were some issues with the community center. They expressed feeling "slightly uncomfortable" about us, that we weren't being entirely clear about our objectives. Yes, we were a neighborhood watch group, but there was a lot of yelling for a community group, and sometimes people came out looking distressed or as if they had just been crying. We were also growing rapidly in size: now nearly twenty of us. It was getting too much, so the church, who were charitable about it, became our next option.

One thing Jean Paul despises, though, is any association with religion. This is not religion; this is community outreach.

You enter through the door behind the altar, which takes you down a narrow set of stairs. The browning carpet smells like grains and then the dark wood smells like tree.

Jean Paul is standing at the lectern, chewing on the apple seeds of his leftover core. I notice the one light in the room hitting the chains on his teeth.

Mary pulls a plastic chair to sit down beside me.

"Evening," she says. "My dear, how is the . . ." She points to her own head of maroon hair.

I peel off the blond wig to show her for a moment.

"I'm rubbing and massaging it a lot. But I bought a new shampoo. I think the K.A.G. one was too drying. It wasn't working so well."

"Oh, that one works perfectly for me, that one. But, yes, might be too drying for some." She crosses one leg over the other.

Two more members appear at the bottom of the stairs. They go over and share banter with Jean Paul. Then they grab a plastic chair from the stack and Jean Paul's face resolves into its usual impassiveness. He looks down to his iPad sitting on the lectern. Scratches his teeth.

38 **K.A.G. HAS STARTED SELLING BED** frames and bedding. Only two models of the bed frames, but an entire range of bedding and quilts. Comfortable, impossible-to-resist fabrics. The waffle duvet, the cream chunky-knit throw, ultra-soft jersey stem fibre.

Luis has brought some new covers home tonight. He never tells me whether they're paid for, whether he's testing and writing notes on them, or whether he's just plucked them off the shelf and taken them home for free. Our new K.A.G. Oak Floating Bed is the only thing properly set up in the new house right now, so naturally he's focused on dressing that. He's the main dresser at K.A.G.—a humble but highly important role. He makes for a good manager in that way. He takes after a servant king, what Jesus is like; he has a humility that allows him to move in silence.

He's been doing all the cooking and serves the food with a tenderness, kissing me on the forehead before sitting himself down. He explains that he learned how to cook proficiently from his mother, who always included him and his brothers in the process. It was something deeply important in his family, to be in the kitchen together, to enjoy food together. Something that wasn't as familiar in my own. Food, just a means to an end.

The kitchen in our new spot is a dream. Our routines have become united in a wonderful, easygoing way. We are able to play music loudly without his roommate objecting or the neighbors complaining. We left his roommate to find a new roommate himself. We didn't care either way. To succeed, it has to be about the timing. We can't slow down our process to be courteous; that's not what people of fine success do.

And now we're living in one of Par Mars's most beautiful, lush estates: the Beverley. We have entered a new culture: where the trees are carefully curated, plucked from the ground in some other, more untouched country then brought over here. Each plant species has been scientifically studied and modified, so as to ensure there will be chance of growth in any climate. Still, sometimes they will die. Climate is the one thing which cannot be altered, even in these estates.

It was the other week, when I was helping Luis move some furniture, that I noticed that the house across the road from ours was decorated only with succulents. Then, on the day we moved, the house had obtained two fully grown palm trees sitting on either side of it.

See, the Beverley Estate is the estate that features the earthy, concrete houses, resembling a combination of futurist and neo-brutalist exteriors—the roundness and the edges combined, the handsome raw concrete. Beechwood and gray stone, mid-century modern interiors. The houses are mostly built in the shape of what looks similar to an Xbox console, curved but square in nature, slightly futurist in the subtleties, yet with the harshness of brutalist monolithic geometry. The windows are expansive, the balconies blend into the horizontality. To have no plants would render it some sort of militarized complex from the outside. Each house casts a satisfying shadow of what appears to be a brick of softened butter. Melting and falling into a river of the freshly dried asphalt road.

There is a park with many trees scattered around the edges to shade a cyclically paved footpath. Universal trees that suggest both tropical and cottage-reminiscent forestry. This big bed of greenery is the moor of the perfect body of our sculpture-like homes.

There are already large, comforting palm trees in front of the house we've adopted, no need to import them. Matted beige flooring. Archway openings. A spiral ash-wood staircase and brown beams across the ceiling. Imitation of natural wood growth. Indoor spa in the main bathroom, looking like a cavity dug from the earth. Strange bulbous edges, perfect for young offspring, perfect for tired eyes.

We've been living here for a week. Everything is neat for now. There are boxes, but the ones we have opened have all been unpacked fully, so that there are only whole objects in this house. Upstairs, there are two smaller rooms. Luis wants to turn one into a home office or perhaps a gym room. We store the boxes up there for now, so that the negative space downstairs is for our feet and for our eyes to loll over.

When I arrive home tonight, I remove my shoes, slide them against the wall. Luis is cooking kimchi hotpot, which I taught him how to make. During the move, and even before that, he has fallen into the habit of having the food ready before I get home. He's wrapped his habits around my schedule and I've done the same for him, arriving at work an hour early so that he has a ride. At nights, any Watch activity that Jean Paul conducts, whether Resisting Act or meeting, doesn't usually finish until 7:30 and Luis is often hungry by then. This is often the hinge of all our recent arguments. He suspects it's a new-age kind of thing that I'm attending to, and he is conflicted when trying to understand the consistency of the meetups, the allegiance I have to them. Whenever it becomes an argument, I tell him it's not so much that I'd *like* to be there, it's more that I am the only one who can do what I do properly. Nobody knows the role better than I do. Then he tells me he just misses me, that's all. He'd like someone to shed the day with.

I would never admit that it's the driving that has become an addictive form of meditation for me. That this practice is what sheds off the day for *me*. To drive is to become nothing momentarily; this is the way it has morphed around my schedule.

After these moments of disagreement, Luis will usually bring up his work as if to fill in the gap. He'll quote something, usually a philosophy, that reinforces what K.A.G. claims about themselves as a brand. A few days ago, he said, "Did you know that K.A.G. stands for the Chinese pinyin for *lovely*? Was it, *ke ay*, kee ar? Mindy told me that yesterday. She's from Guangzhou. She says there's mini K.A.G.s everywhere there."

"Ke-r ai?"

"Yeah, that's it."

K.A.G. has now bought out the six unlucky stores that previously sat beside it—three on each side. And they've expanded enormously. The staff wear linen aprons and earpieces. At the beginning, they had hired a range of "ethnic and culturally diverse faces," but now they're hiring mostly bilingual or trilingual speakers.

This means that Luis is able to practice his Spanish. Though the amount he knows is slightly tinged with the Puerto Rican accent his mother carries. He says there is only a slight difference between the way his father speaks and the way his mother does, but in a hurried sentence it is easy to miss. The *d* sound is often dropped; he gives me an example.

I say a big difference between Mandarin and Cantonese is all in the emphasis. For Toisanese and Cantonese, the distinction is more fleeting before the ear. With their similar tones, the distinction relies more on the shape of the mouth.

Luis asks, "Would it be easy to transition between the three?"

"I think I'd find it harder knowing one."

"Does your father speak English too?"

"Well, he was always definitely the better English speaker. It allowed him to be versatile in his work."

"Yeah my father is Portuguese-, Spanish-, and English-speaking."

He explains that he's always been very intimidated by his father. His father is many men in one is the best way to describe him. Then again, most academics he has come across are like this. As if they are existing in one world to survive, the other to justify why they would like to.

We're serving the kimchi hotpot with the beautiful K.A.G. Woodgrain Server Ladle. The red of the stew steams from the branch-like spoon. It streams into the Teak-Shell Wooden Bowls. We are seated at the table, sitting on thin-cotton cushions, wooden chairs with legs that match the utensils. The house is currently sitting at a perfect temperature. The system beeps and shuts the heating and cooling off automatically.

After a few spoonfuls of the kimchi, Luis says, "I think we're buying out the art store. Did you hear about the manager? He was there *forever*, the pervy one?"

I shake my head, a bubble in my cheeks.

"Well, he left a month ago. About time he resigned. The store wasn't doing well before he left, but he was very . . . strong-willed. He wouldn't have ever let that store go down. It was his whole existence. So, yeah, the board wants to get them while they're down."

"Oh, okay . . . and what about all the young people who work there? That really sucks," I murmur.

"Don't play that card, Leen." Luis shakes his head. "You know it's not me. The whole board in Sham Tseng, they don't see us. It's not as personal to them." He says Sham Tseng like *shaam seng.*

Sometimes if we're not too tired, we'll take a dreamy walk around the estate after dinner. The houses are magnificent and addictive to look at. Outside one of the houses, a few doors down, there is a flat-screen monitor mounted on a section of a front-facing wall, not north-facing, so you can see the digital billboard playing an ad of their child's acting showreel, a telephone number spelling out, traversing from one end of the screen to the other. Every time we pass it, Luis cracks up laughing and I have to hide his face in case they're all there at the window, trying to figure out if the mechanism is unsuccessful or if their kid is just shit at acting.

Outside one of the houses, there are always the same two parent-aged-looking people smoking a pungent joint, one sitting on the pavement, the other sitting on the step. There's an oval around the corner with the adult exercise equipment. The stretching setup that people with sore joints and limbs use to cast resistance. Big dogs in the suburbs. The mentality that draws apart the kinds of dogs in the cities versus the kinds of dogs in the suburbs is that big dogs are to keep us safe, little dogs are good for loneliness.

In the Territories, it was not totally uncommon to keep a dog—there were shelters where people could take strays home—but it was nothing like in Par Mars where the walking, the presence, and the breed of a dog is symbolic of the certain type of life you live. For example: though there is a significant amount of families who are recent immigrants to Par Mars, it feels as if it is more uncommon for them to keep dogs here. Here in this estate is a man who immigrated five years ago, at age fifty. He calls himself Mr. Kumar. At around the time we usually set off for a walk in the evenings, he stands in his section of the park, right by a shit bin, as his big dog strolls freely around the trees.

Mr. Kumar's dog is a large, humorous-looking dog with a soft face and animatedly ginger hair. It is the most cartoon-looking animal I've ever seen. The dog is not something you would be afraid of. A dog that you'd stop to laugh at or talk to with a baby-voiced coo if you were breaking and entering. Something crossed between a puppet from a children's show and a giant bulldog.

Mr. Kumar has explained how rare this dog is but has never told us the breed itself.

Tonight we are leaning toward not taking a walk. Luis has some test reports to go through and two or three new employee registrations. He's doing it by the electric fire.

I stand behind Luis on the sofa and stare into the red light of our fireplace before continuing over to our bedroom with a mug of miso soup. I feel relieved that there is no actual fire, that this gleam and licking is electric. It's something that has always been foreign to me. I have never lived in a home with a fireplace before and would not know how to maintain it. When I saw them in films, I'd ask my mother and she would say, "Fire is known as 'the clinging.' Fire is yang. If there is too much yang—too much vanity, aggression, passion—then you need to balance the elements in the house."

When Luis says, "Kiki," the new compact home controller will do anything for him.

Turning up air humidifier . . . Turning off kitchen lights.

I come into our bedroom, reading a message from Jean Paul on my phone: *Leen my friend, just wanted to let you know that I loved your point tonight about the hypnotizing effect of the shopping complex design. Fantastic stuff. Remember to check the forum tonight, I'll be posting some unfortunate news about an excommunicated member around 10 p.m.*

Tepid air circulating. I pull off my K.A.G. Basic Tee and uncurl the Woolen Monotone Socks from my feet, fold them both, and place them on the end of the bed. Wearing just a bra and some old Guess jeans unbuttoned and unzipped. I sit myself on the carpet of our bedroom floor. My back against the end of the bed, spine pressing on cold, feeling the arch of the blades out. Faced out into the living room. Feeling expansive. My stomach hanging sadly.

I'm brushing my wig, occasionally looking at what Luis is doing. He'll be in the middle of writing up reports or thinking about the objects he is testing. He'll stand and look at the pots, observing how the base meets the stove burner, how it curves at its edges, how it is the perfect completeness of stainless steel. Caressing the handle between the length of his thumb. He'll just hold it sometimes, standing in the middle of our kitchen. Then he'll extend his arms out, as if he were passing the pot to somebody else, pulling his elbows in halfway.

As we progress the state of the decor, our home will look like a display area that Luis dresses in the mornings.

And I'll probably really like it.

K.A.G. is about to launch its first home controller device, Kiki, in a few days. They need people who are proficient at technology to sell it, so Luis has been going through the short-listed contenders—a few have come in from the mega Digi-Buy on 96. The current model of Kiki is a bit like a hybrid of an iPad and a doughnut humidifier. Peaceful home living.

And everyone'll probably really like it.

There will be new versions of the Kiki released every few months. Luis is testing with the third generation right now. Its features connection to the heating and cooling, the lighting. There is also a kitchen function. Luis has been informed that K.A.G. will be buying out another store in order to have a specialized Kiki consultation area. The store in question is the pharmacy.

The twenty K.A.G. franchise managers selected around the world to test the Kiki in their own homes have signed up to test it for life. The pay is substantially higher than what a regular manager would make. Mostly because they have allowed this machinery to enter their lives and dictate the climate of their habitat.

As much as I see the entire K.A.G. movement as a strange propagation, I do learn from its branding and philosophies. Most things in my studio are now from K.A.G. People come in because it just looks like another display room—this is comfortable. K.A.G. is a signpost for modern sophistication and self-awareness of our consumption patterns.

There's a knot in my wig. I brush at it vigorously with the K.A.G. Detangling Beechwood Wooden Comb. As it breaks up, it begins to look like a clump of blood. It's funny to me that I could ask Doms and she'd be able to tell me whether it's genuine blood or not.

Currently, Doms, Vic, and I are maintaining a strictly FaceTime relationship. I organize a call every week or so. Just to see how they are. There's no room in their house for me. Vic has left the pharmacy for good. There is too much work with the business to entertain the idea of a day job.

I called, maybe a fortnight ago, and they had both suddenly changed in appearance. They looked skinnier. Vic's auntie was back from her trip and Vic got her to braid his hair, but Doms had her hair the same way too and she'd shaved off her eyebrows. When I asked Doms why she'd decided to get the cornrows, she told me it was necessary because her hair fell out too easily and could get in the way of keeping liquids sterile.

The way she carried her face with this new hair was unfamiliar. I felt that these physical artifacts—these ways that she and I were carrying our bodies, and the way we used our actions to excuse this state of them—were indications of our boredom and neglect of them. Meanwhile, Vic seemed very comfortable, even though he's stopped going to the gym and has been running or lifting only at home. He looked extremely healthy. It was a version he had not been before the attack but it was a version that seemed virtually impossible to assume immediately after the attack too. Although there was health, a look of love for himself and his surroundings, there was still, above all, a mellow sadness.

They were keeping themselves from everybody. They were nowadays either at home except for grocery shopping or out for walks just around their area. Since it is getting cold, it's been easier to just stay in the house, and it's nice having things to do, said Vic. Doms's cousins, who live around Par Mars, had been trying to reach out to her. Doms believed it was all to criticize the two of them and, in turn, the way her late mother had raised her. They had never understood her, and so often she felt as though she lacked any true family. It was just easier to stay inside and get on with your life.

Before we hung up, she told me about the four Chinese women who shaved their heads in protest against the government persecuting their activist-lawyer husbands. Because the words for *hair* and *law* sound similar in Chinese, they'd said that they can go *hairless* but you cannot be *lawless. Wufa.* The Chinese love puns.

It looked like they were doing well, though I couldn't tell if it was because of their new business thriving, if the cold was helping their crops, or if they had experienced good lottery. Either way it seemed as if their lifestyle was working, that the money was coming in somehow on their own terms. And when things don't look like they'll work, but they do—that must be happiness.

. . .

When Luis is done with the report, he watches the NBA with head-phones on. I know not to disturb him.

I sometimes go to bed before him, and when he comes I'll wake up as he kisses me on the head. And I'll know immediately whether or not to seduce him. It's if I can smell the weed or not. If he's high, he'll want to do it; if not, he'll be tired and heavy in a different way, a more earthly manner, and he'll want to curl up on the side of the bed as a fetus and fall asleep that way.

Tonight I go to shave my head in our en suite using clippers, which are not from K.A.G. The shape is unaccustomed to my hand. It feels like a melting slab of cheese; the colors are outrageous, a red and silver. This aches my eyes. As I bring them to my head, I stop and put them down again. I exhale as if there is a ceiling in my throat.

For a moment, I feel it's the first time in a long while that I've witnessed myself in the mirror. Perhaps it's the fantastic lighting in our new home, the warmth of it, the gentle honesty. I notice the eyelids on me taking shape after my mother. Flat lips like my gong-gong, who had studied anatomy too. My only memory of him: in what was supposed to be their living room, but which was more his very own study. My nose after my father, an indifferent nose. The first thing to turn back when he said good night to me at the bedroom door.

I turn the clippers on again—fingers like my popo's—and press them into my scalp.

I have always wondered whether our bodies begin to take shape after the ones we live with, the ones we make love with and imitate aggressions of.

Before I fall into that levitating feeling prior to sleep, I am momentarily satisfied. My head is on the new K.A.G. Cotton Plush and I am using my ear like a cushion. This levitation lasts a longer amount of time than it usually does, this levitation. My phone suddenly lights up. A message from Jean Paul on the home screen: *Leen, I noticed you did not see the forum or respond.*

Tilting on the edge of sleep, with my phone turned off now, I think of a client I have the next day who I am dreading. The majority of clients who learn the routine of our sessions become loyal customers and return when recommended. Others are difficult and try to locate the good in what I do. Suspicious people, defensive of the sixty dollars, feeling as though they're *donating*. Others are suspicious of any mode of inconsistency. They question the scent if it changes, the color of the towel, the hand shape if it differs as I scroll along their backs. Customers find a way of latching onto the consonants you give them, making them into renditions of stability or satisfaction. What is it about routine? You give them routine, it makes them happy. You give them routine within this sense of novelty, this special, foreign treatment—you stay consistently *Chinese*— they enjoy the othering. You create this ecosystem for them and learn to control it. Well, it's always easier to stay the same than to change, so this must be happiness.

Luis's shifting around wakes me at about three. He rolls over, my eyes adjust to the exhausted expression on his face. He stares back at me, and only now do I remember the new state of my head. He says, "You look beautiful."

Pendulous, for however long it is, I stare at the ceiling.

I have a line stuck in my head from a book my mother kept on her bedside table. I forget to call her often.

I texted her a day ago. She wasn't worried in her response and maybe, slowly, she will become less consumed by my location, my timing. She will see me as a self-sustainable being who can adopt routine. And this routine is what will slowly disentangle her from me.

The line goes: *One does less and less until one does nothing at all.*

39 **THERE'S A SONG LUIS HAS** been playing in the mornings lately. I check for it on his phone: "Surfboard" by Esquivel!

Luis is at the kitchen bench and sees me looking at his phone. "What?" He's pouring coffee and can't grab it off me. "That's my work phone. What is it?"

He is sometimes secretive, sometimes not. It's in the habits he holds.

"The song," I say.

"Oh yeah. My dad loved him."

I put the phone down immediately to show that I wouldn't be looking for any other reason. That I am not *like* that. He wipes a splash of coffee from the floorboards. Gives a small smile as he stands, a warmth. And turns back to his coffee process again.

"Hey, really. I do love what you've done with your . . . head. Your beautiful features, I can see them all." The predictable pacing of silence and noise develops when you've lived with somebody for almost three months. Maybe it is the same thing for the neighborhood. The breath of the house, the breath of the neighborhood.

I go to speak as he is about to again, and he snaps his head back.

"You go, babe," he says.

"Thank you. Doing massages, I just feel like my hair gets in the way. It's both a *spiritual* and *physical* change."

A half laugh. "You're even talking wiser."

As he finishes the coffee-making process, he resorts back to his phone. I know he is texting his colleagues from K.A.G. and reading emails from the board. He checks his phone the minute his eyes are open. In the mornings, he has become inaccessible and vacant from his physical body. Living in a different time zone.

"Do you want to make a trip to Asia?" I ask him.

"Eventually. But I'd be pretty busy. So it won't be much of a holiday."

"Yes, you're so in demand." I hug him from behind. Nuzzle my nose into his shoulder blade. He always smells like the blue Versace. A sharp scent. When his bottle runs out, he'll probably smell like the new body aroma mist that K.A.G. will be globally premiering in two months.

He turns, allowing my head to fall into his chest. We sigh together.

After a moment, he says, "Oh yeah, I was gonna ask if you've read the book I lent you? About Cicero?"

"Oh," I say. "I haven't had time or energy to read. I still haven't finished the American cities book, or that violence book."

"Ah," he says. Then, "You're always reading that forum. That's probably why." His mouth broadens into a grin. "Well anyway, I was just going to bring up this bit in the book that describes the violent social atomism of the time. Property accumulation and violence of fighting for power and material possessions. This anarchy happened in an era where capitalist economic structures or capitalist mentalities didn't even *exist*."

"*Right*." I understand the way Luis allows intellectualisms to justify his behavior. He passes me his mug of coffee. I tell my clients not to drink coffee, but I sip a bit of Luis's every day. Though I really do try to stretch every day as I tell them to, even if only in bed. Even a simple supine twist, supta jathara parivartānāsana or eka pāda pavanamuktāsan, happy baby, ānanda bālāsana. Momentarily, before my body starts to accumulate the stoic energy used to imprint onto others.

"I've been having dreams about bombs," I say. "Last night I was sitting next to one on a Hong Kong bus. And I could feel it heating up next to me. But I didn't move."

Luis laughs and holds me, his arms around my waist. He says, "I love it when you wear the beige K.A.G. top. You look really pretty in it."

Lunch in the food court, eating a pea-and-ham sandwich, responding to the thread Jean Paul posted last night about a now-excommunicated member. Apparently one of the members from the supermarket "freaked out" and verbally abused Jean Paul, accusing him of fraudulence. So they had no choice but to carry out a Resisting Act on him. No details of the Resisting Act in question.

There are two middle-aged men sitting at the table beside me, eating the exact same meal.

"I used to enjoy this place. Used to come here for everything."

"It's different, isn't it?"

"Yeah, well."

"It's got a different feel now, doesn't it?"

"They're kicking all the normal stuff out. The art store, I saw, is closing."

"Where the fuck am I supposed to get my gold leaf?"

"You'll need to stock up before they shut down."

"Yeah."

They look at me and continue speaking, a little quieter.

"They're fucking buying up everywhere."

"Don't know what makes them think they can take all this space up in a country that's not theirs."

They're eating one of the salads from the Burrito Bob's. An oblivious pleasure over both their faces.

During the massage therapy course, someone had said that Chinese medicine and therapy methods are mysterious to a lot of Westerners, but this is why it is attractive.

My mother requests a video call around four in the afternoon, but misses me while I'm on my last client for the day. We haven't been doing the video calls lately, mostly because I do not want her to see my shaved head. I know that if I were to tell her why—about my hair falling out—she would immediately blame herself and the genetics she carried over to me. She'd think there was something she could do about it; she would spend days looking at the body as if it were an equation.

When I video call her back, I'm at home and it's six. Luis is not home yet. I've put a beanie on and am holding the phone right up close to my face.

"Did you get your shot for the flu? I read it's killing people."

"It's fine, it's fine." I ask her about her day.

"There was violence today in Lai Chi Kok. I haven't left the office," she says.

I click my tongue. "A-ya."

She takes her glasses off and looks closer into the phone at me. "*Wah*, your skin is looking good. What happened?"

I tell her it's very quiet, I'm sleeping in a king-size bed now.

Foam mattress. From K.A.G.

"Ah, God bless K.A.G. I love K.A.G.," she sighs. "You have a lot of clients—any one of them could have the flu."

I ask her what happened in Lai Chi Kok. She says there was a robbery involving machetes.

"Hope you were careful," I say.

I see her stand, bringing the phone with her. She switches the camera around. Police cars and lights drowning the hollow of the road and the footpaths. Owners standing out the front of their stores.

"See it?" she says.

"Yeah. Siu sum, okay, ma?"

"Yes, I'm staying inside," she says back in English.

When we hang up, I feel a great amount of sadness overcome me. Next I try calling Doms. It distracts me from Luis not being home yet. When he's home it helps to keep a satisfying atmosphere of security. Not only this, it gives me a reason to stay inside. You need distraction from the fact that there are many places outside to look at; there are lots of people to be.

A television is good for this too. Luis has bought us an Eco-TV from the Digi-Buy on 96. It's one that automatically switches off when you leave the room. It has a light sensor and a voice detector that responds in Kiki's voice. It adjusts perfectly to the visual temperature of the room as soon as it turns on. No awful exposure to the iris.

Doms doesn't pick up. It is a new sensation to be alone. I've only experienced this a few select times in my life. And now that my involvement with Jean Paul has slowed, there has been no excuse but to hover in this space. To have a mind that wanders rather than a mind that is yanked into position.

So I walk in circles, around the Eco-Cotton Sofa in Off-White. My feet against the matted floorboards, twisting, rotating from the ball of my foot. Making me feel a sobriety.

I want to go and feel how the rug rolled up in the corner by the sliding doors feels. I untie the rope holding it together. Unravel it against the floor, in the way of the sun coming through the glass. Slowly I press my toes into it. It's a Shaggy-Mix Rug, light, muted brown. The sensation is incredible on the pads of my toes, between them, nestling through. I bring my knees down against it, feeling a soft sinking as if in quicksand. Slowly lie against it, on my side now. My cheek tickled by the delicate filaments. My palm pressed into the buttery coop of it. I roll onto my back. Each particle, pressing me up, holding me down. My back hasn't been able to endure very much; the pain that seizes it often, especially after a day of massaging. I lie here for a long time and look up at the beams along the ceiling. Follow each grain with my eyes, feel the verticality on the tips of my fingers. My eyes follow the wall down, a few new boxes of K.A.G. samples in the corner from yesterday.

I suspect Luis will continue to justify filling up our big house with things by measuring their goodness. My mother's flat in the Territories has barely anything in it because she truly hates waste; she hates to fill up space. She has always said, *All you need are good aromas, good sounds, and good food.* Filling the space in her nostrils, her ears, her belly, and those of others.

After a while, the sun is down and the room is becoming blue. I switch on the Eco-TV for some noise. It needs to be put on an entertainment unit. Luis will take a timber one from K.A.G. when he can. Then he will get a landscaper to plant a tree in return. This is his pattern of thinking. The more you buy, the more you build, the more you plant. But the more you plant just random trees on land—whether you own this land or not—the more you claim of it.

40 **A CLIENT ASKS ME TO** cup them today. I bring out the case of six cups I have in the storage cupboard and sit it on the mirrored bench where the hole for the hair dryer and cords is. I wipe each cup down with the saline sheets I keep in my new K.A.G. fanny pack, hanging off my hip. This storage technique is one I've picked up on to quicken the process, getting me onto the next client as efficiently as possible.

I haven't cupped anybody since Jean Paul. And I certainly didn't expect to be asked to. These days I will do most of what people ask. The act of servitude, or the act of being open, is addictive—as addictive as what they will pay for it.

Light a little flame in the opening using a gas stove lighter. The blisters grow like yellow canary heads on his back. George Orwell admitted once that he thought cupping was something you did to horses. In fact, the arch in the upper back of this client looks like a horse's riding section. Where you put the saddle and wrap the legs. I perform the cupping and the client is gasping. Tensing up. By the third cup, he relaxes a little, but still makes little grunting noises. When we're finished, he pays and leaves without booking another appointment.

Farah watches him leave for a second and then turns to me, coolly. "So, finished?"

I cross my arms. "Yeah, yep."

She stands up while shutting down the computer as though she's got an entire list of other things she needs to get to. She takes her bag from under the desk, slings it around her shoulder, and leaves.

Farah and I have fallen back into a harshness again. For a moment, she was beginning to soften, the pay raise I gave her, the influx of new customers, giving her more commission on top of the pay. But as the weeks have gone by, I've been tired. And I assume I've missed the opportunity to try to reconcile the place we were before.

In the slip lane onto the highway, I wonder about Farah's lifestyle, whether she's made new friends or if she's finished the novel. I soon forget about her; I'm picking up Jean Paul and Huy.

Fires continue in the north today . . . outrage has sparked over . . . two politicians . . . flooding in the eastern areas but no . . .

They're out on the front brick steps, Huy hanging off the iron handrail. They run to the 900.

As usual, Huy refuses to say hello. He just continues: "So that's the thing with Michelangelo's hidden anatomical message: God's neck is the exact anatomy of a brain. People think he placed it there, that it couldn't be an accident. My theory: it was completely unconscious. In our inverse selves, we retain knowledge of every anatomical shape in our body."

"Mmm," Jean Paul hums.

He's been doing this a lot recently. He won't answer you, but he'll make you think he's got a much better idea about it in his head which he's not going to share with you aloud. It gives the other person the impression that they're much less intelligent than him, that he is at a level of intelligence that is virtually unattainable. So much so that he does not even need to speak, to express it.

Every fortnight he has a moment of expansive epiphany, a new manifesto based on the logic of the last one. So that by the time you enter our password-protected forum as a new member, you must go back and read the very first epiphanic message if you want to understand the most recent one posted.

Since Rick, he's normalized the credit card stealing and cash theft for every time we perform a Resisting Act. Jean Paul says it wouldn't work, one without the other. If you just *rob* someone, they'll feel it's untargeted, an act of desperateness, a spontaneous move on a random, richer individual who they envy. And if you just *inflict* the Resisting Act, they'll feel targeted and humiliated, but won't suffer any loss, justifying it as an act of random terror. As a result, they're probably less likely to change their behavior and more likely to merely feel victimized by it. It's to do with their internalized valuing of money as a source that is feeding their ego and identity. If you take from them their access to money, their reminder of their worth in those measures, they will have to confront their own body and their own being.

Whether it is because it is more difficult to make masculine people vulnerable, or whether it is because there is a subconscious element to Jean Paul's thought process, I've noted that of all the victims I've been able to keep track of, it's been mostly women who I've driven to. Almost an 80 to 20 percent ratio of women managerial targets to men. Perhaps the power of these non-men people feels *unnatural* to him and only through this does Jean Paul see that power in itself, power at all, feels unnatural.

Huy's wearing a Fendi pouch which he says he asked his parents to buy him the last time they were away at a pharmaceutical convention.

Jean Paul asks him where the convention was. "Shanghai."

"It's not real," Jean Paul says.

Huy responds that it doesn't matter.

Huy has moved on and is talking about how Lonnie Luther is getting his screenplay made by a director. The director is from just outside of Par Mars and was invited to the Cannes Film Festival last year.

"Lonnie Luther's humble as hell," Huy says.

Jean Paul suddenly says that his girlfriend is getting her thesis published.

I tell them my colleague has been writing a novel on the reception computer for probably almost nine months now, and didn't tell me.

Huy's quiet. Jean Paul says, "Good for her!"

Huy says nothing and then after a moment says, "Yeah, good for her."

I'm just driving.

Huy tells us he's been taking a creative writing unit as an elective. He has to write poetry about the human body. He laughs. "It's good I have so much to write about. With all the stuff we do, how many people we come across, it's interesting to see how bodies differ, how they can like . . . stretch."

Everyone's silent and I turn up the radio.

Freeing the victim . . . of Asian appearance . . . a student was . . .

Jean Paul has sat his phone with the GPS on the center console so I can see.

When I switch the station there's a song playing by a local artist—an acoustic song about the weather and how it parallels a romantic relationship. The broadcaster comes back on: *We're having Randall Stacy in next week, folks . . . stay tuned for that, it's gonna be a great one . . . this is Oscar driving you home.* The next bit between him and his cohost is about products at the supermarket and the way odd things are stacked across from each other. Like canned vegetables and cake mix. I change the station. *What do these people want . . .*

It's strange to be the driver, knowing someone is looking at the way you do it. Because neither of them is speaking, I feel them staring aimlessly at my steering. I suddenly realize I know this route like the back of my hand.

The GPS tells me: *Make a right onto Dawn Crescent.* Now onto the main road.

Make a left at Sicily Street.

We drive into the Beverley Estate.

Well I actually prefer the warmer weather . . . bring me some of that summer weather, I'm waiting . . . (laughter).

I slow down, turn the radio off.

Continue straight.

Jean Paul says, "What are you doing?"

"Aren't we here?"

"No, incorrect," he says. He looks at the phone. "She hasn't said we've arrived. It's further up."

I ask quickly, "What are you doing to this one?"

"What the *fuck*," says Huy, half laughing. "You never ask."

"Just the chloroform. Delusory technique. This is an early stage," Jean Paul says.

He's got his balaclava on.

"We're thinking of doing an explosive soon," says Huy, "but we haven't got all the stuff for that." He says to Jean Paul, "Did you know that fertilizer was the main ingredient for one of the biggest bombs in the last twenty years?"

Jean Paul gathers his stuff together. "Yeah, I knew that."

Arrived at 255 Beverley Estate.

I must be gasping to myself, although Huy and Jean Paul don't take any notice. Huy's got a balaclava on now. I'll breathe normally soon. Just chloroform. It's okay. Depends if he resists. The problem is, I imagine Luis will. They say nothing and slam the back door. They walk staunchly, the way they always do leading up to a Resisting Act. Stomping all over the green lawn the gardener came to fix up yesterday.

I'm most anxious about them seeing my belongings in there. They'll see it all if Luis is in the bedroom. If Luis has been home for at least half an hour, it's likely he will have already picked up my things and put them away. And if he's been there for at least an hour, he'll likely be in the kitchen cooking by now.

It has been tempting to have dinner parties, to cook for others and be seated to talk. These type of things were the things that had once brought my mother and father small moments of joy. Luis and I have talked about it, but we did not know who to invite. It is something everyone says they'll do and never end up doing.

That's what makes Huy and Jean Paul so confident. They know the leaden effort it takes to get into the car every morning and briefly wave *Hello, how are you?* to your neighbor. The shapeshifting of the personality. The disgruntled versus the always-available, always-here-for-you. The promise we make between neighbors before we even meet them, before we even move in right beside them. It's enough to be living between people. It is easier when we don't communicate. Especially if we are unsure about ourselves. The people they target are often very lonely. They are often back in their boxes at night, alone.

Luis is not likely to have anyone over tonight. He has not mentioned anything.

I drive off tentatively around the familiar curve of road. Passing the oval, the usual attractive middle-aged couple stretching after a run. Mr. Kumar walking his humorous dog, which we've now discovered is called a Tibetan mastiff.

In a second, the buzz of my phone. The vibration against the middle section of the car is violent. I stop in the middle of the road. "Hey . . ."

Huy says, "Dude's got people in the house with him. Aborting."

I do a three-point turn and park across the road. Jean Paul and Huy come running over.

"How annoying," says Jean Paul, getting in the passenger side.

Patting his trousers down.

"He's gotta know or something, what the hell," Huy says, buckling his belt aggressively.

"Don't think so. We'll just try tomorrow."

"We have the meeting tomorrow night."

41 **I'M BACK AFTER DROPPING HUY** and Jean Paul home, having also picked up an imported limited-edition K.A.G. desk from a guy over in the next neighborhood. He was selling it secondhand for about a hundred, where it was originally valued at four hundred. Luis found it online the week before. The seller had advertised it as: *Desk doesn't fit new place. Brought over from London, from minimalist fashion store K.A.G. A limited edition.*

I open the back of the 900 and two of the legs roll out horizontally and make a huge clang against the road. It seems to echo. A pause, and then the door of the house across the road opens, the screen door still shut. A middle-aged woman in a flowery dressing gown and a balding man have their heads in the gap, peering and muttering something to themselves. Then, without speaking or motioning to me, they shut the door again.

I pick the two legs up and bring them to the door. Luis goes to bring the rest in.

He has the last piece in his arms at the door. "So they only did one run of this desk and it's the only shelved thing K.A.G. has ever done. They don't do shelves anymore. There's so many pieces to this one, which is very un-K.A.G. But it was actually a collaboration with this beautiful Japanese designer. *Damn.* It'll look so good, man. It's so pretty to look at."

I nod, almost out of breath.

"How was your night?"

"Fine," I say. "The desk guy was sweet. He helped me load everything into the car."

We come inside.

"What'd you do tonight?" I ask. The kitchen is empty and perfectly clean. Just a bowl with a plate on top, my dinner which he's prepared.

He tells me he did more paperwork. Watched the news. He says, "They're looking for this woman who broke into a property over on Bent Street, destroyed some things for no apparent reason. The image they showed looked just like Mary. You know Mary who was the manager but does the registers at the supermarket now?" Luis laughs. "Bizarre."

I laugh too. "Yeah, imagine if your doppelgänger lived down the road from you. Of all the places in the world, imagine walking down the block and seeing your doppelgänger in the Bell Street bottle shop."

Luis is laughing as he leans against the pristine marble island bench, watching me. His eyes are red, he's slowly blinking.

"So you really didn't do much tonight?" I ask him. To test him, I watch his hands. He doesn't like people's attention there. He follows my gaze and folds his arms up.

"Nope," he says.

I thank him for cooking. I go to hold him tight. He unwraps his arms from one another and places them around me. Then I heat the food up, a stew, in the microwave and eat it on our beautiful Eco-Cotton Sofa in Off-White.

He assembles the desk and admires it.

42 **THERE IS NO UNCERTAINTY IF** there has never been certainty in the first place.

It's a Sunday and there is fresh fruit set in a new Acacia Wooden Bowl, which hadn't been there the night before. I realize the fruit is also wooden. I should've known: Luis gets agitated if fruit is left out of the fridge. It's because he doesn't want to end up wasting it, though I cannot tell whether it's truly that, or whether it's that he feels entitled to the imperishability of everything he owns. I had previously always assigned fake food to the idea of a lack of wealth, my auntie having had plastic flowers and pears decorating her home all the time. Perhaps it was the difference between wood and plastic.

For a house made up of so many brand-new products, it certainly still looks very natural, as if it has grown straight out of the ground. Peering eyes of woodgrain, very close to earth.

There are some plants in gray stone pots. I never water them—Luis does it all. Though now I am not entirely sure they're real. If they're not, you'd still have to dust them, and this requires time. I try to cast my mind back, to recall whether Luis had been dusting or watering. Which act, over time, had he begun to repeat so much that I had forgotten whether it had been a feather in his hand or a vessel of water? Working less and less, hiring more and more hands, so that you may do less of the putting-together and more of the maintaining, more watering or dusting, fussing, pottering around.

Maintaining your acquired plants: that must be happiness. You control everything in your space—your control is what makes it yours.

I'm standing up against the counter, peeling the skin off a green apple. Staring at the plants across the room. Luis is on a call in one of the spare rooms upstairs. I realize I haven't been up there very much. I wonder what that does to the energy of the house. I stand at the bottom of the smooth railing. Look up at the warm, milky light casting itself down, touching the tiniest portion of my forehead. I can hear Luis's voice muffled, speaking with a calm sternness, seemingly to somebody whose second language is English by the way he is enunciating his words.

I curl my palm over the thick stair railing and let my fingers trail after it. How it begins to scoop up. My feet cold and without circulation. I inhale, regulated temperature, humidity. Exhale, a longing to be in the Territories at my mother's apartment with hotness seeping through open windows. Yelling of the market ladies, red fruit-stall lights, mixed smells of food, sewage, and gasoline.

In the last week I have been feeling like an interrupter of this house. I wonder if it is the effect of Jean Paul and Huy pulling up and running across our lawn. The way their sneakers had set into our freshly mown grass. Or whether it is the moments when I go to put away the forks where the forks are not supposed to go. And Luis comes to correct me quietly. I always forget we have the Acacia Cutlery Holder now. I forget most times since we've had it and I put the forks away in the drawers still; it's the way my body has been set into functioning inside of a kitchen. The way my limbs have developed around the blueprint of a kitchen.

Luis has expressed that he does not like having drawers, thinks that it encourages hoarding. He says: *We need to stop hoarding*, and I agree that it helps the earth, it helps our mentality. But I've never hoarded—there was never enough time or space. I have always romanticized the idea of having a lot of things. To me hoarding was a sign of confused, timidly new wealth. If you look at the way my mother kept our house when we first moved to Par Mars, I suppose it might have looked a bit like hoarding. Only because she had never been able to buy so freely—she had never had this much space. And so she was unable to measure the "appropriateness" of items. When she moved back home, she avoided this habit at all costs. Doms, I suppose, was hoarding all of her mother's old belongings in the spare room, only to confuse her belongings for her mother.

It's something Luis talks about often. Modesty in storage. Modesty in design. Letting the interior be a foundation for your living rather than trying to get it to define you.

He has said many times: *I hate the word* minimalism. *It is not minimalism. It is reduction.* In light news segments, I hear the word *minimalism* constantly. In home renovation programs, I hear the words *Zen* and *feng shui*.

Luis appears at the top of the staircase. He smiles and comes down to wrap a hug around my waist.

"What are you doing up so early on a Sunday?" He squeezes my shoulders gently. "You should be resting those."

We spend the day lying on the grass outside. There is a lot of it out here, though there are only two trees, one in each corner along the back fencing. There is sun today and it is feeling nice on my skin. We are playing music out of the new version of Kiki that Luis is testing now: the Kiki X. The engineering of the sound quality in this model is quite good.

I look at Luis and ask him if this is where he thought he'd be a year ago.

He tells me there was nothing indicating it would be this way. He had been ready to succumb to the carpentry thing, an apprenticeship for the company his brothers work at, before the psychic reading. It really scared him, he said. Because it felt very possible, what the psychic had said. That he was not focused enough for it. He says it will make sense to his family why he refused that apprenticeship when they see this home. That all the passion for architectonics was placed in his design, his lifestyle philosophy. The true nature of his character will materialize from the way the staircase wraps around itself, the way the beams stretch across the ceiling. It will make sense to them—who he is and what they don't understand. This was his life's mission; to please them, to be an individual to them.

He returns the question. Turns to his side to face me, blocking one side of his face with his strained-looking hand.

I tell him this is exactly where I wanted to be, where I had pictured myself. It was all the stuff in between that I'd not thought of, the reoccurrence of my binge-eating habit, my autoimmune symptoms, things I thought I'd already overcome. Desires for intense control, things I thought were issues of the past.

"But this makes my answer a little boring," I say.

"No, it doesn't."

Silence.

I say, "Funny how we think once we've overcome something, it's completely gone."

"Funny."

"I don't like to *want control*."

"You don't seem to."

"Hmm?"

"You don't seem to *want* control. You're not very controlling."

"Really?"

"You're very . . . easygoing."

"And if I were controlling?"

"My mamá," laughs Luis. "I'm used to it, if that's what you're asking."

"So I guess you see it more as *caring*?"

"Yeah, yeah."

"You don't think I care?" I smile. A breath.

"It's hard to see when you do care, if I'm honest."

I turn to my side, look him in the eyes.

"I do, though."

"I know you do. I just think . . . you do what you want. I like that about you. You just do what you want and I think it's very strong."

He sits up now, rubbing the side of my arm as he does. I breathe in, allowing the inhale to be easy. Listen to the noise of cicadas like a soft, almost silent screech, and exhale. I lie on my back and the full weight of the sun drops onto my cheeks. I hum, my eyes still shut.

I say, "So, do you think your father—would he be happy then? That you've inherited some of his influences, with the philosophy stuff?"

"Yeah," says Luis. "I think he would be really glad my job is like half and half. My mamá is a very hands-on person. And he's very . . . all up here." He draws galaxies over his head, brings his hands down to play with my fingers in the grass. He says contemplatively, "You never talk about your dad."

"He's all up there too, I guess. But the difference is, he isn't up there by choice. It's like he's been trapped there for a very long time, like he's forgotten there are things *above* the ceiling of his own brain. Does that make any sense?"

"Yeah . . . yes. Like he's just doing the same old?"

"Right."

"What's he like?"

"To be honest," I say, "he likes fishing. He wants me to find someone to marry. That's his main conversation with me, but from there he won't go anywhere else. He's not spiritual . . . he's nothing like my mother. They never got along, really. I suppose that's why he doesn't like to talk about relationships, he just asks about them to see if they exist. But he helped me with the studio and I guess it's his way of telling me he loves me."

"See, my mamá always hassles me about the marriage thing too. But they were both clear when it came to how they showed their love. I know I'm lucky, but I was never like my brothers. They grew up with our culture and understood themselves, but I was born here. I felt strange having them always try to figure out what's different about me. So I just want them to understand me. See themselves in me. That's a big thing for us in our family—connection."

We're lying on the Eco-Cotton Sofa in Off-White and the sun is pouring its final streams of orange through the window. On the television there is a news segment. A report of another attack, which had taken place in a citizen's home. Footage of the victim being taken away on a stretcher. *Par Mars residents are being urged to contact 1300 . . . for neighborhood watch . . . a new system implemented . . . though there have been no fatalities or serious injuries . . . back to you . . . Robert.*

Luis looks at me suddenly. "Did we get more linguini or do we just have the spirals?"

Later, as we're brushing our teeth, I ask whether he got any new toothpaste from K.A.G. Tell him we're running out.

Luis goes upstairs and brings down two more cartons of K.A.G. charcoal toothpaste. A clear tube of sedimented paste.

"What was your night job?" I ask when we're in bed.

"Mover, you know—I told you."

He decides he wants to fuck, rolls over, and burrows his nose into the cavity in my shoulder.

"What'd you move again?"

He ignores me. Kissing, slobbering.

"What'd you move?" I ask again.

"Rubbish."

He's undoing the drawstring of my pants. Pulling them down.

"Can you elaborate?"

"Clutter, boxes, mess."

I push him off a little so that we're looking at each other in the eyes, my knees now bent up, my thighs against my stomach.

He says, "I love it when you wear the K.A.G. pajamas. You look sexy in them."

They're the humble-beige, long-sleeved silk set. Peaceful nightwear designed to soften the skin between the K.A.G. sheet and covers set. *To fall into sleep with modesty.*

The pillowcases have changed—they're silk now. I only notice as I turn onto my cheek to face him. Let the silk melt against my skin.

Eventually he stops trying and I fall asleep within an hour.

The next morning I decide to wear my loose-fitting Calvin Klein T-shirt, the one I wore as loungewear when I was a teenager, being brought to the verge of tears if I thought I'd lost it or left it behind in a previous home.

I put it on and already feel better. Nostalgic. Comfort.

A potbelly is growing on me today. I suspect it is from the heavy mushroom stew we ate at such a late hour.

In the kitchen, Luis has just finished meditating and is heading to our coffee-making materials. Esquivel! is playing again and I am annoyed by this for some reason.

"Good morning." He kisses me on the back of my head.

Only when he turns around does he look at me properly. He turns back again and empties the coffee granules into the plug. He has his favorite mug out, a brown, beautifully shaped ceramic one from K.A.G.

"Kiki," he says. "Could you turn the stove on."

There is nothing on the stove.

"That's okay. Turn it on."

Turning the stove on low heat.

He draws the water into the bottom of the percolator and fixes the coffee over it. Carries the percolator onto the stovetop. Without looking, he says, "Why don't you wear your other T-shirt?"

"Which?"

He doesn't answer.

I know he is trying to get me to wear the K.A.G. one. Perhaps he can't stand to look at this house unless everything in it is matching.

43 **THIRTY TO FIFTY PERCENT OF** *injuries during earthquakes are caused by falling objects*, says Fumio Sasaki. Reducing things reduces injury. Imagine the things that we keep to keep us emotionally safe every day then physically killing us.

Luis and I are talking softly about these ideas. Today he was chloroformed and knocked out in our home, then dragged out onto the footpath for the public to look at him. The reason for this is because the public around us are a *wealthy* public. *And they could learn a thing or two from this, it could really transliterate.*

He'd woken up to Mr. Kumar and his Tibetan mastiff drooling over him in almost-blackness.

I'm comforting him on the Eco-Cotton Sofa in Off-White while he is on painkillers, crying into my breasts.

Chloroforming is not a good idea, I want to say to Jean Paul and Huy. Because I know Luis thrives off his defensiveness, always has. He'll become paranoid immediately and work his employees harder. He'll become persistent in proving himself and enforcing a dubious masculinity. It is not personal to anyone who may be feeling the brunt of this, it is personal to him that he's "failed." And this, I'm beginning to realize, is the flaw of Jean Paul's process. That it cannot be personal, because it is systemic. There are people above Luis who will not see this, and therefore will not care. Even if one person is erased, the system will continue. But I suppose this is how he'd responded to Berta's disappearance, as if it was personal, forcing his way into her house and squeezing the children for their tears to dampen his guilt. Luis is a hard worker with two separate minds. It is only tonight that I have fully understood this. Still, all of a sudden, I realize this uncomfortable desire I have to want to marry Luis.

I kiss his forehead. He has a bruise on his upper arm and neck.

I have a hickey on mine, I remember, as I trace my fingertip over his purpling bubble.

Otherwise, he seems to be fine physically. Although I've never seen him so emotionally dejected. He looks disappointed in himself, embarrassed, will not make eye contact. I attempt to distract him by talking about his favorite things, K.A.G.'s philosophy about attachment to physical objects.

He agrees tiredly: "You become the physical space you live in."

I say softly to him, "What if we were married?"

He mumbles something indistinctly then eventually falls asleep.

An ode to the comfort of the K.A.G. Eco-Cotton Sofa.

I stare at the K.A.G. handbook, which has appeared on our new Oak Wooden Bubble Coffee Table in the last few days. On the first page, it talks about ions getting stuck in the corners of houses. The places where you burn incense and sage and vacuum and mop are the same all the time. Even the way you clean becomes routine, so that eventually the cleanliness you think you're implementing isn't even really effective cleanliness anymore. The handbook asks: *Do you know what the previous owners of the house were like? Did they have negative energy, illnesses, vulgarity?* To make a new home is to consider what is inside the walls and to not accumulate too much to blockade any leftover energies that need to be released. Accumulating too much can encourage being overly affected not only by "stuff" but also each wall and the ions inside them.

I am stuck here on this Eco-Cotton Sofa. I want to prepare incense, like how my mother does, but Luis is lying across me, keeping me warm.

Tracing my eyes up the fireplace, along the beams, the apex of the ceiling, perfectly vacuumed corners. Our plants breathing in and out. Warm annular downlights, no dust circulating.

The edges of our dining chairs. So smooth.

If something bad happens in a house, can you feel where it happened? I'm wondering *where* Jean Paul and Huy chloroformed Luis today. If I knew the exact time, I'd probably be able to tell.

Half an hour later I'm speaking to Doms on the phone, Luis still draped over me. The news switched on, a report on a fundraiser for children. When I activate my camera, I wave and see that Doms has a K.A.G. face mask over the bottom part of her face.

I'm whispering so that Luis won't wake.

"I miss you," she whispers, adjusting herself where she's sitting.

I miss her too.

"Our business is keeping me really busy," she says. "People from everywhere just *want* fake piss *all* the time. Directors and theaters want blood. Did I tell you I got a request for a quote from George Lucas's old production company?"

She tells me they've mastered imitation. The key is experimentation of the model substance on different surfaces to see how it spills, how it becomes absorbed. And also patience.

"Where do you get the actual *model substance* from? Is it your own?" I ask.

Doms lets out a huge laugh. I turn the volume down. "No. Ours? That would be the worst model substance."

"Then how do you get model substances?"

"Don't worry," she says. "Little secret."

I tell her I'm getting tired of secrets these days.

"It'll sound weird if I say it. I'm not an artist. Artists can get away with heaps. What's his name ... *Michelangelo* was dissecting bodies from graveyards as a teenager."

44 IT'S A SATURDAY MORNING AND I decide I'm going to force my way into Jean Paul's apartment and confront him about Luis. Wearing my white work coat.

The corridor leading to his front door from the elevator is carpeted, one rectangle window at the end of it shining white light through. It's one of the newer, more gentrified apartment blocks in Par Mars. The walls are perfectly gray. Jean Paul's neighbor's door is open, someone vacuuming inside.

It's such a long, skinny hallway.

I knock on Jean Paul's door a few times. Ring his phone once, knock again. My breath is stuck.

An older woman comes out of the neighbor's apartment; she looks tired, is a cleaner of some sort—holding a vacuum in one hand, a dust pan clenched between her arm and breast. She gives one quick nod—a sort of nod of solidarity, or understanding, or something, locking the door behind her. She checks her Samsung and gathers her things. I watch her lumber down the hall, hunched over, her weary black hair, tied in a falling bun. Adjusting the vacuum cleaner, looping the tube around her arm.

Jean Paul opens the door, half-naked and mossy-eyed. He's on the phone. He stops and stares, quickly says something in French and hangs up. He's blocking the door with his arm outstretched as if just leaning, but I know he is attempting to keep it brief with me. Keep me outside. I exhale, I think about bringing up Luis right here, right now. I say instead,

"I'm giving you a massage and an ear clean." I exhale and try to shoulder past him, a strong urge pulling me in. "You've been doing so much work recently."

He tries to stop me with his arm, but he's tired. I knew he would be. He never messages or posts on the forum before 8:30 but is always up after 8:00. This is the small space of time when his body hasn't woken up yet.

I wrestle my way through the door and find I'm looking down a narrow hallway. The bathroom is to my left. I walk with confidence, him grabbing my shoulders and me pushing him off. All of these actions performed with an awkward passive-aggression.

I feel him looking at the hickey on my neck.

Doms admitted on the call last night how they get their real samples of blood and urine. They've negotiated a deal with a nurse who takes blood tests at the hospital. She takes a bit more blood from a healthy patient and leaves a small vial for them in a pot plant by their door. Obviously, the name of the patient is not disclosed. For every sample, they leave twenty-five dollars for her under the mat. "Everyone has different blood," Doms had said when she told me.

At the end of Jean Paul's hallway is a big room with open light, paneled windows. A desk sits at the farthest end of the room with a chunky white computer on it and about fifteen to twenty exercise books. The kitchen is against the wall closest to the entry corridor and has a fridge, a microwave, and half-cut-up vegetables on the island bench. The bowl has no fruit in it.

It's otherwise empty except for the piles of books scattered on sections of the floor, as though a child has made a city out of them.

Jean Paul is standing behind me. I don't know what to say to him. I'm mostly finding a way to exhale.

I ask if he's moving.

He has this face: somewhat bewildered, somewhat childlike. "Uh, no, I'm not moving. I just . . ." he begins. "I just don't really have much.

For you to look at. I buy things sometimes but always end up selling them again. I'm eBay's favorite seller." His laugh is distant.

"Where's your girlfriend today?"

He sighs and leans against the kitchen counter, rubbing his face.

"Fuck," he mutters. He waits a moment, then tells me they broke up about eight months ago. He says that he's been dating, once or twice. He hasn't brought anyone home yet. There is a woman, Peta.

Something about the subject of romantic partners is tense.

I wonder if it's because he'd seen my things at Luis's the day before, or perhaps it's because I've never seen him like this, as someone who longs for personal connection, someone who's had their heart broken.

I'm about to say something about minimalism and Luis's theory of reduction in the living space, but it doesn't feel right saying it to Jean Paul, who looks like a little child standing in the center of his messy bedroom. Deliberate minimalism—I think about this.

We look out the big window, the main attraction. Across the road is a laundry and behind that, a sad little park where a woman with a hat on is walking an empty stroller.

He tells me he has this rare book he knows would sell for over two hundred. It is from that professor, whose house we stopped by a while ago.

I flick through some of his books, working up the courage to ask him to not perform another Resisting Act on Luis. He is playing with the pores on his face in front of the reflection on the microwave.

I say, "So how's the community group going? Do you think?"

"As planned," he says, pausing for a moment to look at me. He slowly turns back to the microwave.

"Everything working, you think?"

He doesn't answer, just says, "Fuck!"

The guide to clear skin is clear space. This is something Luis says while washing his face with minimal splash.

"I think . . . dust won't help . . . your skin," I say, the nervousness apparent in my voice.

He turns again from the microwave. "Dust?" he says with an air of disdain.

"Well, if your books are in stacks everywhere, it creates more clusters of dust accumulation, you know?"

He scoffs. "You think *my place* would accumulate dust? Leen, I don't even have a table. I stand at the *bench* to eat my breakfast."

"Right."

"Leen, have you ever, *ever* lived alone before?"

"Not really."

"Correct." He lets out a set of endearing laughs, coiling them into a cruel patronization. "If you've ever paid rent on your own, you'd understand . . . why shelving is not the first thing on my mind. And I don't think *dust* is the only thing getting my skin down."

"Right, sorry." I watch him turn back around. He looks at himself for a few more seconds and then comes over, leans against the back of the counter to face me.

"No, don't apologize." He grins. "I'm just saying."

"How long've you lived here?"

"I used to be at a shittier place. It was after I'd gone abroad to study, to get some life experience. You can't really talk shit unless you've done that really. Come back from experiencing other forms of reality and realizing that you can't be a regular person with a nice house and a car *and* be interesting with all these experiences."

Quick breath. He looks at me dead in the eyes before launching back into his account.

"I had to come back. I couldn't afford it anymore, who was I kidding? And then I was somewhere shittier. I was studying again. I was doing life and realizing how stupid I was in my twenties. Then everything seemed okay and I moved here. And I love the light, it's north-facing. Light is all you need, so that you can read."

A quick breath. Looks out the window.

He continues, "I'm very used to this *now*, you know. No furniture. That's why it upsets me when people who work with big expensive items like furniture can just *take* them."

A silence.

"You know, it's not what you think in the movies. When you chloroform someone, they don't pass out immediately. It takes a good ten minutes."

It occurs to me as I'm driving back to the complex that eight months ago was when he started this entire thing.

When I arrive home after a few hours with clients, Luis is not there. I yell out for him, run up the stairs, and peek my head into both rooms. I run out the back door barefoot, my feet pressing into the slightly damp lawn.

He answers his phone, says he's okay, he'll be home in a few hours. He says to me, "I love you."

It's four in the afternoon. I haven't eaten yet and there is a holey feeling in my stomach. I go to the fridge. There's a green-tea-and-milk carton with the white K.A.G. square label on it. I wonder if Luis just relabels everything we have with the K.A.G. labels or whether K.A.G. has just released a new milk tea line which he's testing. It does look beautiful.

The air conditioner is on.

I fall asleep after eating two bags of the same flavored potato chips and watching *Friends*.

When I wake, it's just about dark. The sky is a stocking color, just as opaque.

The back light is on. The grass in our backyard is looking nicely combed. I notice two shadowy figures right up against the fence

A big animal tied to a pole. Luis, and a horse.

He takes a few moments, then comes over to me at the screen door.

"Hey, Leen." He kisses me on my forehead.

I clutch the Ecru Waffle-Weave Blanket.

He goes to the fridge and comes back with a handful of raw vegetables, touches my head as he passes, and disappears out the door again. The horse is shuffling and the moon is out. It's shining on the horse's glistening wet back.

When Luis comes back inside, I slide the glass door open for him. He wipes his shoes on the bit of concrete. Removes wet grass from his soles. If I had it my way, there wouldn't be any shoes or shoe-walking in our house—the way it's always been in my other households. Luis insists that having shoes in the house is okay because it means we are not too attached to our floors. To be too comfortable in a space is to spoil it.

"What's going on?" I ask.

He glances outside. The horse is standing completely still. Then shudders its head and bends over, sniffs.

"That's Moleskine." He turns back around and grins, an exhilarated look in his eye.

"Why? Why do we have a horse?"

"She's mine. You have your 900, I have Moleskine."

Since Moleskine arrived two days ago, Luis has been spending almost all his time brushing her.

On Monday, I go to the studio at about nine and leave him standing outside brushing the horse, claiming he had a day off. I come back at around six after a full day of back-to-back massages and some ear cleans and see him still standing out there, now with a big coat on.

The air conditioner's on too.

I think about talking to him about the incident, the Resisting Act. Maybe it has triggered a kind of quarter-life crisis in him, manifesting in the physical form of a horse named after a notebook. He is twenty-nine, he's had a hard couple of months maybe. He has never been physically attacked like this before. Perhaps I needed to take him to some sort of therapy.

When he comes inside, he has a vacant look in his eyes, though he is smiling largely.

"You okay?" I ask.

"Yes, I feel really good. Really good."

My father once told me about the Horse-Faces. They were the guardians of hell alongside Ox-Heads—occupation as muscle. Together they performed inductions of souls into the underworld. I had many nightmares about them as a child. Because they almost always first appeared in the form of angels.

45 **I START TO WARM TO** the horse, but only because it keeps Luis from the excessive cleaning, online purchasing, rearranging of everything, taking things apart, and putting them elsewhere. Keeps him less tired, more preserved for his workdays. He seems happier too.

I cook us a pasta. I don't recognize myself: a brown headscarf wrapped around my head, the same way the humble-looking model has it in the spread of the latest K.A.G. catalog. I'm setting the table and putting a glass of water on a coaster for him. I stand there admiring the table. The cold slips in as Luis holds the door open, wiping his shoes on the concrete. I go to Kiki X and press the control button, she responds: *Yes?* And I say to turn up the heating.

There are red and blue flashing lights outside the window. A moment of a siren, but switches off immediately after.

Luis goes to the window and pulls the curtain away a little, ignoring the soil coming off his shoes. I join him and see that the man across the road is looking out from his half-open blinds as well. We make brief eye contact. He shuts his first.

A police car is patrolling. Luis stops staring and lets the curtain fall back.

"Hmm," he says. "They don't usually patrol in this area. They're only ever in the south areas of Par Mars. You reckon it's cause of those idiots? Those *kids*?" He inhales forcefully.

We return to the living area.

"Someone would have had to call," he says.

I bring the pasta simmering in the pot and empty it into the serving bowl at the dining able. We sit.

"No one ever snitched where we were in the last house. Even though we all despised each other in that block." Luis raises his eyebrow. "Oh well."

I watch as he scrapes the fork around the bowl, finding more crumbs to eat. "There's more in the pot."

When he stands, I say, looking toward the window again: "Do you think the more you're *not* left alone, the more unsafe you feel?"

"Yeah, yes, but . . ." Luis licks his finger. Doesn't finish the thought. Instead, he places his hands flat on the table, exhales and rubs one hand over his head. "So, my old job, I was a bit like a . . . what do you call it? Like a henchman. For this guy. He was my plug for a bit, that's how we met. He dealt a lot of the hard stuff, you know? Some stuff you wouldn't even believe. Stuff that you couldn't get anywhere else, these really special prescription drugs. I mean, I never had to do anything. Everyone was normal. Everyone was nice, a lot of middle-aged customers. Don't laugh at me—he was a twig. Innocent-looking guy."

He grins and offers his hand across the table.

I take it and laugh. "What would you've done if someone really did something?"

"Pssht," laughs Luis. "I don't want to sound bad, but honestly from the first time I picked up from him, he probably thought my uncle was in cartels or some shit . . . or . . . the smart kid thought other people would think like that, and often they did—no one ever fucked with us."

"Mmm," I say. "We're so visual."

46 **ANOTHER CHATEAU PARTY AT PEGGY'S** tonight. She's big on community during times of uncertainty. This afternoon, a robbery had been reported in one of the units of Luis's old block. Luis didn't say anything about it except that it wasn't surprising—high crime rate there.

I'm in the gallery room where Peggy had done her reading the first time. There is Mary, sitting across the room with a woman who has her hand on her upper arm. Mary looks very happy, her limbs seem softer than usual. I don't recognize anybody else from Jean Paul's cult here and it's ten.

Vic is sitting cross-legged in front of me, inhaling nitrous oxide. Peggy is trying to gather a shroud of people to watch her play the piano.

She's favoring Luis tonight. She keeps parading him around, her arm around him, kissing the top of his head often while she's drunk. Her husband doesn't mind. It's him that sits on the front porch, smoking a cigar, with his large, slightly asymmetrical moustache. So big, I wonder if the smoke gets tangled in it.

Peggy finally sits at the piano with a gathered group of five standing around. It's a Fazioli with the gold rim and black high gloss. She sits Luis on the bench with her. He has his hands in his pockets, looking up to the ceiling at God.

She starts to play. I think it's something by Elton John. Nobody sings along and she looks back to see if anybody knows the song. Nobody seems to.

Vic falls back into my lap. When he sits up again, I ask him where Doms is.

Ramon, the butler, is standing in the doorway. Observing the scene peacefully. He takes a cloth from his pocket and wipes down one of the seats someone has stood up from. I watch how carefully he sways his hand around.

Doms comes in lighting a joint. She's smiling a large, suffocating smile at Ramon who seems to be debating whether or not to tell her to smoke outside.

"Which one's Luis, anyway?" she asks me. "I thought I'd finally get to meet him tonight." Doms has gotten a nose job. And her nails are done too. The braids are in.

Vic is drinking something. He says, "And *you know us*. This is the *one* time in six months we'll come out. Man's got five more hours to show." He laughs, but there is a sort of contrition to it.

Doms has an empty smile. "We work to stay in our houses, but never end up leaving them."

She and Vic thrust a laugh together.

They're both turning twenty-six this year. They both look slightly guilty.

Doms is posting more and more pictures now. She has about 650 followers. She's begun to gain some as she practices taking photos in different lightings around the house, around the neighborhood. I assume this is how she gets her socialization.

She's staring at my top.

"K.A.G.'s?" she asks.

"Yep."

"K.A.G. is getting sexier. Look at that neckline."

Vic collapses into Doms's lap. He arrives again, sitting up as he resolves into reality. "Hippie crack," he says, wiping saliva from his mouth. He stands to grab another drink from the ice bucket by the front door.

"Horse tranquilizer," says Doms as he leaves, exhaling smoke at me. "He's been on that too. He *rarely* does it. We usually just make brownies and have one night like that a week. It gets monotonous staying at home and guarding our elixirs, watching them and playing the whole online game. The packaging, the waiting for responses. You know ketamine?"

I think about a horse under tranquilizers. I think I have seen it once before. A horse paralyzed, its giant tongue lolling, a defeated sight.

"Sometimes there's this point where you go from semi-control to none. A K-hole. Vic's been down it, just *one* time. He said it felt like something was weighing him down. That he had relocated, lying by the side of the pool, his shoulders hung over the edge of the water. That he was bleeding from his nose. He was watching me and I was standing in the middle of the pool not doing anything, with his favorite Balmain top on. But to me, he was stuck in this position on the couch for nearly an hour." Doms shows me with her body, contorting it.

Spice Girls is playing now, a tune I recognize from the CD store that had once been at Topic Heights years ago. They would play a cycle of fifteen songs. When it ended, it would start again. We used to sit outside the store after school most days, my friend from high school and me, eating candy and waiting for this sonic eclipse.

Doms says the thing with their process is that the more euphoric they become, the better batches they make. Because dissociation helps us travel to where we want to be. So we are able to be in contact with our blood cells, the systems in our bodies. She says that Vic hadn't wanted to go down that path at first. He wanted to quit altogether—everything all at once. But she managed to convince him that it was okay, there was freedom to it and it was okay to embrace that freedom.

"Are you sure Vic will be okay?" I ask her.

"Vic is *fine*." She lowers her voice. "Leen, the sex is good again."

She relights the end of the joint, smothering it, and offers it to me.

I try to recall whether Jean Paul had plans for the Chateau tonight. I know he and Huy had a vague plan to come to the party and spike some drinks or something minuscule, almost petty, like that. Just to cause slight unrest. *Better than nothing*, Huy had said.

I'd found out that the batch of weed going around the first time at Peggy's had actually been sourced from Huy, who knew it was laced; a batch of medicinal thrown out at the pharmacy after a mass product recall.

I look at Mary, who's giggling, fixing her hair. She looks at me, squeezes an affectionate smile.

I take a hit and look down.

"White Widow," says Doms.

"What?"

"The strain." She rubs her lips together.

Outside the room I call Huy. He says he and Lonnie Luther are still at home playing Monopoly, but if they get bored they might come hang out. He tells me the game's been going for an hour.

I ask what Jean Paul is doing.

"Uh . . ." He hesitates for a moment. "Not sure, sorry."

I try to call Jean Paul but he's not picking up.

The hallways look almost blue from the themed lighting, and people are draping over the staircase.

Later upstairs, Mary is fixing an IP camera to Peggy's pot plant. Her delicate fingers secure them behind a few of the leaves, framing the little eye of the camera.

"I *adore* a good monstera plant. I have two at home," she says, barely loud enough for me to hear.

"Oh yeah, it's nice," I murmur.

Mary winks at me as I knock on the door to the bathroom.

Inside, a baby monitor beside the basin is playing a nocturne by Chopin. It's one I recognize my auntie playing in her home in the Territories on an electric keyboard, the sound not so brilliant. Barely distinguishable. I remember my father telling me I should learn this piece. My father asking, *Are you practicing piano? Why don't you learn that beautiful song you like so much?* And I would always say, *I don't know how to learn it, I don't know what song it is,* whenever we arrived home to our apartment. I had never asked for the name of the composition.

The bathroom smells like lavender, which induces nausea in me. The olfactory nature of it reminds me of too much. Seventeenth floor, the sacrificial altar built into the flat. Apples and pomelo. Cheap lavender-scented candles.

I begin to think about Peggy's genuine longing to please people and bring them together. Then it makes me feel a little sad, thinking about what Jean Paul could do to her, what it would mean for us as her tenants.

The little light bits in the sheen of my pupils gleam through with wetness. I bend over, about to throw up. The wall forming at the back of my throat. But I just sit here, chin hovering over the toilet bowl. And I look at the popcorn walls, the details so wonderful.

When I come downstairs, Luis is playing the piano and I realize that he had been on the other side of the monitor playing that nocturne.

I wonder if Peggy has adult children or anybody who would miss her in a way that wasn't purely symbolic. I wonder if she suspects anything.

I wonder if she's set up this mass gathering party so as to die with a congregation around her, or less morbidly, to seek protection, seeking witnesses.

This house doesn't tell you much about her, or her husband. And it unsettles me. There are only things everywhere, mostly ornate things. Making it even more inexplicable.

I peer into the large room from the bottom of the staircase and watch Peggy breathing down Luis's neck. The way he bundles the notes together, ignoring everyone. Fingers contorting, relaxing, as if carving a sculpture. When he reaches for the note up the top, he nods his head as though he has been considering the entire piece and has now reached an epiphany. He starts to build the volume and Peggy roars, "Ho!" The little moments of explosive mannerisms she has, full of innocent emotion. She has her hand lightly on his back.

Luis looks sad as he concludes the piece, almost dormant, nearly pitiful. His fingers twinkle rapidly one final time at the top and then they fall back down around the middle C.

The room applauds and he stands with a blank expression, pursing his lips at Peggy who is hugging him around the shoulders.

"I *told* you to play," she's saying.

She shows him off.

"I *told* him to play. I knew it, I knew it. A born natural. Look at those fingers."

We're sitting on the front step of the Chateau and we can smell the aroma of the cigar Peggy's husband is smoking a few meters away. He's looking at the big round moon from his stoop on this hill. As if he's waiting for *quiet*, asking the moon for it.

"I felt like crying when you played," I tell Luis.

"I'm very talented." He's finally grinning.

I nudge him. Tell him that I knew the song by ear but not by name. Tell him I used to try to play it by ear. Picking it apart, pulling every feeling from it, trying to place them on the keys.

"Opus nine? Number two."

We're holding hands.

I see Farah at the bottom of the hill stepping out of a car. An Uber, or maybe it's her dad's car. She takes one look up the hill and sees me. She reluctantly gives a half wave and fixes her shoe.

I wave back.

"You're good at waving," says Luis. "Thank you," I say.

Farah is taking on the hill in baby-blue pumps. Something that was in fashion maybe four years ago. Tonight she's dressed to impress. I stand and we hug each other, which hasn't happened in a while.

"I finished," she says.

"What?"

"I finished the novel. I'm moving away to the city. For real."

My face doesn't decide to change. I'm probably high.

Farah has a lighter in her hand now.

"You don't smoke," I say.

"Well, I'm hanging out with different people now." A puff of it in my face. "Also . . . your friend, Jean Paul, he gave me Lexapro. It's really helping. I feel really good."

My mouth is hanging slightly open. I press my lips together, nodding.

She proceeds to walk into the house. "See you later."

Behind me, Luis is indifferent. "It's been a rough week, hasn't it?"

He takes something from his pocket. He wants to snort it, I think.

"Where'd you get that?" I say.

"Oh, his name's Huy," he tells me. "Huy's the guy I . . . you know, worked with. I met him at community college. He used to come over and play video games. But, yeah, his family owns the pharmacy, or he works there or something. So he's got access to all the—you know, all the prescriptions I was telling you about."

I have my fingers splayed out like a star.

"Oh," I say. I look at the powder. Don't know how to tell.

"We used to call him Sprite, cause he's so tiny, he's like a twig. He looks so harmless that it's kinda funny."

"Right." I pause. Inhale, lowering the cortisol, the stress hormone. "Do you, like, know when you got that?"

"I've had this bag for a while."

Exhale, expand, and contract. Feel the nervous system.

Luis stands and goes to the table Peggy's husband is sitting at. He lines the powder without saying anything to the husband, though Luis *knows* who he is. This is how formidable K.A.G. is. A world where Luis is seemingly more powerful than a man who owns a big shell of commercial assortments. A successful business franchise trumps a large cavity for potential tiny commercial failures.

He offers Peggy's husband some and he shakes his head, not even flinching, not saying a word. Inside, "Pass That Dutch" suddenly plays, the bass apparent. I peer through the door and find that the crowd of people is dancing poorly to it.

Luis leans over the table. "You know I'm not supposed to let anyone know about next season's products, but K.A.G. is importing a whole bunch of designs that are ideal for long-term storage."

He wipes his nose.

"I thought the idea was weird at first because of the way the board presented the catalog. They showed me these photos of apocalypse preparation. You know the celebrity bunkers—their underground homes in case of an apocalypse or disaster? It was like a catalog full of them."

The idea of having an enclosed space with very few objects in it; just efficient solid storage, with everything you need in there, he explains.

He says, "Have you heard that 30 to 50 percent of injuries in earthquakes are from falling objects in the house?"

I tell him he told me that when he was gacked up on painkillers that night.

"You know the Chateau Marmont is supposed to be earthquakeproof?" I ask him.

He says I've told him that before.

I think of going to introduce Luis to Doms and Vic, but suddenly there is a big noise overhead. It is a helicopter, or a hovering UFO, a strange shape. Shining lights on the horizon. Being up on this hill, we can see everything and it mesmerizes us. Someone is running up toward us, a figure with a bag. We realize it's a delivery of food. He leaves it with us without saying a word and runs back down the hill to his electric scooter.

We eat the food shamelessly. Someone will forget they ordered it. Only after we eat it do we feel slightly guilty and decide to drive home.

I'm driving us down the highway. The 900 with the top down. Someone has left a banner up on the side of an overhanging bridge: JESUS

LOVES YOU. On the radio: *The recessive gene . . . a factory strike in Bangladesh . . . motor vehicle . . . if you ask me.*

Luis turns off the radio and plays "Violets for Your Furs" from his phone's speaker.

47 **THE DAYS ARE STRANGE FOLLOWING** the night at the Chateau. In a corridor leading to the restrooms in Topic Heights, a woman is standing still, as though someone has pressed pause on her mid-walk. I approach and sort of look at her out of the side of my eyes, my bladder stressed. Notice that her eyes are following mine, pleading at me with a violent pressing.

I wash my hands. All three basins are blocked up full of water. I stall and fix the two loose ends of a scarf wrapped around my head, pulling them tighter. Wipe the corner of my nose, where oil and dirt become trapped. My hair has been growing again on my body, everywhere except my head. My mother would say it's something to do with hormones, testosterone becoming apparent in the body. I wonder if my hair will grow back, whether the alopecia will continue. I rub the edge of my smooth forehead.

When I come out of the restroom, the woman is still standing there in the exact same position. I think I hear her speaking.

"Are you okay?" I say.

Her eyes start flittering around, though she doesn't blink.

I continue down the corridor to the relief of the public walkway. A woman with a baby carriage shakes her head as I interrupt her path. I look back and the woman now has her mouth gaping at me. She isn't making any noise. But she is calling for help.

Two people are seated and waiting in my studio today. Farah is having polite conversation with one of them, a woman we've never had before.

When I come in, she introduces herself and asks if there are elevators in Topic Heights. I think about it and realize there is only the service elevator in the fire escape corridors. She then asks if I offer services that are widely accessible. I try to remember whether the massage table I have has a system to adjust its height. In massage school, they highlighted the extreme importance of communication.

"Spinal cord," the woman says, as if reading my mind.

I don't handle the situation well. I think for too long and the woman says, "That's okay. No stress."

The second person, a man, leaves after a long and winding conversation about prices.

Before he exits, he says, "You know, in Chinese medicine, it used to be that you didn't pay your specialist until you were well again."

Of course he isn't reprimanding me, he's just saying.

When I'm home, I feel dejected from the day. Previously, with the lack of customers, there was the worry that there would be no one for my service. But now having customers makes me feel that perhaps it is *my service* that cannot cater to everyone. It makes me think there is one type of person who enjoys the culture of a shopping complex and everybody else has to work around it. And it feels as though I've fallen into the habit of only visualizing this one buyer persona. I slump on the couch.

Luis, meanwhile, is moving our things into the Future-Style Acacia Units that seal up and only unseal again when you push them a certain way with your human thumb. He says he's apocalypse-proofing the place. I think he's messing around with me, but he's very adamant that all of my things go in the boxes too.

He gets me to pack my belongings. Items go into the first box, then the box goes into the unit, and then the unit goes into our beautiful High Wild-Oak Sideboard.

"It will be healthy for you, a mindful practice," he says gently.

My body is aching from the day and my brain is a void.

"You should also read the new K.A.G. catalog. This month's feature editor explains it really well. Living with the foreshadow of disaster makes us appreciate the present."

He helps me lift some of the books I have into a container and then demonstrates how the container fits into the unit. Pulls it out again and lets me continue.

"K.A.G. is always about *mental* lifestyle—internal lifestyle, they call it. Internal ecosystem inspired by your outer, which you have the power to create. Damn. It's inspiring."

"Did you steal these ones?" I ask, looking at the boxes. Like nothing I've felt before: smooth thick wooden material, with steel lining the insides.

"What? No, I don't steal, Leen. You know I don't. This is from the board."

I notice his piercings, the ones in his ear and eyebrow, are out. I ask him why and he tells me the K.A.G. board doesn't like them. They told him at a random checkup today. It's audit season again.

"I like your piercings in."

Piercings and long drives and beer; something I am homesick for. "We change for our money, don't we," I decide to say, sighing. Flicking the pages of the Cicero he lent me.

He doesn't say anything; he's folding his clothes neatly—a skill he's practiced every day, for years probably. I wonder if he still practices, or if he has his employees do it now.

I had a client the week before who told me how they were an employee at K.A.G. A retail assistant.

I asked whether she knew Luis.

"I wish. There are so many employees, you can't imagine. Luis is constantly busy. He's in his office a lot of the time too. They made him a really nice office out of where the art shop used to be, you remember?"

She explained to me that she's overworked and takes up double her duties because the import rate is absolutely ridiculous.

"The amount of 'stuff' we have to sort," she said, tensing up. "K.A.G. is a fast-growing business. It's really picky about who it hires. People usually don't last a week. There's lots of products that come in and there are heaps of people hired just to carry it in. So lots of injuries. Lots of *pushing it under the rug.*"

She explained the reason she came to my studio today was because she had watched this YouTube vlogger a few days ago, who was also a K.A.G. retail assistant somewhere overseas. At a large and ever-growing branch. She'd made a video called *Average day of self-care for a K.A.G. retail assistant.*

In the video, she told me, the vlogger had made it a habit to get massage therapy once a week, to visit the doctor regularly, to take a bath. After a moment of silence, she asked whether I got massage therapy for the physical toll placed on me through massaging others. Transferring my energy into their still, deliberately unoccupied bodies, slanting and bending and excavating into them. No resistance.

"It must be hard," she said. "I feel guilty."

I pressed my forearms into the space where her shoulders separated.

She explained that there's no space for depression and anxiety in her workplace. She talked all through the massage and apologized for it. She got anxiety when there was too much silence. She said it was so cold in K.A.G. They ramped up the cooling and heating to mimic the weather so people would buy the things necessary for that sort of weather. They controlled the climate of the store the way Peggy controlled the mood of the complex. And the way Peggy controlled the climate of the complex on hot days so that customers will think less of how it's hot outside. Their immediate sensory desires are met, so instead they will think about what to buy for the kitchen.

When I offered her the ear-cleaning service, she agreed to it as though it were a side of fries.

"Anything," she said. "Anything to get this gunk out of my brain."

When I usually offer clients the ear cleaning, most of them see through it as a scam. When clients see through you, it either encourages you to lie to them, or to question yourself.

That whole day, and recently, I've been questioning myself. After the client left, I took notice of the way I had engineered the lighting, the temperature of the room, the music I played, the temperament of myself. Wondering if it were a collective dream, or just my own.

Luis runs his hands along the side of my jaw to the emptiness above my ear. Fingertips that only a carpenter, a pianist, could possess. The fingers he uses to fold clothes delicately, place objects thoughtfully. It's a different sort of feeling, as though a swarm of cells are gathering there to mingle, to kiss.

A nocturne is playing through the Kiki X.

"Hey, uh, actually," Luis says, "do you think you could help me shave my head tonight?"

"You want to be just like me."

He grins. "I just want it almost buzzed."

"Okay." He walks out.

He pulls his head back through the door. "Hey, and uh, do you think that friend of yours, who makes the urine, could she provide some for me?"

Doms and Vic come over for the first time the next night and only because they're making a sale to us. These are the only times they'll leave Doms's condo.

The little test tube has a tag with a string wrapped around it, as if a rustic birthday gift.

"The instructions are there and it includes everything you need to know in the case of a drug test, but we'll explain it for you anyway."

Doms takes a seat on the firm Eco-Cotton Sofa in Off-White. Vic stays standing, holding her shoulder. She sorts through her tote bag.

"Great set-up," says Vic, looking around, filling the silence.

"Yeah, right," says Luis with a grin. "No obstructive shapes."

Luis taps something on his watch and music plays, something meditatively dance-like, something he's never played before. I guess he's being adaptable. He's very good at that.

Doms pulls out two packets of something. She holds the tube up around the rim, her nails bitten to the tops of her fingers. "So this. This is really just water, potassium chloride, albumin powder, uric acid . . . and, um, what was it again . . ." She looks at Vic.

"Creatinine," says Vic. He smiles lovingly at her, then looks at us and laughs. His hands move behind his back. Rocking back and forth on his heels. Vic's cheeks are less round and more taut. The beard is growing out. Doms looks so different, her nose done and now possibly her eyes have been pulled upwards at the sides to create a catlike effect. She has the braids tied up into a bun tonight.

"Have you ever done a drug test before, Luis?" Vic asks.

Luis shakes his head. Sitting on the opposite Eco-Cotton Sofa. "So, the testers will come in. What they'll do is separate the compounds of the sample. They'll most likely use the five-panel drug test, which will identify cocaine, amphetamines, THC, opioids, and PCP."

"*Yeah*, right." Luis is nodding with his chin in his hand. He is so easy to love when he is inspired to learn, to listen.

"So you'll pour this synthetic urine into this pouch." Doms holds it up and stretches it. "It's obviously very malleable, smell-proof, and it's been tested to never break. So you can either strap or tape it to yourself, or you can keep it in your underwear."

Doms continues, "But what you'll need to be careful of is the temperature of the urine. Because they also test appearance, smell, and temperature. You could try running it under a tap, that's a good trick . . . but you might not have anything to wipe the bottle with."

Doms looks up again at Vic, who's swaying on his feet.

She holds up the two packets in her lap. "So I've included two sachets of kairo in the deal for just an extra two bucks. These are shake-up heating packs. Shake them up, heat up the mixture in the staffroom and immediately wrap this heat pad around it to keep it at the temperature. That's pretty much it."

Doms stands up and hands over the thin test tube and two sachets to Luis.

"Inconspicuous kit as well," says Vic. "We pride ourselves on the secure packaging." He puts his hands around Doms's stomach, resting his chin in the hollow of her shoulder.

I'm shaving Luis's head in our main bathroom. He's sitting in the square bathtub we've never used, holding a mirror up. The sound of the razor between us, nothing else. The lighting is set to warm, reflections of porcelain sink, dusty gray marble. My feet are cold underneath, but the way the room has been lit by Kiki X is so lovely. Redolent of desert season. Alone together, I hold his head against the enclave of my stomach. He closes his eyes. Presses his lips together as he tilts up and looks at me.

He has no shirt on, his bare back rounding against the porcelain.

We pause a moment, staring. Then I clasp his forehead and continue with the razor.

"Is our heating on really high?" he murmurs.

I turn the razor off. He sits forward, arching his back and stretching out his arms.

He yells, "Kiki, turn down the heating."

I finish and bristle his head with my fingers.

He gets up. "Sorry, I'm sweating so much." He looks in the vanity, runs his hands over his almost-bare head. He appears indifferent towards himself. Runs his hand through the stubble at the top and the shadow of black facial hair growing at the bottom of his chin.

"Did I do okay?"

"Yeah, you did perfect."

An hour later, Luis is doing a line of coke off our Beech Rectangular Coffee Table. A diffuser is emitting a mixed citrus scent to encourage sleeping. The television: *Who will she choose?*

All our things are packed away into our apocalypse-proof units, stored in our built-in robes. There's a rogue monstera plant in a sandstone pot beside the dormant electric fireplace. I'm unsure if this is the best place for it. Unlike humans, these plants cannot just pick themselves up and migrate to a different location in order to manipulate their health circumstances. I learned about plant health in accordance with the moon at a young age—one of the books my mother had urged me to read. But I don't want to suggest moving it. Luis has it there for a reason; he does everything with intention, it is clear in the way his eyes sit. The way his hands react.

The lighting throughout the entire house is set to low to save energy, to set a mood. Luis is vaping on the Eco-Cotton Sofa in Off-White.

"You stopped smoking cigarettes," I say.

"K.A.G. started selling vapes. They're stocking them at the store tomorrow."

It's a beautiful slender bamboo vape mod, and it matches the shade of our new Acacia Moon Bowls and some of the coat hangers. It's chai, smells like cinnamon, a natural aphrodisiac; cardamom, a natural laxative.

I'm tempted to buy one for myself. For the feeling of it between the thumb and finger. The beneficial factors of sweetening your senses, elevating breath control and pace. He offers it to me, and I take it between my index and thumb, a delicate little sheet. I put my lips to it and adore the sensation.

"Mmm," I say. "Good."

"Cinnamon," grins Luis, his face is a changed, euphoric smile. As if the smile itself is dissociative to the rest of his face. I puff another little bit and feel it cooling. Coiling around in the back of my mouth. Luis has said they don't allow managers to offer K.A.G. discounts for friends or family—otherwise no one would buy anything given the number of staff. Even his mother had to pay full price for her beech office set, which included a magazine rack, a bamboo pen holder desk set and book dividers.

Los Tres Ases is what is playing now. A big sneeze from Moleskine outside, shuffling. I widen my eyes and rub underneath them. I find myself unable to experience the transition from silence to noise. There is no action between the two anymore.

It almost seems that inside this house, if Luis thinks it, it happens.

48 I ROTATE MY SHOULDERS, THE way they click into my spine again. I allow my mouth to hang open. Farah is looking at me from her desk, then looks back down again.

The previous night Jean Paul had said something strange in the 900. On our way to pick up Huy along the 96, he said without turning, "I was thinking how easy it would be to blow up K.A.G. But that wouldn't do anything in particular, would it?"

I am about to do a deep tissue on a client, a one-hour, which is rare. I usually only do a twenty-five-minute. It's for a new client, who undresses immediately in the open so that I don't have enough time to turn around before he's almost nude. He still has the bottom of his pant leg scooped around his foot, almost tripping as he approaches me. He comes to stand beside the massage table in his underwear. He lifts the disposable underwear up.

"This for the crotch?"

I am facing the other way to check the water level in the diffuser.

"Yes," I say.

He lies down. "Done." Then, "Stat. I just need you to focus on my upper: the shoulder blades and neck. No oil, just dry. I've got a meeting in seventy-five minutes."

I stare at his pasty, elongated face. He takes off his watch.

Laying my elbow in, I say, "How's the pressure?"

He doesn't answer. There is no talking whatsoever the entire time. He only speaks again to Farah as he's paying for the session.

I come behind Farah when the door shuts. "Was he okay to you?"

"He was fine." Farah doesn't look at me.

I'm about to go back to the massage area when Farah says, "Hey, Leen. You know I wasn't kidding the other night. I actually got into a writers' program." She swallows. "It's . . . it's really in the city. It's three days a week, so I'm using the money I've earned and I'm going to try and move there."

I guess the first thing I think of is that she has to stay for the next week at least, and I'm tempted to tell her right away: *You know, this is your two weeks' notice.* I refrain and flash a smile at her. "Good."

Robert Greene says: *Keep others in suspended terror.*

I decide not to mention it now and she continues to work without saying anything else.

I decide to take a peaceful browse at K.A.G. before I explode. I run my fingers through the soft cotton. Go to the kitchenware section and feel the rim of an Acacia Moon Bowl, breathe in the aroma diffusers. They've started stocking big crockpots, which the label says are good for keeping soybean and kimchi. I notice the beech trays, designed for breakfast in bed. I wonder if Luis has considered performing this act for me, even just as a test run for the product. The ratio between acts he performs for himself versus the acts he performs as test runs for the board is highly uneven.

I run my fingers through the document binders.

Walk through a new section full of clocks, digital and analog. This is where the dollar store once was and now it's just clocks. There is a silent ticking and the whole room vibrates on the minute. I imagine Luis having the resources to assign a staff member to go and fix any hand that falls out of place.

The face towels are soft, feel like a mother's paw.

K.A.G. is only selling products in beige, baby blue, baby pink, gray, black, charcoal, and four different types of white. Today I am wearing what the mannequin is wearing. I look at its pearl-white body, how it pairs well with the design and color of the clothing. And as I keep walking, I pass a mirror and I cringe.

Soft string music plays throughout the store.

I take a seat on the pleasant-looking Cotton-Polyester Feather-Cushioned Sofa in one of the display rooms. My palms run over it. The store is busy today. There are renovations going on in the far north end of the store, to the left of the counter behind temporary walling. Luis hasn't mentioned this.

Siting in this display room is like sitting in my house. Opposite me are the apocalypse-proof consoles in various sizes. The oak is so smooth, it makes you want to rub your cheek up against it, makes you want to put all of your products inside and never see them again.

I buy myself an iced oolong tea and a plastic-wrapped layered dan gou and sit on the couch again.

Someone else is here now: a small Asian girl listening to something in her headphones. She looks about three years old and the very little hair she has is tied like an exclamation point above her head. She bobs her head at the phone she's holding. Her mother is somewhere in the store, most likely. The girl stares at the apocalypse storage consoles. Two teenage schoolboys are leaning against the consoles.

"Yeah, actually, Daphne was looking at me so much today," says one.

"Yeah," says the other.

The first one starts playing with the drawer of the console. "They're not supposed to open easily," says the other. He's reading the description plate on top. He pushes the unit sideways with his human thumb and it subtly pops out. "See."

"Right," says the first one, and tries himself.

"Actually, at my parents' church, they mentioned this store cause they're stocking this stuff like the end of the world is about to happen or something."

"Oh, right."

"Daphne's cool, but are you sure you want a chick that wears pants to school?"

"I don't know, like I really give a shit."

"If I had a bomb-proof storage system, I'd test a bomb out on it."

"Don't even act like you'd know how to start making a bomb, fool."

The first one softly kicks the console. They both laugh and the other one kicks it. Then the little girl stands up and kicks it.

Her mother comes up behind her suddenly and yells, unembarrassed about raising her voice, "Nooo, May Lee! No." She then speaks to her in Cantonese, picking her up to leave the store, two bags of K.A.G. products over her arms. "Mho gun keui *de* . . . so jei, keu de so *jei-ah*."

A few soft bell dings in a lovely melody and then a calming announcement in four languages: the K.A.G. will be closing soon.

It's already five.

I go up the escalator, passing our old spot and continuing to the studio.

Farah is walking out the door, leaving right on time.

Jean Paul is tapping his pen on the lectern, watching Lonnie Luther and Huy in the second row of chairs. Huy with his legs over Lonnie Luther's legs.

"Well, I've heard," says Jean Paul, launching into the meeting a few minutes early, not waiting for everyone to quieten down, "that Peggy, of the Topic Heights complex, did some drug rounds today. Random audits. And I think it's got to do with the Resisting Acts. What do we all think?"

Nods and hums. Someone in the front row clicks their fingers.

"Well, I've also heard that Peggy has started selling more store lots to the K.A.G. franchise."

"Boo!" someone yells from the back. More start booing.

I'm sitting beside Lonnie Luther. He looks at me with his eyes wide and scoffs. He hasn't resonated with the congregational setting much; he says his family were never religious, so he doesn't understand the performance of it or the reigned passion that people can conjure instantaneously. Instead of turning to Huy, he turns to me. He doesn't want to upset Huy by being patronizing.

Besides, Huy is always sitting at the front, as the second-in-charge.

Lonnie Luther can't sit still in these meetings; he only likes them when he's filming. He only ever likes anything when he's filming. He feels a moment is wasted if not captured in some way. The subject could be hacking another man to death and he'd probably still like it if it meant he got to film.

Jean Paul says, "We all agree, don't we, that big corporations like this need to be stopped. The workers working in these big corporations think this—so what does that say?" A forced but charismatic smolder.

Half an hour later, he moves on to the next item on the bulletin. "I am off to a conference for the neighborhood Watch organization. If you want to sponsor me you can—you all know the drill by now." He motions towards the iPad set up in the front row of seats. "This conference is about. Active. Change. Huy and I have already completed tasks like these before."

He motions to Huy who puts his hand up as if to wave at whoever is looking.

Huy says, "I will soon be training our Watch group in ways that we can initiate alternative forms of protest, demanding change in the character of those who have the resources to change the way that we function as a society. After both successful and unsuccessful instances in our tests, I feel we're finally in a place to share what we've learned."

"It's not the person we're testing, it's the routine of power," says Jean Paul, pressing the end of his pen into the lectern. A pause. Then he slaps his hands together in a rhythm. "Remember. That. We are *not* in the mood now, especially today, to be taken advantage of. We are not in the mood to be replaced by machinery. We are not in the mood to be treated *like* machinery. Remind them that you're here."

"Yes!" someone yells from the back.

Jean Paul continues to explain his thinking to the whole congregation. We've known for the past few weeks of Jean Paul's current favorite theorist, Heidegger, and his theory of technology, his view of aimless behavior and overproduction. Jean Paul's love of Greek mythology, his study of Sartre and Nietzsche. He says, as a result, this group is mentally, *intellectually* prepared to commit physical acts, which perhaps they had not been ready for before.

"Physicality," says Jean Paul, "is often uncontrollable. But with the right intention, what is seemingly violent will become not violent. What is usually bad behavior becomes an act of sacrifice."

Jean Paul calls this physical morph the *magnification*, the highest form of membership in a Watch system. It demonstrates immense control and absolute intentions.

He says, "While the provision of these Acts may initially set an alarm off in your head—you may say, 'Jean Paul, they seem . . . *unnecessary* . . . too violent'—I want to give you a reminder of *epiphenomenalism*."

The room is embarrassingly silent.

"Which we learned two weeks ago . . . in which subjectivity in the mental state depends entirely on objectivity in physical and biochemical realms. *People*"—he comes out from behind the lectern and takes a woman's hand in the front row—"*you* are the physical event that will change their meaningless, drawling lives, help repurpose their energy elsewhere."

The woman turns to the rest of the crowd as Jean Paul returns to the lectern. She gives a flat smile to us.

"So here we use three tactics to physically trigger and break open their manipulated minds. Sensory, pharmacological, and degradation—or as I like to call it: *delusion*. These tactics feed into the depersonalization and disconnection of their mind to their situation. Without leaving your own fingerprint, you remind them of their humanity. You reflect to the community around you, the symbolic violence of these big faceless corporations. Physicality is important here. After all . . . we forget our hands are here and how much we can do with them, how much can be done without them."

Huy and I are now standing upstairs at the doors to the nave. The front doors opposite us are wide open, a mild breeze coming through. The sounds of cars starting. Gravel crunching, people chatting. There is certainly a social aspect to this to be enjoyed. Huy is playing with a pack of pills. I watch him for a moment and he holds them up.

"Flun-itra-ze-pam," I read on the pack.

Jean Paul is carrying the fold-up table he uses to have one-on-one consultations with his members. When he has these one-on-ones, his only rule is that they have to know what they want. It's a quick-fire exchange. It's a test to see if they are thinking with long-term intentions rather than with impulsive, ill intent. They are essentially pitching him a business deal—he just takes notes. It's the only opportunity his loyal members have to manifest a Resisting Act of their own initiative. He phrases it as if it's his way of screening his members. *This table is sacred*, he says. *Do not offend it.*

Jean Paul is making sure all the legs are locked in before putting the table into the storage cupboard. He's polite, never skips a step, does things properly. He has a lot of patience until he doesn't. He was destined to be a great leader. But I think about people who decide to adopt political bodies and people who decide to believe in apocalypses versus people who are born into the state of it, who are living these circumstances without choice.

He goes downstairs again and I say to Huy, "I have a feeling Jean Paul isn't really thinking about anyone's requests seriously right now."

"Yeah, he's *really* concerned about K.A.G., isn't he?"

"Mmm."

Huy shifts his feet. "Now that I've fallen for someone . . ." He shifts into a half-hearted tenderness: "I realize."

He looks over at the stairs where Jean Paul will be coming back up soon.

I raise my head, my eyes doing something strange. "Mmm."

"And Luis—I know he's a good guy at heart." He's now whispering.

I drop Jean Paul off. Make a scary face at myself in the rear-view mirror. Eyes widen until it hurts. I must be exhausted. Pull them down.

Every night I cannot remember whether I sleep. It's strange.

Luis has ensured that at night there is complete darkness—at least within the design of this house. He needs to be fresh every day. Me, even more so. The K.A.G. curtains, though thin and linen, are double-layered and can be tailored to become triple-layered in order to keep the light out. There's been talk of getting some kind of awning or shutter for the exterior part of the window, ones that will seal the home shut. It would then be completely dark with no assurance of the outside, maybe only some occasional noise, if it's very loud. It will be like lying inside a sealed case, guessing what the people around you are doing.

There are teenagers next door, children of a wealthy doctor and surgeon. During the nights that their parents have shifts, they have friends over, drinking and yelling. There are cars that sometimes bust an engine speeding through the curvy streets of the estate because they haven't installed the speed humps yet. Sometimes strange sirens. Sometimes an explosion in the distance.

There are builders currently doing work on Moleskine's stable from five in the morning because Luis insists they do it while he's on the property.

Sometimes, I swear, Luis will get up after two hours of sleep and put on a movie. If I look out the door I can see a blue light shining through the darkness, creating an apex. I hear the heating or cooling system turn on. I try to sleep again. When I call out to Kiki, it doesn't work—she hasn't been programmed to my voice, she's locked only to Luis's. In the next update, they may allow more than one user to have their voice programmed. Luis is constantly getting updates for this development. An upgrade has been done so that Kiki X is installed in all rooms now, connected at the one center.

When Luis eventually crawls back into bed, I'm left awake while he drifts off again. One night I whispered, "You know if I don't get enough sleep, I could hurt people and be sued." And he didn't get up for the next three nights, but then began to again on the fourth.

The only peace I get is in my 900. Just me and the empty beige leather seats. When I drive, I feel so good I could fall asleep. It feels infinite when you drive the same route alone. Over and over. Like a skin-care routine. But no mirrors, no phone, no home controller, no human contact, no guilt about not speaking to anybody, no guilt about not calling my parents. *Be safe*, they say. *Don't think about anything except the lines on the road.*

I do so. I drive as if time's paused.

It's better without the music too. You hear each pothole and feel it simultaneously. Hearing the braking. Hearing the underwater-like reflections of other drivers' sound systems, pulsing against the skin of your car. The skin of my 900.

At the front door now. And I hear Luis calling out all of a sudden, "Kiki, turn up the cooling."

It's so hot in here.

He's high, the way his arms are, redness in his eyes. And he's dropping some bone marrow into water. It splashes back onto the tiles.

"So late," he says softly, but loud enough so I can hear it as I walk barefoot down the short corridor into the main living area. My shoes are on the Metal-Oak Shoe Rack.

"What?" I call out.

"Nothing."

He's sweating when I get into the kitchen. His limbs are slack.

"Too hot for soup," I say.

"Kiki, turn up the cooling," he says, wiping his hand on the tea towel.

Turning up cooling.

The house gushes out some air, but stops soon after. Luis doesn't notice.

"How was K.A.G. today, with the drug tests and everything?"

"Almost all of us did it." He shrugs. "I used the synthetic bag. It was yeah, as you'd expect. It worked. You have talented friends. They're really changing the game, aren't they?" He pauses. "Peggy came down for a visit."

He serves soup with the Woodgrain Server Ladle.

"It's like the heat is cooking *us*." He goes over to the Kiki X and looks at it for a moment, as if it *can't* be wrong, comes back.

We sit at the table, the Weave Placemats under the Acacia Moon Bowls.

Moleskine makes a noise outside and we look. There are shadows of trees blowing, nothing else worth noting.

"It's okay. Heat is better than cold," I suggest. "Better for the joints. Sweating is good for releasing toxins trapped on the surface of skin."

Luis gives a considerate nod. He swallows hastily, the soup clearly burning his lips. He grabs his water immediately to chase it down his throat.

. . .

Healing studio owner and yet I am unable to heal this poor residual man lying next to me in our wonderful king-size bed, Microfiber Deluxe Topper. He kicks the duvet off himself.

"I'm burning up," he says, as if to himself. All his clothes off.

I trace his bruising with my eyes as he lies beside me, attempting to be still. He has no time to think about his physical self. This is something I'd say to a customer. He has no time to trace the bruising with his own eyes, so I do it for him.

"Why don't you go outside and see Moleskine?" I say. "Get some fresh air."

49 **AT THE KITCHEN BENCH A** few nights later, I'm reading a local newsletter which gets sent out to our business emails. There is an article this week about an outdoor shopping mall being built, only ten minutes down the road from Topic Heights. They're calling it a walled city.

It' ll be like The Grove, says the CEO. *The architecture will be designed to be inclusive for all types of people. It will be carbon-friendly, and have eco-friendly bathrooms and prayer rooms. It will all be outdoors; the food court range will be curated to cater to a large diversity of eating requirements; the parking lot will have vehicle charging stations. Bike lock-ups will be available.*

It's going to be sensational, an absolute superb spectacle of a shopping experience, Peggy is quoted as saying.

I wonder if Peggy is at all feeling as though this shopping complex will mean the last of Topic Heights. This new complex promises the delivery of more places to feel included, to park your car and spend time, meaning less time at hers. Especially if the complex will be outdoors— less guilt about being crammed inside a synthetic-oxygen tank, but more rain too. All the same, being outdoors is quite stylish right now.

On the television, the local news is covering a story about a new estate opening in six months. *It recalls a specific style in architecture history, Pueblo Revival . . . wonderful . . . designed by John Ericsson . . . Breaking news . . . an unknown explosion . . . off the 96 . . . no injuries . . .*

Luis comes back inside from feeding Moleskine, sliding the door shut so that our Double-Layered Linen Curtains jump from the surge of air.

I shudder slightly.

"I thought I heard something out there," he says, coming to stand on the opposite side of the countertop.

"The wind? Or the neighbors?" I go to shut the curtains properly.

"Yeah," he says, his face pale. He looks back outside the window, pulling the curtain slightly away.

He goes to the table, takes his Acacia Cylinder out and prepares a line of cocaine.

In the food court, Peggy is sitting at a table, weeping to herself. It's right after five p.m. the next night and the security guard is standing nearby in the archway leading to the restrooms. Just staring at her.

I've come down the escalator to find somewhere to throw our trash. I've got a garbage bag slung over my shoulder. I pause, thinking of ways to avoid Peggy's eyeline. When she lets out a huge moan, I put the bag on a nearby table and approach her.

"What is it?" I ask her.

"It's my security cameras," she says. "I've just realized I've been watching the same video of the *same* day, the *same* activities, the *same* people walking past, the *same* mannerisms for the last . . . I don't even know . . . *three* weeks." She is a big crier. The drip from her nose elongates. "Do you know what that means, Leen?"

"Sure." I reluctantly pat her on her back. She's sweaty.

"It means. No. SE-CUR-I-TY. For the last *month*. People could have been shagging doggy style on the bench outside the Target for all I know."

I simply nod, a sympathetic face. She lets out another huge moan and I sit on the chair diagonal to her.

"And you know what *sick* joke made me realize this?"

"What's that?"

She leans in and whispers, "Someone swapped footage of my own home onto my screen. When I went to check the connection, I realized it was playing on a different web address . . . the complex cameras have been disconnected, replaced with footage from my own house."

She begins to sob again.

"Oh, it's so hard, Leen, you have no idea," she wails softly.

A tortured whisper. "You have no idea how hard it is."

An email is sent out to all Topic Heights tenants saying Peggy is taking her long service leave and that she's on a plane to Ohio.

"She's from Ohio," says Huy.

It's the afternoon after I saw Peggy crying. I'm sitting with Huy and Lonnie Luther in the back section of the pharmacy while Jean Paul's at the desk, sorting through the next morning's prescriptions.

"Yeah, don't ask me how I know that," Huy says, fiddling with stuff in his teeth.

"*Huy*," says Lonnie Luther, pulling Huy's hand out of his mouth. "Stop it."

"My parents were her suppliers, but they may as well have been paid therapy money on top of that. The way she'd just talk *at* them," says Huy. "Anyway, she bought a lot of our drugs. Did you know she and her husband bought both shopping complexes? They bought the Galleria, but he gave her Topic Heights to manage." Huy slides his hands under his thighs. "It's odd, I think most people know her. She's probably one of the most popular people in Par Mars. She's one of those people who is embarrassed about their power. So it's kind of corny if you ever talk to her, she wants to be a normal person, you know."

"I think it's hard to own a business," I say.

"As a woman too," Lonnie Luther adds, averting his gaze. As if he sees ghosts in the room that no one else is seeing.

"Even Lonnie knew her before he started hanging out here," Huy says to me, pointing his thumb at Lonnie Luther. "My parents pitied her. She didn't know what was coming to her, owning this dying shopping complex, but at least *we* can move, right?"

I stare at Lonnie Luther and realize it was him with the camcorder at Peggy's first Chateau party. Behind the red dot, by the door. Hired to film the night.

"She's a troubled lady," Huy says. "I think very lonely."

"Poor thing," I say.

Lonnie Luther looks at me. He's getting a relationship body and has stubble growing around his jaw. He leans his head on Huy. "Yeah, why did we attack *her* again? She's not really the problem." Lonnie Luther swallows. Holding a lot of weight in his throat.

"I just feel horrible," says Lonnie Luther. "I didn't really think about it."

We look at each other.

"Your idea wasn't too violent, though," I say.

"It still feels like it."

Huy shifts so his arm is over Lonnie Luther's shoulders. He flattens his lips, looks up in the direction of the prescription counter. In Jean Paul's general direction. He darts his eyes again, looks at me looking at Lonnie Luther.

"So I've been watching *Teen Wolf*."

We're grabbing our bags from the staff room and getting ready to leave for St. Bernard's when the microwave blows up behind us. Jean Paul's next to it, coughing.

"How long did you heat it for?" I yell. "It's only supposed to be three minutes, you asshole."

There's smoke coming out of it and a small fire starts. Jean Paul sprays it with the tiny extinguisher hanging beside the evacuation poster. He puts the extinguisher down and coughs again into his hands.

"Don't worry, Leen," he says annoyed, hacking up saliva. "It's old as fuck—"

"How *old* are you, Jean Paul? Don't you know how to heat up food? You have to open the lid a little."

Huy laughs from the couch. He gets off his phone and stands up.

"All good?" Lonnie Luther is sort of laughing too, but there is a torture in his eyes.

Jean Paul has been irritable recently. And he looks exhausted. Lonnie Luther and Huy are laughing hysterically around him, but it's almost as if he doesn't hear them. He cleans the bit of mess on the bench and then we leave the staffroom, back down the passageway and through the complex to the staff parking lot.

Jean Paul in the passenger seat, Lonnie Luther and Huy in the back. On our way to St. Bernard's. Due in fifteen minutes.

I think everyone is on something tonight, something from the pharmacy maybe. Can't tell. Someone's on the electric organ upstairs though. It's towards the end of the hour we have here.

It was a spontaneous call-to-meeting tonight. And I think, if I can tell by Jean Paul's suddenly fixed smirk, that it's in celebration of Peggy going on long service leave. Mary is on her laptop, wearing a casual blazer, sitting on one of the chairs to the side. I come to sit beside her.

"My stomach is so happy," she says to me, typing away. Her wrinkling fingers. "I've been eating so well—I've been *so* disciplined since knowing Jean Paul. He's absolutely transformed the way I think about my lifestyle."

"How's that?"

"That routine shouldn't be something your body is forced into! Routine is something you choose consciously!"

"Interesting."

Heavy typing. She seems to be writing an essay.

"You know, even furniture can put you into a routine. The way walls put you into a house." Mary stops typing, looks up, tilts the reading glasses she's wearing at me.

"Furniture," I repeat. The word swollen in my mouth. As if I can't bring myself to understand the pronunciation.

Jean Paul gathers everyone to bring their plastic chairs to the center. He has both hands pressed into his lectern, his elbows bent so they are slightly collapsed.

"I know what you are thinking." He grins.

A long, precise pause. I can feel Mary buzzing with excitement beside me, or perhaps it is the plugged-in laptop on her lap.

"That we have made quite an impression without making the slightest . . . impression."

Slender laughter.

"But that's incorrect. We have not won. Not yet. Not quite."

He walks out from behind the lectern. The room is at a standstill.

"Sometimes it's not who appears to be in power on the surface who has the most power. Think about Jesus Christ, Mark Zuckerberg . . . 'What are you *saying*, Jean Paul?' I'm saying: our deadly consumption is bigger than the structure of shopping complexes. Our doomed form of consumption is our consumption of concept. Yes . . . we may have temporarily taken down Peggy, poor friend. But what is worse than Peggy?"

"Her husband!" someone yells.

"Incorrect." Jean Paul side-grins. "Not quite, ma'am."

"The new complex!"

"Let me tell you!" Jean Paul says as more people raise their voices over the top of his. "Your local K.A.G. That's a local *and* a global problem that won't just go away on a holiday."

People cheer without noting the details. Just the way Jean Paul's voice inflates is encouraging.

Mary lightly touches her elbow to mine. "*God*, he's a great speaker, isn't he?"

I must be heating up, blushing at my cheeks. I swallow all the weight in my throat.

"Remember that we are not in the mood now or ever to be taken advantage of. We are not in the mood to be replaced by machinery, we are not in the mood to be treated like machinery. Remind them that you're here."

The room clangs with more applause and offbeat, empty merriment.

50 JEAN PAUL, HUY, LONNIE LUTHER, and I are driving out to the ends. Where all the industrial sites and animal farms are; south of Par Mars, the very south. It's called Marshall Hills out here, but most call it Martian Hills because supposedly, over the hills, you are able to see the UFOs. There is often a club of eccentric people, usually middle-aged, who bring their picnic chairs and wine. They come and sit on the large stretches of lawn there, and wait.

Lonnie Luther has a passed-out K.A.G. board member over the top of his lap in the middle back seat. He says, "Marshall Hills is named after the name Marshall, which means love of horses in Scottish." He quickly adds, "Don't *ask* me how I know that."

This makes Huy laugh hysterically into his hand.

Jean Paul, I can feel, is entirely indifferent. I connect my eyes with Lonnie Luther's through the rear view.

He says, "I had to film a horse-riding ad out here once. Before all the horses there died. The ad could never air."

Huy explodes with laughter now and collapses his head onto Lonnie Luther's shoulder.

Red beams cross over the vacant face of the board member. A rare car passing us, flashing its headlights. This is something you do in the ends, on the highways that stretch over big canvases of sand and rock.

"What killed all the horses?" I ask. Staring at the two of them in the back. Huy's phone light dilates over his cheeks.

"Sometimes aliens kill livestock and cattle," Jean Paul says quietly.

"I mean, true, did they die all at once?" Huy asks. His phone light off now.

"Over two nights," says Lonnie Luther. "Like they'd been cut into."

"A sick joke," says Huy.

I can feel Jean Paul becoming indifferent again. It's the way his exhalation changes.

"Like something *we* would do, isn't it?" Huy says, kneeing Jean Paul's seat.

Jean Paul turns his head slightly, not allowing his eyes to meet Huy's.

"Swear to God if you ever hurt a horse, I'll kill you," Lonnie Luther says. "Rich executives, fine. Selfish, repressed store managers, whatever. CEOs of shopping complexes, great. But touch Seabiscuit and I swear."

Huy is laughing hard now, and Jean Paul cuts in quickly, "All right, anywhere here's fine, Leen."

"What a *dumb* name for a horse," Huy whispers.

On the radio they're saying something about the new shopping complex: . . . *and where are they getting all this money to make this place so perfect . . . hippy hub (laughter) . . . what about that, at least a gourmet doughnut . . .*

I think about swerving and crashing the car. I pull to the left quickly. *Now.*

"Whoa." Huy hits the back of the passenger seat. "My stomach is *sensitive.*"

I can feel Jean Paul choosing to not react. This is probably what he'd want. If I were to crash this 900, I would be the only one responsible. Jean Paul has found many ways to corner his friends.

He seems to have picked on lonely people. What happens when you're not a lonely person anymore? I suppose he keeps the remnants of the sort of person you were when you *were* lonely. He has thought this all before.

"Stop. Stop now," Jean Paul whispers sharply. "Stop here."

I do as he says, brake slowly. The sensitivity of a perfect chauffeur.

Our feet on the gravel. Crunching through. I stand by the car while Lonnie Luther and Huy carry the K.A.G. board member.

Jean Paul films. "You're both stronger—my arms are injured from carrying that table up and down those stairs."

Sound of cicadas.

They walk beyond the broken wire fence to a point where I can barely see the red dot on the back of Lonnie's camera. I tap my foot.

A car drives past, honks.

I drop my head down. My ears are peeking out from under my beanie. I pull the beanie over them, tucking my chin in. Letting the arch at the back of my head weigh my head down.

The car is reversing again.

"You need a hand, darlin'?" someone calls out.

"No, nope!" I say, almost aggressively. I don't lift my head up.

The driver pauses. "Just askin'," he snaps. "I got two kids in the back. We've been driving for hours. Christ, wouldn't hurt to be polite." He rolls the window back up.

I glance up very quickly, see that his wife looks apologetic about him. They drive off.

Soon I see two little headlights in the distance. The lights growing larger around the bend. I look out to the distant field. Nearly all black except for a streak of red blemishing the horizon. The form of a hill not too far from here. But no sign of any other human beings.

The car in the distance is speeding up closer, now slowing. To a stop. The window winds down.

"Hop in," says the voice.

I look up. It's a man, maybe in his early thirties, bald, with a Fila T-shirt on.

"No," I say. "I mean, I'm fine. My friends are peeing."

"Oh?" He's just stopped in the middle of the road. "Yeah."

"How far out did they go peeing?" he scoffs.

"Not far, but they're self-conscious."

"It's ranger's property out that way. They could get in trouble. Do you need someone to look for them with you?"

"No," I say, this time angry. "Go on."

He takes something out from his pocket. Shows it to me. A badge. "Highway patrol," he says. "I can place you under arrest under suspicion of criminal behavior. Let me ask you few questions, please."

I screw up my face unwillingly. The side of my mouth mutters, "Fuck."

"Now produce your driver's license, please," he says.

We wait.

"I'll say it again, miss. Please produce your driver's license or any other form of identification."

I reach into my jacket pocket, pass him my license.

"There's been abnormal activity around, you do know that, don't you? Have you not seen the news . . . Ling?" He's shining a torch to the license.

I shake my head. "Don't really watch the news much."

"Well, there's been things happening. Watch the news and stay safe on the road. Don't lie about having friends. If you need a nap on the road or if you need to take a piss . . . perfectly fine if you pull over safely." He folds his lips into his mouth. "Now this isn't really *safely*, is it? You're barely off the road. It's a hazard. We'd rather you find a spot with more dirt on the side. Not my words. Words of the law."

"That's it?" I look behind me. I can see figures moving towards us.

"That's it. See, no need to be scared. Just be honest next time. And be careful where you stop." He flashes a horrible-looking smile that morphs into a sleazy one. "Have a good night now."

He looks me up and down, lingers too long. As if he's done his dirty work and now he's wondering if I'd like to fuck.

I turn slightly. The figures are visible now. The three of them.

They wouldn't be able to tell it's a cop who's with me.

The cop is still here looking at me, attempting to produce a vague expression of seduction, a mixture of that as well as a sort of carnivorousness. He doesn't flinch or notice the others. Perhaps his eyes haven't adjusted to the dark yet.

"Bye," I say, flashing a careful smile.

I imagine if I get back in the car he might follow his eyes around to where they may begin to adjust; a possibility he could see the three of them. Jean Paul may be bloodied, depending on whether the board member had woken up in the process. Either way, at the very least, there would be dirt all over their shoes and the smell of Clive Christian on them.

At home, Luis has got the builders over again. They're finishing up Moleskine's stable. He's asked them to consider also building concrete shutters for our house. Luis had seen it done in a K.A.G. home-tour video of this Korean architect. The purpose of them is to be able to close yourself inside in a case of bad weather, a natural disaster, an apocalypse or a home invasion. For complete silence, all you'd have to do is press a remote control or call on Kiki.

I take my shoes off and put them on the Metal-Oak Shoe Rack.

There are no extra shoes there.

The builders and Luis are sitting around the K.A.G. Beech Pearl-Circle Table. The builders all have their shoes on. One of them looks vaguely familiar. He turns to look at me, smirking. The other one is drawing something up. I give Luis a look. He thinks it's about the shoes and he almost smiles in response. But really it's about how unusual it is to see other people in this house. And I think about whether Luis really did have somebody over that night, when Jean Paul had first attempted to ambush him.

The builders leave after an hour and Luis comes to me on the Eco-Cotton Sofa in Off-White. Lies across it, his head in my lap. I bristle my fingers through his hair and look at the dining table, sheets of paper stacked into a neat pile.

"Hey," I say. "Remember that night I brought home the desk?"

"Yeah."

"Did you have someone over?"

"Oh, um . . ."

"Can't remember?"

"No, I can." He swallows. "It was the K.A.G. board. They came to install and brief me on the upgrade of Kiki, when they did Kiki X. They had to do a proper setup to connect her to the heating and cooling, the stove and the bathroom and everything else."

"Oh, right," I sigh.

"It was strictly confidential."

He flinches when I touch his forehead, where the bruising sprouts up like vines. He's developing this reaction. We don't talk about it. I hate to waste time talking about the little things we can't help. When you're in a relationship and the both of you are running highly successful businesses built on spirituality and holistic healing, time when business is not involved shouldn't be wasted—it should be used to remind ourselves why we are in that business; that is, for gratitude and simply *living*.

I think about offering him a massage, but he'd say no. And even if he said yes, he'd probably turn it very quickly into sex. So we just stare at one another.

The humidifier is going. If I breathe consciously through my nostrils, I can feel it. If I pay attention, I can feel the air without looking at the home controller. Something Luis can't seem to do as quickly—it's why he has trouble with the heating and cooling system nowadays. Sometimes he'll have the heater, cooler, humidifier, and diffuser going all at once. And when I ask him why, he'll pretend it was a deliberate decision. Something scientific, something pseudo feng shui.

I'm surprised he hasn't killed the horse, the way he's been relying on Kiki X recently. The one thing this K.A.G. home controller cannot take care of is the goddamn horse. But I can't speak about this with him because he takes this horse so seriously.

When we're in bed, I lie so still I can't feel my hands anymore. I imagine Jean Paul sleeping on a cold, hard ground. Just to say he did it.

Luis keeps turning over and over in our king-size bed. I can hear Moleskine moving around outside. I switch my phone on to the forum. A recent upload of Jean Paul pulping the board member in grasslands.

The builders wake me up the next morning. A high-pitched drilling sound.

Luis is looking at me when I open my eyes.

Immediately, he says, "Sorry, I wanted them to start as soon as possible." And touches my cheek.

I shake my head without saying anything and roll over, pull myself up out of our bed, out of the K.A.G. Elegant Cross-Hatch Sheets in a shade of blue that comforts.

The floor is always cold in the mornings. The concrete floor, with our Shaggy-Mix Rug in light brown, which lies limply over a quarter of the room. A Reversible-Bath-Style Rug in our ensuite, which feels like a refrigerator this morning.

I look in the big, perfect mirror. I'm wearing my K.A.G. Insulating Fleece Pajamas, white thin stripes and beige everything else. These are not my sexy pajamas; they're slightly different. If I'm not in my sexy ones, I'm not in the mood. It's a silent language.

I run my fingers over the bareness of my head, feeling the dome shape of it, holding it, pattering it, a different kind of stimulation. The flat of my palm, my fingers fluttering.

I see Luis coming up behind me. He's grown a bit of a loose stomach. Like he's been eating too little, too much of the wrong thing. He looks in the mirror and smiles at me in there. Plays with my ears.

"My parents," he says, "they're going to come over. They want to."

I look at him in the mirror.

I have my K.A.G. Frosted-Glass Toothbrush in my mouth.

I brush up and down, not side to side.

"Okay," I nod. "I'd love to meet them."

"Well, actually. I was thinking I could have them here alone."

I nod again, deliberately similar to the first nod. So as to make a slightly aggressive point. "Okay."

Silence.

Then I say, "You know I've helped pay for this house too, don't you?"

He raises his voice slightly, "I just want them to know how I designed and invested careful time in this property. I want them to know I've worked hard on the look of it. Leen, I just want them to be proud of me . . . you know about this. You get it."

I rinse my mouth with the K.A.G. Tooth Protection Formula.

"Yeah, yeah," I say.

He stands perfectly still as his hands float to his sides. In the mirror, his posture is perfect.

"Yeah, I get it," I say.

I turn and take his shoulders and his body flinches, his shoulders freezing up. He has a look of sadness, of weariness.

51 "SUCCESS BECOMES ADDICTIVE," JEAN PAUL says.

I'm sitting in the pharmacy, and it's fifteen minutes before the studio will open. I have seven unique customers booked. Seven unique bodies with different needs at different stages.

Jean Paul's opening the pharmacy again today. He puts his white coat on. "I swear, the fucking manager, if he doesn't show up on time again . . ."

He passes me a bottle of bitter orange.

"Anyway, Leen, *easy* success becomes addictive. But *long-term hard work*, that's *real* success. Poor friend . . . that Vic. You don't keep in touch with him anymore, do you? He doesn't know how big of a mistake he's making. Easy success, leader of his own empire. Exploitative. When you own a company, you either sell out or you sell off. He's in a big trap, poor friend. But you know what it is, they're *lazy*. Vic is lazy. That's what happens when you have a partner who's won the lottery. He's lazy . . . he's disappointing."

"Actually," I say, "I think they're doing really well. Working all day and night. But they're happy."

"Cop-outs," he mutters.

These days at the complex, more people come just to hang around, not to shop. Mostly they sit in the food court, one arm slinked over the back of a chair.

Peggy isn't here to watch the cameras. She hadn't been doing so for months apparently. Still, she represented the fact that somebody *was* watching. It was something intangible but her position represented something just as domineering as the bodies with badges and weapons on their hips. People know she's not here now and that means something.

I'm walking to my studio. Someone is following my every step. I turn around suddenly.

"Watch it," the person behind me says.

Just a man carrying his grocery bags. He walks around me, shaking his head. Disdain in the way he holds his bottom lip.

I look down over the balcony. Five customers are going into the Target as the roller doors open.

I keep walking. Pass the escalators.

I look down again. K.A.G. hasn't opened yet, but the lights are on inside and I know Luis has already been here for an hour. The plastic screens still out. There are about ten to fifteen eager customers waiting to go inside. Some fidgeting with their clothes, some on their phones, all waiting to go in.

It's a sales tactic, I know.

As Robert Greene says: *Use absence to increase respect and honor. Create value through scarcity.* Luis knows this all too well.

I continue walking and cross to the opposite side of the balcony.

In our studio, the warm low lamps are on to entice drowsy guests, a place to repose.

Farah is sitting at the computer, ready for the day. She has her hair up.

"You look good," I say to her.

She gives me a tight-lipped smile. "Thanks."

It seems better.

"Let's go heat up lunch together today," I say. There's a week left with Farah here. I'll be alone after that.

She nods with a complacent smile. "Okay."

Law 48 according to Robert Greene is to assume formlessness.

He says: Keep yourself adaptable. Taking form makes it easy for enemies to grasp. *No law is fixed. The best way to protect yourself is to be as fluid and formless as water.* Quite similar to Tao Te Ching 78.

We're waiting by the new microwave as it drones, then three beeps go off. Farah makes a habit of waiting an extra ten seconds so that any radiation roiling inside doesn't get released when opening the door.

She pulls the ends of her sleeves over her hands and grabs the red Tupperware container, steam coiling out from it. I'm looking at my phone for a moment, observing how on the forum the video of Jean Paul beating the K.A.G. board member has disappeared.

"It's jeera aloo," she says. "Trying to go vegetarian."

"That's great," I say, shutting my phone.

We sit on the couch. Me on one side, Farah on the other. I watch her spinning the fork with her fingers.

"So as a writer, do you pay attention to a lot of detail, then?" She nods, her mouth hanging slightly open, airing the hot food.

"Yeah, I like to people-watch."

"Topic Heights is good for that."

I cross one leg over the other. I try to smile, but my pride is suspending my face into its true look of disappointment. It must appear strange to Farah.

"Mmm," she says, her mouth full. "Yeah."

Silence.

Finally, I tell her, "I'm proud of you."

She puts her container down. "You know," she says, "you're selfish." She wipes her tongue over her two front teeth.

"Oh?"

"Yeah." She looks down at her food, a hard frown forming over her eyes. She's running out of breath, as if she can't breathe properly.

She picks the container up and starts prodding around in it. "You want to be seen by everybody as successful," she says, "but at the expense of others. You make money and you make your own ego out of that shit. You always complain; you never think about how it affects me." She laughs breathlessly. "Why would you be so upset every time I do something for myself? Why would you ever assume that I belong to your ambition and your ambition only?"

I want her to leave for the city now. I suppose this is her method of detaching ourselves from one another. Making it an easier transition for me.

Jean Paul gives me a Halcion.

I'm back in the staff room at the end of the day, thinking about whether Farah was being genuine. If that was really her speaking or if it was her inability to move forward without feeling guilty about it.

"What?" I say to Jean Paul.

"For your stressing. You look ridiculous stressing like this."

I read the box.

"I know you," he says.

I'm sitting on the kitchenette bench.

"I did it," he whispers, leaning in closely.

A K.A.G. worker, an older Eastern European-looking man, is sitting nearby, sewing a name tag onto his linen K.A.G. apron.

"What?"

He opens his notebook. It says: *Steel ball bearings, push button switches, battery connectors, cables. Thermite.*

"Jean Paul, I've had a long day of ploughing my arms into people's bones. Please let me have a moment?" I take a sip from a plastic bottle. I take the Halcion because it's there.

"Acetone peroxide," he says.

"How'd you learn to make that?"

"The internet. There are recipes online." Jean Paul laughs. "One guy, he made forty grams by accident. He was watching the colors, seeing if they changed, and made a bomb."

"And the ingredients?"

"Oh, you kind of just . . ."

"What?"

He crosses his arms around his chest and squeezes either side of himself.

"Well, I used Huy's student card and stuff to access the labs, but he didn't mind." He lets a breath run out quickly.

"He probably thought you were *reading*."

"He didn't mind."

Quiet. I hop off the bench, start to walk away.

"What I'm saying is, Leen"—he grabs my arm, grits through his chained teeth—"it'd be much too easy for an actual criminal to make it."

"You won't use it, right? That would make you an *actual criminal*."

Jean Paul pauses, crosses his arms over his chest again. It makes him look so small. "I've done so much work, though. So much research." He looks at his Rolex. "I have to close up."

The K.A.G. worker is sort of peering at us out the corner of his eye.

I whisper as he turns to leave, "You'll hurt people."

The look on his face reorganizes itself into a foreign expression—an expression of ferocious mockery. "We already hurt people." It feels like match point—his face calls it.

I make my way to the staff parking lot, lean against the car, and text Jean Paul to ask how long he'll be. He doesn't respond. I decide to wait a little while longer. Out in the distance beyond the ledge of the rooftop are muted mountain ranges, subliminal against the haze. The clouds are depleting in a way that takes after the crumbing of expired milk. I inhale: simple pleasures, standing here witnessing the natural fluctuations of land mass. Exhale, the sweat between the webbing of my fingers, the unnatural climatic shift from inside to outside.

I think about the sounds that had once kept me up at night while living at my mother's here and at Doms's, the intermittent exchange between the sound of loud cracks and the moments of one round alto eruption, somewhere in the distance.

Around the time we had first moved to Par Mars, my mother told me they might be the sound of tests. Just like how we'd heard the sound of cows moaning before dawn while on vacation in the country. They didn't want to worry people during the day, so they did it while we were sleeping.

"Who?" I asked. I'd been sitting at the dining table, peeling garlic. She was at the bench, squelching her hands around in a bowl full of raw meat.

"The people who create weapons for distribution. How do you think they know they work?"

"They shoot people to test?" I exclaimed.

She laughed. "No, of course not."

I asked her why they made them at all if it was something that needed to be hidden. Why would the sounds of cows crying upset us if we already ate them?

She stopped to look at me, at this point. "Why so many questions?" And then, going back to her marinating, "People want to get things done quickly." She shook her head. "I don't like eating meat."

A sort of grimness had entered her voice.

"I feel the stress of the animal as I bite into the flesh. But we rely on it now because it's given to us like that. If it wasn't given to us like that, everything would be different. They'd be killed differently, maybe they wouldn't scream so loud. We love to eat it how they've made it for us to eat, though. It is in everything, Leen—the way our fruit is picked, the way our vegetables are packed. If we didn't have people finding out how we like to eat things . . . If we didn't have people testing weapons—" She stopped, she looked confused. One of the first times I'd seen her like this. She began to heat the oil.

I'd finished with the garlic and turned to look at the television as I passed my mother the bowl of it. Footage of a mushroom cloud was being shown as part of a montage to advertise a news program. My mother looked too, then began to tilt the pan, letting the oil permeate. Combining the garlic, impregnating the flesh of it with fat from the oil.

"Quickness," she said softly, after a while. "They need to do things as quickly as possible if they want to really make money first. And I think it makes people comfortable, to have someone else do the difficult things for them. It just works for the business, Leen."

52 JEAN PAUL NEVER CAME OUT from the pharmacy so I drive Lonnie Luther to St. Bernard's. Huy hasn't been at Topic Heights today either.

We drive there in relative peace, laughing about moments from the last meeting, how certain members demanded attention from Jean Paul, the way they'd *lick his boots*.

I park at St. Bernard's and Mary, who's just parked as well, tells us Jean Paul had been driven there by one of her supermarket colleagues.

Now, I'm sitting with Lonnie Luther outside the nave of St. Bernard's, waiting for Huy to text back, see if he needs a lift tonight. Lonnie Luther's been busy all day with a video project for the local school, making its end-of-year environmental fundraiser campaign. Soon all the local TV and pre-film ads will be directed by Lonnie Luther—his frame will be the only frame to view through.

"Call him. My phone's out of battery," Lonnie Luther says.

I call Huy. Just one ring and he picks up. "Did you get a lift to the meeting?" I ask.

"I'm *grounded*," says Huy. A tinge of injustice to his intonation.

"You're nineteen. How're you *grounded*?"

Lonnie Luther cracks up laughing, slapping his thighs. "Asian families, man."

"I'm under house arrest then, whatever. A whole bunch of stuff was stolen from the pharmacy." Huy suspects it was Jean Paul this time. He thinks maybe the haul had been Jean Paul's trade for some uranium on eBay. "Jean Paul was saying you either had to be a friend of a uranium buyer or you had to offer a really good trade."

"Why does he want uranium?"

"He wants to try a dirty bomb. That guy, he's so ambitious. He wants to do everything just to do it."

I'm quiet.

"I think he's settled on trying napalm though."

Huy sort of laughs. "My parents trust him since the new manager started slacking. He's been opening and closing, doing a lot better than the new manager lately. So they didn't believe me when I told them. It's not like I've never stolen from their supplies. They found out about all of that too. So I'm grounded."

Lonnie Luther's listening on the other side of my phone. He looks at me when Huy says this.

I'm quiet. Lump in my throat.

"Oh yeah, so guess what I found out while I've been bored shitless here at home?" Huy says. "Jean Paul is, like, thirty-six. He's studied everything on the face of the planet. He's in *so much debt*. He traveled and spent all of his inheritance from his grandfather who invented the pancake-sandwich press. He's a fucking reckless bastard." Huy laughs. "He's worked as a . . . what are those lawyer things? Like, he studied to be a barrister. Then he worked on a farm, one in Mexico and one in Barcelona. He speaks fluent Spanish as well as Montreal-French, you know? It's *crazy*, guys. Plus he went to jail for tax evasion. He's so experienced, he's lived the life."

He explains that he found his birth name on a university database in Bradford in England. His name is Stephen Simmons. Then Huy found a police record with his name on it. It said that he was part of some brotherhood while he was in prison.

"Do you think he'll actually do it?" asks Lonnie Luther.

"Do what?"

"He's got all the materials, right? For an explosive?"

"Yeah, he had them a week ago. My parents only found out when they got back a few days ago. What was missing."

"When would he do it, Huy?" asks Lonnie Luther.

It's a few hours until Jean Paul will want to blow up me and Luis's home.

"Leen?" Huy says over the phone. "You there?"

"I mean . . ."

"I know . . ." says Huy. "You worried right now?"

Lonnie Luther moves away from the phone to look in my eyes mournfully.

"Does he know Luis's address off by heart?" I ask. "It's saved in his maps, remember."

"Well, what if I don't drive him?"

"Someone else will."

The night's clear, pinkish, when we step outside after our call with Huy. Our feet against the gravel, they feel like sinking. Across the ample stretch of road, a man has stopped his car and is filming St. Bernard's. He does this for a moment and then gets back in his car again.

I don't want to go down to the meeting. It's as if I'm afraid that being there, listening to the adrenaline charging and coursing among the embittered spirits of the Watch members, will convince me that perhaps it *is* a good idea after all, to obliterate our house.

The sound of Jean Paul shouting and his congregation shouting in return makes me nauseous. Though, because I cannot hear anything else, I wonder if it is just the nonlinear frequency still ringing in my ears from all the other nights. Just echoes, making me feel how hollow my stomach, how cold my skin is.

We pace, waiting for the meeting to finish so that we can speak to him. If we can just convince him before he goes.

Lonnie Luther says, "Would it be a better idea to . . . just get Luis out of the house before Jean Paul goes over? Would Jean Paul really want to listen to you? He's been really . . . I don't know . . . lately."

"I don't know," I say.

Robert Greene says: *Win through your actions, never through argument.*

"Why does he want to jump to the explosives?" Lonnie Luther asks. "Did Luis aggravate him in some way?"

Robert Greene says: *Keep your hands clean.*

I suggest that perhaps he still wants to draw attention to himself. Without *showing* himself. He seems to love the idea of being a symbol without occupying any physical body. He wants to embody his ideas, let them eat him up and morph him into something intangible, that people will look at in awe. This is what the idea of celebrity is—and this is what Jean Paul has found to be most successful in controlling behavior around him. Any physical being is never enough. Jean Paul wants to be everywhere and everyone at once.

Lonnie Luther laughs, a dark handsome laugh. "Fuck."

The members come out now. The regular chatting, a few of them smoking cigarettes together. We wait until the cars have cleared. And then we get out. Mary waves at us from her car, smiling. "Yoo hoo," she tries calling over.

Inside the nave it is a forbidding sort of cold and emptiness that rushes to greet us. We see the door to the basement is locked.

We're driving home.

Robert Greene says: *Your hands are never to be soiled by mistakes and nasty deeds. Maintain such a spotless appearance by using others as scapegoats and cat's-paws to disguise your involvement.*

The sky is ocean-blue. Maybe the tint on my windows. At the big gas station I see the lights flickering on for the first time tonight. It must be exactly a quarter to six. Somebody overtakes me. Lonnie Luther sitting dead still beside me. I notice he's filming. I don't know how to feel about that, maybe safe.

The sky suddenly twists into a peach color as we come off the highway.

The sun sets its orange bloom onto the Home store; there's a big stripe across it.

The McDonald's at the front. Children on the play equipment.

It's the idle coil before sunset; the reflection of the sunlight on the road bounces up to pierce the eyes, and I can't tell if it's an orange or green light.

Traffic is about 70 and 100 kilometers per hour here. I reduce my speed reluctantly.

It's a talent of mine: if I drive somewhere once, I know how to get there forever, speed limits and twists and turns and all.

The scatter of trees occasionally keeps it from looking exactly like a sparse, abandoned military site.

We don't have our windows down; it smells like cigarettes in here.

We pass by Brandt Boulevard, where you turn down to get to Doms's place.

Turn right, another long road, and then another right down Dawn Crescent.

Now onto the paralleling main road, making a left at Sicily Street.

Palm trees. Footpaths that look like honey, dipped in sun. Now driving into the Beverley Estate.

APOCALYPSE

LUIS

THE CONCRETE SHUTTERS CAN NOW respond to Kiki X. It's been a three-week-long project, and it's something he's really proud of. First the stable, which had also been a two-week-long process. Now this. Look how much can be done in a month with this kind of attitude. It's hot. The shutters are closed to glue them in position—they'll have to stay like this overnight and they'll come back to see if the hinge is working the next day. It's nearly nighttime anyway. He'll test-run the voice commands and the connection to Kiki X tomorrow afternoon. And a brilliant sun will shine through, the feeling of completion, of creating something so functional and beautiful.

For now, there's dinner. He holds the pot, feeling the way it curves. He smiles to himself. The handle is sturdy, it does not make his wrist bend uncomfortably. He holds the pot to his stomach, the arch, the coldness of the stainless steel, feeling like the freshness of a moon.

These exercises, though a sort of burden, have been making him feel an odd peace, a subtle gratitude. For the objects available to him. He finds absolute quiet when he focuses on one object at a time. If only this was something he'd implemented in his teenage years rather than all the drugs and video games.

There's a chemical smell. It's quite strong. But Leen's old car isn't in the garage. Whatever this is, it smells like petrol but worse. He thinks he may have left the gas stove on.

"Kiki, turn off the gas stove."

Turning off the gas stove.

He thinks he can hear a high-pitched hum. Or feel a presence. Gas stoves, they feel like ghosts when they're on. He can't be sure. *It's better to be safe than sorry*, his mother had said.

"Kiki, pause the music."

Pausing "Estate" by João Gilberto.

The music doesn't pause.

The precise articulation of the lyrics is licking his ear—that the sun binds us together, that the sunsets are beautiful, burning only now with fury.

The power blows with a bellowing bang. A short circuit maybe. He reaches for his phone. It's not where he thought he'd left it. He has never lived in such a large space. He had grown up sharing a room with two of his brothers. There was never privacy.

It's hot, overwhelmingly. If Luis looked to his arm now he'd see it has burnt off.

Luis remains, on the exterior, in a calm state. He crawls one way, then crawls the other using just his knees and one arm to nudge him along.

The house feels as though it is closing in. Completely dark now except for the large ominous flame coming from the east side of the house. It's licking the Double-Layered Linen Curtains. It's slurping up the Shaggy Mix Rug in beige. The horse. Moleskine is screaming outside. The stable isn't fucking fireproof.

Had he organized this test run? To try out the new apocalypse-proof line? Was he not supposed to be home tonight? He remembers the idea and having that meeting with the two board members that night. That night when he'd sent Leen to pick up the desk. How long ago that had been. The board members had been impressed by the way he had done up the house.

But the fire would not have been good for Leen, especially at that time. They had just got settled. Perhaps the board has organized it without his consent? Misunderstanding him. Was it detailed in the last contract he signed, one he hadn't bothered to read closely? In many ways, he can't be angry—only practical now.

One eyelid is dripping down over his eye.

"Kiki!" he yells. "Kiki, activate the emergency system!"

His fingers on his available arm are curling into themselves. He won't be able to open the shutters with his fingertips withering off. What he needs is oxygen. But it's all been sucked out. Why hasn't the fire system been activated? This was a new objective of the Kiki.

"Kiki, open the shutters!

"Kiki, open the shutters.

"Kiki, cool down the house. Kiki, the fire system. Kiki, humidifier please."

Concrete oven, he thinks. He's locked himself into a concrete oven.

"Kiki, open the shutters.

"Kiki, open the shutters. Please."

His mouth has filled up with his own saliva, a bit like soap. He laughs.
"Kiki."

Still the sound of the sensible, low voice, singing about a love long gone. Dilation of strings. He remembers Leen saying something about the dilation of strings.

He only wishes now that his parents had come to see the place sooner.

He's thinking about the loving look in his mother's eyes, and his father's strange arm movements, his considering face.

The voice murmuring, under the sudden sound of the bright but matted flute, about another winter coming, how he cannot remember the love he had, without the summer.

"Kiki," he tries one more time. "Open the shutters."

She looks paler than usual. Beside her, a tall man in black.

THE CLOSING

53 "WHAT ARE YOU DOING? WHY are you just sitting here?"

He is bent over the Beech Rectangular Coffee Table as if in prayer.

Tears droop into the corners of my lips. And though the skin on my neck stings, is peeling back and crisping, I feel a sort of tender warmth between my muscle and bone. The feeling of my fatigued limbs being held by a low orange simmer. And inside this hotness, there is a curious feeling of home.

Then maybe I hear him say, "I think our things are safe. It's fine. I think our things are safe."

ACKNOWLEDGMENTS

This book is for Anna Lee and Caroline Lee. Thank you to my family, Christina, Adrian, Nate, Anna, Marina, George, and Clara. Particularly to my mother, Christina: this book began with you and ended with you, your support, and your passing down of knowledge to me. Thank you to my father, who's supported me in my writing and shared so much wisdom. Anna and Nate, thank you for all of your enthusiasm to share stories and our artistic practices together.

To everyone who has worked on this book with me. I've had the privilege of learning from so many brilliant people. Gratitude to my agent, Barbara Zitwer, my editor Danny Vazquez, Rola Harb, everyone at Astra, and those who worked on the previous editions with me: Ellie Freedman, Lee Brackstone, Vanessa Radnidge, Camha Pham, and Elena Gomez. Thank you to Rodrigo Corral Studio for the incredible cover.

Gunk Baby would not have been possible without the aid of community I have around me. Thank you to Creative Victoria for funding this project so generously. Thank you to The Melbourne Prize Trust, Readings, and Melbourne University Centre of Visual Arts, who provided space for me to write this novel at the Norma Redpath Studio, where I began and completed the first draft of this book.

The country this book was written on, and which the fictional world within it resembles, is stolen land. As a settler I'd like to pay my respects to the Wurundjeri and Boonwurrung people of the Kulin Nation and their Elders past, present, and emerging. *Gunk Baby* is dedicated to storytellers of color, who inspire me to continue to ask questions, reflect truth, and demand change.

AUTHOR PHOTO BY JESSE MERCIECA

ABOUT THE AUTHOR

Jamie Marina Lau is a twenty-five-year-old multidisciplinary artist and writer. Her debut novel, *Pink Mountain on Locust Island*, won the 2018 Melbourne Prize Readings Residency Award and was short-listed for the 2019 Stella Prize, the 2019 New South Wales Premier's Literary Awards, the 2018 Readings Prize for New Australian Fiction, and the Australia Literature Society Gold Medal. Her writing can also be found in various publications. More info on jm-lau.com or on Instagram @babyzzks.

It takes a village to get from a manuscript to the printed book in your hands. The team at Astra House would like to thank everyone who helped to publish *Gunk Baby*.

EDITORIAL
Danny Vazquez
Rola Harb

PUBLICITY
Rachael Small
Alexis Nowicki

SALES & MARKETING
Jack W. Perry
Tiffany Gonzalez
Sarah Christensen Fu

DESIGN
Jacket: Rodrigo Corral Studio
Interior: Richard Oriolo

PRODUCTION
Lisa Taylor
Alisa Trager
Elizabeth Koehler
Olivia Dontsov

COPYEDITING
Janine Barlow

COMPOSITION
Westchester Publishing Services

ABOUT ASTRA HOUSE

Astra House is dedicated to publishing authors across genres and from around the world. We value works that are authentic, ask new questions, present counter-narratives and original thinking, challenge our assumptions, and broaden and deepen our understanding of the world. Our mission is to advocate for authors who experience their subject deeply and personally, and who have a strong point of view; writers who represent multifaceted expressions of intellectual thought and personal experience, and who can introduce readers to new perspectives about their everyday lives as well as the lives of others.